Being Committed

Being Committed

Anna Maxted

10 ReganBooks
Celebrating Ten Bestselling Years
An Imprint of HarperCollins*Publishers*

The Library of Congress has cataloged the hardcover edition as follows:
Maxted, Anna.
    Being committed : a novel / Anna Maxted.—1st ed.
        p.   cm.
    ISBN 0-06-009669-1
        1. Commitment (Psychology)—Fiction. 2. England—Fiction. I. Title.
    PR6063.A8665B45 2004
    823'.914—dc22   2004045347

ISBN 0-06-009670-5 (pbk.)

05 06 07 08 09 RRD 10 9 8 7 6 5 4 3 2

For Nettie Edelman
Imagine, everyone,
the best sort of grandma

Acknowledgments

As Oscar might say, a bigger, taller thank you to:

Phil Robinson, Jonny Geller, Deborah Schneider, Cassie Jones, Judith Regan, Sharyn Rosenblum, and the crack team at Regan-Books, Mary Miller, Paul Hawkes, Gary Akres, Pamela Walker, everyone at Garden Suburb Theatre, Maryanne Hillier, Maria Yiannikaris, Andrew Robinson, Kirsty Fowkes, Mary Maxted, Sarah Spear, Jacquie Drewe, Duncan Heath, Frank Tallis, Carol Jackson, Douglas Kean, Suzanne McIlduff, Anna Moore, Laura Dubiner, John Nathan, Tiffany Smith, Rupert Reece, Geoff Robertson, Jo Eccleshare, Sarah Hurley, Caroline Glass, Rory Aird, Ben Figgis, Justin Thomson, Lesley Diamond, and Dr. Howard Myers.

Being Committed

1.

Every woman likes to be proposed to, even if she means to refuse. At least, until I'd racked up a couple of marriage offers myself, that's what I believed. Aged fifteen, I read of one thirtysomething who'd totted up five and was happy to boast of it in a national newspaper. Then, I considered her lucky, glamorous, popular with boys. Everything that I, as a teenager, wasn't. (My adolescence can be summarized by one incident in which I took a gobstopper out of my mouth on a train. A man leaned forward in his seat and said, "Oh! I thought you were deformed.")

Years later, I realized that the proposal collector and I were a lot alike. You have to be quite a twit to allow matters to escalate to the point where some guy assumes you'll agree to rely on him for your life's entertainment when you have no intention of doing any such thing. (No man pops the question unless he is convinced of a yes. Which says not very much for the perception and self-regard of quite a few men.)

I'm being harsh. If it happens once, it's understandable. There are certain men who need to get married, for whom the woman is almost incidental to proceedings. The wife is the tedious yet necessary ingredient, similar to yeast in bread. This sort of man fixes on his target rather like a pit bull, and any girl who can't run fast enough is at risk. Then it's not her fault.

That said, sometimes it is. A persistence in finding you perfect can transform even a man of moderate charms into an accidental fiancé. I know that women, as a gender, are renowned for hankering after men one politely describes as "a challenge." But I'll bet that even those men have at one point (perhaps by having sex with us) given the impression of finding us attractive. *I* think it's instinct to gravitate toward those who find us delightful.

Disagree, but you'll disagree until the day you meet a person who dislikes you on sight and doesn't bother to hide it. Then you'll realize there's little more repellent. You won't be able to get away quick enough.

So, putting you at the right end of the desirability scale as it does, it's no wonder that a marriage offer is glorious in *fantasy*. A man, not noticeably defective, falling at your feet with a shower of gifts: flowers, jewels, big dinners, himself. A vitamin shot to the ego. The fact that out of all the millions of women he has met in his life, you are the one he finds most bewitching. (Or who he thinks will have him.)

Alas. The reality of an unwanted proposal is spitefully different from the dream format—I discovered this the embarrassing way. And, as I believe that it cheers the spirit to hear of another person's romantic woes now and then, I feel it's only my duty to share. Patience, however. As I said, I have had *two* marriage offers—wait! *Three,* now that I think about it—one of which was successful. I'm going to detail one here and, to reassert my dignity—presently making for the hills—I've decided not to tell you which it is just yet.

I hope you're sitting comfortably. Even if you don't deserve to.

Jason drove. And not just because our weekend away in St. Ives was to celebrate my birthday. He always drove. As I was unbothered about who drove and of the implications were Jason ever to be seen in public being driven by a woman, I let him drive. Indeed, whenever we traveled together, I'd head for his car, no question. I'm all for granting favors at no cost to myself. Driving is an activity that men engage in to boost their self-esteem, which I can relate to but not in a Fiat. Anyway, as we both discovered awhile back when I directed him to Swindon out of spite (we were supposed to be going to Oxford), the navigator holds the real power.

Perhaps I'm not giving the greatest impression of myself. My sister-in-law Gabrielle says this is inevitable as I grew up in Hampstead Garden Suburb. She means that a typical native of "the Suburb"—a seemingly quaint residential area of London, characterized by big beautiful houses, trim heathland, and fierce conservation orders—is a rude rich person who drives a large car badly (when your nose is that high in the air, it's hard to see the road) and serially mistreats au pairs, cleaners, waiters, and anyone apparently poor—that is, who takes home less than £1 million a year.

I've reminded Gabrielle that I drive a Vauxhall and am comfortably unsuccessful, but her reply is "Yes, darling, but for some reason you're still *rude*."

If that's true, I apologize, and offer the weaselly excuse that I'm only being defensive. Gabrielle has a point. The Suburb, though picturesque and exclusive, is a bitchy village with a high concentration of unhappy families who resent their neighbors. Even though a friend of mine who's plod—pardon, a police officer—says they have zero to sneer about because half of them are bent. Still, if you don't conform—say, you smile at a gardener or divorce (or worse, divorce, *then* smile at a gardener)—you are shunned like the traitor you are. It's an environment that stunts your natural affability, if you had any to begin with.

My job doesn't help. I'm a private investigator, but not a very good one. You can imagine how that went down with Next Door. If

I'm not in the mood to offend (rare), I tell people I'm in public relations. Which isn't a lie. Occasionally—when I don't botch things—I *do* help the public with their relations.

Pretty much the rest of my time is spent tracing people, which I hope sounds glamorous. Actually, all that tracing usually entails is a series of chats in which I invariably pretend to be someone I'm not. Anyone could do it. Really, it's no different from dating. Anyhow, Greg, my boss, finds me amusing, which is the reason I'm not on the street.

At the time I'm speaking of, the one part of my life under control was my relationship with Jason. Mainly, I have to admit, thanks to Jason. Given the chance, I would have messed up. But Jason was that rarest of men, a real sweetheart. Don't ask me why, he liked difficult women. (Well, I'd hesitate to introduce myself as "easy.") "Difficult" gives an impression of being wild, independent, untamable, which I like. But, stripped of its cute, coltish associations, I fear the true translation of "difficult" is "bad-tempered."

Jason has stood me for five years. When a person describes themselves as "easygoing," I say nah. (Although I have the nous to say it in my head.) What they mean is, they're too lazy to organize themselves, so they let someone else do it. The true test of being easygoing is whether you accept someone else's choice when it proves to be the exact opposite of what you would have chosen for yourself. Most self-proclaimed easygoing types flip out on seeing that the wrong brand of juice has been procured from the supermarket. Easygoing is Jason Brocklehurst. Five years is a long time to let your girlfriend have her own way.

The day before I turned thirty-one, I was feeling fine. I'm a London girl, but it's always a relief to escape the fight. Also, Jason kept saying, "I can't wait to give you your birthday present," so I knew he'd bought me a bath. That must sound strange, but my bath was green and reenameled and it *flaked*. (Never reenamel a bath, it doesn't work.) I'd sit in it and feel dirtier than before I'd washed. I was convinced that particles of dead skin from the bottoms of my flat's previous owners were caught in its scratchy surface. The thought made me feel slightly sick.

As a result, my baths lasted a mean two minutes. The deprivation was beginning to affect my sanity. My dream bath was a designer rip-off. Philip Stuck? Something like that. It was white, sleek, freestanding, with gently sloping sides, and it cost a cool £700 in the *sale*. I didn't expect that Jason had bought the bath and hidden it in the Fiat boot (a bath tap would barely fit in the Fiat boot), but I guessed he was planning to present me with a picture of the bath. The excitement was affecting my sleep, which I'm not ashamed of. People who don't get excited about receiving gifts are tired of life. (Nor do I buy that "more pleasure in giving" blather, unless you give in anonymity. If you give in grinning person, you might as well be getting—it all reflects back to the ego.)

My birthday journey to St. Ives took a while longer than it should have, because Jason had to accomplish everything on his to-do list. Task twenty-eight was "Buy water en route for hotel."

As Jason emerged from the petrol station, carrying seven monster Evian bottles, I showed my teeth. One of those babies (well, they're the size of babies) can last me a fortnight. My excuse is, they're too heavy to lift, and by the time they're not, the water's gone stale. London tap water has been—cute euphemism—recycled seven times, and when I bought a water filter I emptied it so rarely that all the lovely, pure, filtered water turned green. Consequently I'm as hydrated as the food NASA gives astronauts to take into space.

Only a week back, Jason had stuck a pink note to the toilet lid:

URINE TOO YELLOW. CORRECT SHADE: PALE STRAW. DRINK MORE CLEAR FLUIDS. We'd gone out that night. I'd drunk seven vodkas just to oblige him.

"There you go."

Jason dropped a stunted bottle of Evian into my lap. "Even you can lift that."

"Oh, sweet of you. Thanks. Though I won't drink it now or we'll have to keep stopping."

Jason glanced at me. "We'll stop anyway, Hannah."

"Yeah, but we don't want to have to stop *immediately*."

Jason laughed. "Your skin will dry up and you'll get wrinkles. You have to drink enough water to hydrate every organ in your body before your skin even gets a drop."

"Ah well," I said.

Jason sighed. "What music do you want?"

Now I laughed. "You're determined to be nice."

He smiled. "It's your birthday tomorrow, Gorgeous. We're in love, and we're on an adventure. What could be nicer?"

"Jason. People say things like that in films, then in the next scene they die in a car crash."

"Hannah!"

"Sorry. I just like to guard against the worst-case scenario by preempting it."

Jason shook his head. Aware that I was crushing the mood like a small child stamping on berries, I chose *Scott 3* and the rest of the journey was harmonious.

Jason had booked us into a castle because he knew I loved castles, and he was appalled to find it was a fake.

"It *looked* old on the website!" he kept saying as we stared at its newly crenellated walls. There is a silence familiar to long relation-ships, which people refer to as "comfortable." This wasn't one of those.

"We can go home," said Jason.

"Don't be silly. Anyway, it *is* old," I murmured as the porter slammed our bedroom door behind us and we surveyed the 1960s decor. Jason looked as though he might cry.

"Jase," I said. "Look at the view."

From our window we could see the buxom curves of the coast-line, the sun casting diamonds on the water, and the sultry blue summer sky.

I squeezed Jason's hand. "We're going to have a great weekend.

"Let's go for a walk," I added. Walks, I presume, are the point of being in the country. "And let's go out tonight and eat baked pota-toes and fudge."

Jason got a stiff look on his face, as if he'd sat on a pin.

"What?" I said. I was having trouble warding off my own stiff looks. I was about to be thirty-one. I was past the age where rough-ing it meant I was cool. Now, roughing it meant I hadn't done very well in life. It was a sore point.

"I'm happy to do whatever you like," said Jason.

"But?"

"It's all-inclusive."

Don't think he was mean. He wasn't. He knew I hated to owe him. On my pay it was inevitable, but he liked to help limit the damage. We went to the restaurant for dinner after a dutiful walk by the sea. Twelve minutes of piped Charles Aznavour and tinned run-ner beans, and we left the restaurant *and* dinner.

"God, I'm sorry," said Jason.

He drove into St. Ives and I sat in the car while he purchased two baked potatoes. (Cottage cheese and salad, no butter for him. Cheddar cheese, butter, and tuna mayonnaise for me. I feel that Jason is healthy enough for both of us.)

"Hooray," I said as he passed me our food. I balanced the yellow container on my knees and undid the catch. It made a scratchy squeak that gave me goose pimples.

"No!" said Jason, tapping the lid of my carton.

"Oh!"

"Wait until we get back to the castle."

"Why?"

"Because."

It was unlike Jason to give orders, and this made me uncomfortable. I wondered suddenly if he was intending to dump me. It was an intriguing thought. Some men think that to conclude a relationship in civilized surroundings reduces a woman's disappointment. These men are mad. What a surprise if Jason were one of them. Neither of us spoke until we reached our room. I made a second lunge for my potato. If I were about to lose my man, best to cover the loss of my appetite.

"Leave the potato!" said Jason as if I were a dog. (Working, as I do, for a firm called Hound Dog Investigations, the issue has been raised.)

"Why don't you lie on the bed and read," he added, "and I'll lay the table."

I belly-flopped onto the bed, snatched my book, and pretended to read. Jason dragged an ornamental table and two chairs over to the window, pulled two small bottles of champagne from the minibar, fuffed about with napkins and plastic cutlery, arranged the potatoes on two fruit plates. Then he attached the dinkiest speakers to his portable stereo and pressed *play*.

The strains of "Brown Eyed Girl" filled the room. I curled my toes. In a past life I'd attended an exercise class run by a woman named Gertrude who I have no doubt was a corporal on leave from the German army. "Brown Eyed Girl" was the tune she made us squat to, and I can never hear it without suffering a flashback. Van Morrison croons, "Everywhere I go," and Gertrude screams, "BEND LOWER, BUTTOCKS OUT!"

"I'll be one sec," said Jason and vanished into the bathroom.

Twenty minutes later I knocked on the door. "Jase?"

Jason has an irritable bowel and spends as long in the toilet as other people spend in the pub. I was going to demand special dispensation to eat my potato before it rotted.

"Jase?"

I pushed open the door. And there was Jason sprawled lifeless in front of the toilet.

"Jason!" I screamed. He was facedown and I had a mad vision of turning him over to see half of his head had been eaten away. Happily it was all there. He was pale but warm. He blinked.

"Careful," I said as he struggled to sit. "You must have fainted."

"Fainted," Jason repeated. He struggled with his trousers, which were at his ankles. "Hannah, will you marry me?"

"What?"

"Will you marry me?" said Jason. He was beaming now, and ferreting in his pocket.

"Come away from the toilet," I said.

I hope, for the sake of humanity, that I am alone in replying to the question "Will you marry me?" with "Come away from the toilet."

"Did you hit your head?" I added.

Neither of us were really listening to the other.

Jason flashed open his left hand, and I recognized his grandmother's engagement ring. He'd shown it to me before, and it reminded me of a big wart. Encrusted with red and black stones, it reeked of evil and belonged to a dead woman. Not my thing. I'd yet to see an engagement ring that was.

Jason sank to the floor again, this time on purpose. I was shocked that he wanted to do this.

"Hannah," he said. "I've waited nearly five years to make you mine. Please marry me."

I took his hand and kissed it.

"Jason," I said. "You are a wonderful, gorgeous man. I'm so very sorry. But . . . no."

2.

When I introduced Jason to a member of my family as "my boyfriend," six months after we first met, Gabrielle's reaction was "poor kid." She referred to Jason's being younger than I was and moony-eyed, but it still annoyed me. Who did she think I was, Heidi Fleiss? I reasoned that Gabrielle was blissfully married to my brother, Oliver, so perhaps she believed she had the monopoly on love. Her husband thought so too. When Gabrielle told him I was seeing Jason, he left a message on my answer machine:

"Ner!"—"Hannah" is too much of a stretch for Oliver—"I hear you're banging Jason! I think it's hilarious!"

Neither Jason nor I—we were in my kitchen discussing what we should eat from the freezer at the time—agreed with him.

"It's because we're younger than them," I said, deleting the message. "They think they can patronize us. Oh, and because Gab and Oliver are *married*. You'd think they invented it."

Jason laughed. He often laughed at things I said, surprising me. I never thought I was funny till I got together with Jason.

That I got together with Jason at all was unlikely. He'd attended the same school as Oliver. Our older brothers had been in the same class. His family lived in Highgate, in a huge white house. The first time I set eyes on Jason, I felt I knew him. And I don't mean that in the you-complete-me sense. I felt I knew him simply because I knew hundreds of boys like him. The dark hair, the brown eyes, the wealthy family, the five-a-side football on Sunday mornings. I took one look at him and I knew which university he'd attended and that his mother had sent him food parcels once a week all through term.

As it happened, his mother hadn't sent him food parcels all through term because she'd died when he was thirteen. She dropped dead of a heart attack in the street. She was buying nuts for a party. When he mentioned it, I remembered. Bad news is social currency—I was going to say "when you're a teenager," but on second thoughts, I'll amend that to "when you're a human being." Aged fifteen, I had no idea how you treated someone with a dead parent, so I'd played safe and ignored him if we passed in the school corridor. I did apologize about that, later. He *had* noticed. He was a sensitive boy. On our third date he said, "Were you breast-fed?" I nearly ended it there. I didn't, though, because he was delightful. He was enthusiastic, without cynicism, like a new puppy.

Jason and I met in the kitchen, at a New Year's Eve party. I hate those things. I'd rather sit on my own, see in January first looking up medical complaints on Google. It was ten to twelve and I was about to leave—I'd decided I'd prefer to spend midnight in the Vauxhall than with these people and I was hoping to filch some peanuts for the road. I was starving—people never provide anything *substantial* for guests under twenty-five; do they think hunger hits only in middle age?

I'd just tipped the dusty remains of a packet of Doritos down my throat when I realized that I wasn't alone. I turned round and there was this guy staring at me. Twit, I thought. It's the first rule of surveillance. Never stare directly at the back of the subject's head because chances are they will turn round and look at you. It's *instinct*.

"Yes? Can I help you?" I said.

If I sounded harsh, it's because I hadn't had a good year.

He replied, "I like the back of your head," and I laughed before I could stop myself. If he'd thought of a better line I don't think I would have stayed.

"I'm not even meant to be here," I told him. (The host was a friend of Oliver, which was fine, but he and Gabrielle had said they'd meet me there and they hadn't turned up.)

"I'm not meant to be here either," said Jason, who turned out to be the host's younger brother. He was meant to be surfing in Australia, but the holiday firm he'd paid a grand had collapsed three days before and he hadn't taken out travel insurance *yet*.

"So when were you planning to take it out?" I said. I cracked a smile. "On the flight home?"

He talked to me about surfing and to my surprise, we were still in that kitchen at 5 A.M. Jason fell in love with surfing after seeing Sean Pertwee star in *Blue Juice* with Catherine Zeta-Jones. Not her finest hour, although it probably was Sean Pertwee's. I was touched to meet the man who could claim with a straight face that he had been influenced by *Blue Juice*. I'm sure it's why I let him kiss me.

Truth was, Jason wanted to impress, and I wanted to be impressed. A few weeks after we got together, I even tried surfing. It was his idea, not mine. I've never felt the need to encroach on a partner's interests. Not least when they take place in Polzeath. I believe a crucial element in the success of any relationship is the quality time you spend apart.

I wasn't enthralled at wearing a wet suit. As bodies go, mine is like the Vauxhall. It does its job but isn't flash. I accept that, but there's a difference between compromising one's dignity and taking liberties with it. I had the air of a walrus, and my thighs squeaked as I approached the water. Though the dress code was nothing to the sport itself. Surfing made me realize how little I enjoy exerting myself. Also, I wear contacts so was forced to keep my eyes screwed up the entire time I was in the sea. It was a tense eight minutes.

I might not have taken to his hobbies, but I took to Jason. For six years, I'd been sleepliving. He woke me up.

I'd skipped college, become what my boss Greg calls a "blagger." A blagger is a low life-form in the world of PIs. I worked for a trace agency. The years became a blur. Your every day is spent ringing people to blag information out of them. You can do this in a nice way, but truth is, you choose the quickest. You reveal a little of your chosen persona. If I was claiming to be from the Department of Social Security, it might be, "We've just had a new system installed, it's a nightmare." I was paid less than the minimum wage, I know it. It was not great for one's self-esteem. Jason was the boot in the ass I needed. The week after we met, I talked my way into a job at Hound Dog Investigations.

Jason was still a student then, and keen to save the world. After "uni," he'd been to Tibet and wouldn't shut up about it. When he completed his "postgrad" law degree, he planned to specialize in human rights. He recycled his lemonade cans and copies of *The Guardian*. I noticed that unlike some of his peers, he treated women with reverence. Maybe, in his eyes, we all were potential mothers. Whatever, I found him charming. Old-fashioned, a real gentleman. He was an antidote to my entire lifestyle. He took me to see *Hamlet* at the National and sat there for nearly four hours, wet-eyed. My eyes stayed dry. My seat nearly didn't.

"What did you think?" he breathed, afterward.

"Yeah," I said. "I've dated men like him."

I'd never dated a man like Jason. Gabrielle and Oliver might scoff but we had a lot in common. Jason thought it would "spoil things" if you lived together before you got married. I couldn't agree more. I was twenty-six years old and I liked my own space. There wasn't much of it, which made me value it all the more. I had an apartment that was pretty much all corridor, in Camden. It was a basement flat, and the lounge window was at pavement level. As I viewed the place, a tramp lifted her skirt and relieved herself in front of *my* railings. Even the estate agent was shocked when I made an offer. I didn't care about tramps' bottoms. I thought it was sad but funny. Presumably, the estate agent wouldn't have been offended had she been a dog.

I don't think Jason was impressed with my home, but he wasn't repelled by it either. As he still lived with his father at the age of twenty-four, I think he saw it as some achievement that I could stuff crisp wrappers down the side of my sofa without being yelled at. Actually, I didn't do this as often as I might. I'm a messy person who is obsessively tidy in bouts. When the flat lapses into a state worthy of *Grime Watch,* I'll spend until 3 A.M. scrubbing. I find I have the eyesight of an eagle, and at 4 A.M. I'll still be pouncing on a rice grain on the kitchen floor or a biscuit crumb near the leg of the lounge table.

It would make sense to employ a cleaner, but I don't. Even though Gabrielle taunts me, "It's your heritage." Gabrielle gets a lot of mileage from the fact I was born in the Suburb. This isn't a whine. Because I get even more from the fact that she was born in Mill Hill. *Miw Hiw,* I call it, in deference to the local accent (at the end of each word draw down both corners of your mouth as far as they'll go).

Actually, there's nothing wrong with Miw Hiw except that it's a long hike out of London and not exactly kicking. I've spent no time in Miw Hiw, but I sense that its female inhabitants attend the local salon weekly for a *do,* carry bags that match their tan and demin leather uppers, and refuse to step outside unless their long acrylic nails are painted red. If ever I want to annoy Gabrielle I'll describe a client with the words, "She was a bit *Miw Hiw.*" Gabrielle will shriek, "Shut up, you've never even set foot in the place." I tell her, "You live in northwest London all your life, Gabrielle, you get an instinct for these things."

Gabrielle has changed since the days she let a woman who'd escaped from an asylum and into *Snippits* perm and dye her hair. Oliver once showed me an old photo and I did myself an injury. She had eye makeup like Ozzy Osbourne and a hairstyle like Axl Rose.

Twelve years and one child later, Gabrielle resides in Belsize Park with my brother and has adjusted her image—though I wouldn't say *accordingly.* Belsize Park isn't short on high-maintenance women, but I can't believe there are many who spend quite so much on their appearance as my sister-in-law. Last September, when Jude was four months old, Oliver found a £3,000 suede coat in a plastic bag in their bedroom. Next to a box of £545 stilettos. Jimmy Shoes, I think she said they were. Anyway, Oliver gently suggested to Gabrielle that per-haps shopping was becoming "an emotional crutch"?

Her reply: "*Du-uh!*"

Their part-time nanny was employed shortly after, enabling Gabrielle to resume her work—she designs and makes wedding dresses—and her health club membership. I think the shopping bills decreased, a little. She claims she needs to dress well for her career, as brides-to-be want first-sight evidence of your good taste even if they don't know they do. I'm giving attitude but secretly I defer to everything she says. Fashion is not my thing. It is hers. She reads *Women's Wear Daily* like a preacher reading from the Bible. Only on occasion do I doubt its influence. One morning she knocked on my door and I opened it in my Snoopy nightie. She cried, "Hannah, I *love* your look!"

When I first introduced Gabrielle and Jason, four and a half years ago, I reckoned they'd get on. Gabrielle's knowledge of what to wear, now and in the *future,* what will suit, where to get your hair cut, which restaurant is hot, what wine to order, is exhaustive (and exhausting). If her mission as an ex-inmate of Miw Hiw was to become sophisticated, she succeeded. Becoming a mother cramped her glamorous style for about five minutes. *But,* but. Like Jason, she has a warm, loving heart and traditional leanings. Some minor celebrity got hitched in a dress that I swear was modeled on a toilet-roll-holder doll, and I made the error of commenting on it.

In a voice of ice, Gabrielle said, "You know, Hannah, you should take a day off. Every girl who gets married has a secret image of herself. Of how she wants to look on her wedding day. And I believe in her right to look beautiful, if only for once in her life, and for everyone to be on her side for that moment. And it is true that brides are radiant. Even the plainest, plumpest girl is transformed. I get very angry if ever I hear someone say anything against a bride."

I felt like shit. I deserved to.

I was surprised that Gabrielle didn't take to Jason. I remember, early in our relationship, Jason sauntering into a café to fetch us some coffees while I sat outside. A blonde made cat-eyes at him as he passed. He didn't notice, which amused me, so on his return I remarked on it. The conversation wandered to fidelity. Cheating, he told me, wasn't in his nature. "My father never had an affair," he said, as if that explained it.

His words reminded me of something Gabrielle had said when I'd mentioned a case I was working on: older guy, young wife, he suspected her of cheating with her fitness instructor, and he was right.

With real exasperation, Gabrielle had said, " '*To the exclusion of all others.*' Why don't people *get* that?"

How could those two not adore each other?

Well, they didn't. They were mutually polite, ever so respectful and attentive. But they had trouble stretching civilities beyond two minutes. It was inconvenient. I couldn't even read a magazine on Gabrielle and Oliver's luxury toilet. Or as Gabrielle once called it, "*luxe* toilet." What the hell does that mean? Jason would loiter outside the bathroom, sighing. Gabrielle would suddenly recall she had an urgent e-mail to write. ("Like *what*?" I grumbled to Jason after she used this excuse once too often. " 'Cancel the black satin. On second thoughts, I'll make this one white.' ")

Their indifference bothered me, but not that much. It's not as if my faith in Gabrielle was absolute. I was happy to let her correct me on the zeitgeist. (Now I no longer pronounce St. Tropez, "Saint Trowpez," or Merlot, "Mer*lot*.") But I put her straight on quite a few things too. She was so naive. One time she had her purse stolen. A while later, she got a call at home from the Barclaycard Fraud Department. "We've found your credit card, madam. To establish your identity, please state your mother's maiden name, your credit limit, and your date of birth." It was pure luck I was there and over-heard the conversation.

As Gabrielle opened her mouth to tell all, I pressed my thumb on the receiver cradle and cut off the caller.

"What did you do that for?" shouted Gabrielle.

I rolled my eyes. "You give the details, that guy runs up three and a half grand on your card."

As it happened, it *was* Barclaycard Fraud Department. But it might not have been.

3.

When I turned down Jason's marriage offer, he squirmed his hand out of my grasp and ran it over his face.

"This isn't happening," he said. "Tell me this isn't happening." He shook his head at the ceiling and laughed, a nasty sound. Tears came and he smudged them away with his thumbs.

I watched in horror. "Jase," I said. I reached out to touch him. He jerked away, shaking his head, one hand held up as if to ward off the devil.

"Jason," I said. "I'm sorry."

The understatement of the year, but the truth. I *was* sorry. I was sorry he'd blown our future by asking such a stupid question. That sounds mean, but really. If you don't like Chinese food, say, and your partner takes you to a Chinese restaurant for your birthday, even if it's the best Chinese in the city ("yeah, you say you don't like Chinese food, but wait till you taste this, this is different, you'll *love* it"), there is a part of you that's going to be irked. The action of treating one's beloved to a large meal is seemingly above reproach, but this sort of deed has an evangelical selfishness to it. The undertone is "Your opinion is wrong, let me convert you to *my* way of thinking, you'll be much happier . . ." When in my experience, if ya don't like Chinese food, ya just don't like it.

Well, *I* don't like Chinese food, but I prefer it to marriage. Not marriage in general. Some of my best friends are married. Just marriage for *me*. Jason knew this. I feel, therefore, I had a right to be annoyed.

Jason stumbled away, out of the bathroom. I followed, my heart at boot level. Jason has the body of a young god and—in theory—

18

should have been able to protect me in a fight. I'm not saying that's what most women look for, but in these mean times it's a bonus, whether you care to admit it or not. I had no doubt that if ever I was attacked in Jason's presence, he'd leap to my aid and faint on the spot, leaving my aggressor to stamp on my head. (I'd hope to defend myself, but I suspect that if I tried to throw a punch I'd break my knuckles. I never drank enough milk.)

My point is, there has always been a softness to Jason, which I liked. I saw where I was needed. *I* could protect him. He trusted people and I thought that was admirable, if foolish. I could take care of him, in that sense. The second time we met, he took me back to his dad's place. It was January fifth. Jason, who likes order, had thrown away the previous year's contents of his Filofax. There it was, in his bin, the entire diary. I didn't expect Jason to possess a two-way shredder (we've pieced together a document shredded one way before, but that's rare, it's just that at Hound Dog, time is someone else's money). Still, most crooks are lazy; at least invest in a one-way shredder! He hadn't even torn each page in half!

"Jason," I said. "What are you going to do with that?"

"Throw it in the rubbish." He laughed. "I *was* going to recycle it, but . . . I didn't want it cluttering up the corner of my room for a week."

I looked severe.

"What?" said Jason.

"I burn my rubbish," I said. "All of it."

"You do? Why?"

"I'm not paranoid," I said—he was doing a bad job of looking unalarmed—"I know how people work. And you're leaving a data trail behind you that can be abused. They can go through your bins, take your name, proof of address, your credit card details, your bank details, steal your whole identity. They can take out loans in your name. All they need are two, three items with your home address on them, and they can walk into PC World. Before you know it, you've bought five computers at two grand each. Worst-case scenario, the bailiffs come knocking, your credit rating is destroyed, you've got years of aggro trying to clean it up."

"Gosh," said Jason. He marched over to the bin, fished out his Filofax papers, and placed them at the back of his sock drawer.

I smiled. I could keep this man from being hurt.

Now, five years later, I was doing the hurting. It made me want to get away. I couldn't stand to be around him when he was in this delicate state. It repelled me. Not a noble feeling to admit to but, I'm hoping, a human one. It's instinct to remove yourself from the person most likely to get eaten. (Primitively speaking.) That didn't stop me from feeling ashamed. I'd always presumed that my desire to protect Jason from harm was because I loved him. Now I wondered if it was because I couldn't stand a man to exhibit *weakness*.

"Jason," I said, "I am so sorry. I *do* . . . you know . . . feel the same way. But . . . ." I didn't want to sound piqued but it was hard not to. "I . . . was surprised you asked. Knowing how I feel about marriage."

Jason's face turned a pinchy red and white with rage. "You say that like it's a bloody computer program!" he shouted. "*Marriage* is only as bad or good as the people in it, you, you *fool!*"

"I—"

"Five years," he said. "Five years. What, did you think we'd just meander on like this forever? I'm twenty-nine and you've wasted my time. What is so *scary* about getting married, having kids? I don't get it, what's wrong with you? What's wrong with doing what normal people do?"

I felt my eyeballs swell. I always find something to say, even if it's irrelevant. Half the time you can't shut me up. But at that moment, I hadn't a word. Some people plod on for years pleasing everyone but themselves, only revealing their discontent when they run amok with a machine gun. Jason didn't quite make this category but it felt like a close thing. He'd seemed happy enough. And then, after all this time I find that not only has the man secretly been buying *Brides* magazine and stashing it under his mattress, he's desperate for me to make him a father. For all I knew he'd been pricking holes in condoms for years.

"Twenty-nine isn't that old," I said. "Some men don't have kids till they're fifty."

Jason was holding a Biro, and when I said this, he made a face like Jack Nicholson in *The Shining* and snapped it in half.

"I'm just saying," I said.

Jason clutched at his hair. "Do you," he screeched, "even live on this *planet*? Because, you don't seem to have any *EM-PA-THEEE*!"

The person next door banged on the wall.

"Then," I replied, "why do you want to marry me?"

Jason marched to the door and yanked it open and stamped out.

Perhaps he wanted me to chase him, but as I wasn't doing a great job of sensing his needs just then, I decided to stay put. I sat on the floor and closed my eyes. My head felt like it might go pop. I'm not that different from most people, I hate confrontation. The worst element of my job—there are a few contenders—is process serving. There was a time when, if I had to do a serve, I'd take Maisie—Greg's old, fat black Labrador—as protection. As a good idea it ranked with giving lone female drivers a lifesize man doll to prop in their passenger seat and frighten off attackers.

My *Turner and Hooch* act came to a sorry end when I served the owner of two young, lean Alsatians and found myself running down three flights of stairs with Maisie over my shoulder. It wasn't funny. I had to have physio three times a week for a month. Greg called me a berk and refused to pay for it. Unpleasant, the entire episode, but compared with the slow death of my relationship, I reassessed it as not that bad.

I sighed. The room was hot and smelled of baked potatoes. I glanced at the table. Our dinner had shriveled. My stomach growled. I did my best to ignore it. It growled louder. I shot another look at the table. That wrinkly potato was the mermaid to my sailor. What harm would it do? Maybe if I ate quickly. Naturally, Jason reappeared when my mouth was full. I stopped chewing, but I knew it looked bad. Callous, even.

He gave me a look of disgust, dragged his suitcase from under the bed, and turned his back.

I swallowed. The sight of his big, sad back—sad in *posture,* for those pedants among you—just hit me. All my strength left me as I got what this meant. No Jason, anymore.

A life bereft of his warmth and his *goodness*.

For him—for anyone, I suppose—proposing was an ultimatum. I'd called his bluff, or he'd called mine. I was used to having him around. He was my appreciative audience. I'm aware that this description falls a little short of romantic, but we had been together for five years. If you can stand each other after being whapped over the head with the saucepan of reality, I call that real love. Any idiot can *fall* in love, that's the fun bit. It's the ability to stay there that counts.

It annoyed me that when Jason read a book, he licked his finger to turn the page. It annoyed me that when he stayed over at my flat he snored. (Causing me to ask him once, "Can you stop breathing?" And it wasn't a Freudian slip.) It annoyed me that, no matter how often I told him it was a scam, if Jason opened the door to a kid selling dishcloths, he'd buy a stack of them. There was a whole pile of unwanted household items under his sink—dusters, washing-up gloves, wrapping paper—all purchased at vast expense from some little villain with an honest face and a smart mouth.

All these attributes drove me nuts, but I still loved him.

Likewise, it enraged Jason that I left my dental floss on the side of the sink. One time he spun a spiderweb of floss around the hot tap to demonstrate the error of my ways. (I unwound it, amused.) Nor was he overawed with my line of work, but he had the good grace to keep quiet on the matter. I think he assumed I'd grow out of it. It pained him that I never paid a bill unless I got a phone call.

He hated it that I'd write Christmas cards and not send them because I couldn't locate my friends' addresses. He loathed it that I wrote my friends' addresses on random scraps of paper instead of in my address book. He couldn't stand that I'd use my entire body weight to crush down my kitchen refuse to squeeze in another egg carton, preferring to empty the bin only when its contents acquired the density of mercury. (At which stage, Jason would feel obliged to step in, as the bag was so firmly wedged against the bin's sides that only a bodybuilder could shift it. Then it would split, spilling a week's worth of rotting food over the floor tiles. I know that, momentarily, this made him hate me.)

And yet. He adored me.

Which made it all the more surprising that, four weeks after his proposal to me, he got engaged to someone else.

4.

Her name was Lucy and she was his next-door neighbor.

"Well!" I said to my boggle-eyed parents. "If that's all it took, lucky he doesn't live next door to an old tramp.

"Then again.

"So. I find out a bit about her. I discover she *bakes* for him."

My father sat forward in his cream leather armchair and tried not to look impressed.

"Treacle sponge, jam roly-poly, if you can believe that. I only ever baked for Jason once."

My mother, hovering behind the cream leather armchair like a parlor maid, tried not to look shocked.

"I made him a cake for his twenty-sixth birthday. Took me a day; looked and tasted like I'd dug it out of Pompeii. By the time I'd shaved off all the black bits, it was the size of a scone.

"Oh," I added. "According to Martine, Lucy is also a 'proficient seamstress.' I presume I've misheard. I'm thinking she's said 'dominatrix.' 'Worse,' says Martine. 'She's good at sewing.' I say, '*What?*' And Martine shouts, 'She's a homemaker!' "

"And what makes Martine the expert?" snapped my father. He was red in the face with annoyance.

Martine was an old friend who for political reasons had remained in touch with Jason. "Oh," I said. "Martine likes to talk."

I made a joke of the seamstress stuff, but it had shaken me. Sewing. When I was fourteen, I was forced to make a skirt at school. The pattern was unnecessarily complicated, so I just cut out two squares of material and sewed them together. I felt threatened by the idea of a grown woman who sewed for *fun*.

I'd also realized that if Jason and Lucy were official, I couldn't put it off any longer. I would have to update my parents. I hadn't even told them we'd split. So here I was, fighting a sofa like quicksand, trying to make it sound as if nothing was my fault. I'd called my father on his private line, to check he was home, then driven round. My mother had answered the door.

"Hi," I'd said. "Is Daddy there?"

Even Jason teased me about that, calling my father "Daddy."

"What a *baby*!" Just about everyone I know has some issue with it. I refer them to their therapists. Though even Daddy prefers me to call him 'Roger.' (His name.)

"Hello, love, are you all right?" My mother always wanted to talk.

"I'm fine. Is he upstairs?"

"I'll call him down for you, shall I?" She sounded thrilled at the chance to be of service.

"Could you."

It's obvious, but I'll say it. I was a lot closer to my father than my mother. I didn't respect my mother. She had no life of her own. She just clung to his. He was patient with her. Because, in MTV-speak, my mother brought nothing to the party. She was like a winter garden in that she maintained herself to the exact level required to survive her environment. Nothing more. She had no dangerous opinions. Whatever made you happy made *her* happy. For goodness' sake. Women like that set the rest of us back about fifty years. She didn't work, although she was a qualified accountant. Considering we were the one family in our road with a mortgage (I checked with the land registry), I thought it rather louche of her.

When I broke it that Jason was engaged to someone who wasn't me, my mother paused. She shot a nervous glance at my father. Then she said to me, "How do you feel?"

"Terrible," I said, testing her.

"It *is* terrible," she replied. Had I told her I felt "wonderful" she would have replied, "It *is* wonderful."

She added, "But you'll be okay about it, won't you?"

"I'll live," I said.

My father was more direct. "What! The bastard! What a prick! How *dare* he treat my daughter like this? I won't allow it! My God, you waited *five* years for that little schnip! He'll come back! Don't you worry! This tart next door is a rebound relationship, it won't last! I'll go and have a word, if you like."

I did my best to put him off. This wasn't idle talk. My father would go and have a word. Next thing I'd know, I'd be married to Jason. Jason was *petrified* of my father. Jason's own father was a bully, and I don't think Jason could shake off the idea that all fathers were bullies. Also, I suspect he was a little jealous of our relationship. My father was my great friend. I know that Jason felt threatened by this. Perhaps, having lost one woman, he was forever in anticipation of losing another.

I reassured my father that, while I was distraught over Jason's defection, I would slowly piece together the shards of my life. You might think it strange, my father ignoring the fact that *I* was the one who had first rejected Jason.

Actually it wasn't strange, because I hadn't told him. My father was a true son of the Suburb, in that one of his ambitions was to inform the neighbors that his daughter was a Mrs. I'm a lazy girl who likes an easy life and I saw no benefit to me *or* my father in telling him the truth. Honesty is an overrated virtue.

Which might explain why my father was also under the misapprehension that I'd been waiting five years for Jason to propose. My father has a reputation as a maverick—which, in the Suburb, can mean anything from mowing your own lawn to buying a German car—but which in his case means that he refuses to be shocked by what I do. However, he's not *that* much of a maverick that he's content for me to remain single my entire life. I know this, because he is not very good at keeping his opinions to himself.

As I walked down the garden path of my family home, head hanging, my father banged on the window and—when I looked—pulled a sad face.

I felt unaccountably teary.

Soon after this, it became apparent that the brilliance of the rejected lover act I was staging for my parents' benefit wasn't entirely down to my acting abilities. This had a lot to do with everyone I know presuming I must be utterly distraught. It hit me that I was more of a loser than I'd thought, because it was insultingly obvious that all my friends believed I'd blown my one fluky chance of hooking a man. I'd never been a "Someone likes me! Oh hooray!" kind of girl, but from the way they were behaving, perhaps I should have been. Jason and I had never warmed to each other's pals. I'd always thought that, if ever we were to split, this would be a bonus. Now I discovered it made no difference. They all took *his* side.

At this point, I was forced into introspection. Which I hate. My problem with self-analysis is that—as far as I can tell from listening to other people drone on—you never discover anything *good*.

Since Jason had left, I had reverted to instinct. Instinct is important in a job like mine. At least that's what Greg said when he employed me. I agreed with him. I've since found that he was talking about hunches. How very Chandleresque! To me, a hunch is a lucky guess. *I* was talking about taking the easiest, quickest route in any given situation. Apparently, laziness is actually instinct. This is why women's magazines moan about men trying to skip foreplay. I felt guilty when I read that because if I've ever had the opportunity *I'll* try to skip foreplay. It's like doing a crossword puzzle. Ultimately, it's *unnecessary*.

This, I supposed, could be why my friends were pessimistic about my chances of mating ever again. As I said, I'd reverted to instinct. Drinking little or no water, beyond what happened to be contained in my food. Staying up till one in the morning for no reason, flicking from channel to channel in the futile search for the elusive, brilliant program that was worth being tired for. Buying those plastic individual coffee filters that are such a foul reckless waste of the earth's resources. Not phoning people who'd phoned me unless I was pretty much certain they were out.

Jason had been such a civilizing influence. At first I hadn't missed him. Perhaps because—as with a bereavement—I couldn't really believe he was gone. I enjoyed pleasing myself. It was nice not to wake to a reproachful roar from the bathroom because I hadn't bothered to place a new toilet roll in the toilet roll holder. To Jason, this mattered profoundly. He set a lot of store by order, that boy. Everything had its place.

But as the weeks rolled on, I began to feel like a child whose stern parent had finally disclaimed responsibility. I needed an opposing force to push against. With Jason gone, life was one dreary constant; there were no happy little zigzags of dispute. I could eat Bolognese I'd warmed straight from the freezer and no one would say, "Hannah, if you want to live, you might want to stick that in the microwave for three more minutes on high."

I bet Lucy never ate from the microwave. She was probably dining on Jason's vegetable lasagna at this very moment. (That, by the way, is not some filthy innuendo. Jason could cook only three dishes, but over the last sixteen years, he'd perfected them. His lasagna was my favorite.) The thought of Lucy's eating *my* lasagna enraged me, and I threw my chicken vindaloo, still in its plastic container, in the bin. Then, come 1 A.M., of course I was starving and there was nothing to eat. I got up to stare inside the empty fridge regardless, knocked the remote control off the sofa, and it fell hard on my toe. A further consequence of Jason's desertion was the discovery that a sulk is meaningless in isolation.

The next day, as with most days at the Hound Dog office, I had to type a report. I'd just finished a case that had surprised me. A guy had called, wanting us to trace his ex-girlfriend from fifteen years ago. He didn't want to get in contact with her. He just wanted to make sure she was okay.

Jesus Christ!

Anyhow, I'd traced her. It had taken me an hour. I didn't tell the client this, of course. Clients need to believe you've been tramping the streets for days in your fedora and beige mac with a magnifying glass in your black-gloved hand; otherwise they feel you've over-charged them.

Greg is strict about presentation. Because, inevitably, we do a little less than we wish to *appear* to have done. It's important that our reports look professional.

Each report begins with "THE SITUATION." This is a summary of our instructions from the client, on the date they were given, and the name of the subject. We also include an instruction sheet, with the client's name, contact details, the agreed budget (essential—it's a shock to people that a day of three-man surveillance costs £1,000), and a copy of all written contact with the client. Then, of course, we enclose a breakdown of our invoice, and the detailed "RESULTS OF OUR INVESTIGATION." In this instance, typing up the report took me longer than the investigation itself. I wrote the address on the envelope and posted it.

As Greg whipped past, he glanced at my computer screen.

"What's that?" he said.

"The address of th— oh fuck."

I'd written the name of the client on the envelope. But I'd sent it to the subject.

Greg narrowed his eyes, peered at the address. "Reading," he said. "I'll expect you in late tomorrow."

The next day, at 5 A.M., I was heading up the motorway to one of the plainest towns in Britain. I parked a discreet distance from the girlfriend's house at precisely 6:34 A.M. and fell on the Mars bar I'd procured from a petrol station. I don't eat while I'm driving. I don't have many standards, but I feel that once you commit to a habit like eating while driving, it's going to be about as hard to kick as heroin.

The postman finally made an appearance at noon. I hurled myself in his path.

"Oh, *God*," I wailed, "you have got to help me."

The sob in my voice was surprisingly authentic. And not just because he was holding the envelope with the girlfriend's address scrawled in my thicko handwriting. "I've driven from London to catch you . . . My only hope is that you're a kind man . . . you see, I . . . I . . . I wrote a letter to my husband . . . telling him I . . . wanted to leave him and . . . I've made the worst mistake of my life." I pointed at the envelope and nodded toward the girlfriend's house.

After my early start, I didn't look fabulous. But I think it worked in my favor. He glanced over his shoulder, handed me the envelope, and said, "There you go, pet. Good luck the two of you."

When I'd composed myself, I called Jason.

5.

My father had said that Jason would come back, so perhaps I should have waited. Truth was, I couldn't. Patience is another virtue I find overrated. (In fact, I can't think of one virtue that isn't. They're like West End plays, in that sense.) My view is, I have to exercise enough patience in my job, I don't see why it should impinge on my social life. I *knew* Gabrielle would think it wrong of me to try and pinch Jason off Lucy, but I believe that both members of a couple face temptation, and if your relationship is good enough, you'll resist.

Jason didn't return my call.

Three days later, a Friday afternoon, I rang his office. "Hi. Is Jason there?" I said. "It's his girlfriend."

"Lucy!" said the person on the end of the line. "Oh, hello!"

I held the phone away from my ear and gave it a dirty look.

"Er, *no*," I replied. "It's Hannah. Who *is* this?"

"Ah, Hannah. Jason's ex. I'm Kathleen. Jason's PA. I've been his PA for, let's see now, four years."

"Oh, come off it, Kathleen," I said. "You didn't recognize me either." (Pardon me, but there's nothing more tedious than people who have a problem voicing their anger *directly*. Not only do they want you to feel guilty, they want you to guess the reason why. Jesus. We're all busy people. I find the best way to deal with someone who tries to delicately hint you into feeling dreadful is to run at them with a direct attack. They react like a vampire in the Bahamas. They just can't take it.)

A long silence, then Kathleen said, "He's gone surfing in Polzeath, Hann-*arr*."

There you go: stumped.

I put down the phone, sighed, grabbed my car keys.

As I arrived in Polzeath, the wind just about blasted the features off my face. The last time I'd been here, I'd asked Jason if he couldn't find somewhere to surf that was a bit less blowy. He thought this was hilarious and related it to his mutant surfing friends, who'd all ha-ha-ha'd in my face. So I'd said, "Yeah, funny, but you've got to admit, this is a bit pissy compared to Australia." They shut up.

However, five years on, I returned to Polzeath in a contrite spirit. Which sounds like a sports car, but alas, no. I coughed up for a B&B, because I wanted to shower before approaching Jason. Put on makeup, even. I'm not good with makeup. I never learned to apply it—I don't know, what do other women do, watch their mothers? On the rare occasions that I bother, I end up looking like Jude Law in *A.I.* Gabrielle keeps her lipstick in the fridge. I keep mine on the radiator. (There's a radiator in my bathroom, next to the sink, instead of a shelf—what can I tell you?)

Saturday morning, I ate as much sausage and egg as the landlady could put in front of me. If there's food on offer that I didn't cook, I find it hard to say no. I'll even clear my tray in economy class. I left the breakfast table having doubled my weight.

Then I riffled through the magazines on her hall table until I found one that was postseventies. It was a choice between *Bella* and *The Lady* (and *Able Seaman,* but I'm not that stupid). The woman on the front of *The Lady* was, I reckoned, in her fifties, but the woman on the front of *Bella,* though young, had gold eye shadow. I found this confusing, so I chose the lady on *The Lady* as a template. At least her blusher had distinct boundaries. Twenty-five painstaking minutes later, I zipped my makeup bag and left for the beach.

I knew Jason would be there. He never wasted a moment. I admired that. It was good to be with a man who was passionate about something, even if it was surfing. "It's a magical feeling," he once said. "When you're watching the waves begin to form, it's like being hypnotized. They're like big green mountains rolling toward you. Sometimes you see dolphins out there."

I loved that description. Like how a child might say it. I saw him as a lost boy, then, and it caught at my heart.

"Jase!" I shouted when he finally waded ashore. In his black wet suit, carrying his board, unshaven, he looked more of a rugged personality than he was. I ran up to him, and he yelped.

"Hannah! What are you doing here? I didn't recognize you. What happened to your skin?"

My smile twitched. "What do you mean?"

He bent in concern.

I touched my face and felt powder. "I'm wearing *blusher*. I made an effort."

Jason took a step back. "So you are. Wow. It's, er—nice. You remind me of my grandma."

"Good-bye." I turned to go.

"Wait!" He was laughing now. "So, what are you doing here?"

I tried to rub off the blusher with my sleeves. Bloody *Lady* magazine.

I said, "Jason. I'll be honest"—when people say this, you know they're lying—"I feel I was a bit . . . *hasty* to turn down your proposal. I . . . miss you. It's not the same without you. I feel like a . . . stray cat. I realize you're with that other girl now and I respect that, but it was a pretty quick turnaround and I wouldn't want you to rush into marriage on the bounce"—I saw the look on his face and paused.

"*Do* you respect that I'm with Lucy?" said Jason.

Did he *want* me to lie?

"Jason. You have to fight for what you want. I don't believe in suffering in silence."

"I know."

Jason was not being as friendly as I'd hoped. This last remark was plain cheeky. Where suffering was concerned, Jason was king. A few years back, he'd sworn he had a brain tumor, as he kept seeing flashes of white light. After months of this, I put it to him that, as his flat was on a main road by a junction, the flashes of white light were from a speed camera. I heard nothing more about the brain tumor after that. Yet if ever he had a headache, he wouldn't say, like a normal person, "Do you have any headache pills?" He'd say, "Do you have any *painkillers*?" The drama, it was like living with Barbra Streisand.

I stared at the sand. "Look," I said. "You must be freezing. I just wanted to talk, but maybe now isn't the best time. We could always meet up next week after work."

I waited for him to contradict me. Instead, he nodded. A slow grin spread across his face.

"I like that idea," he said.

I smiled, touched my hand to his cold cheek. Breakthrough!

Jason had given me the details of what looked like a posh address in town. I presumed it to be some po-faced private club.

"I presumed it to be some po-faced private club," I shouted.

"Have I ever, since you've known me, shown any inclination to join some po-faced private club?" said Jason.

"People change."

"You don't."

You have, I thought. I wasn't used to a Jason who answered back. Nor was I used to a Jason who tricked me into attending his *therapy* session.

I chose the chair farthest from the shrink. Jason chose the one nearest. I kept my arms crossed and my coat on.

"You look uncomfortable," said the shrink.

"I *am* uncomfortable."

The shrink, a portly woman in her fifties, took this opportunity to explain why I was here. "One of the driving forces in Gefilte therapy"—I think she said—"is the concept of unfinished business. Jason has been using the 'empty chair' technique. If you have unresolved issues, for instance, your father treated you cruelly but your father died and you didn't have the chance to confront him, you imagine that your father is in the chair and you tell him what you think of him. It's a helpful way of achieving closure. People get really engaged and involved, and everything they've bottled up comes out."

"Jason's father is still alive," I said.

She smiled. "I'm speaking theoretically. Jason asked you to come here today because he feels that he and *you* have unresolved issues. We thought it might be helpful if we had a discussion." She added, "Jason employed the empty chair technique with you but he found it didn't suit him."

"I didn't have the imagination," said Jason, blushing.

"Right," I said. "So what are we discussing?"

The shrink cleared her throat. I didn't like her. "Jason is having a few problems, and it would be very helpful if you could give us your take on things. It might be that Jason is distorting . . ."

"He looks fine to me," I said. Neither she or Jason smiled.

"We hope that you can help me get a more balanced view of what's gone on."

It's always a pleasure to be requested to hold court. (Not an invitation that comes my way so often.) Particularly if the subject is someone else's shortcomings.

"Great!" I said.

The shrink coughed. "Jason feels there was a lack of intimacy in your relationship. What do you think of that?"

I raised an eyebrow at Jason. "First I've heard of it."

"I see. So, what was your impression of the relationship's level of intimacy?"

"I thought it was fine."

"How would *you* define intimacy, Hannah?"

"Being intimate?"

The shrink looked disappointed. She reminded me of my English teacher when I described *Animal Farm* as "a book about pigs."

"Can you recall an instance where you felt that you and Jason were sharing an intimate moment?"

I thought for a second. "Yes!" I said.

The shrink beamed.

I hesitated. "It is . . . *fairly* intimate. I don't want to offend you."

"Oh," she replied. "There's very little that can offend me. Just as long as you feel comfortable sharing."

"Okay." I glanced at Jason. He gave me a terse nod.

"We were in Jason's flat. We'd just been to dinner at not a very good restaurant. I'd had the chicken. Jason thought he smelled of oil from the kitchens, so he was having a bath. Suddenly I got cramps. Really bad cramps. Jason only has one toilet and it's in his bathroom. Normally, he doesn't like us to—but it was an emergency, I rushed to the toilet, sat down, I had *the* most terrible diarrhea. So terrible, in fact, that Jason was sick in his own bath."

I smiled at the shrink. She looked offended. I looked at Jason. His hand was covering his eyes.

The shrink sighed. She tried to hide it by letting her breath out slowly. "I see," she said. "And when you think of an intimate moment in your relationship, that's the scene that springs to mind?"

"Yes." I paused. "Why? Did you want a *sex* moment?"

"This isn't about what *I* want. It's about what intimacy means to you. And you've . . . told me." She coughed. "Thank you."

I nodded. "Don't mention it."

She scribbled something on a pad. "Hannah," she said. "It looks to me as though you define intimacy as being familiar enough with a person to disregard polite social convention." She seemed to be trying hard to keep her tone neutral. "What do you think of that?"

"I think," I replied, "that that is *most* people's definition of intimacy."

"I see. But would you accept that some people might have a different interpretation of what intimacy means?"

"Well, yeah, a few, but what?"

"Perhaps some people might interpret intimacy as being emotionally open."

"Oh, right."

"Would it be right to say that you don't feel entirely comfortable with the concept of emotional openness?"

My lawyer wasn't present and I'd had enough. "I really don't see the point of this. If Jason had such a problem with my levels of intimacy, why did he ask me to marry him?" I glanced at Jason and saw him look hopefully at the shrink. "*She* doesn't know!" I said. "*You* answer."

"I hoped you'd relax more," he replied. "And. I loved you anyway. Love you." The last two words were muttered.

"Jason," I said. "That's very sweet, but why are you bothered about what I think *now*? You appear to have moved on."

Jason rocked forward in his chair. "Hannah. I brought you here because what you said in Polzeath confused me. I *do* still love you. I am still in love with you. And yet if you don't want the same things as me, then, however much I love you, I can't spend my life with you. I am very fond of Lucy and . . . she wants what I want. I could be very happy with Lucy. But, Hannah, *you* are the love of my life. What you said in Polzeath gave me hope. That maybe we could be together. But this time, if we were to do it, we would have to do it properly. Not just jump into it. Address the issues that need to be addressed. Do some changing."

I swallowed. He sounded like a country western, the worst sort of song. Whiny.

The shrink smiled at Jason. I could tell she loved it when people turned their insides out. I smiled at him too, although my smile was a little more tense than hers. Don't get me wrong. I was delighted that he still loved me. I felt similarly toward him. But being the love of someone's life puts you under pressure. The shrink saw her chance.

"Hannah. Would you agree with the idea that you are uncomfortable being emotionally open?"

I looked straight at her, speaking slowly and emphasizing the important words so that she'd understand. "The job I do is not about emotion, it is about *fact*. I am not used to dealing in the reason *why*. In the job I do, the reason why is not *important*. In fact, it is essential for the success of my work that I am the *opposite* of emotionally open. Emotionally *closed*," I added for her benefit.

Her mouth fell open slightly.

I was about to add "I am an information mercenary" when I glanced at Jason and saw him roll his eyeballs at the ceiling and mouth "I am an information mercenary"—a phrase I *might* have employed before. I settled for, "So, yes. I would agree with that last idea of yours."

The shrink licked her lower lip. "You know, in a way, Hannah, being a therapist is rather like being a detective. You're looking for clues about a person and encouraging them to show you the landscape inside them."

If this was a stab at getting me to *bond* with her, it failed. When I said nothing, just pried out something sticky from under a fingernail, she added briskly, "Hannah, has there ever been a point in your life that you can recall where you were more comfortable with being emotionally open than you are now?"

I made a clicking sound with my tongue. "Why do you ask?"

She glanced at her watch. She pretended she was looking for

something on her desk, but I saw her gaze hover at her wrist. "I'm thinking that perhaps there has been an event or experience in your life that has possibly *influenced* your belief."

"What belief?"

"Your belief that being emotionally open is dangerous."

"In my job being emotionally open *is* dangerous. Highly dangerous. I mean if you're undercover and—"

"She's not talking about your fucking job!" shouted Jason.

The shrink looked apologetic. "Hannah, Jason, I'm afraid we're nearly out of time. Is there anything anyone would like to add?"

"Yes," said Jason. "I would like to add that I know I have my faults, but *she* has more, and now, her saying she wants another chance, it's thrown me into turmoil. I mean, I feel terrible about Lucy, but I want to give Hannah another chance, but I think, for it to work, she has to learn to give a little, adapt—"

The shrink shifted in her seat. "Jason, I'm so sorry. We have to finish in a second. I have a patient waiting downstairs."

"Okay, but I just want her to know that if only she could acknowledge why she is *like* this it would make all the difference, I mean, she hasn't even told you." He glared at me.

The shrink stood up. "I'm afraid we have to end *right* now." She paused. "Told me?"

I frowned at Jason. Then I understood. "Oh!" I said. "I've been married before. When I was twenty. For five months. I'm a raddled old divorcée consumed with bitterness and regret. Is that relevant?"

6.

It's the one thing I have in common with Jennifer Lopez. (Apart from the size of our bottoms, I suppose I should add but won't. I'm not as good at putting myself down as I should be.) God, it was embarrassing. This wedding was *massive*. My father wanted a fuss. I'm quite a show-off, so I was happy to cooperate. In my head I was crowing, "*I* am the bride! You have all *got* to be nice to me!" Your wedding day is the day you can get your own way, no matter what. Up to a point.

My friend Martine—we went to school together—was a bridesmaid. She said, "You're only asking me because I'm fat."

"You're right," I told her. "I only asked you because I thought you'd make me look *grrrreat!*"

She grinned. "Yeah, go on then."

Martine was one of the few friends who didn't think my marriage to Jack was a mistake. (My various relatives were torn. A cousin's wife's *father*, a man I've met twice in my life, said to me, "Congratulations. I don't hold with these feminists, what do they call themselves, '*singleones*'? A woman's life is pointless unless she has a ring on her finger.") The point is, most of my relations couldn't decide whether to sanction my decision or condemn it. Was it about time I became respectable, or was I tying myself down when I was barely out of my teens?

As the cousin's wife said, "Hannah, marrying at this age is not normal when you're middle class and educated. You're supposed to want a career and the freedom to explore other relationships first." (As opposed to simultaneously, you imagine.) I looked at her like she was mad. First, I wasn't *that* educated. Second, why should marriage hinder my career? If anything it would help it as, with any luck, I'd no longer be trawling the streets for men at all hours. Third, did she think that Jack was, as she'd put it, "my *first*"? (I resent people who use phrases like "my *first*," so the person they're speaking to is practically obliged to imagine them having sex in order to complete the sentence. It's not nice.)

My father, though, was delighted. He loved Jack. So did my mother, I could tell. And so did I. He was a shit, which I liked. He started out as a solicitor for a city firm that had a reputation for employing beautiful people. He was arrogant and rude, but funny and good-looking so he mostly got away with it. Like Jason, he went to my school, but the two boys never really got acquainted, as Jack only joined for the sixth form and Jase was three years younger. Unlike Jason, though, Jack didn't seem to be wild about me. Turned out we'd attended the same junior school—maybe he remembered me from the days when I used to chase boys round the playground with a booger on my fingertip. Our relationship reminded me of a cat toying with a mouse. I didn't mind. I liked playing games, I got bored otherwise. Jack amused me.

He was an insane Elvis fan, but not in that tedious, showy way that people often are. Jack was a purist about Presley, which I found acceptable. I asked him, "Would you rather I died if it meant Elvis came back to life?"

He paused. Then he said, "Would I get to hang out with him?"

We used to compete to annoy each other. A particular favorite of mine was calling his mobile when I knew he was on the train. "Where are you?"

"On the train."

"Pardon?"

"I'm on the train."

"Sorry?"

"I'M ON THE—oh piss off, Ratfink!"

He called me Ratfink. Not what you'd call romantic, but I thought it was cute.

I mainly agreed to marry him because I thought it would wind him up. How right I was. He actually put a lot of thought into the proposal. It *started* (bear with me) on Christmas night. I'd fled my family in their red paper hats as soon as was decently possible and raced to his flat, a tiny space on a main road above a Greek restaurant. Jack hadn't moved back home after university, and nor would you, if you had his parents. They were half human, half glacier.

On tearing the wrapping off my gift, I was enraged to find that he'd bought me a *jigsaw* puzzle. A thousand pieces, the bastard. There was no picture on the box, so I said, "This better be good. What's it of?"

He smiled and said, "One way to find out."

At about 3 P.M. Boxing Day (I got distracted, also I'm not good at jigsaw puzzles), I pressed in the last piece, in a disbelieving daze. The whole damn thing was black, except for five words in white. "Ratfink, will you marry me?"

I rubbed my eyes, blinked. My head felt as if it were full of helium and my hands shook. I turned round to see Jack leaning in the doorway, a strange look on his face.

I said, "Yes, okay, now where's my real present?"

Jack was not a gushy person, and because he didn't bombard me with romantic verse (I had a Hallmark idea of love, aged twenty), I assumed he was in control of his feelings. So I fought to control mine. I'd take what I could get, not make a fuss. My grandma Nellie said, "It's not the hen that cackles most that lays the largest egg," but I wasn't inclined to listen to her. When I told Martine that Jack had asked me to marry him, her mouth fell open like a trap. She said, "I didn't think men like Jack proposed. I thought men like him were shaggers." I thought so, too. Ever since I'd known Jack, he'd seemed aloof.

We were on nodding terms at school. We got together (although it was less formal than that) outside the Everyman cinema in Hampstead, after going to see *Hard Boiled,* separately. I trod on

42

his foot in the foyer, apologized, said, "Oh! Hello!" checked to see if he was alone, like me.

I got this surge of adrenaline, standing close to him; it was insane. He didn't move away.

"What did you think, Hannah?" he said.

I felt a bolt of pleasure, that he remembered my name. It meant something, made me reckless. I said, "All that killing, it makes me want to kiss you."

He stared at me, and I thought he was going to say, "Fuck off." He said, "Go on then."

I stood on tiptoe and kissed him quickly on the cheek. I pulled away and saw that he was smiling.

"What?" I said.

He touched a finger to my mouth and said slowly, "There was an awful lot of killing in that film."

The sex was—excuse my limited grasp of the superlative—*amazing*. It freaked me out, to be honest. I didn't like to think about it.

I'll tell you about the wedding, though. It was not the style of wedding Jack would have chosen. It was the style of wedding my father had chosen, and as he was paying, we'd let him choose. He'd been so excited. He bought all the magazines and kept ringing me at odd hours. Once it was "I've seen these cuff links, they're bloody superb! One cuff link says 'Dream' and the other says 'Man.' What do you think?"

What I thought was that Jack would rather one cuff link said "Dick" and the other said "Head." What I said was "Roger, they sound hilarious. But I think Jack already has cuff links. Why don't you get them for yourself?"

There would be a silence, during which I'd hold my breath. Then, "Great idea! *I'll* wear them!"

Or, it would be "Hannah. Freeze-dried rose petals or feather-fetti?"

"Roger," I said, "what *are* you talking about?"

He kept delegating chores to my mother, at one point encouraging her to undergo a makeup trial at the hands of a "makeup artist." Judging from the results, this woman was more of a graffiti artist. My mother did her duty. She sourced bouquets, tiaras, cakes, all according to my father's direction. I was grateful to her. It's not as if we don't *speak*. We have a formal relationship, that's all.

As for Roger, I was pleased to be making him happy. Not many fathers get involved like that. Martine reported an exchange with *her* father. She'd told him about my dress. I'm not an elaborate kind of girl, but to my surprise, the straight-down, no-fuss designs, far from turning me into Grace Kelly—even Gene Kelly would have been nice—made me look like a white post. It was the, what does Gabrielle call it, flouncy Cinderella-style skirt that suited me. Even I could see the difference. Then I saw the price tag. *Two thousand pounds.* My father didn't blink.

Anyway, Martine was about to get to this bit when her dad interrupted. He said, "So how much does a wedding dress cost these days? A hundred pounds?"

Martine found this amusing. Truth was, at that point, I thought a wedding dress cost a hundred pounds.

If you believe in wiffle-waffle, there were bad signs. I was having my hair fiddled with at some salon, five hours before I trotted down the aisle. The girl jammed the tiara into my scalp and said, "Are you in a play?"

Jack had got wrecked the night before and looked like death. *I* hadn't got wrecked. The decision was pure vanity.

It was a strange day. Jack's parents were there, scowling at each other. I'd say his mother lowered the room temperature by about ten degrees. They separated the following year. I kept them a distance from my father. He was on a high; I didn't want their sourness to taint him. My mother cried from the ceremony to the carriages. By midnight her face had puffed up like a chipmunk. Jack was very serious. Probably, I thought, he was wondering what he'd got himself into. He'd chosen his suit, bought me a gold ring so thin as to be barely visible (my choice), and turned up. That was his contribution.

I'm not complaining. *I* made a list of my friends, which took four minutes, and fit into my dress. I was happy to hand over to Roger, and Jack was busy on other projects. All the same, the end result was a shock. It was a bit . . . *Miw Hiw.* My father had booked "Original 1930s London Taxis" for both me and Jack. I felt a right prat. (Even though when we stopped at the lights, a cyclist smiled at me and mouthed "You look beautiful." What a doll.) My father wore a lime silk waistcoat, which made him look like a jockey. At the reception, we discovered personalized candles on every table. If there's one superfluity in life, it's personalized candles. The photographer and the toastmaster were like a pair of failed television personalities. It was a tough call who was the bigger moron.

The whole event, including fish, must have set my father back twenty grand. That's quite a lot of notes to stuff down the toilet. I've not looked at our wedding photos since, and my dress is scrunched up in a big white ball at the top of my wardrobe. You do feel bad. It feels fraudulent, to go through all that clamor—my father's friends and business associates were there—only to quit the relationship five months later. I had to call every guest, announce the news, and send back their presents. (Which in some instances, where a cut-glass vase was involved, was a pleasure.)

The end of the marriage was a shock. Despite everything, I do think on that day Jack and I were happy. Scared, but happy. We chose a first dance (they make you). I can't remember the title, but the chorus was "When you're with me, baby, the skies will be blue for all my life." Jack held on to me so tight I struggled for breath.

Now I see it differently. A man doesn't propose at age twenty-one unless he is in the grip of a very strong emotion. Nor does a woman accept. But I was such a *baby*, one year younger than Jack, and I think it was significant. I had no perception. I never considered that he might assume he had married me for life—I couldn't envision that far—I thought thirty was death. I couldn't see beyond the next day. I was obsessed with Jack and trying not to be. Even marriage didn't convince me he loved me; even when he said, "I love you," I wasn't convinced.

Apart from my stupidity, the trouble—*one* of the troubles—was that Jack had decided that he no longer wanted to be a lawyer. He was ambitious. He wanted to be a theatrical agent. At first I didn't believe him. I didn't want to. I suppose that I feared that any sort of change would take him away from me. I said, "A theatrical agent? What, did you read that in a book?" But he was serious. He took voluntary redundancy and set about establishing himself in his new career.

This involved getting work experience at a large agency and spending every spare minute at the theater. He'd go to what he called "crappy rep" and amateur dramatic society performances and drama schools, theater groups; he'd even attend school plays, watch a bunch of fifteen-year-olds hamming it up in an assembly hall—anyplace where he might spot an undiscovered talent. I laughed at him about the assembly hall bit and he replied, "Hannah. There are *so* many parts for teenagers." Not that anyone would have taken notice of him then, but it was useful. He chatted to other agents, casting directors; it got his face known.

The marital home was, for financial reasons, the tiny flat above the Greek restaurant. And, for a while, it felt like a palace. His wedding present to me was a huge carved oak wooden bowl, containing what looked like two dinosaur eggs. They were smooth ovals, polished gray brown stone, heavy, and beautiful.

"They're fertility stones," he said. Then, "Probably pinched from some poor village in Africa."

My wedding present to him was a new bed. It was also oak. It was a sleek colonial-style four-poster, and I wasn't sure if you were meant to drape white organza over the top to create a canopy. We didn't, but I liked the idea that we *might*.

I had allowed myself to relax, briefly. After the ceremony, Jack had been so uncharacteristically tender. I woke up one morning to find him stroking my face. I opened my eyes and he turned the stroke into a nose-pinch. For two months we saw no one but each other. Jack liked to cook, and he cooked for me. Thai jungle curries that filled the flat with the aromas of lemongrass, lime, and coriander. Coconut milk sticky rice with mangoes. "I like to watch you eat," he'd say as I tried to scrape out my bowl with chopsticks, and we'd fall on each other. He'd pepper my face with hot chili kisses.

Now it's as clear as a poke in the eye, but it wasn't then. I was naive, convinced that love was not about giving of yourself; I thought it was about holding back. And so, when Jack's new career stole his attention from me like a mistress, I pulled away from him, wrapping myself in solitude. I convinced myself that he was away from me because he wanted to be. It didn't occur that he was looking ahead, to how he could make things better for us in time. Simply, we didn't talk enough. I didn't have the emotional vocabulary nor did he.

I became the housekeeper by default, a role I resisted. The dishes stacked up like stalagmites. Damp towels moldered in piles. In Jack's absence, I refused to do a weekly shop. The mere idea of it and I imagined myself trudging round the same branch of Tesco every Thursday for the rest of my life. I preferred to subsist on whatever I found in the kitchen cupboards.

Once Jack came in and I was eating a dinner of dates, followed by teaspoons of ground almond. Ground almond *rapes* your mouth of moisture; I had to swallow five times before I could speak. Jack accused me of ignoring him—not my style. I think, in retrospect, he was bewildered by my sudden coldness and, perhaps because of his upbringing, his reflex was to match it.

It was a pity it ended how it did. I'd always thought we understood each other. We didn't. There were huge swaths of each other's personalities that we'd misread entirely.

Well. I hadn't seen Jack for ten years. Meanwhile, here was Jason offering me a second chance, despite my poor performance in the therapy session. Jason was a far nicer person than Jack or me. Jack and I were sensible to divorce, despite the terrible pain we caused our families. My father. We were too alike, we would have destroyed each other. Our relationship was far too uncontrolled.

Meanwhile, I had an opportunity to realign my life with Jason, a pure, sunny person, a good—not to mention gorgeous—man. Jason would lift me up where I belonged. As for his conditions, they didn't bother me; he was as menacing as a kitten. There was also the small, unworthy thought that I had invested too much time *not* to persevere with Jason. As Grandma Nellie liked to say (to any woman older than ten), "You're not getting any younger."

We stood outside the shrink's office and I squinted up at him. The sun was in my eyes. I said, "I can learn to give a little, Jase. Just tell me what to do."

1.

When Jason listed his conditions, I was shocked. I'm not often contrite, but when I am, I expect that in itself to make people relent. Often when someone is angry with you, all they want is for you to admit they're right. Once you accept blame—or at least give the *appearance* of accepting blame—their anger fades. Jason was breaking my rules, which meant that all of a sudden, I was a person with a lot of problems. This annoyed me because none of them were my fault.

I drove straight round to see my father.

I could conclude only that Jason's love for me was less reckless than it once had been, because what he was asking of me was just a *little* more than I'd expected. I respected him that much more. Even if it did mean trouble. But Roger would know what to do. I had absolute faith in my father, which, I think, is important. Most people I regard as idiots. Talking of whom, Martine rang as I was speeding down the Bishop's Avenue (the most vulgar building site in London) to ask where the hell I was, she was sitting in the pub eating a bag of crisps and a man had just made oinking noises at her.

Any other day, this would be nothing to do with me (it's unjust that fat people are given a hard time by strangers for eating in public, but I have no sympathy for Martine, as she enjoys provoking them), but I was reminded that we *had* arranged to meet. I explained. Martine choked on a crisp. Through the coughing, I determined a croaked intention to come to my father's house.

"N—" I said, but she'd hung up. I sighed, and went via the pub.

Happily, my mother was out. My father came to the door looking rumpled, shirtsleeves rolled to his elbows.

"Hann-ahh!" he said and held out his arms. Relieved, I fell into them. We hadn't spoken for a week. He was working on his screenplay and his mood soared or soured according to the health of the creative process. I'd presumed he was at a delicate point and couldn't afford any kinks in his stream of consciousness. However, we tended to speak most days, so if he didn't return my calls, my conscience played tricks on me.

"How are you?" I said. "How's work?"

"Both *marrrrrrrrvellous*, darling."

His official career was in corporate PR. He was codirector of the company. If you asked him what his official role was, he'd say something like "We promote or defend a company's interest in the public arena. Anything that is written or said about a company has an impact on its employees, their families, and the people who do business with that company. The media is incredibly powerful. It can ruin careers, shut down businesses. But how does society protect itself against the media? By hiring people like us. We ensure that what is written is fair, *the better truth.*"

And unofficially? "We lie a lot."

The rest of the time, he wrote and acted. He was a leading member of Inimitable Theatre, one of northwest London's most respected amateur dramatic societies. I liked to go and see him in plays, mainly because it was nice to sit still for a few hours. I was grateful that he always kept his clothes on. IT's most recent production had required Mrs. Caroline Epstein to stand onstage and shout at the audience while naked. While I realized it was art, I would have rather she'd worn pants.

"Hello there, Martine."

"All right, Mister L."

Martine was quite *blushy* around my father. I didn't know whether to be pleased or appalled. I compromised on saying, "Yes, but you fancy Roger," if ever she was in danger of winning an argument.

Roger led us into the garden. "So what's up?" he said. He was wearing shades so it was difficult to see his expression.

I opened my mouth to explain, and gargled with dead air. It's so much an instinct to screen my words before I speak, I rarely have to think about it. In this instance, I should have. Was I crazy? I couldn't tell my father that Jason had set me a great long toilet roll list of Rumplestiltskinesque conditions, only the fulfillment of which would persuade him to reconsider my suitability as a life partner. I couldn't tell Roger this because it contradicted a previous fabrication, namely, that it was *Jason* who had ended the relationship, not me.

I rubbed my throat. "One second. I need a glass of water." An unlikely excuse, but one that would give me time to construct a story. I didn't bargain on Martine. I tripped back into the sunlight, to hear her loud voice shattering the tense stillness of Hampstead Garden Suburb's atmosphere.

"Yeah, but fair-doos to Jason. He was desiccated—sorry what yeah—devastated when Hannah turned down his proposal. This Lucy thing was just him showing her he wasn't. I think it was all a trick and I think it's worked. It's a bit much, him setting conditions, but I think it might do Hannah good to do what he wants for a change, don't you think, Roger?"

I imagined myself as Schwarzenegger in, well, any of his movies, running in slow motion toward the disaster consuming his family, shouting "*Noooooooooooooooo!*" I decided against it as I didn't want to trip on the step.

Forcing my face into a bland expression, I sauntered into the garden. I ignored Martine (there was no point in rage, she just doesn't think, it would be like trying to punish an owl). I glanced at my father. He raised an eyebrow above his shades. I've been trained not to incriminate myself, even in the face of intractable evidence. So I smiled.

My father waggled his shades with the tip of one finger. "Martine here brings me the intriguing news that young Jason proposed and was rejected. Whereas I seem to recall being told that *you* were desperate to marry and *he* was the scoundrel. What do you say to that, madam?"

Martine made as if to lift her enormous butt off the sun chair. As ever, her G-string rode high over her jeans. I leaned heavily on her shoulder. Not so fast.

I coughed. Truth, he didn't sound too bothered, which I simply could not believe. Not only had I lied to him (an insult, as I knew he regarded me as one of his best friends), I had lied to him about a matter of monstrous import. Roger was not someone who lost his temper, but even with the sedative of Martine's presence, I'd expected rage.

"Roger," I said. "That was then. I made a mistake. Now I *am* desperate to marry." A porker, but I *had* inched closer to considering the possibility, which I felt justified the exaggeration. "Now it's Jason who's creating obstacles, which is why I'm here. To ask your advice."

My view is that very few human beings on this earth can resist the almighty compliment of their instruction being sought. The implication is, you prostrate your lowly self before their greater wisdom. People love that.

My father shoved his shades to the top of his head and glared at me. "You were a fucking fool not to accept him in the first place," he said. Then he smiled. "But what's done is done. Go on. What?"

Deal with it, I told myself. You deserved that. He's reacted with remarkable calm, considering.

"Jason does want to get back with me," I said, spitting the words to keep my voice steady. "But he wants me to change. And amid his many and various bizarre demands—"

"Such as?"

"—Such as, I should take a little more care with my"—I grit my teeth—"appearance, try and look a bit more grrr*feminine.*"

Martine and Roger burst out laughing. I scowled. "Shall I continue or not?"

They nodded.

"Yes, please," said Martine, which set them off again.

"He wants me to 'seek closure' with Jack."

There was a silence.

"*Never!*" said Martine, who I'll bet had no idea what this meant. (As it was, I'd had to ask Jason to elaborate.)

My father stretched his arms behind his head and grinned. Then he nodded, slowly, seriously, as if considering the proposition.

I couldn't be bothered to maintain composure. I burst out, "Isn't anyone going to ask *why*?"

"Why?" said Martine.

"Because he thinks I have problems relating in a healthy adult way which stem from my failed marriage with Jack!"

"His words, I presume," murmured my father.

"Daddy, what do *you* think? Is he totally *insane*?"

My father stroked his chin. "Actually, I think he's rather sensible."

I stared at him. He must have wanted me to marry Jason very much. "Roger, you know I haven't seen Jack in ten years."

Martine's head swiveled right, left, right, left as we spoke. As if she were watching a game of Ping-Pong. Her mouth hung open, and if she wasn't careful, someone was going to shove an apple in it.

"And what does that say about you?" said Martine, who had obviously been watching *Oprah.*

"I have absolutely no idea," I replied.

"Me neither," said Martine.

We both looked at Roger. He flipped his shades down over his eyes. "I think," he said, "you owe it to Jason." He paused. "And yourself, not to mention your doting father, to do what he asks."

I swallowed a sigh. My father was right. "Okay, Roger. I will."

He beamed and ruffled my hair. "Good girl."

Gabrielle squinted over a satin dress that, with its fancy bows and laced bodice, reminded me of Cinderella's most elaborate ball gown. Its rich cream contours billowed over her slender arms and set off her tan. Her stomach rumbled. I said, "Eat something."

Gabrielle shook her head. I wasn't surprised. There was a scrawled note stuck on the fridge downstairs that read GOD I'M SO FAT. I knew Oliver hadn't written it. Even though Gabrielle was about as fat as a rake. She had a love-hate relationship with food. She won't eat chocolate unless she's "hungry enough to eat a banana," because "that's the greed test." She is also author of one of the most bizarre sentences I've ever heard. I offered her a date, being out of biscuits, and she said, "Ooooh, I'd *die* for a date!"

Once, before she had Jude, she'd embarked on a regime that permitted her to eat only foods beginning with "ch." She'd got the idea from an article that mentioned that some male film star—whose name I forget except that he was married to another film star, if that helps—had gone through a phase of eating only orange foods. She had a peculiar faith in famous people's diets. The "ch" adaptation had been made because Gabrielle disliked citrus fruit; however, despite the twin blessings of chicken and cherries, it had failed for a host of reasons, including chocolate, chips, chana masala, and cheese.

"Whose diet is it this time?" I inquired.

"The editor of *Vogue*."

"Oh yeah."

"A lot of wine, and meat." She made a face.

"Hey, Gab," I said. "Wouldn't it be funny if it turned out that you didn't gain weight from eating, you gained it from sleeping on your back instead of on your front?"

"No, it wouldn't. Anyway . . . Stop changing the subject. Tell me *all*."

I shifted in my seat. "How's Jude?"

"Asleep."

I nodded approval. Jude knows I'm scared of babies and therefore shows me the contempt I deserve. If ever Gabrielle hands him over, he arches himself violently backward like a large salmon until I hand him back.

"Go on, Hannah."

I giggled. "Remember that time I came round to see you and a fly flew up your calypso pants?"

"Palazzo pants."

It was hilarious. There was a muted buzzing, and Gabrielle started screaming and jumping. Then, still screaming and jumping, she unzipped her white palazzo pants and ripped them off. At which point, Oliver walked in and said, "*Hel*-lo!" It was one of those big lazy fat flies that can barely shift ass off the ground, it w—

"Hannah, stop stalling and get on with it."

Bother. I took a breath. "This is Jason's idea of me doing penance," I said.

Gabrielle looked unimpressed.

"If I want to be with him—"

"*Do* you want to be with him?"

"Absolutely."

"Why?"

"Ah, Gabrielle, you know."

"No, I don't."

"He"—I smiled—"Just the thought of him makes me smile."

"That's it?"

"No!" I paused. "He is easy to live with, he's a good person, he makes me feel at peace."

"None of this is saying 'love' to me."

I sighed. She didn't *like* Jason; I couldn't hope to make her understand. She had an intractable definition of love. She was a love Nazi, a party member of the "At First Sight" brigade. I don't think she realized quite how offensive and annoying this was to the millions of people who got to know their partners before letting their emotions get the better of them. Jason and I *went* together nicely. We were comfortable, we complemented each other. Not like Jack and me: our relationship had been like a train's steel wheels braking too fast along a track: all speed, sparks, and shrieking.

I gestured round loosely at her study. "I do . . ."

"What?"

"Love Jason."

"Jesus, it's like someone has to prize the words out of your mouth with a wrench."

"I think he thinks that's part of the problem."

No answer.

"He thinks it goes back to Jack."

"And does it?"

"Gabrielle, you *know* it does."

"Yeah, well."

"So my mission is to find Jack and, I suppose, sort out any unfinished business."

Gabrielle, who had three pins sticking out of her mouth and

looked like a Barbie version of *Hellraiser,* spat them onto the floor. "Excuse me. *WHAT?*"

"Yes, I know. Well, it gets worse. I asked Roger's advice and he agrees with Jason."

"Serves you right for asking Roger's advice."

"He only wants the best for me," I said.

Gabrielle, with the tenderness of a lover, laid the wedding dress to one side. Then she grasped my hands. "Hannah," she said. She looked as if she was on the verge of saying something profound. If she was, however, she changed her mind. "You know what. I agree with Roger. Marriage is *not* just a piece of paper. As you know. It requires maturity and responsibility. I think Jason is entitled to ask you to sort out the baggage from Jack." She hesitated. "After all, Hannah," she said, "Jack did divorce you because you cheated on him."

8.

That makes me sound terrible. It wasn't as bad as all that. Gabrielle is merciless where fidelity is concerned. And God, so am I. Now. If I said it was a brief indiscretion, committed at the dawn of our acquaintance before I realized it might go somewhere, when Jack and I were little more than cheeky nighttime phone calls and flirtatious rows over drinks, perhaps you'll see that I'm not a *totally* cold bitch with no concept of decency or loyalty. And I was only nineteen. Oh well. I won't beg.

I feel that apologies and explanations serve only to confirm the severity of your offense. If ever you're confronted by the subject when on surveillance—it's happened to me only once, and I blame the client, who wouldn't pay for an ABC (three-man team)—you deny everything.

"You're following me, who are you?"

"Who are *you*? You mad? What, you famous or something?"

You can rely on people's remarkable faith in their own paranoia. They mumble an apology, can't get away from you fast enough, think they're going crazy. In Britain, it is considered rude to confront people, particularly strangers. So even if, when on surveillance, your own paranoia leads you to fear you've been pinged (rumbled, for the *Famous Five* fans among you), it rarely happens. However, in this instance, suspecting that if my reputation sank any further it would drown, I think I will have a go at defending myself.

Jack was possessive, a trait that has been idealized as romantic and very male in pulp fiction but in reality is highly boring. I wouldn't have minded except he didn't show himself to be keen in any way, beyond suspecting all the men I was friends with of fancying me when they didn't. I wanted him to get to know the people I was fond of, but this was impossible, as he was so rude and aggressive that they stopped calling. Men are breathtakingly lazy in a way that women just aren't. If a woman likes a man, she'll make the effort to keep in touch. If there's work involved, men won't bother. It's the Mars bar attitude to friendship. If you're at home and it's in the cupboard, you'll eat it. If it's in the shop, you won't.

Although there was one guy—his name *was* Guy—whom I'd met through work before I got together with Jack. Guy was an actor, researching a part as a low-life detective. The guy who ran the trace agency had palmed him off on his most junior blagger, me. I didn't mind, being only too pleased to talk about myself. Also, I liked the look of Guy. He was self-deprecating in a way that didn't quite hide his enormous arrogance. He also had a nominal girlfriend, one of those ghostly apparitions often referred to but never seen. I understood the code and wasn't offended. If he felt he was so damn attractive he had to haul around an invisible buffer zone, then maybe he *was*. Being a confidence trickster myself, I felt it was professional courtesy to admire the skill in others.

As soon as he realized I wasn't about to fling myself at him, I became a contender. I wouldn't say it was Guy's mission to get me into bed, because even that would indicate in some small way that it was about *me*. But you get the gist. I was more than happy to restore his faith in himself. (I'm not sure I agree with the concept of women being used by men. You have to be a bit of a mutt to get *nothing* out of it.) One time I was interviewed for a tinpot cable TV program— they wanted a female detective, I was the best they could do. The sound guy stuck a mic down my top, but it didn't pick up and he had to ferret around my bra while we were on air. The host said, through gritted teeth, "Cheap thrill for him."

I wasn't about to let him get away with *that*. I replied. "For me too."

That pretty much described my relationship with Guy. Our friendship was spiderweb thin, despite the fact we liked each other. The world was full of people you could waste a lot of time liking; you had to pare it down. Our affinity rested on the promise of an occasional fuck. Once we were getting up to no good in his lounge and he said, "What would you do if my girlfriend walked in now?"

I love that! What would *I* do?!

So when I met Jack at the cinema a few months later, I didn't feel obliged to explain myself to either man. When a bloke takes you out (in the dinner sense), what do you owe him? Nothing, I believe is the correct answer. I didn't feel it my duty to give Jack a rundown of my petty misdemeanors. Anyhow, Guy went missing, so I presumed he'd found some other part to research.

Jack and I continued to see each other. But nothing, beyond

sex, implied it was exclusive. There was no automated Saturday-night reservation. If Thursday rolled by and we hadn't spoken, I'd assume myself free that weekend. Which didn't preclude me from making my own arrangements on Wednesday morning. So when Guy rang, out of the blue, sleazy with charm, wanting to take me to a comedy night, I thought, *yeah*.

If you'd asked me then to explain myself, I'd have pointed to my most shallow impulse, that Guy had been on the telly. (Two lines in *Coronation Street,* presenter of a segment on treasure hunting in Wales for a travel show pilot that never got made—he was almost famous.)

But no. If I was honest with myself (and I wasn't), Jack was a man who rendered all others invisible. At least he did to me. I felt weak, I hated it, and maybe I hated him for it. The whole time I was with him, I had a sick, unsettled feeling. I played tough, but I felt that Jack was in charge and knew it. If anyone had asked, I'd have probably said the stars and the moon were his doing. Allowing Guy to chase me was my inarticulate way of regaining power. And then, because my motives were confused and I barely understood them, the situation slid from my control.

I'd parked my car outside Guy's flat, so when Guy asked me to come inside to watch his show reel, it was easy to say yes. Even though I suspected that "show reel" was a modern term for etchings. He was sweetly proud of his show reel, all two minutes of it, so I said nice things. He kissed my ear, and I let him.

"Stay," he whispered.

"I can't," I said. In my scumbag heart, I thought Jack might ring at 3 A.M. Which he sometimes did. Then, my lousiest move. I added, "But you can come home with me if you want."

He said, "Don't worry about it."

I drove home. (Although "home" was a bit of a fanciful description of my rented abode—one room that closed in on you and a bed that fell out of the wall.) It was around two in the morning. I parked the car aways down the road near the roundabout—it was hell for parking where I lived—and trotted toward my block.

I knew someone was following me. For a start, they hadn't bothered crossing to the other side of the road. Which meant they didn't care if I saw them. This was bad news. I started to run and—for good measure—screamed, "Help, help, fire, *FIYEEEERRR!*" (I wouldn't ever waste my breath shouting "Rape!" or "Murder!" Samaritans are choosy these days, they respond only to "Fire!")

"Hannah, shut the hell up, it's me, Jack!"

I stopped and span. How embarrassing. I signaled to various neighbors peering blearily from windows to return to bed. "Jack, you psycho. What were you—"

I saw he had a bottle of champagne in one hand and a bedraggled bunch of sweet peas in the other. I like sweet peas. They have a beautiful scent and aren't half as brash or mindless as roses. I feel that a person who gives you sweet peas has put thought into their choice. I had mentioned this theory to Jack, weeks before. My heart beat fast and my cheeks burned red. I was grateful for the dark.

He jerked his head in the direction of the roundabout. The council had planted grass and a few shrubs on it. "Waiting for you. I think I fell asleep under a bush. Where have you been?"

"Out," I said. "But now I'm back." I touched his face. "Look at you. You've got moss in your hair."

He grabbed me, tipping me backward in a flamboyant embrace.

All the way upstairs I told myself I hadn't done anything wrong. Well, I *hadn't*. But I could have. I could have arrived home with Guy in tow. And if I had, it would have been *my* choice. I felt like a person who misses a flight that subsequently crashes. I was shaken. I never called Guy again, and he never called me, so I exonerated myself. I wasn't to know that Jack would choose that night to turn smoochy on me. It was very unlike him.

But our relationship changed. Most people exist in their own little worlds—I've done a hundred and forty-three miles on a follow, and the bloke didn't have a clue. He never looked in his rearview mirror. There's too much going on in people's minds for them to notice what's around them. That's why there are so many car accidents. And yet, evolution does well with the poor materials at her disposal. Whenever we connect with anyone in an investigation, we don't look them in the eye. We look at their chest. If you look someone in the eye, they'll remember your face forever. Even if they're not that bright, there's some genetic program that triggers their memory. Not what you want, when you're walking down their street a few days later.

Jack had never seemed entirely present when he was with me. This—as I mentioned—made me feel jittery, and yet, perversely, I also found it reassuring. I don't like being smothered with attention, I start feeling shifty, I prefer to have space to breathe. Whatever was going on in Jack's mind that prevented him from totally committing to being with me even when he *was* with me, I was grateful for. Some men need to be master of their woman's soul—I wasn't sure I had one.

And yet, the night I slunk home from Guy's place, the instinct that whispers something isn't right kicked through Jack's self-absorption. There was nothing unusual in my getting home late or being evasive. But it was as if Jack sensed a change in the air.

For the first time, I could feel that he wasn't holding back. He behaved like a man in love, a man who realized that he might have something to lose. It was a rush. As most scary experiences are. Another of my grandma Nellie's unheeded sayings was "Be careful what you wish for." I was nineteen, an age at which you reject any club that would have you as a member. Without using anything as advanced as words, I showed Jack that I preferred him as his old unbothered self.

He snapped out of it. I told myself I was pleased. I didn't want him to *need* stuff from me; I didn't find that attractive. I was more comfortable with his treating me as a challenging pastime. That's how I treated him. I do realize that in a relationship you are required to give support. But you're happier to give it when you know it's a luxury, not an essential. Otherwise it's a duty, not a kindness. It's the difference between feeling good about the two of you, or bad. Jack slid back into his sarcastic skin with ease. Which was why I was so surprised when, five months later, at Christmas, he asked me to marry him.

The wedding you know about. That's where I differ in opinion from Gabrielle. She sees a wedding as a marvelous celebration of everlasting love. I see it—as I see all the significant occasions in our lives—as an opportunity for other people to make money. Perhaps this is because of what happened to Jack and me afterward. We might have survived my housekeeping and his travels. (Even though I think if you believe that absence *does* make the heart grow fonder you'd be well advised to check with yourself whether you like your partner.) But then Jack and I went to dinner at my friend Evie's.

She was a relatively new acquaintance. She'd had a slew of different jobs and did a few weeks of blagging before leaving for a stint in telesales. I told her a lot, for me. What I mean is, she knew about Guy.

I don't mean to sound Dolly Parton about it, but Evie, who wore her thick honey-blond hair in a great luscious rope of a ponytail, could have *had* Guy, if she'd chosen. But, sitting across the dingy room, she saw me make the conscious effort not to chew my Biro when our boss brought him over to my desk, and didn't try anything. I'm not great with girly rituals and pacts but even I understood that as Evie had courteously passed on Guy for my benefit, it was expected that I throw her a scrap of gossip about what she'd missed.

Anyhow, when Evie's dinner invitation was issued, Jack and I had been married for five months, and I hadn't seen Evie since our wedding. And of course, there'd been no chance to talk then. The man Evie was dating had forced Jack into another room to see, of all things, a treadmill—this bloke was picturesque but *the* most boring person ever. I was watching Evie tip a jar of Chicken Tonight into a pot and telling her how Guy had made the decision that had changed my life.

She flicked a satin strand of hair out of her face. "So you ask Guy to come for a shag at *your* place, and just because he can't be bothered to drive ten minutes for sex, he turns you down—and that's the *one* night that Jack surprises you with sweet peas and champagne. *My god,* Hannah. I bet Jack wouldn't have married you had he known."

There was a loud *crack* behind us as Jack banged his wineglass down on the table with enough force to snap it.

"You bet right," he said, and our marriage was over.

As the door shut, I caught the look on Evie's face. I'd call it a smile of horror. I found it hard to talk to her after that, and we lost touch around the same time Jack moved out.

Which was the following day.

I know that sounds extreme. But, oh the irony, I think it was only then that I began to understand my husband. *He* had been under the impression that we had been in an exclusive relationship for months before the sweet pea night. Meanwhile, there was his girlfriend, trying to organize a fuck with another man. Jack loved me, but I hadn't believed it, I needed him to build me the Taj Mahal.

"So you've been screwing this bloke."

"*No!* Well. Yes. Once. Ages ago. We had a thing. But not that night! We kissed, nothing . . . serious."

I tried to explain, but I fumbled it. Terror wiped fifty points off my IQ as I stood there. My panicked mind blurred the lines, I couldn't give Jack straight answers. The joke of it was, under acute stress it was plain that Guy was nothing to me, whereas Jack was everything. I could see him, putting two and two together, making five. He'd been away a lot recently . . . I'd been cold toward him. . . . I'd cheated on him . . . now . . . then . . . what difference?

He could have ordered me out of the flat, but instead he went to stay with his elder sister, Margaret. I rang him at her house in Richmond, to try to explain again . . . *better,* but in my heart I knew it was futile. There would always be doubt, and Jack needed to be a 100 percent certain. He was too proud to accept less. He couldn't choose his parents, but he could choose his wife. And now, he found, he'd chosen wrong.

Jack allowed me to lie to friends and family about our reasons for divorce to save himself from embarrassment, not me. We said we never saw each other and we'd grown apart. (Keep it bland and people will believe you.) He thought the truth would make him seem undignified. Even though the reality is most people don't think like that. Rightly, they see the shame as being all on the adulterer's side.

Ten years on, I summoned the memories, and the shame of it felt like yesterday. At the time, people said I was coping well, and the more they said it, the better I coped. This will hurt only if you let it,

I told myself, and remember, no one's died. I succeeded in *not* thinking about Jack, and what might have been—a feat I achieved by working hard and watching an awful lot of television. I found that the less I did, the less I wanted to do, until I could barely do anything. That might not sound ideal, but it had the required effect. Everything was reduced—feelings, ambitions, energies, desires— my existence became nicely muffled as if I were living under a layer of snow.

Jason had dragged me out of my stupor. So, you see, I owed him a lot. Even so. I cannot express how much I did not want to contact Jack.

But my father insisted.

9.

I could have traced Jack in ten minutes, but Peter rang and I had to deal with him.

Peter was a regular client of Hound Dog. His problem was an obsession with a woman who had no interest in him. Katya was young and very pretty, from Bulgaria. She had a boyfriend back home. She'd taken a cleaning job at Peter's house. Other people give their cleaners five-pound tips; Peter gave his a Mercedes. Her only collusion in his fantasy was to accept it. I quite admire that. He insisted she have it, so she took it. Maybe she thought, What a kind man. And if she didn't, I admire that also. Peter hadn't *said*, "If you take it, I expect sex," so I say fair enough. If you can't say what you mean, don't be surprised if people don't do what you want.

66

Greg refused to install a video camera in Katya's bedroom, as this was "perverted." He did, however, bug her kitchen.

Greg had made an exception for Peter. Normally, if a person comes in convinced that their partner is cheating, Greg asks, "Are there children?"

His second question is, "Are you in business together?"

If the response to both these inquiries is no, he replies, "Dump them. You haven't got a relationship. Your relationship has broken down."

But Peter was prepared to spend any amount of money and Greg had four boys to put through private school. Peter therefore had not brought out the best in Greg, who was reluctant to be reminded of this and had thus assigned all dealings with Peter to *me*.

Peter was ringing because something he'd heard had convinced him that Katya *was* in love with him.

He'd heard her say to a friend *on tape,* "I really want Peter tonight."

I'd listened to the tape myself on his instruction and—having hit *rewind* seventeen times—I had bad news.

"Peter," I said. "She didn't say, 'I really want Peter tonight.' She said, 'I really want pizza tonight.' Peter? Hello? Peter? Are you still there?"

I sighed and replaced the receiver. Then I sighed and picked it up again.

My plan was to call Jack's mother and, failing that, Jack's father. I had numbers for both, and I couldn't imagine either one had moved house. They weren't the type. I could pinch my nose and pretend to be from the good old DSS claiming to have sent National Insurance contribution forms for Jack to the wrong address. Nothing to worry about, we can send out another set, but he needs to sign and return them, where should we . . . ? Or, I could be myself.

Before I met Jack's mother I made a few assumptions about her. Based on Jack and his high self-opinion, I decided that from the moment he was born to, possibly, last week, she hadn't stopped telling him, "You are *so* handsome, you're such a beautiful baby, you're the most handsome, clever baby in all the world, you are *such* a clever boy, your mummy loves you *so* much, she thinks you're gorgeous and funny and clever and *so* kind, there's no other baby as special as you."

I was mistaken.

I have rarely met a person so devoid of warmth. It was as if she had no soul. I guessed she must be very unhappy. She chain-smoked throughout our visit, mostly in my face. I refrained from flapping my hand in front of my nose, as I didn't want to be as rude as she was. I noticed how tidy the house was. It was like an ornate and immaculate ashtray.

Every china ornament had its place. The carpet was white. There were huge sofas in a flowery print that looked as if they'd never been sat on. The matching armchairs had clear plastic casing over their arms to prevent the material being sullied by human touch. I saw only two family photos, stiff studio poses in silver frames. Didn't they possess their own camera? This was a serious indication, I felt, of a dysfunctional family.

Gabrielle and Oliver's place was higgledy-piggledy with pictures—although, to be fair, Ollie *is* a photographer—but still, I saw it as a sign of joy and health. Gabrielle and Oliver getting married, Gabrielle and Oliver in the Maldives, Gabrielle and Oliver in New York, Gabrielle and Oliver in Thailand, Gabrielle and Oliver in Hyde Park, and—later—Gabrielle, Oliver, and Jude in the hospital, Jude and Gabrielle in the garden, Jude and Oliver in bed, Gabrielle,

Oliver, and Jude in Sardinia, Jude, Jude, Jude, Jude, Jude, Jude, Jude.

Before Jude was born, Gabrielle had declared that she didn't want the house overrun with children's toys and baby paraphernalia. After Jude was born, she told me, "It's his home too. Why shouldn't he have a presence?" This was after I tripped over a garish push-along trolley in the hall. As I rubbed my shin, red lights flashed, a computerized voice said, "I-am-an-ape," and then burst into a jaunty rendition of "London Bridge Is Falling Down."

In Jack's parents' house, he didn't have a presence. He was twenty, but there was nothing to indicate he had *ever* lived here. Jack's mother didn't offer us a cup of tea or a biscuit. I couldn't imagine Jack running around as a seven-year-old playing cowboys and Indians with his older sister, Margaret. (I'd met her—against all odds, she was a laugh.) I couldn't imagine him stamping the mud off his Wellington boots in the pristine kitchen with its ugly cork matting. Cork matting was surely in fashion about a hundred years ago, but this floor looked like new. I couldn't imagine that Jack had ever been allowed to look after the school rabbit, let alone entertain the thought of owning a puppy. She didn't kiss Jack hello when we walked in. She didn't touch him, which made me want to.

I decided to pinch my nose and be from the DSS.

As I searched for the number, hands trembling, I thought about other things. Jason. Roger. The two men who mattered to me were convinced that this was the right thing to do. I swallowed, in a futile attempt to introduce moisture into my dry throat. I wanted to believe them.

My father had said, "Hannah, my darling girl. You made a bloody mess of your first marriage, and my feeling has always been that it *could* have worked, had you stuck at it. I suspect that's *your* secret feeling too. And I'm certain that the sense of failure that goes with a failed marriage"—I'd wished he'd stop using the word "fail"—"*has* impacted on your relationship with Jason. Particularly as it now emerges that you've been resisting a fresh start. You need to thrash it out with Jack. Say all the things that went unsaid. You were both young and immature and silly. But I think you've been scarred by the mistakes you made, and the consequent fear is preventing you from committing to a new life with Jason."

He had to be right. I *had* been affected by the death of my first marriage, particularly as—I now realize—I was its killer. In the ten years that I hadn't seen Jack, my work had given me a thousand opportunities to observe other people messing up their relationships. It was remarkably easy to do. But . . . all the same, what was I going to *say* to Jack that would magically cleanse my soul? Just because you watch *ER* doesn't make you a brain surgeon. I wasn't sure that I had learned much that was useful from my job. Of course, I'd picked up some stuff, but I couldn't swear that it would help me conduct a second marriage with any more *heart*.

My knowledge became applicable only when it was too late.

I knew the signs of a cheat. (It varies slightly, depending if the cheater is male or female.)

A man is likely to tell his suspicious partner that she's mad. "You're imagining it. It's all in your head. You need to see someone. . . ." That sort of rubbish. But something will have changed. He may invest in a phallic object, like a car. A purchase that makes him feel younger, even if his mistress is the same age as him. Balding men also tend to do something with their hair. He might cause arguments to give himself the excuse to storm out—and go and see his lover. He's *not* likely to get new underpants as, I'm sorry to report, in most households women still do the washing. He might though, become more attentive, do the dishes, for instance. Guilt.

Cheating women change their hair, lose weight, buy new

underwear. They're also more devious. Men aren't so clever. They'll leave texts on their mobile phones, e-mails on their computer. This is because they still believe that women are useless with technology.

Trouble was, as a detective, I was interested in fact, not feelings. There's always a reason people cheat, but I never got to see it. At Hound Dog, we rarely hear the end of the story. We do ask the client, What do you want to achieve? If we do find out he's having an affair, What are you going to do about it? Greg says we ask because we don't want to wreck their life for no reason. Although my personal view is that if they come to us, it's already wrecked. Often they're pretty much certain of what's going on but they want it confirmed.

So I was excellent at recognizing the evidence that a person had left a relationship emotionally, but I had no professional need to discover *why*. As a result, I suspected I was no better equipped to clear the slate with Jack than I had been ten years ago.

I tipped back my chair and stared at the wall. Bang in the middle of it was a framed note from a client. She was adopted, I'd traced her mother. She'd typed the note with an old-fashioned typewriter onto thick cream paper.

It said,

Dear Hannah,
    Last week, I met my real mother for the first time and it was both weird and wonderful. Thank you so much, you have changed my life.
    Love . . .

She'd stuck an old-fashioned magnifying glass over the text and framed it. It made me smile every time I looked at it.

Perhaps I *was* being too harsh. I'd gleaned some idea about the way people lived together; it was unavoidable. When a husband or wife (usually a wife) came in, fearing their partner was playing away, you'd ask about a change in habits and they'd spew out their whole life story. You had to be quite a counselor, which I wasn't. I got around this by mostly keeping quiet and nodding at pertinent intervals. That was all, I realized, that most people required. After an eternity of talking to the human equivalent of a stone wall, they were gasping to be *heard*.

And occasionally you were surprised.

One woman came in and asked us to do surveillance on her husband. She was lovely, but she talked too much. Her tone never varied and I found it impossible to tell if she was talking about something really important or very banal. Anyhow, her husband's behavior had changed. Instead of coming home from work every night, he'd be out till ten. She didn't believe his excuses; she suspected he was having an affair. We put two men on him (one of whom was me) every night for a week. And every night, we watched this guy go to an old-fashioned pub and, over two hours, drink a pint of bitter by himself.

We showed her the tape and she got the message. We all did. It subdued the whole office, even Greg.

And then there was the woman who was convinced her husband was going to prostitutes. I had to ring to tell her it was a transsexual, and all she said was "Okay. Thank you. Good-bye."

God, what was I talking about? I'd learned masses. Mainly, I'd learned how low most people will stoop. But I'd also learned a little about what it was like to feel betrayed. You don't always need to hear a great long speech. Sometimes "Okay. Thank you. Good-bye" says it all. Maybe I was equipped to face Jack again.

Anyway, I wasn't facing him yet, I was facing his mother. I picked up the phone and dialed. Perhaps if I hadn't been so wrapped up in the past, I'd have paid more attention to the present. As it was, when a male voice said, "Hello," I launched into my spiel on reflex. I'd just got to the bit where I kindly reassured the quaking taxpayer that he had nothing to worry about when the person on the end of the line interrupted.

"Bullshit you're from the DSS. That's Hannah Lovekin, what the fuck do *you* want?"

Forget outraged denial and counteraccusations of madness and delusion.

"Oh, er," I squeaked. "Hello, Jack!"

10.

I thought fast. "I didn't want to upset your mother by ringing in person," I said. "I just wanted to get your current address. I thought that would be the least painful way of getting it."

"And what would you *just* want with my current address?"

"It's hard to explain over the phone. I thought if we could perhaps meet—"

"I don't think so," said Jack, and cut me off.

I smiled crossly and said in a singsong voice, "That went well." Then I slumped over my desk. My legs felt light and hot, as if they might give way if I tested them.

"Not personal problems, I hope," said Greg from the doorway. I sprang to attention. Greg was holding a bowl of porridge and looking unconcerned. I knew for a fact that porridge was stone cold, but he'd still eat it. He made it every morning, stirring it on the stove until it turned gluey. Then, inevitably, something would distract him and he'd end up grabbing a spoonful here and there throughout the day. I liked seeing Greg wander around the office with his bowl of cold porridge. It made me feel at home. But not today. It was a matter of pride that I did not bring the dramas of my personal life to work. We spent all day dealing with other people's dramas, there simply wasn't room for our own.

Also, when Greg had interviewed me, I'd mentioned that I was divorced and asked him if this mattered. "I prefer divorced people, actually," he'd said. "Divorced people are more stable, even if they're depressed."

"*I'm* not depressed," I'd replied. "I'm pretty happy."

"Good. So tell me, how are you going to feel about telling people their husbands are cheating on them?"

"I'd be sorry to tell anyone bad news," I'd said in what I thought was a diplomatic manner, "but my view would be, they deserve to know, they *want* to know, and they should know."

"They *think* they want to know." Greg had paused. "I'm quite amoral. What we do *is* amoral. My fear is, people coming in here with their fucking morals and judging me."

I'd leaned forward at this point. "Judge you for what? Finding out the truth? If someone feels uncomfortable with you for exposing cheats, chances are they're one themselves. *You're* not the one who should be made to feel guilty. You're the messenger. Unless someone has been hurt, you aren't employed."

Greg had smiled at me then. He'd nodded slowly, eyes half closed. "I like that," he'd said.

Therefore, it was a matter of honor that I was seen to be stable. The voice of reason. "No personal problems," I said. I sighed in a Partridge Family–type manner, tilting my head toward a sunny tomorrow. "Life just couldn't be any better!"

Greg placed his bowl of porridge on my desk. For one nasty second, I thought he might make me eat it as a punishment for lying. "Go on, girl," he said. "I have so many secrets—one more won't hurt."

He grinned at me, and I made a face back. I could imagine that when he was younger, women fell over themselves. They kind of still did. He looked good, if haggard. And he was intelligent, without making a big deal about it.

"I'll tell you," I said. "But keep it quiet."

I decided to stick to the facts and leave emotion out of it. He'd appreciate that. I've heard of offices where women actually cry in front of their boss. Gabrielle once worked on the fashion desk at *Harpers & Queen* and she said that at any given moment you could bet your lunch there'd be a staff member weeping in the toilets. The kind of information that made me glad I worked where I did. You don't do that sort of thing here (unless you're a client). I don't like to see people cry. It frightens me. When someone cries in front of you, *anything* could happen.

"I need something from my ex-husband, so I called him. He wasn't pleased to hear from me."

Greg made the appropriate face. "Must be an important something."

"It is. Which is why I will find a way of getting it."

I don't like to look less than capable in front of Greg. People are unforgiving like that. You can be as accomplished as Michelangelo, then you screw up *once* and that's all they care about.

"Anticipating a fight then?"

"It's looking possible."

Greg smiled. "I'd like to meet the man who's a match for you, Hannah."

I'd like to tell you that Greg thinks of me as the daughter he never had, but it wouldn't be true. I think people overuse that phrase. However, he's fond of me in an idle way. I feel that fondness sometimes leads people to be familiar, which in turn leads them to take liberties. This was one.

"He isn't a match for me," I replied, scowling. "That's why we're divorced and I haven't seen him in ten years."

Then I smiled to show I was unaffected.

"What's he do then, this ex-husband of yours?"

"He's a theatrical agent." I rolled my eyes to demonstrate what a silly job this was. But, being king of the silly job ("I get paid for a lot of tomfoolery," he once said), Greg was keen to hear of a kindred spirit.

"Interesting. Who's he represent? What's his name?"

"I don't know."

"You must know his name, girl, you married him!"

"You know what I meant. I don't know who he *represents,* Greg. His name's Jack Forrester."

Greg frowned. "I've heard that name."

"Oh! Are you sure?"

"Wait there." Greg padded out of my office, leaving his congealed porridge on my desk. I moved it out of my eyeline. No doubt Jack was marvelously, marvelously successful. Well. If so, he deserved it. He'd not exactly shied away from work. He'd wanted to get into the industry because, he said, it sounded like fun. "Looking after people who dress up for a living." But if I knew Jack, it was a lot more than that. I could imagine him doing well in a business that required you to be hard *and* charming. Jack got what he wanted by not quitting. (Except with me.) I couldn't begrudge him that.

The phone rang, scattering my thoughts.

"Hannah?"

"Yes."

"It's me. Jason."

"Hell-*o,* Jase! How are you?"

"Really well, thanks. And you? I was ringing to find out how you were getting on. With my"—he paused—"requirements."

He coughed. Jason was hyperalert to the faintest squeak of innuendo, which, in this brash modern world, I found sweet. Did I say, he would never *ever* pass anyone, man or woman, an upright banana. I formed this theory on casual observation, then tested him, over the years. Horizontal, always. God forbid it should remind them of a standy-up you-know-what.

"Oh," I said. "Great."

"Good. It's just that I feel that it would be best for our relationship in the long term."

"I agree."

"Love you."

"Thank you."

There was a sigh.

"Hannah?"

"I'm still here, aren't I?"

He sighed again. Just as it is hard for some women to accept that their man does not believe in Valentine's Day (what a crock), I knew it was hard for Jase to accept that I was not an "I love you" person. I showed my affection by making fun of people. I made fun of him the most. Ergo, I *adored* him!

"All right, Hannah," he said. "We should meet in, say, a week, for a progress report."

"Definitely."

He sighed for a third time and put the phone down.

A *progress report*? This was ridiculous. All the same, I had to be impressed. Jason, being assertive. How mmmmmmmanly! Meanwhile, I was uncomfortably aware that so far I'd achieved nothing. I'd put off all the fuff about taking more care of my appearance, because in this day and age I could barely believe he was serious.

My hesitation was not on feminism's behalf. It was based on the principle that you should accept a person for who they are. Oh hell.

That is such a *lie*. We accept people for who they are only *until* we marry them. Then we dispense with the froth and get down to the serious business of shaping them with a scalpel. Jason was being honest, and for that, I had to applaud him.

Furthermore. An admission. That day I was a bride? Gabrielle was right. Even I had been transformed. It was a kick to be told by a stranger, "You look beautiful." And when Jack saw me, tromping up the aisle, despite the surreal horror of what we were doing, I recognized that look, a look of awe, a look that men usually reserve for women like Sophia Loren and Cindy Lauper—I mean, Cindy Crawford. Call me outdated—it was one of my proudest moments. It would be nice to get that look again off a man. Jason, I mean.

I picked up the phone and dialed Jack's mother. This time, the snow queen herself answered.

"Hello, Mrs. Forrester? Is Jack there by any chance? It's Sylvia, a friend of his, I'm from school, he might not remember me."

I hoped if I gave her all the information she needed, the conversation would be short.

She must have cupped her hand over the phone. There was muffled discussion, then, "Hello?"

"Yeah, Jack, sorry, it's me again."

"You don't give up, do you."

It wasn't a question, but I smiled. A trait he valued in himself. People get sentimental about that kind of thing. It causes them to make rash decisions. "You're right," I said. "We don't have to meet. But I *do* want to speak to you. Please. It won't take long."

You don't frighten people off by abruptly dumping a great big time-gobbling effort-heavy demand on them. You kindly request them to grant you a small easy favor, *then,* when you've wriggled your way into their confidence, you ask for a little bit more and . . . a little bit more.

Silence. Then he said, "What's your number? I'll call you back."
And he did. After fifty-seven minutes.

"This is going to be short. I'm busy. And I have nothing to say
to you."

"Got it," I said, scribbling down his caller ID.

It was Jack's nature to be mean. Even when he made you laugh,
it was by being nasty. I remembered him reading out a problem,
written to an alternative therapist in a Sunday supplement. Some
poor woman had had a hysterectomy and was suffering night
sweats.

" 'I have tried agnus castus, black cohosh and sage tincture, but
am still struggling,' " Jack had quoted. " 'What else can I try?' Hmm,
a fucking *doctor*? Jesus, something really horrible's happened to you!
Stop eating weeds! Get some proper *medicine*."

He was cruel and he was clever, a devastating combination.
Especially so when he no longer liked you.

I wondered if I should tell him the truth. Bloody hell. The truth
was only the entire point of the exercise!

"I'm getting married," I said. "Probably. The bloke has suggested
I, er, clear up some dead wood first."

"What?"

Quite. I tried again. "He wants me to"—I squirmed—"make my
peace with you before we—"

"You're getting married."

"Yes, I—"

"*Me*? Peace with *me*? What the fuck have I got to do with
anything?"

I swallowed. Was the connection bad? He was hardly making
sense. "He thinks I"—I made a face—"he says I hold back because
of . . . stuff. What happened. With us."

"You told him you're a cheat?"

"Ah, Jack. Maybe I *was,* once, in a way, but it was never like you thought. But yes, I've told Jason the whole truth."

"What about your family?"

I felt a twinge of pity. Jack had liked my family. Especially my mother and Gabrielle. Despite how I felt about my mother, I hadn't minded. I'd wanted Jack to have all the love he could get, he had been so deprived of it. When we divorced, his loss was the greater, and I wondered if he blamed me for that, too. It would be painful for him, even now, to think that I'd told my family about messing around with Guy. Jack would feel diminished in their minds, I knew it. He'd hate that.

"*God,* no," I said, compassion making me an idiot. "If Daddy knew we split because I'd been stupid with another man, he would . . . he wouldn't respect me. He'd despise me. It would be *horrible.*"

Jack was silent. Then he said, "Oh, you don't know, Hannah. The experience might do you good."

11.

I put the phone down on him, which, I realized after I did it, was the reflex of an idiot. It wasn't even in anger. It was from *fear,* like a child smashing a window, then drawing the curtain; there, now it hasn't happened.

When people discover I'm a detective, they always ask, "Have you ever been shot at?" No. Why would I be?

With my personal relationships it was different. A miracle that a loved one hadn't shot at me. But if Jack were to tell my father the truth about why our marriage ended, he could inflict as much damage. I found it hurtful that he still hated me.

80

Over the decade, my feelings toward Jack had softened and I'd remembered him with goodwill. So it was a shock to speak to him after all this time and realize that *his* interpretation of our breakup had not been refined; the years had only intensified his anger.

I didn't think it was Jack's style to tell tales. He'd had ten years to blab and hadn't. But the news that I planned to remarry hadn't pleased him. Now I had a niggling anxiety, to add to my other worries. My father had a *thing* about infidelity.

Should I call Jack back? In a hostage situation, negotiators advise that the captive maintain dialogue with their kidnapper to increase their chances of survival. But what if the captive's dialogue is whiny and irritating? If I tried to maintain a dialogue with Jack, I might take a metaphorical shot in the heart.

Or should I never contact him again? I do believe that if you ignore a problem, it goes away. For a bit. I always feel, when faced with an unwelcome situation, "Now is not a good time. If this had happened *next* week, I would have been able to deal with it much better."

I didn't want to deal with it at all. I would just tell Jason that Jack still bore a grudge and refused to see me. I'd tried. I hoped that would be enough for Jason. If it wasn't, I was in trouble. I dreaded the idea of telling Roger that I'd failed with Jack—again—and that my marriage to Jason was therefore off.

I sniffed and smelled oats. I glared at the porridge, snatched up the bowl, and marched toward Greg's office. I reached it, took a slow, deep breath, put a smile on my face, and knocked.

"Yup," he said. "Come in."

"I believe this belongs to you."

"Thanks, girl." He paused, signaling that our conversation was over and my presence superfluous. Too bad.

"You said the name Jack Forrester rang a bell and ran off. I wondered if you'd met him."

Greg shook his head. "I've read about him. He's done well for himself. He looks after some big names. A lot of young actresses." He grinned.

"What a boy," I said. "Good old Jack, I'm so pleased for him."

I turned to leave the room.

"Hey."

I turned back.

Greg winked at me. "Keep me informed."

I drove to Hampstead Garden Suburb after work in silence. I'd realized that, if I failed to sort out my "baggage" and Jason no longer wanted me, I had very little in my life.

Ah well.

I had more immediate concerns. Terence Rattigan's *Separate Tables,* for one. The casting and selecting committee of Inimitable Theatre had voted to stage this play, a 1950s British classic, according to my father. He was director (as well as a star), and tonight they were doing a tech. Which, for the Martines among you, is short for a technical rehearsal. I'd said I'd help out—an idea I blame on the guilt reserves swishing about my insides. I hoped Roger would be too busy bossing to ask after my love life. I parked the car, dragged two jumpers out of the boot—wherever IT rehearsed, the cold was polar—and hurried into the assembly hall of the local grammar school.

I liked pretty much everyone in IT. It was a friendly company. Whole families were members. A woman might join because she loved acting, and persuade her fiancé to join too. They'd marry, and when their children were old enough, they'd probably take part in the yearly pantomine. Eventually, they might decide they preferred to work behind the scenes, doing costumes or choreography. My mother joined because my father asked her to, but rarely mingled. Once, one of the more Am Dram members boomed, "Angela, whenever I see you, I always think of a cup of tea!"

There she was, face, hair, posture sagging, sweeping the floor in front of the stage. It was thick with sawdust—it looked like they'd just finished building the set. I nodded hello. Roger was standing in the middle of the hall, in crisp attire, pinching his chin between finger and thumb and murmuring to William, the stage manager. He was fond of saying, as everyone scurried around him, adjusting lights, sound level, scenery, "I'm not the director of *this*, I'm a worker like everybody else," but it wasn't true. Even his laugh sounded lordly. Although IT was not short on men with deep laughs.

I decided not to bother my father; he was obviously busy.

I beelined for Diana, a primary school teacher. She hadn't been with the company long, found it hard to say no, and was therefore apportioned the work of ten men. That evening she was taping cable wires to the skirting boards, so no old dear would trip and sue.

"I can help you with that," I said.

I was sneaking backstage to find scissors when Roger cried, "Hann-arrr!"

Blow. I approached Roger. He had a pencil tucked behind his ear.

"Hiya, Daddy, how's it going?"

"Appallingly. Miriam wheeled the fireplace from the garage on the trolley, left it outside, and some bastard's gone and pinched it."

"What, the *trolley*?"

"The trolley. The ugly, four wheels, platform and a handle *trolley*. What possible use could anyone have for the damn thing?"

I wrinkled my nose. "People will tea leaf anything these days, Roger."

"I don't know where you learned to speak like that, but it certainly wasn't in my house." He groaned. "*And,*" he added, "Nettie is refusing to wear a wig, so Peggy's going to have to spray her hair with orange dye."

I sucked air through my teeth. Peggy was seventy-six, and whenever she sipped her customary Earl Grey, her hands shook so violently the cup just about shattered the saucer. Nettie was in all probability about to be sprayed all over orange; her head would look like a clementine.

"Anything else?" I said, biting my lip.

"Rosie drifted off while she was meant to be prompting, and Sefton was left hissing 'line, *line.*' Hardly a tragedy, but he stormed offstage, bellowing, 'This! Is the last production I'll ever do for this company!' "

"Roger, he always says that."

My father ran his hands through his hair. "I know, but it doesn't make my job any easier." He suddenly produced a stopwatch and shouted, "This is the big one! Right! Let's change the scenery. Any able-bodied person! Could we have interval music? Just get it all off! No discussions! ONE MINUTE!"

Everyone sprang (or tottered) into action, and my father started pacing. I saw my chance and murmured, "I'll just go and help Diana," but Roger grabbed my wrist. Seven minutes later, when Peggy was still meandering round the stage clutching a framed picture of a horse, Roger said to William, "Take over, will you?" and propelled me by my neck to the back of the hall. He gestured to a chair. I sat down, and so did he.

"Make me smile," he said.

"OK. Know the one where the camel walks into a bar?"

"Hann.Er."

I sighed and flopped forward. "Roger, I've *tried* talking to Jack, but it's impossible. He's all bitter. It was a mistake to contact him. I really think it's best to leave him be. I don't know what that means for me and Jason, but—"

My father stood up and walked away. Perhaps he'd suddenly remembered to remind William of something and would return in a second. But he didn't. He didn't look at me again the entire evening.

12.

I rang my father first thing. "I'm meeting Jack later," I said.

Roger laughed. "Oh, bravo! That's my girl."

I beamed down the phone.

"If I was distracted last night, darling, you must forgive me. You know I mean nothing by it. I rather fear I wandered off midconversation like an old loon . . . I didn't, did I?"

"Oh, *no,* Roger, don't worry about it. I know what rehearsals are like; your attention's in a hundred places."

"At the very least. Anyway, must dash. But let me know what happens with Jack. And don't let him bully you. I won't have any man bully my daughter."

I put the phone down, still smiling.

I also rang Gabrielle to tell her the news. The tone of her voice surprised me. "Are you all right?" I said.

"Fine. I'm just in the middle of something."

"Work?"

"No . . . no. Cleaning the bathroom."

"I thought you had a cleaner."

"I sacked her."

"Oh. Why?"

"Why do you think?"

"She was thieving?"

"God, Hannah. Not *everyone* is a master criminal." She took a breath and brought it down a level. "She just wasn't very good at cleaning."

"Gab," I said, "*no* cleaner is good at cleaning, because it's a job that it's impossible to care about. The last cleaner I had was like a cat burglar. Left no trace. Your mind-set when hiring a cleaner has got to be 'This will be marginally better than not cleaning my house at all.' "

There was an unimpressed pause. "I can't think like that. Anyway, I can do a better job myself."

"Are you sure, Gab? It's a big old house you've got there."

"What are you implying?"

"I don't imply things. I *say* them. And I'm saying it's a lot to manage, your job, Jude, *and* the house. And," I added, "I bet you do all the paperwork, knowing Oliver."

"We have Nanny Amanda."

"Yes, but nannies don't do paperwork. And she's only part-time, isn't she?"

"Well, yes, of course. If I hand over my child wholesale to another woman, what's the point of having him?"

"No, no . . . I agree."

"It's not like I have *four* children. It would be a bit sad if I couldn't manage *one* child."

I was unsure what we were arguing about, so I gently eased the conversation to a close. I'd tell Gabrielle about Jack when she was more herself. When you have your head down a toilet (even a luxe one), scrubbing shit, it's hard not to see it as symbolic of your life. Even if your life is as lovely as Gabrielle's.

*   *   *

At work, I was good for nothing. Even though I had a corporate insurance case to amuse me. It seems that half the country is at home on full pay after injuring themselves at work. Greg likes corporate business because they give you a budget and tell you to get on with it. Matrimonial cases tend to be more interesting, but when they say adultery doesn't pay, they're right. You can't make a living out of adultery. It's awkward when some poor wife rings up and says, "I can't afford for you to watch him today," then, five minutes later, "He's not home yet—can you go out and find him?"

Insurance companies are less emotional. They just want you to find out whether Mr. Bloggs really *does* have a serious spinal injury from slipping on a grape on company premises or whether he hobbles in public, then does backflips around his garden, and they're generous because we save them a fortune. It's not that easy, though; we put the work in. If someone *is* defrauding an insurance company they're usually cocky about it. They'll limp all the way to their front door, and then you'll *see* them sauntering around their lounge, miraculously healed. They won't even bother to draw their curtains, because they know it's illegal to film someone through a window. The law is designed to help crooks.

I had grand ambitions of fighting crime, but didn't. I thought about Jack. After leaving the *Separate Tables* rehearsal, I'd rung and said, "Please. Let me explain myself. You never allowed it." I took a breath. "It might make *you* feel better too, Jack." When he paused, I'd added, "Even murderers get a chance to defend themselves in court."

"Yeah, well the law's an ass," he'd said. "And so am I. Jesus Christ. But we'll meet on *my* terms."

I sat at my desk, chewed my pencil, and replayed his voice in my head. I felt sick at the thought of seeing him. I stood in front of the mirror, stretching my cheeks toward my ears, to see how I'd aged since Jack had last seen me. My stomach curdled. I feared that the mere sight of him would turn me into the naive little girl I'd been ten years ago. Maybe he'd cancel our meeting and I wouldn't have to go through with it.

But I knew he wouldn't. Jack made decisions, acted on them. As I knew to my cost.

We were meeting at seven in a restaurant that, according to *Time Out,* was a second home to celebrities and "media people." I'd not heard of it. It was strange to imagine Jack hanging out with celebrities. I didn't want to give him any credit, but I had to. I bet he was a good agent. He wasn't impressed by fame. Or, rather, he was less impressed by fame than most of us. I claim not to be, but I fear that I am. If someone is kind enough to point out a famous person to me, I feel highly excited. Unfortunately, I never know who they are. I am nonetheless thrilled by the idea of their fame, and of the happy chance to brush past it.

Maybe Jack was different now. Perhaps he'd shed all his old friends and mixed only with the well known. I wondered if he'd turn up in a velvet suit. Or if he wore an earring. That was the one twittish thing about Guy (who, as far as I knew, had never made the Evel Knievel three-bus leap from obscurity). Guy wore an earring. I'd remarked on it—"Mmm, nice earring"—and he told me that he got a new earring every time he got a new girl. Profound. This one was represented by a cat. I said it seemed to me as though she'd be more accurately represented by a mat, which earned me a cold stare.

Jack didn't turn up in a velvet suit. But he looked a lot different from when I'd last seen him. If I was the blushing sort, I'd have gone scarlet. My heart beat so hard, I picked at my shirt, as if he might detect a tremor in the material. I felt he could see right through me to the bone.

His dark hair was very short, very *Black Hawk Down.* There was a hint of stubble. When we were on friendlier terms I'd teased him about it—his facial hair naturally grew in a Mexican bandit style. He was thinner than he had been aged twenty-two, which made his deep-set eyes look even more sunken. His teeth were still his best weapon. An upper premolar on each side of his mouth had poked through the gum but never bothered to emerge further, which I'd found ridiculously sexy. (Although, described, it sounds revolting.)

He was wearing a beautiful orange shirt, artfully faded jeans, and scuffed trainers. He was carrying a mobile that looked as though it might cook dinner for you if you asked. His appearance suggested a fraught diary, success, and no effort.

I'd made an effort, but not so that he'd notice. I wanted to look sharp, in control of my life, but not as though I was trying to attract him. If you desperately need something off someone, you don't arrive looking like a beggar. You arrive looking well fed (within reason) and prosperous. So I'd cleaned my glasses. (My contact lenses were out of action. My fault for always running out of saline solution and leaving them in tap water overnight, licking them before popping them back in. Jason insisted I'd go blind with this regimen, but it wasn't that. They were scratchy; some sort of calcium deposit had built up on them.) I'd washed the shine off my face and brushed my teeth. And checked my clothes for stains.

I was wearing my work gear, which, since you ask, is whatever I feel like wearing on the day. On the rare occasions you need a disguise—only when you're spending a long time on the street—you put on a hat, to break up the features of the face, or change your jacket. Otherwise you just try to blend in. Be a Ms. Nobody but a Ms. Everybody. A gray woman who doesn't stand out. Although sometimes you have to stand out to fit in. I've worn a hard hat and a fluorescent green jacket and carried a clipboard so as not to be noticed.

Happily, though, this wasn't today's outfit.

Jack saw me sitting in my favorite spot of any establishment—corner table, back facing the wall—and gave me a reluctant smile. (To be honest, I hadn't *chosen* this spot, I'd been led to it, when I announced who I was meeting.) I found myself briefly speechless. I stood up—I don't know why—and said, "I see that tooth still hasn't grown."

He huffed amusement, then frowned. I could tell he regretted the smile. But I felt more cheerful than I had a moment before. I didn't want things to turn nasty, and it looked as if they might not have to.

"You look old," he said.

Then again.

"What a rude remark," I said. I was shocked at his lack of gallantry. I wanted to bite back, but I clenched my teeth.

Jack shrugged.

I said, "Do you want a drink, rude person?"

He flipped open his mobile, flipped it shut, stared at me. "No. I want this to be over with. This isn't a *social* meeting."

I stared back. "Relax, Jack. You're not that irresistible."

When the waiter approached, I ordered a red wine, drank it. My hands shook, I sat on them.

"Nervous?" said Jack.

"Hung over."

"I think you're nervous, seeing me again."

"Yes, I am, and you know why that is? Because you're such a colossal *a*-hole." I stared hopefully at the bottom of my glass. "Jesus. I thought we could be civilized for five minutes. I fucking forgot who I was fucking dealing with."

My language always deteriorated when I was with Jack. Five minutes in his company, my mouth became a filth pit.

"So what did you want to discuss? Why you were seeing some-one else when you were seeing me? How things are at the office? Who you're cheating on now? James? Jason. Didn't *he* make a sacri-fice for all mankind."

"Jack. You're so chippy. Are you jealous?"

"Oh, yeah. That's what's missing from my life. Marriage to a woman who makes me miserable. *Darrrling.*"

I jumped. A thin blonde with eyes slightly too close together was standing by our table, trying to focus on Jack. She gave me a huge white grin before bending low to kiss Jack on both cheeks and give him a bird's-eye view of her cleavage.

I yawned and looked around.

I had a fine view of the entire restaurant. Which could only mean that Jack Forrester commanded the best table. Way beyond, by the crisscross stained-glass windows—which allowed in light, but no goggling from the street—I saw a few grumpy types eating. They knew they'd been relegated to restaurant Siberia. Nearer, I spotted a soap-star hard man in a pink flowery shirt picking at a frilly salad. And, walking up to the table next to ours was an oldish guy I could have sworn was a famed actor. I think he was in that *Hobbit* film. The two women sitting there stood up and one smoothly said to the other, "You know Ian," as he reached to kiss her cheek.

After murmuring about a "project" currently "on hold" but "about to be green lit," the thin blonde strode back to her table.

"So she's your darling," I said.

Jack looked down his nose. "I call people 'darling,' " he said, "when I can't remember their names."

I fiddled with the stem of my wineglass. "So how *are* things at the office?"

He laughed.

"No, really. I hear it's going well."

"Yeah? How'd you hear?"

"Well, gosh, Jack, I bugged your office." I gave him a disgusted look. Then I said, "My boss knew of you and mentioned it."

Jack rubbed the back of his neck. "Right," he said. In a more civil tone, he added, "I've got some nice clients. You know one of them."

"Me?" I laughed. "I don't know anyone."

"Jonathan Coates. Mr. Coates?"

"*Mr. Coates!*" I laughed. "What, Mr. Coates who taught drama at my infant school?"

"*My* infant school too."

"Yeah, I know. Why would you represent him?"

"He's a very talented voice-over artist."

"You would say that. You're his agent. How funny."

"He found me in the *Artists & Agents Year Book,* recognized my name, why is that funny?"

Jack glanced at his phone again.

"Are you in a rush?" I said.

"Yes. So say what you have to say. Then we can part forever."

He was too cruel. I tried to think of what I wanted to say and then say it, but it was as if my tongue had furred over with moss. To my horror, my nose tingled, which I vaguely recalled as a precursor of tears.

Here was the thing. I needed to grovel. Not only did Jason want me to purge my soul, he wanted *written* proof that Jack and I were—as he put it—"best friends again." An eventuality that looked as likely as peace in the Middle East.

"Look," I said. "I'm sorry about what happened, but I really don't think it was quite as terrible as you've always thought. I didn't actually *do* anything . . . much with Guy. Not when it got serious with you. I mean, there's always a vague period at the beginning of every relationship and—"

Jack drummed his fingers on the table.

"What's wrong?"

"Hannah. This isn't sounding like an apology to me."

"Well, no. It's not an apology. It's an explanation. I had odd ideas about relationships when I met you. Jason is quite into"—I winced—"therapy, and looking back to, er, go forward. He feels that if you understood the truth, you might forgive me. And feel better about the whole . . . episode . . ."

"Yeah. That's not going to happen."

"But," I stammered, "give me a chance."

Jack threw himself forward, resting both arms on the table, making me start. "Hannah. He wants the impossible. You're saying he wants us to work through our past, picking out the issues and the problems like, like *weevils* out of a cow's leg and resolving them, leaving you pure and clean, absolved of guilt, a born-again innocent."

I nodded. I was still trying to grasp the relevance of the cow's leg. "Yes. That's exactly what he wants. Even if you are being sarcastic. So why . . . ?"

"Because there *is* no resolution, and part of the problem is that you will never understand that. Once you cheat on someone, the relationship can never be the same again. It's like breaking a plate. You betrayed me, Hannah, when I loved you more than any woman I will ever love, and you never saw it, you never acknowledged it— you still can't, you don't have the mental apparatus, you *lack* the appropriate emotion, it's like you're fucking . . . *autistic*—I can't forgive you for what you did to me, you changed me as a person for the worse, and I hate you for that."

Well. There it was. Straight from the heart. Or the knuckle. It was more information than I'd ever had about how Jack felt about my behavior. I should have fallen at his feet, breathless with regret. But I couldn't. He irritated the hell out of me. He was a self-pitying, pompous pig who just wouldn't *listen*.

"You absolute fool, get over yourself," I said, and walked out.

13.

I was buzzing with anger, and red-faced. This was so typical of Jack and me. Our rows went from 0 to 60 in ten seconds. I could still hear Jack saying "I hate you." I made a gargle of rage in the back of my throat. I wasn't used to uproar in my private life. Then, right in front of me, a woman stubbed out a cigarette under her shoe. She ground it out like she wished it was a person.

She was pretty. I pretended to check my phone messages. This is a ruse more advanced than rummaging in your bag because it allows you to loiter *and* stare. No point hanging around if all you can see is a crumbly tissue and a bunch of spare change. I let my eyes flicker over her face again. The sense I got was of someone carefully put together.

Her shoes were black and white, wildly pointed at the toe, with a pattern punched in the leather and a tiny heel. These, instinct told me, were fashion. Ugly and awkward as they were, they managed to be superior, to suggest, "I know something you don't, *poor* you." I found it hard not to stare at them; it was like trying not to stare at a birthmark. If Gabrielle had taught me anything, they were designer and cost three hundred quid. Still, her cardigan was buttoned up wrong. I know little of the ways of men, but I suspect this clunkiness gave her more *ooh la la.*

She stepped into the restaurant I'd just left, and as she did, it struck me that if I didn't start walking, I'd still be there when Jack emerged. I took one step toward anywhere, then stopped. Then I followed Ms. Pointy-Toes indoors. Just far enough that I could see where she was headed. I said "Mm-hm" into my phone, while signing a cool "one moment" at the receptionist.

Ms. Pointy-Toes walked right up to Jack. I saw her kiss him on the mouth and saw him kiss her back. I actually put my hand to my throat, like some old grandmama on seeing a woman astride a horse. Then I nodded, unsmiling, at the receptionist—who returned the compliment—and stalked into the street.

I brushed my hand over my face. My heart felt curled up and burnt into a little black cinder. *What exactly,* I asked myself, *were you hoping for here?* I felt sick and foolish. Jack had a beautiful, glamorous girlfriend. Admittedly, my evidence was thin. She could be a friend. Yeah, right. As a PI you have to learn to distinguish between fact and supposition; it's like boning a chicken. That said, I've never boned a chicken, and on occasion I've found supposition priceless. Like, say, on *this* occasion.

I reminded myself that I had come to see Jack for *one* purpose. To facilitate a second marriage proposal from Jason. It shouldn't bother me who Jack was fucking. Maybe it was because she was a blonde. They might be ten a penny in, say, Sweden, but in Britain a blonde is seen as extra-special, like a Ferrero Rocher. It riled me to have been succeeded by a model who the nation would regard as aesthetically superior. I'd have liked Jack to have downgraded to an old woman with a wart on her nose. Or maybe a man.

I tensed my jaw and turned away. Get a grip, Hannah. Our meeting confirmed that divorce had been the correct answer. Jack had moved on. I should too. But how the hell could I if he wouldn't allow me to fulfill Jason's conditions? Jason was right. I *should* sort out the clotted confusion that ruined my first marriage before embarking on a second.

Jack said he *hated* me. Hate is a strong word. I blinked, saw Jack kissing the blonde, his hand resting on her hip. Jack was a lost cause. I held my breath for a bit—forget him, concentrate on Jason. I'd devote myself to Jason, whatever it took.

"Crazy," said Martine when I told her the next day. "Hey, are Jack's premolars still retarded?"

Martine was a dental assistant. She existed in her own head and in romance novels, which was lucky, considering her job. It was a living death, although she worked for a nice man. Marvin. He adored being a dentist. The man loved teeth. He also never stopped talking. Or turned off Capital Radio. He spoke every thought aloud, over the ads for car insurance and bonehead DJs, all day in one tiny room.

"I wonder what the thought for today is on the Sensodyne calendar; Martine, tear off the slip, will you, it's usually something to do with brushing, silly Sensodyne thoughts. . . ." I would have shot myself. I think Martine barely heard a word.

"Yeah," I replied. "And so's Jack."

Martine looked up from her plate. We were in her local pizzeria. I'd had food poisoning from there, twice. "No, he's not," she said. "We've all got our pride. He thought you were doing the dirty on him. He can't forget that. He can't respect you. He's a romantic."

Martine picked a black olive off her pizza with her nails. I imagined little arms and legs waving in horror as it was transported to her mouth.

"Respect is not a fundamental of many marriages," I said. "Really. I know."

I treated Martine to the example of a recent case. A woman had an ABC follow her fiancé for three months because she thought he was cheating. We had a van outside his house, the lot. She spent *forty thousand pounds,* for which we kindly confirmed her suspicions. But then, in the last month, he stopped cheating. Weeks later, this woman rang Greg to invite him to the Brompton Oratory. "We're having a blessing for our wedding," she told him. "I'd love you to be there."

Greg, eating a fried breakfast at the time, swallowed a large chunk of sausage whole. "How," he replied, "do you think you'll feel, spiritually, with *me* there? And where do you want me to stand? Behind a pillar?"

"*My* marriage won't be like that," said Martine. "My husband—when I meet him, that is—we won't have even *one* secret from each other."

We are all stupid. It depends on the criteria by which we are judged. Martine appeared to be more stupid than others. Even though my private belief was that she wasn't quite as dense as she pretended. She has four elder brothers, and a certain level of helplessness was expected of her, even rewarded. Anyway, I preferred people who kept a bit of themselves back.

"I won't be *getting* married when Jason finds out that I failed to resolve anything with Jack."

Martine gasped. I thought she was choking on a wad of dough until she said, "Roger would know what to do!"

"Genius, Martine," I said.

"But," roared my father, leaping off his deck chair for emphasis, "for heaven's sake, why *won't* he sit down with you like a rational *adult* and talk matters through? This is ridiculous! Ten years have gone by! Surely he doesn't want to stand in the way of your last chance at happiness?"

I held my untouched glass of water in two hands and stared into it.

I felt low; Jack had turfed up a lot of bad memories. It was like meeting the big shot from school ten years on. No matter how grand you are in your life now, you revert to the relationship you had then. I was different, I was urbane, for god's sake, urbane! But with Jack I was still that silly teenager who couldn't commit. My father wasn't helping.

"He's still upset with me," I said.

"Why, though!" shouted Roger. I could sense the neighbors, holding their breath on their sunken patio. "It doesn't make sense! Give me his number! Where does he live? *I'll* go and talk to him, I'll have a word, bloody chutzpah!"

My heart seemed to make a lunge for my throat. "No!" I said.

My father took off his shades and stared at me.

"There's no need for that, Daddy," I said, calmer. "I'm . . . I'm sure Jason won't mind if I don't return waving a peace treaty from my ex-husband."

"For Christ's sake! Forge the note! Forge it! Who cares? Bloody stupid idea! What Jason doesn't know won't hurt him!"

"Well, I—" I stopped. That phrase summed up my relationship history, with everyone. It made me no better than Brompton Oratory woman. I was not going to forge anything for Jason. This was supposed to be my new start, not a sly recycling of old attitudes.

"So you haven't answered my question!" boomed Roger. "Why's Jack being so bloody contrary, what does he care? What aren't you telling me? You're not telling me something. Pumpkin! What is it? Don't lie to me! I'm in corporate PR, madam, I know an economy with the truth when I see it, come on, spit it out, spit it out!"

My mouth opened and shut.

More than anything, I feared my father thinking less of me. He said the most curious thing once. It was my mother's birthday. I'm always nicer to my mother on that day, it's like a gun amnesty. We'd all gone to the theater. It was a first night and my mother had recognized the playwright, a grizzled old thing sitting in the row in front. I noticed he didn't laugh once. Hey, maybe *he* noticed *I* didn't laugh once. When the actors finally took their many bows and everyone scrambled to leave, my mother giggled.

"What?" I said.

She covered her mouth. "He passed me, and I thought, what if I was to shout, 'What utter rubbish!' What if I'd shouted that out during the play? Or what if I'd jumped out of my seat and attacked an actor?"

"Don't be ridiculous," said my father.

Gabrielle was with us to dispel the tension—Oliver had to work—and she'd slipped her arm into my mother's. "*I* know what you mean, Angela. I think that sort of thing, too. If I'm at a magazine do with Ollie, talking to the picture editor, I sometimes think, What if I were to throw my drink in his face? It's . . . Well. It's not because you're a rebel."

We all laughed. Except Daddy.

"I think," added Gabrielle, "it's because you think it's the *worst possible thing* you could *ever* do. You fear authority, you fear other people's disapproval."

"Oh dear, do I?" said my mother.

I felt a brief flutter of affection. "Yes, Angela," I said, "you do. You shouldn't. You're . . ." I didn't want to say she was as good as them, but now I couldn't *not* say it without flouting the gun amnesty, ". . . as good as them."

"Hannah, your forehead," said my father. "Do you have an allergy?"

"Oh! No," I said. "It's just a few spots."

As Gabrielle and my mother wandered on ahead, my father mused, almost to himself, "Shame."

"What is?" I said.

"The way you disregard your appearance. Sometimes I think of how pretty you were as a little girl and I look at you now and I feel disappointment. All that promise, *blown*. Like biting into a . . . sour cherry."

I was a bit hurt.

I blinked away the memory as Roger clapped his hands in my face. "Hello-o! Earth to Hannah! Spit it out! You did something to antagonize Jack! What did you do? Out with it!"

Ah, Christ. I was determined to be straight with Jason. Surely my father deserved the same treatment.

I swallowed. "All right, Daddy. If you really want to know. The reason Jack still dislikes me so intensely is because he thought I cheated on him. He found out after we married."

I wanted to explain that it was more a technicality than a physicality. But Roger didn't give me the chance. He stared as if I had morphed into a different person, maybe not even a person, more like a variety of toad.

He said, "Then you're no better than your mother."

My father turned his back and let me go. I was trembling, but I wasn't surprised, because my father has a thing about cheats. He has never forgiven my mother for cheating on him. And neither have I.

14.

I used to be close to my mother when I was little. I was very girly then. The memories are fragmented but if I choose to, I can pick out glinting shards.

She bought me a green velvet dress; I used to stroke it on my lap like a cat. And a pair of black patent shoes.

I can still remember the breathless thrill I got from seeing my feet in those shoes. I remember my five-year-old self, whispering those magic words *"black patent shoes."* I wore them for parties, for going to special places, and when I fastened their silver buckles I could barely believe they were mine, that I was a girl who wore black patent shoes.

Shoes like these had the power to transform me into something I was not. All the people I wanted to be (my mother, ballerinas, princesses) wore such pretty shoes: pink, satiny, ribbony, high-heeled, shiny, pointy-toed, or *open*-toed, for which you painted your toenails lovely colors. If I tried on Mummy's shoes, my legs became a *lady's* legs. My mother was very ladylike. She used to apply pearl lipstick, then blot it twice with a tissue.

Although there was something guarded about her even then. I have an old black-and-white photograph—I came across it recently, digging through my desk drawer—my father must have taken it on holiday in Portugal or Spain. Angela is sitting on the sand in a flowery swimsuit on a small stripey towel, her hands clasping her knees. She is slender and brown and her eyes are closed. I don't think she knew he was taking the picture, she is too inside herself, absorbing the sunshine. I like her feline grace in this picture; she looks as if she might be purring, but maybe it is her wariness I relate to. Ollie and I are nowhere to be seen. The beach is packed with people perched on clusters of deck chairs in the distance, and the sea is a thin blue strip beyond them, but my mother is sitting on the pale sand, all by herself.

I don't remember much, certainly nothing of our very early relationship. Grandma Nellie once mentioned Angela having "difficulties" after I was born. I presumed Grandma Nellie meant women's problems and didn't inquire further. So maybe we weren't that close at first. It's funny how before the age of five your consciousness takes it all in . . . and lets it float out again. Apart from the disembodied lipstick blotting and the recollection of my black patent shoes, there are no active memories.

Photographs, still lifes, are all the evidence I have. I know Angela has a picture of us together, on her dressing table, still. We are in the garden and she is showing me a leaf. I'm no expert on kids, but I'd guess I was around two. We are both frowning in concentration over this leaf—maybe it was an oak leaf—and my baby hands look small and chubby next to her slim ones.

Until it all went wrong, I hoped to be exactly like her.

My father did a good job of taking over, though. There is a further memory blank around the time it happened. But you get a sense. I wouldn't admit this to, say, Greg, but I believe that if something bad happens in a place, sadness seeps into its walls and is held in suspension by the structure that bore witness to the crime. That's maybe why I don't like Hampstead Garden Suburb, our house. It holds the lingering scent of regret and unhappiness. If the sin has not been absolved, there is nowhere for it to go.

I recall a brief period of shouting, then silence.

I have an image of standing in our hallway, watching my mother leave by the front door. And from another time, my entering that hallway and running up the stairs, holding the sobs in my throat. I don't recall who let me in, but I ignored whoever it was. I don't know what happened when I reached the top of the stairs. I remember hating family mealtimes. Concentrating on the food on my plate, willing it to disappear so I could leave the table. I spent a lot of time in my Wendy house—a sheet draped over an enormous cardboard box—arranging its contents, making the kitchen neat.

I'm not sure who retreated first, me or my mother. But the person she was seemed to fade away. Even when she looked at you, you felt she was looking through you. What changed was, she *bought* more for us, for Ollie and me, but it wasn't fun. *Did* less, bought more.

She got lazy. She stopped putting Scott Walker on the stereo and singing "Jackie" in a breathy American accent while she made us our breakfast.

I used to love the way I'd come downstairs and she'd have every element of the morning under control. I'd lie cozy in bed for ten warm minutes before getting up, listening to her clank utensils, draw the blinds, open the sash window, lay the table, splash water into the lily vase. She bought a bunch of white lilies every week for the table, because when Ollie was a baby, they were the only flower he took notice of. She'd tried daffodils, roses—no response—but whenever he saw the big, beautiful lilies, with their bold petals and strong scent, he'd point a fat finger at them and say, "*da!*"

If you believed Grandma Nellie—who was forever regaling us with tales of our once-blissful childhood—nothing was too much trouble for my mother then. A specialty of Angela's was a *boobala*— that's what she called it, I think it's a Yiddish word and she learned it from *her* grandmother. A *boobala* is, from an objective viewpoint, a disgusting concept. It is a cross between a pancake and an omelette except fluffier, and you sprinkle sugar and lemon on it, or strawberry jam. If she wasn't making us boobalas, it was bacon and eggs, with runny yolk. (Her ideologies were blurred.)

Then she started buying breakfast. Crepes from the supermarket and squeezy bottles of syrup. Chocolate sauce. We were allowed Ricicles. White toast and butter and marmalade. Peanut butter. Banana Nesquik. Simplicity was, for a short time, a novelty. Ollie ate and chattered, and my mother smiled in his vague direction. I just ate. Once I made a triple-decker sandwich of five crepes, sprinkled each layer with Ricicles, squeezed swirls and swirls of chocolate sauce and golden syrup, crushed it down with my hands, then rolled it into a sausage and ate it like Homer Simpson eating a bratwurst. All the while beady-eying my mother, but she never said a word. Just stared into her coffee like there was a gold coin at the bottom of it. Ollie noticed, however, and mouthed, "*Pig.*"

My breakfast habits around the age of seven may well account for my eating habits now. I can eat *anything.* Because he has no imagination and can't be bothered, Ollie gives me a mammoth bar of chocolate at Christmas. So on January 1, while a large proportion of the female population are committing to their soy and sackcloth diet, I'm thinking I could crumble some Dairy Milk onto my oats. I can eat chocolate with tuna, for god's sake, I can eat it between slices of bread. I have no concept of a food being "too rich." Too *rich*?! What *is* that?

After a year or so of the bought crepes—during which, I presume, I got fat—my mother changed again. She dressed, rather than dropping us off at school in her pajamas. She'd even gone through a phase, I can't remember how long it lasted, until my father found out, I expect, of booking a cab to pick us up from the house at 8 A.M. every morning. And collect us at 3:30 P.M. Really, that year, it was money no object. Ollie accumulated a trumpet, a guitar, a piano, and a water gun the size of a cannon. *I* got face creams. Lots and lots of face creams. Not to use on my face, because I was no longer interested in all that, but to mix with purple and black paint, to concoct magic potions. When my father traveled to Birmingham for work, he brought back the tiny complimentary bottles of shampoo and conditioner from his hotel bathroom.

I kept all my potions in a cardboard box, which I painted with black glitter nail varnish and labeled MY WITCHES SET. I had a big squashy covered notebook with rough yellow paper on which I wrote evil spells. I scraped pollen from the flowers in the garden and red juice from poisonous berries. I added shampoo, mud, and turmeric. I'm not sure who I thought was the witch—me or my mother. I stopped short of offering her a coffee and pouring a potion into it. She'd have realized anyway (all of my potions foamed). My venture into sorcery predated the British cappuccino.

The year of plenty was over, and if you judged by appearances, my mother was back. Up early, hair clean, pearly lips—although her mouth looked chapped underneath and made me lick my lips. Ricicles were contrabrand again, and boobalas and bacon and eggs were on the menu once more. I refused them and ate toast. I didn't like her. Whereas once her every action, every word, her whole being pulsed love for us, this new model was a too-jolly imposter. She drove us hither and thither, to friends, to the park, to swimming. I had a bet with Ollie, who could swallow the most water. It was a certainty that it was 40 percent urine but I didn't care, even when I vomited and they had to clear the pool, that's how much I loathed my mother. I found her spiritless and *servile*. And so, I could see, did Roger. Angela was the perfect Hampstead Garden Suburb housewife, but she never sang anymore.

My relationship with my father, meanwhile, improved no end.

And now that, too, was ruined. Difference was, *I* had ruined it. In some ways, I was a naive child. I didn't know about sex, affairs, the terminology. When I watched *Dallas*—I was around eight—Clive told Lucy, or was it Sue-Ellen? that he was "impotent," and this made her cry. I asked a classmate, "What's 'impotent'?" and she laughed at me and said, "You are." I gritted my teeth and pinched the soft bit of her arm until she screamed. So, while it was in my head that my mother had had an affair, I didn't really know what this meant. All I knew was, it was the gravest of offenses, a bad, evil, wicked thing—a crime that got me and Ollie whispered about at school. It made my father and me very unhappy and hate her. It was all her fault.

Even as a child I could see that Daddy wasn't quite like Mum in capability, but I was patient with him. Funny thing is, I see it now, with Jude and Oliver. The kid is one year old and he already expects less of his father. Mummy is the one in charge, who knows what she's doing. Daddy is more for *fun*. My daddy was certainly more fun. As Angela became increasingly dreary, with her dutiful cooking, endless tidying, constant fussing, and near silence, he picked up her slack. But he had no clue about parenting *rules*.

He was a shocker. He let us stay up so late on schoolnights, we'd fall asleep on the lounge sofa. He'd let us watch *the* most violent films you ever saw in your life. *Manhunter* was one. In another, I distinctly remember Bob Hoskins ordering a man's leg to be sawn off. One day Roger decided to take over the cooking of dinner. I remember seeing a crab on the sideboard, going *clack clack clack*. Then my father bashed it dead with the *House Beautiful* cookbook. (After that, he tended to avoid the kitchen.) He bought us as much raisin and lemon cheesecake as we could eat.

My mother didn't interfere. I wasn't sure if she didn't dare or she didn't care. She was like a lodger. No, more like a housekeeper. My father had the run of our lives. He was a very dramatic parent. He was terrible at DIY, and once ran the lawn mower over his foot. I was sitting in the crook of my favorite tree in our garden, and he roared, "Aaaaaooooooow! Aaaaaaaaaaaooooooow! Aaaaaaaaaaaaooooooooooow!" Then shouted for good measure, "That really *huuuuuurrrrrrt!*" The opposite of *her*. Once she was chopping onions and cut off the top of her finger. There was blood all over the chopping board, but she didn't say a word. It was as if she didn't feel it.

At least my father's response to pain was *honest*. She made no sense. Also, I wanted to please my father, so I took his lead. When he was in a good mood, he was exhilarating to be around. He took Ollie and me to parties with his actor friends. I'm not sure how old I was, I'd guess about eight—I remember barging through a sea of waists belted with gold chains, to reach the Matchmakers. Daddy bought me a pink bow that he liked me to wear in my hair. I tolerated this because it got me attention from the other grown-ups, which gratified him.

Sometimes he allowed me to bunk off school and go to work with him. He had an office with lots of windows at the end of a corridor. It contained a desk the size of a Ping-Pong table. I liked going there because his assistant was purveyor of fancy biscuits and treated me as a VIP. Also, his business partner had a black collie, who permitted me to feed her chocolate digestives, then prop myself against her rough warm back while I devised spells in ye olde handwriting. Her breath was *awful*. Ollie refused to bunk off school. As he got older, I felt his disapproval of my father. I tried to ignore it. I knew I was my father's favorite.

And now I'd fucked it up. As I drove away from the house, I didn't know how I could bear what I'd done. I'd betrayed my father as *she'd* betrayed him, and the pain he must be enduring seemed to swell inside me, too big for my body; it was like a great inflating balloon, growing bigger and bigger, sucking up the air in the car, leaving no room for me to move or breathe. I pulled over.

Well. I could do one thing for my father. Just to ensure that take two with Jason ran smoothly.

I forged the note from Jack and mailed it.

15.

By return of post, I received a brown parcel marked FRAGILE and a banana plant. The parcel contained two big beautiful white ceramic mugs, made in Italy and decorated with hand-painted red hearts. I smiled. Jason had never liked it that none of my twelve mugs were a "matching *pair*." There was a pale blue envelope stuck to the plant pot. Neatly printed on it were the words "Here's to a new leaf!" I looked and, there was a stiff green baby leaf tightly furled at the head of the banana plant.

It occurred to me only later that there might be a message *inside* the envelope. It read,

> *Dear Hannah,*
> *You rock!*
> *I'm so glad it's all going so well. It sounds from his note as if Jack was delighted to have the chance to clear things up! I'm in Kenya on business for two weeks as from tomorrow. I look forward to seeing you upon my return,*
> *Smackeroonies,*
> *Jase xx*

I felt unworthy. I think that all many women want is for their man to keep them *in mind*. They don't much care if he buys flowers or dog food. Flowers are sweet, but the fact that he was out and thought—"Dog food! If I don't get it, *she'll* have to make a special trip, I'll save her the trouble!"—that's great too. I placed the banana plant in a nice draft to keep it cool and thought about how Jason kept me in mind. It made my heart melt a little (not the core metal, you understand, just the outer steel).

He deserved to have everything he'd asked of me. Every single thing. He hadn't asked for much. The essence of his requests was that I make an effort for him. It wouldn't hurt me to wear a skirt once in a while. Nor would it kill me to talk about my emotions, if I spotted any. I could become the sort of female who applied lipstick to shower.

Trouble was—here I went, always an excuse—Jason had tried to spruce me up before and failed. Baby doll nighties, lipstick, they worked perfectly well on *other* women, but not me. We weren't a natural pairing.

He once bought me a container of a deep red substance called a "splash gloss" for my birthday. I smeared it on my mouth out of curiosity before we went to a restaurant for dinner, spent half an hour grinning at all the waiters like the novice I was, then happened to glance at the wall mirror, and, horror, the stuff was all over my teeth. Oh, my God, I was one of those women with lipstick on her teeth, they're usually about *fifty*.

And there was the time he returned from Selfridges with a pink nightie the size of a dishcloth that looked adorable in its lush wrapping, but appalling on me. "Your pajamas are all holey," he'd said.

I struggled into the garment. It was made of a stretchy material, clingy and transparent. You could see nipples, pubes, the lot; it was like a free show. It skimmed my upper thighs, strained over every lump. The pretty little pink ribbon and pink lace edging strove for a delicate effect, but their efforts were futile, overshadowed by the nipples and pubes. I'm not obese, but this thing made me look like an elephant seal in drag. A supermodel would have looked *okay* in

109

it. I wore it that night and lay there bolt awake, it was so prickly, like sleeping on thistles.

"I'm sorry," I told Jason, having retrieved my pajamas from the kitchen bin. "The nightie doesn't fit. Guess I'm not a baby doll."

How mean and ungrateful I was. I hadn't even persevered with the nightie. (It had cost him ninety quid, which worked out at forty-five quid per square inch of material.) But I hated that nightie on sight. It reminded me of the fact that some women obviously feel obliged to look alluring in their sleep. I feel quite strongly that this is one time you should be allowed to relax.

Now I felt nauseous with shame.

Okay. This was what I would do. I'd grant every request on Jason's wish list. I'd reinvent myself to please him. I was going to learn to cook quiche. I was going to transform my appearance from ho-hum to *da-na*! I was going to out-girly Barbie, become a super-dolly. By the time I'd finished, Lucy and her sewing kit were going to look about as fucking feminine as a rugby player next to me. Oh yeah, and I was going to clean up my language.

One tiny snag in my grand plan. I didn't have the first clue.

I dialed Gabrielle.

The expression on my sister-in-law's face was making me nervous. I'd expected her to be delighted.

"I just don't see why you're doing this. For Jason."

"Gab. I messed him about for five years. I've just ruined his chance to lead a nice life with a normal woman. Lucy," I added, to be clear. "This is a second chance for both of us. I want to show willing." She looked unconvinced, so I reached for my trump card. "We *may* get married. I want to give us a fighting chance."

If my argument was philosophically unsound, Gabrielle didn't notice. As expected, she reacted to the "m" word like a dog to a minute steak.

"Married?" she breathed. "Hannah, I didn't realize! My God, congratulations! Oh, then, of *course!*"

Jesus, what is it with people and marriage? It turns them into nincompoops. Funny, that, because no one likes going to weddings.

"Brilliant," I said. "Is now okay to start? Or is it a bad time?"

I smiled at her, hoping. As far as I could tell, if you had off-spring under twenty, any time was a bad time. I hardly rang, because whenever I wanted to, I'd think, "But she'll be busy now."

Gab was dolloping a pink lumpy mixture flecked with orange into an ice cube tray. It looked like vomit, but I knew it was pureed homemade haute cuisine for Jude. She owned about ten recipe books for babies and they were all full of salmon à la croute and chicken chassis. That kid ate like a king, he didn't know his luck.

"I've got to label this and stick it in the freezer, then I'll be done," she said. I watched her squeeze the trays into a compartment crammed to the brim with ice cubes of pureed chicken l'orange and mashed-up prawn cocktail with garlic mayonnaise, so I presumed. She slammed the freezer door, stood up, and said, "*God,* that's satisfying."

I must have looked mystified because she added, "I pride myself that he's never eaten from a jar. He's got *such* a good appetite. I love to make him healthy food and know that he'll eat it. You know, if he doesn't finish his lunch, I'm in a bad mood for the rest of the day."

I smiled at her again. But I was thinking, that's a little intense. I looked at her standing there, all high on good mothering, in her beautiful kitchen, I looked at her fiercely fought-for figure, her girl band clothes (no point in having the figure if you couldn't say ha-ha to the world), and I wondered what Gabrielle would do if her perfect life got a chip in it.

Which reminded me. "Did you get a new cleaner?"

"No, not yet. But it's fine. I do it myself, at night."

"Right."

There was a lot else I could have said, but I chose not to. I had asked Gabrielle to do a "makeup over" on me (that's what they call it on *This Morning*), and while I was not a powder puff sort of girl, even I knew that a makeup over is something women do to each other as a shortcut to being really great friends. It bypasses the need for one of them to go through a trauma and for the other to be there for her.

And yet, despite this peacock display of familiarity, I felt that Gabrielle and I were exchanging less information than we ever had in all the time I'd known her. I suddenly understood what Jason's shrink meant about intimacy. Yeah, you could go to the toilet in front of someone, but that didn't mean much unless you knew what they were thinking *as you went.*

Gabrielle seemed to have forgotten that to meet Jason's demands, I'd had to see Jack. If she'd remembered, she wasn't interested enough to ask about it. I found that incredible. It stuns me how unimportant the minutiae of our lives are to even those closest to us. It's good to be reminded of this occasionally. It keeps you alert. Plainly, *I* had no life, as *I* recalled that Jude had attended a peer's first birthday at the weekend.

"Did Jude enjoy the party?" I said.

"What? Oh. No." Gabrielle put her fist to her forehead and bared her teeth. "I thought the invitation said three o'clock. They'd hired Monkey Music to entertain the babies. So we get there at three, and Robson's mother opens the door and says, 'You're too late!' So I said, 'But the invitation said three.' She swore she'd put one but said maybe she'd made a mistake. I get home, find the invitation. It says, '1300 hrs.' *Thirteen hundred hours!* What, are Jude and Robson in the army? She's German, so maybe it's more normal in Europe. But I'm from Mill Hill! I don't go by the twenty-four-hour clock, I—oh, look, why am I going on about this, anyway, he's with my parents today, they're taking him to the seaside, so at least he'll have a nice day today."

"Good," I said. "But I'm sure he was fine yesterday too."

"I don't like making mistakes."

A distraction was needed. I said, "Lucky you're not me, then."

Gabrielle laughed and the spell was broken.

"Right," she said, flexing her fingers. "Coffee. Then we'll go to my study and you can get undressed."

"What?"

Gabrielle gave me a reproving glance. "If I'm to be your new stylist/dietitian, I need to have a good look at you."

"I'm not going on a diet. I never said anything about dieting. I can't eat less than I *need,* Gabrielle. If I even think I might be tricked out of food I start bulk-eating. Put me on a diet, it'll have the opposite effect, I'll be twice the size before you know it."

I wasn't exaggerating. I take hunger very seriously. Sometimes I'll be eating a piece of chocolate and swallow it accidentally before I mean to. I feel it going down my throat in a lump, and the fact that a taste experience has been squandered is a cause for *severe regret.* I'll think about that chocolate going down whole several times again that day and feel intensely annoyed about it each time. If you're like me, you cannot diet; your nerves can't take it.

Gabrielle held up a hand. "Calm down, dear. I'm not talking about deprivation, I'm talking about health."

One and the same. I took my coffee and slowly followed her upstairs. Of course I would be wearing old fraying knickers and a graying bra. Gabrielle is a woman who kits herself out in matching white lace underwear every day of her life. She even calls it *lingerie,* that's how chic she is. I reminded myself that I was going to do anything it took to make myself worthy of Jason. I was going to be a born-again girly.

Gabrielle took my coffee cup out of my hands and placed it on the side. "Okay. First thing you'll need to do, Hannah, is take off the hat. It's not a good look. Oh my God, neither's that."

I was wearing a baseball cap. She'd wrenched it off before I could stop her.

"Hairdressers are so expensive," I said. "Anyone can cut a fringe."

"Plainly not."

"It kept looking wonky, I had to keep cutting."

"You idiot. When did you do this?"

"Last night. I was bored. There was nothing on TV."

My sister-in-law made a face.

I added, "Gabrielle, if you must know, I felt bad about . . . something I did to Jason, okay? I felt remorseful. I did it out of remorse."

It was true enough. I kept eyeing my banana plant—procured under false pretenses—and wincing.

She hauled me to the mirror, her grip just about squeezed the marrow out of my bones, I was surprised not to see it squirl from between her fingers like Play-Doh. "Remorseful. Uh-huh. You look like Jim Carrey in *Dumb and Dumber.* Bet you feel remorseful *now.* You twit!"

I shifted from foot to foot. It was fair to say that I had made myself look a bit simple. Nonetheless, I was impressed that Gabrielle had seen *Dumb and Dumber.* "I do a bit," I said in a small voice.

"Second thing, I'm going to have to send you to my hair stylist."

"Don't you mean first thing?"

"No. First thing, we need to get you some new clothes."

"Why?"

"Because you can't just go to Michel"—Meeeshell, she pronounced it—"in a tracksuit. Well, I suppose you could, but it would have to be Dior."

"What! You mean you *dress up* to go to your hairdresser?" I could barely believe it! What was the world coming to? But she was nodding!

"You bet. And full makeup. And that's another thing. Do you even pluck your eyebrows?"

"No."

"Take off all your clothes."

"Wh—?"

"Take them OFF!"

Miserably, I obeyed.

There was a sharp intake of breath. Maybe I'd grown a tail and not noticed. This time I knew better than to say "What?"

Gabrielle lunged for the phone and pressed five on her speed dial.

"Hello?" she said. "Gabrielle Goldstein here. I have an appointment with Michel tomorrow at noon. This is a courtesy call to say that my sister-in-law, Hannah, will be coming in my place. She sleepwalks, I'm afraid, and last night she cut her own hair while she slept, yes, poor thing, only Michel could save her. Thank you. Now, please transfer me to the spa desk. Sybil? Darling. It's Gabrielle. Yes. An emergency. No, my sister-in-law. Full-leg and Brazilian. Eyebrows. Mustache—"

This was too much. I did *not* have a mustache. But I did have work. "I have work t—"

Gabrielle pressed hold. "Take the day off!" She paused. "You can get dressed now."

Good, because I was starting to feel undignified, standing there stark naked having my physical and mental imperfections openly mocked.

"Sybil? Yes. Manicure. Pedicure. Probably a Thalgo marine algae wrap. And a St. Tropez for the day after. No. I'll deal with the face. Yes. Thank you. Bye."

She ended the call and grinned at me. I grinned back. Brazil, St. Tropez, these were nice places. Beauty treatments with such lovely names couldn't be that bad. Gab ordered me to be back at her house the following morning at nine sharp, and I didn't protest. I was actually looking forward to this. Doing penance was going to be *fun*.

16.

"Lovely, now can you pull your cheeks apart for me?"

I can't speak for the rest of society but it's not often I find myself pantless on all fours on a table, spreading my buttocks so that a glamorous blonde can rip out the hairs obscuring my anus. Maybe other, harder women get used to this. But me personally, call me a wuss, I couldn't get over the unusual fact that my anus was in her face. She was staring right at it. Oh, there it was, my bottom hole inches from her ski jump nose. I couldn't believe people voluntarily did this. And I'm not talking about sexual sadists. Normal women. I mean, it isn't *right*.

I blushed right the way through to the back of my head. At the least, I blushed on all four cheeks. When she was tearing the hair off my legs, I'd managed to bluster through my embarrassment.

But this? Nothing! No words could cover this!

116

I shut up. The Brazilian silenced me as effectively as a bullet. I couldn't have spoken even if I'd wanted to. This was a social situation that gunned down etiquette and left it bleeding; there was no form of words on earth, no correct behavior available to the human race that would normalize *this* and make it comfortable. Monstrous mortification dwarfed the pain, which, experienced in isolation—an Iraqi prison, say—would have been excruciating.

I supposed if there was a God and he was looking down on me (I hope not), he'd have said I was being punished for my sins. Even so, I would kill Gabrielle, I would *kill* her for what she'd put me through. The day had been a horror, right from the second I'd set eyes on her that morning.

To my surprise, Oliver had opened the door, with Jude in his arms. Jude—who was wearing a white fashion item, a cotton leotard—screamed when he saw me, from fright or delight, I wasn't sure.

"Why aren't you at work?" I said (to Oliver, not Jude).

"Why aren't you?" he replied.

"I got the day off."

"And I'm freelance, remember?"

Oliver gently placed Jude on the ground. That child had the fattest feet I'd ever seen. There were creases in his thighs, they were so pudgy. This, for some reason, was enormously pleasing.

"Go and see what your mother is doing, darling," said Ollie, and Jude tottered off on his fat baby legs.

When I first heard Ollie speak to Jude, it choked me; he used a voice I'd never heard before, insufferably tender. But when he said that, *Go and see what your mother is doing, darling,* I felt a sick jerk in my throat, like someone had hooked a noose round my neck and was tugging. I wanted to throw myself on the floor and wail.

I had no idea why.

I gulped and stared at him, as if his face might give me the answer, but he grinned and waggled his ears at me—a trick he'd mastered at age seven and, some might argue, the peak of his talents. I smiled stiffly, and seconds later, Gabrielle appeared, Jude at her hip.

Within minutes, she'd whisked me upstairs and was preaching about the proper use of face creams. It emerges you *don't* mix them with black paint and poisonous berries and chant spells over them; you put them on your face. As she talked me through the moisture-replenishing, wrinkle-reducing, cancer-zapping, eternal life-giving powers of a tiny pot of gunk entitled Dolphin Aromatic Soothing Cream (or something), I felt a swell of suspicion. Then she told me it cost forty-five quid.

"The smaller the pot, the more expensive, normally," she added, as if this explained it.

"Gabrielle," I said. "This is . . . I mean . . . it's oil and water and pink dye. It's . . . it's . . . tarted-up Vaseline. Those pseudoscientists in their fake laboratories, they must sit there in their white coats pissing themselves."

Gabrielle set her mouth in a cold, straight line, which led me to understand she had a vested interest in the Dolphin scientists being geniuses and the Soothing Cream being everything it said on the instructions. Instructions! (*"Stick finger in pot . . ."*).

I knew it was foolish to continue, but I couldn't stop myself.

"So when Jude gets his baby eczema, you reach for the Dolphin Aromatic Soothing Cream, do you? I mean, he has the best of everything, Gab. He'll be a bit peeved when he learns to watch TV and he finds out you've been treating his skin with crappy old Sudocrem from a *gray tub*. What are you going to tell him, it's because he wasn't worth—?"

"It's *Darphin*. Now do you want me to help you impress Jason or not?" shouted Gabrielle.

"Sorry," I said. "Go on."

"This is Givenchy Balancing Mist; it's a moisturizing toner—you spritz it on after you've cleansed your face."

Since when, I wanted to ask, did a perfectly fine word like "cleaned" become "*cleansed*"? Cleansed had a bibilical ring to it, and I wanted to know just how dirty those beauty scientists thought women were. I kept my mouth shut, which was lucky because Gabrielle held up the bottle and squirted it right at me. It was cold and nasty like someone spat in your face.

Then she'd taken me to Brent Cross Shopping Centre. Most of my friends growing up spent more time in Brent Cross Shopping Centre than they did in their own homes. This is because traditionally, northwest London mothers have used Brent Cross Shopping Centre as an alternative to open prison for their kids. That place is pure evil. Husbands and wives walk through its doors holding hands. Minutes later they're at each other's throats. It's the Bermuda Triangle for happiness.

I hadn't been there for years and was sad to see that Top Shop hadn't shut down. As I remembered, you had to be master of the dirty look to survive in that store. Gabrielle dragged me in there—it was full of fourteen-year-olds, I felt like a pumpkin in a carrot field—and bullied me into some asymmetrical clothes.

And then, just when I thought the torture couldn't get any more sadistic, she'd driven me into town and introduced me to Sybil. Thank heaven that I couldn't have an algae wrap on the same day I'd had a leg and bikini wax. "That's fine," I joked, scrambling into my knickers. "I prefer cheese and lettuce."

Sybil gave me an odd look. I imagined it was "You revolt me."

When I checked out what she'd done to me, later that day, I went hot with shame. I looked like a porn star. There was no way I was going back. Sybil could stick her algae wrap and her St. Tropez.

She'd explained what they were. I could fly to India, get amoebic dysentery, and it would have identical effects *and* save me money.

Gabrielle rang. "So how are you feeling?" she inquired in a voice that suggested she expected thanks.

"I feel"—I paused. "Bald."

Gabrielle chuckled. "And Michel's a star, isn't he?"

My lips pursed of their own accord. I'd been shunted from the clutches of Sybil to the razor-wielding Michel, a rude Frenchman. He seemed to take the state of my fringe as a personal insult. Then, in a five-second frenzy of rage, he'd given me a cut that transformed me into a cross between Myra Hindley and his mother. I now had what I feared were sideburns. I'd spent forty minutes with the blow-dryer trying to merge them with the rest of my hair.

"Now, listen," said Gabrielle. "I've got to go in five minutes, I've got a client coming round. But I wanted to tell you. If you want to learn to cook your way into Jason's stomach, or whatever the phrase is, I'm not your woman. I only do baby food. However. I do know the perfect person."

"Really?" I said. "And she wouldn't mind helping me? I don't only need to know how to cook a dinner, I need to know how to *present* it."

"You're serious about this."

"Yes," I said. "I am. I want to give Jason what he . . . wants."

And I wanted to exorcise my guilt. Despite the Brazilian and the sideburns, it hadn't abated. It was there, coiled like a snake, inside me.

"And your father."

"What?"

"You partly want to get back with Jason to please your father, don't you?"

120

"You can't object to a parent *approving* of his daughter's choice of partner," I said.

"Can I ask," added Gabrielle, "does this new you last until death do you part? Or does it last until the end of next week, when you tire of making *choux* pastry and neglecting your own needs?"

Shoe pastry? What was she on about? "I assure you," I replied, "I am not a person who neglects her own needs. My need right now is Jason. And if he's happy, I'm happy."

"You know," said Gabrielle in a flat voice, "people say that. But personally I don't find it to be true."

Ah, me neither, every doofus knows that that phrase is just talk. You think it makes you sound fab, but it makes you sound like a loser. Even if you love someone, their happiness can never be a substitute for yours. If it was, I'd be out of a job.

I was simply trying to convey my sincerity using ready-made words. As for skivvying after Jason for the rest of my days, well, maybe I'd get hit by a bus before I turned forty. Meanwhile, I doubted if I'd be able to maintain the cleanse, moisturize, tone regime for more than a month without a bank loan, but I was really, really going to try. I wanted to see the look on Jason's face when, day after day, I served up roast chicken in high heels. (Me in high heels, not the chicken.)

Jason and I had the capacity to have a great relationship. I was aware that for the last five years I'd operated within it on half power, while he zipped around on full throttle. If only I could find it in me not to be quite so *lazy* with him, we could be content. Roast chicken, I felt, was an important part of that.

"Gab, are you okay?" I said. "Your mood seems to have dropped. Are you still not eating carbohydrates?"

(Not that long ago, Gab had come over and I'd bought a bread at the Italian deli called ciabatta. All the rage, apparently. I knew instinctively that Gabrielle was a ciabatta kind of girl. So I served it up with butter and cheese, and from the look on her face, you'd have thought it was a cowpat.

"I'm sorry, Hannah," she'd said. "But ciabatta is like *poison* to me. It's white bread, it's nutritionally void. Its glycemic index is, like, about a *hundred*." She ate the cheese. I ate the ciabatta, expecting to fall down dead every time I swallowed.)

"It's not that. I'm fine. Just tired. Anyway. Come round tomorrow at eight, after Jude's in bed, for a lesson in How to Be Jason's Ideal Wife." Pause. "Knock, don't ring, there'll be a baby asleep in the house," she added, and cut off.

I shook my head. She was both ends of the seesaw, that one.

My hair didn't cause an uproar at work, but only because someone else was the focus of ridicule for a change. One of our freelancers, Ron, had been on surveillance in a van, across the road from a subject's house, and decided—after seven hours of monotony, broken only by some kid bouncing a tennis ball off the side of his vehicle for forty minutes—to smoke a cigarette. A neighbor had seen smoke, assumed the van was on fire, and called 911. Ron's nicotine high was cut short by six burly blokes in helmets wrenching open the back doors of the van and spraying him at close range in ten tons of foam.

Ron's excuse to the firefighters had been "My missus doesn't let me smoke in the house."

Naturally, they'd believed him because men secretly think that all wives are like that. I couldn't blame them, *I* secretly thought that all wives were like that.

It got me thinking as I rang Gab and Oliver's doorbell. What was I trying to be? A traditional wife? A good wife? An unhappy wife? Or a pastiche of a wife?

As Martine once said, "God, I'm becoming a pistachio of myself."

I didn't want to be a pistachio of a wife. All I was doing, I reassured myself, was extending my choices. If it looked a little subservient and antifeminist to some people, I would refer them, myself included, to the lack of respect I'd shown Jason . . . previously. I had to make it up somehow.

"I told you to KNOCK," said Gabrielle in a voice loud enough to wake every baby in the neighborhood. "And"—dragging me into the house by my wrist—"why are you still *white*? What happened to your St. Tropez?"

"I'll rebook it," I lied.

"No, *I'll* rebook it. I don't trust you."

We glared at each other.

Then I noticed a navy blue shoulder bag on the floor. It had an anchor insignia and yellow rope trim. My shoulders tensed.

"Whose is that?" I said.

"Hannah, I—" began Gabrielle.

"Hello," cried my mother, peeping from behind the kitchen door with her best impression of a confident smile. "It's me!"

17.

"Oh," I said.

There was a tone I reserved for my mother. Its use had become habit over the years. Slightly bored, a frosty edge, but not downright rude. Nothing, were she ever to challenge me, that I couldn't attribute to being busy or tired. But she never had challenged me. Our relationship had slowly disintegrated like bread in water and she had allowed it to happen. Occasionally I'd marveled at her stupidity. If one course of action isn't working, it is basic logic to try another. Even rats know that. And yet my mother still clung to the same position, meek, obedient.

Didn't she know that the nicer you are, the nastier others treat you? Did she imagine that one day my reaction to her watchful, beseeching eyes would change? I resented her because I felt that if she'd cared enough, she would have taken charge of my anger and shaken it out of me. At first I was probably too young to know what I was hating her for. My dislike was instinctive, so I thought, based on the knowledge that she had deeply hurt my father. Later, when I was mature enough to understand the meaning of an affair, my disgust reformed anew at a conscious level.

She was led by *me,* whereas everyone knows that the job of a mother is to show her children the way.

I'm not saying I never felt affection for her—if ever you've experienced a "Joy to the World" type mood you'll understand. You catch yourself in a moment where all's well with you, and you feel a spontaneous swell of goodwill to pretty much anyone. It's rare, I admit. But if one of those moods ever hit me, nostalgia would sneak up on the back of it. I'd yearn for the days when life was uncomplicated. When my ability to drink from a beaker was a great achievement and Mummy would sit close to my high chair, applauding.

But then, I'd *see* her, an aged cardboard replica of her young self, and she'd say something annoying. I'd get an unfriendly expression on my face without even trying.

I knew Gabrielle wished we were friends. She was the best of friends with her mother. They borrowed each other's clothes. This was a bad idea, as no sixty-year-old—however black her tan and blond her roots—looks good in a crop top. They also discussed their sex lives. I'd rather not have a sex life than discuss it with my mother.

I said as much to Gabrielle, so she knew to keep out of it.

She tried her best. Gab was a compulsively energetic person; part of her charm was that she was enthusiastic about her friends, not just herself and her immediate family. So it was hard for her not to interfere, to try to get us to pull ourselves together. Perhaps Ollie warned her. (Ollie preferred to let things be. His motto was "Ah well.") Or maybe she knew that if she wanted to keep our friendship, she had to keep quiet on the matter. She had to appreciate that I was quite reserved (not about other people's business, you understand, just my own). Also, she wasn't the victim in this.

But now and then her need to shape us into a cozy family unit overpowered common sense.

"Angela," I said. "Can you wait a minute? I have something I need to discuss with Gabrielle."

Against her will, my sister-in-law followed me into the lounge.

"What are you *doing*? I said.

"Hannah, you have to admit that no one is better at traditional house*wifery* than your mother."

"Gabrielle," I said, speaking in a slow, patient voice as if to a very stupid person. "What do you think you are achieving? Tricking me here."

"You don't give her a chance," burst out Gabrielle. "You have no *idea* what it's like for her! How you treat her, it's offensive!"

"But she—"

"I know, and you know what, there are worse things!"

I gave her a nasty look. "You're *insane* about fidelity in marriage."

"There are many ways in which you can betray a partner."

"Like?"

"Mental cruelty—"

"What are you talking about?"

"I know your mother loves you—"

"Oh, come off it—"

"Hannah, you don't get it, everything she could have said to alienate you from—but she wouldn't because she knows how much you—"

"What?"

"Nothing."

All the anger left Gabrielle in a visible "*puff!*"

"I just," she added, "don't think you know how intense it is being a mother. And I cannot imagine anything worse than having your daughter hate you. You think about your children twenty-four hours a day, they fill your head so there's barely room for anything else, their well-being, their present, their future, their happiness, you want to guard them from danger for the rest of their lives, you worry about the people they will meet, today, tomorrow, forever, those who will love them, hurt them, how you can ensure their safety after your own death, you gaze at photos of them smiling and wish you could preserve them in that moment, because in that moment they are safe, you worry every time they get in a car, every time they're out of your sight, you look on everyone as somebody's baby once, and yet you assess everyone as a potential threat, you creep into their bedroom and watch them as they sleep, listen to their breathing, check the window lock in case a pedoph—"

"Gabrielle, Gabrielle!"

She stopped.

"Gabrielle. That's not *my* mother. That's not a lot of mothers I know. That's you." And then I added more softly, because her face had crumpled, "You are such a good mother. Jude is such a credit to you."

She burst into tears.

"Gab, Gab, what is it?" I patted her on the shoulder. She sniffed and pulled away.

"I, I get so scared. I worry that he's going to die, that someone will take him away from me, and I'm so tired, he sleeps okay now, and I'm *still* so tired, I can't concentrate on anything, there's no time, even when I'm with Jude I feel I'm half elsewhere, I feel guilty when I'm with him, guilty when I'm not with him, and his food, the bloody freezer, that bloody useless freezer, I made a huge batch of chicken and vegetables for him yesterday, my whole evening, and today I went to show the nanny and the superfrost button hadn't worked and the chicken was *soggy,* I had to throw it all away, and I was just so *angry,* and I forget things, I forgot I had a bride coming round last week and I didn't have her fitting ready, it was awful, it had gone out of my head, you know, I can walk out of the lounge and Ollie will say 'switch on the kettle' and by the time I've reached the kitchen I'll have forgotten what he's asked me, and it's all such an *effort,* some days I don't even wash my face, and like, last week-end, Ollie and I finally made it out of the house to take Jude to the park and we're walking along and this bird, this disgusting bird, I feel this horrible *splash!* on my head and shoulder and this bird has *poohed* on me, purple berry pooh, and I want to scream, and run home and shower, but I'm so desperate to get to the park with my family for, like, five minutes of being a family, that I just get Ollie to wipe off the worst with a nappy wipe, and then"—she covered her mouth with her hand—"that night, I'm so so tired, I don't . . . wash my hair until the next morning! Me, *me,* can you *imagine, me* doing that, so disgusting!"

She stared at me, forlorn, from the sofa. She was wearing white; her hair was tied back in a sleek ponytail, the picture of glamour. Although, if I looked closely, there was a weariness around her eyes. Actually one eye. Her left brow was beautifully plucked. The other was . . . bushy.

I took a deep breath. I am mediocre at giving advice. I wished there was a superhero I could call on; if only Cat Woman existed. Alas, it was going to have to be me. "Gabrielle," I said, "the first thing we are going to do is to get you a cleaner. You cannot do every single thing. You are already running two lives. Possibly three, if I know Oliver. It's too much. Now. Jude is fine. That is the main thing. But also, equally, you are *not* fine. So we have to think of what will make you fine. I think, more sleep. What time do you go to bed?"

"Oh, well, midnight, usually."

"What time do you get up?"

"Six. Five-thirty. Depends on Jude."

"The little rat! You need to be in bed by ten-thirty, latest."

She nodded. "But—"

"No buts. You must *do* this. It is very simple. But it will make a lot of difference to your mood."

"But that's when I make Jude's foo—"

"I'll make his food, goddammit!" She looked unsure, so I added, "I'll make some of it. You tell me what to do, I'll do it." Why, why, why, you rash fool, moaned a voice in my head; at least offer something you're capable of!

"I suppose," said Gabrielle, "I could ask my mother to do some of it. She'd love to. It's just that I, I like to do everything myself. I don't trust anyone else to . . . do it as well as me."

A woman after my own heart, but I wasn't going to admit it. "Gab, you have this need to control everything, including the weather. But I suspect that being a parent means being out of control, to an extent. I think it might help if you learn to accept that. You're a brilliant mother. But no one can be perfect. It's not possible and it's not . . . necessary. Better to allow yourself to make a few mistakes. If you're anxious the whole time, Jude will pick up on it. As for some of your other problems. Some of them can be solved by referring to your diary. Writing lists. Lists are good. You tick off things, Jason's always doing that, and then you have a sense of achievement. Meanwhile, you do, and always have, look immaculate. You . . . you, might want to pluck that other eyebrow, though. But your skin looks great, your hair looks great. If that's what bird pooh does to your hair, well, someone better tell those beauty scientists."

Gabrielle clapped her hand to her brow. Then giggled.

I felt a flutter of relief.

"You're good," she said. "At practical stuff. I feel a lot better. You're right. A lot of it is simple. I'll go to bed earlier. Delegate a little."

I smiled. And yet I sensed that she was leaving something out. Rather like a play splashing "'INCREDIBLE'' over its posters, when the critic actually wrote: "An incredible waste of time and money, the worst show I've ever seen in my life, abysmal. . . ." What was Gabrielle leaving out?

She had mentioned that she was terrified of Jude dying, but— Jesus, I had no answer to that! There was no answer. Not the answer *she* required. ("No, he is never going to die. Never. I guarantee it.") The kid had to take his chances like the rest of us!

I cleared my throat. "Gab," I said, "Jude is going to be fine. He is surrounded by many people who love him and take great care of him. It's natural to worry, but don't let it spoil the joy of having him. He is fine, and he *will* be fine."

I could see her drinking in my words. If society didn't have rules about such things, I sensed she would have sucked them out of my mouth. Her smile lit her face. "Yes. Yes, I know. You're right. Thanks, Hannah."

I had a hard time not looking shifty. I present optimistic guesswork as fact, and because she wants to believe it, she does and is reassured, even though she is a fully grown adult who in her rational mind knows it is guesswork because it can't be fact.

Women. I tell you, they're amazing.

The front door of Gabrielle's house clicked shut. She jumped up. "Angela!" she gasped. She flipped open the wooden shutters and we peered through the window. My mother was plodding down the path, a brittle figure, clutching Waitrose bags.

My sister-in-law shot me a pleading look.

I regarded the smooth polished oak floor and murmured, "Oh, let her go."

18.

"You know her mother isn't well," said Gabrielle, crossing her arms.

"What? No. No, I didn't."

At a cousin's wedding, years ago, Grandma Nellie embarrassed herself by screaming at my father. She kept shouting, in her wavery voice, "Shame on you!" She had white flecks at the corners of her shrunken lips, congealed spit. I never wanted to kiss her. We hadn't been close; she'd always favored Ollie. I think she thought boys were more important than girls. My father had said, "Calm yourself, Nellie," kept his cool. But I was furious with her. What did *he* have to be ashamed of? *Her* daughter was the cheat. It was tense in the car on the way home. After that, I only ever saw my grandmother at family events, and after a few years, the fact I never visited made it too awkward for me to suddenly appear on her doorstep bearing cake.

I paused. "How not well?"

"Ill," said Gabrielle. "Hospital ill. She wanted to tell you to your face, but you never seem to go round when she's home."

I swallowed; apparently there was a pebble lodged in my throat. "Oh, right," I said and ran after my mother.

I caught her as she was stepping into the Volvo. My parents have a car each, as do most residents of the Suburb. While the place is a wasp nest of conservation orders and the unspoken threat of citizen's arrest if you don't trim your hedge to the ordained height, locals see no irony in owning an average of three great gas-guzzling vehicles per family.

"Angela, wait."

My mother stepped out of the car backward, banging her head hard on the door frame. She didn't react, she just gave me a nervous smile. "I thought you—" she stopped.

"I got caught up in there, with Gabrielle," I said. (It was a matter of policy, I never said the word "sorry" to my mother.) "We were talking." (Another policy; never explain more than you *absolutely* need. If you blather it starts to sound like an excuse, which weakens your position.) "I'd still like to cook, if there's still time." A part of me remembered eating chocolate cake dough from the mixing bowl while my mother checked the oven. I preferred it raw. My grandmother always said I'd get a stomachache, but Angela still let me. "I didn't know Grandma Nellie was in hospital. Is she okay?" I added, "Did you hurt your head?"

It annoys me, people who are stalwart about physical pain. It makes the rest of us look like whiners. I could conclude only that they do it to impress those around them or to conform to some

British Standard of Painbearing, set down in the 1700s by a bored lord. I find it ridiculous, it is *your* pain, not anyone else's; you should make as big a deal of it as you see fit without having to tip-toe around everyone's tiresome sensibilities. There is no need to be like Jason, who never shuts up, even if he bites his tongue. But why couldn't my mother say "Ouch!"?

"I'm fine," replied my mother. "Grandma's fine too. I thought you'd changed your mind . . . about the cooking."

I reached down to take a shopping bag, and together we walked toward the front door. Even that was awkward. We weren't used to walking together, we hadn't got the who-goes-where arrangement sorted out—she waited for me to go first, I waited for her. She was being polite. I hated people walking behind me. I had this irrational fear of being shot in the the head. After a jerky stumbling-over-our-own-feet episode, she went ahead, I followed.

"What's wrong with Grandma?" I said. As I said it, I realized she had a choice of interpretations.

"She had a mild stroke."

"Oh, God."

This kind of conversation incapacitated me. Jesus, it was like *I'd* had the stroke. I never knew what to say, what the appropriate response was. I always ended up asking irrelevant questions, like "What route did the ambulance driver take to the hospital?"

"Was she, er, dressed when she had it?"

Ah, God, be *quiet,* Hannah. The only other question fighting to take the death leap off the tip of my tongue was "Have you canceled her milk?" (You don't want milk bottles lining up on your doorstep, it says "Coo-ee!" to burglars.) I managed to swallow it.

"She was in her housecoat," replied my mother.

I nodded briskly. "Great, great."

"The kitchen's ready for you," cried Gabrielle, God bless her.

"I'll be in my study if you want me." Angela and I both reacted to this news as if it meant the difference between life and death.

"It's nice," ventured my mother, "that you want to do this for Jason."

Yes, I wanted to say. I thought it might make up for lying to him, do you know what I mean?

"Yes," I said.

My mother blushed. "Well," she said, "I've bought a cookbook and the ingredients."

"Great," I said. "How much do I owe you?"

I had more small talk with my neighbor's cat. (A Siamese, they have a surprising amount to say to humans, considering they're cats.)

"Don't worry about it."

I was about to argue when I saw the cookbook she was holding. *Are You Hungry Tonight? Elvis' Favorite Recipes.*

"Oh!"

She smiled, looking down at the table. "Jack gave me this, for Christmas once."

"He likes Elvis," I said unnecessarily. I felt a tweak of annoyance. Talk about untactful! We were cooking for *Jason*. Not only that, my mother had to know that Jason was not a fried peanut butter kind of guy. "What recipes were you planning on making?"

"I thought we'd start with meat loaf and mushroom gravy." She paused, to give me the opportunity to faint where I stood.

"It's very easy," she added when I didn't. "Only five ingredients for the loaf, and five for the gravy."

That's ten, I thought.

"You just mix everything together for the loaf, then place it in the oven for an hour. As for the gravy. It's really about frying the onion and mushroom in butter, then adding some stock. You mix flour and water in a separate bowl, then add that. It's mainly stir-ring." She added, "What do you think?"

"It doesn't sound too terrible. Do I have to make anything with it?"

"Jacket potatoes are fine. Put them in the oven with the loaf. And beans. Cover them with a drop of water, and cling film. They can be done in the microwave in three minutes."

Music to my ears.

"Drench them in butter, or grate Parmesan cheese over them, to shooche them up a bit."

She meant, jazz them up. Except she said "shooche." I can't even *write* how that word sounds, it's so weird. I don't know where she got it from, she's the only person living I know who uses it. It is a sad word. It reminds me of a hairdresser fluffing up an old woman's thinning hair.

"And for dessert. I know Jason likes to maintain his figure"—agh, she made him sound like a girl—"so I thought, Spicy Baked Apples. Again, it's mainly mixing ingredients." She hesitated. "It does say baste every fifteen minutes, but I think you might skip that part."

My mother talked me through each recipe, making me stir and chop. Once she corrected my hold on the knife, and her hand trembled slightly. She was used to taking orders, not giving them.

"I've copied out the recipes for you," she said. "I'll lend you a baking tray. You can buy most of the ingredients, but I've bought you a tin of Marigold Swiss vegetable bouillon powder, for the mushroom gravy. Make up half a pint. One tablespoon of powder mixed with boiling water. See?"—she pointed to the side of the tin with a varnished fingernail—"the letters 'tsp' stand for 'tablespoon.' Two tsp per pint. Simple. But it's important you get it right. Remember, if in doubt, add more powder. It increases the flavor."

I nodded. "Right."

She took over for the gravy. I paid close attention without standing too near. The atmosphere was roughly the same as when I took my driving test. Except, I suppose, she was a little more excited than my examiner to have the honor of my company. She dropped an onion, then a fork, and then a serving spoon, splatting hot butter over Gabrielle's immaculate tiles. She never quite met my eye.

I never met hers either. I had a brief thought that maybe these recipes, easy as they were, weren't entirely suitable for someone with an irritable bowel, but my mother was aware of his complaint, and in matters culinary, I trusted her. While we waited for the meat loaf and baked apples to cook, Angela showed me how to give the appearance of almighty, backbreaking effort.

One, put flowers on the table. (In a vase, not just lying there.) Also, not sunflowers. A small and delicate bloom.

Two, serviettes. Plain, not patterned or jokey. Fold them in half triangular-ways, then again, so they prop up themselves.

Three, heat the plates in the microwave for two minutes.

Four, wear an apron to answer the door.

Five, spray *oh de cologne* on your wrists. (I'd have to buy some.)

Six, bleach the toilet.

Seven, arrange a row of tea lights on the table (these are small candles) and dim the overhead light. Remember, it's not an interrogation.

Eight, wear a light lipstick (pale red, she suggested), a skirt, and heels.

Nine, provide wine, and Japanese rice crackers in nice bowls.

Ten, turn off the TV before you let him in.

I'm not sure this was the correct order. Also, I couldn't quite tell the difference between the *appearance* of almighty backbreaking effort and actual almighty backbreaking effort. I never turned off the TV. The TV was my *friend*. It was great for filling in gaps in the conversation. Maybe I could turn it down?

Already I was aching to bend the rules. I should do what she said and press the *off* switch. It wouldn't hurt to try. Much.

I wanted to show my mother I was grateful, without excessive physical contact. "This was very kind of you," I said carefully. "I appreciate it. I wondered," I added in a rush, "if you needed me to do anything for Grandma Nellie. Is her house secure? Her kitchen has a stable door. Now, most people think you can get away with just locking the lower half, and securing the bolt. But you have to lock the upper door too. Otherwise someone can smash through the window, unbolt the bolt, and climb in. And does she have a security letter flap? It's very fashionable for thieves to hook keys off hall tables with a fishing rod; it's easy with a normal letter box. They're usually after the car keys, but they can equally let themselves in and raid the house. They usually do it between four and six in the morning. What she needs is a security letter flap—you can stick a pole through it, but it snaps shut so you can't pull anything back out. There are other measures she can take, hook mortice bolts and reinforcing strips for the door. And is her alarm in good working order? She should read the small print of her house insurance contract, because they're shockers, that lot. And have you canceled her milk? I mean, temporarily canceled her milk? And her *Daily Express*? And there should be some lights on all night to give the appearance of habitation. And curtains should be drawn, downstairs at the back. And windows locked. Each window should have its own lock, a generic lock is fine. I can recommend a good locksmith. Her extension has a flat roof, so that's a weak point, security wise. She doesn't have any garden ladders laying around, does she, because that's a no-no—"

I stopped, because my mother was looking supremely uncomfortable. As if she felt she ought to speak but didn't want to. I smiled impatiently and raised my eyebrows.

My mother twisted her wedding ring back and forth, back and forth, at speed. "I thought I'd mentioned it," she said. "I must have forgotten. Grandma Nellie moved into a home eight months ago."

She hadn't forgotten. I'd forgotten. It was shocking how great chunks of significant information passed in and out of my ears like ghosts.

"Oh, right, yes, of course." I went hot. My mouth felt dry and the forbidden word strained at my lips. It was strange, actually, that I had forgotten Grandma Nellie's move to a home, because at the time I'd thought about it a lot. I'll be honest. I don't do a lot of deep thinking on my personal relationships. In fact, I spend more time agonizing about relationships that don't actually exist. For instance,

Oh, Susanna, don't you cry for me,
I'm off to Alabama with a banjo on my knee!

I heard the tune on one of Jude's plastic toys and recalled the words out of nowhere. And wondered why Susanna would waste her time moping after a man who was so plainly a conceited idiot—moseying off to Alabama with a banjo, daring to imagine her distraught?! She was probably glad to see the back of him—him, his silly banjo, and his unrealistic view of job opportunities in the music business. Susanna—I imagined her demure and blond, in a checked pinafore, baby blue and white—was probably too well brought up to tell him she loathed his banjo playing and him.

I don't know why I do this. But in between fretting about imaginary Susannas, I did think about my grandmother going to a home. I didn't like to dwell on it, because such a move so plainly signified the End for Grandma Nellie. As Gabrielle is always reminding me—or was—the whole world is not as seedy as I imagine it. When her mother was in hospital with pneumonia, the nurses were wonderful, kind and caring. But Martine's elderly uncle had Alzheimer's and when Martine complained to a nurse that he was ignoring her, she replied, "Oh, I give a sharp tug on his nasal tube, that gets his attention." After a tale like that, it's hard to conjure up Florence Nightingale. Despite our troubled history, I didn't like to think of Grandma Nellie at the mercy of strangers. So I suppose I blanked it.

"But," said Angela, "there, there, there is one thing you can do, if, if, if you like. I know Grandma Nellie would be delighted." I cringed. Did I really make her stammer? And it was embarrassing, after the meat loaf and baked apple, to forget that my grandmother had been packed off to a home.

"Sure," I said. "What is it?"

My mother coughed delicately, placing her fingertips in front of her pearly lipsticked mouth. "She'd love you to visit her in hospital."

"Of COURSE!" I boomed. "Whenever you like, it would be a pleasure!"

Jesus, Mary, Joseph and the Technicolored Dreamcoat, kill me now, I'd rather die.

19.

The specter of Grandma Nellie—or maybe that's tempting fate—the *looming* visit to Grandma Nellie got me thinking. I'm not claiming anything profound. Just, life is over pretty quick—mine seems to jump in bursts of six months, in accord with dental appointments—and so many people make a mess of theirs. I was at work, two weeks later, and Greg was telling me about a case he'd taken on for a Mrs. Speck. It was standard.

They lived in Dover. He was in London overnight for business. Mr. Speck told his wife that he was meeting a male colleague for dinner at a restaurant called No Boo. Or something. She'd rung No Boo, who'd confirmed the reservation, but she was still suspicious.

"Anyway," said Greg. "I put a static on it"—a one-man observation—"and he follows him back to the hotel."

I was relaxing into the story, I loved the way Greg used the lingo. It made me feel like a member of an elite club. *Static. "Get some victor"* (video footage). *"Sunray"* (the client). *"Alpha one"* (the male subject). Once, when we were on surveillance, he said the words "Alpha one in pole position indicating right"—meaning, the geezer was at the traffic lights in the right-hand lane—I got a silly little shiver down my spine. I think Greg knew this, because he spoke plain English to everybody else.

"So after an hour, he comes down from his hotel room with a gorgeous Oriental woman. At that point, I put the full team on him. He goes to a cash machine. Hands her some notes. Then she gets a cab back to Kensal Rise."

What a scummer. I was no longer relaxed. It depressed me. There was Grandma Nellie on the brink, and here was Mr. Speck banging prostitutes while his wife sat at home phoning No Boo. And what killed me was, she knew. Or she would, when Greg filed his report. And then what would she do?

Divorcing aged twenty is enough of a blow, but at least you haven't squandered too much of anyone's time. When you were Mrs. Speck it was different. She was stuffed. Either she ignored Greg's findings and accepted that she would waste her entire life on a man who wasn't worthy of her. Or she accepted that she'd wasted half her life on a man who wasn't worthy of her but that *possibly* there were better men out there, and jumped into the harsh, desperate world of middle-aged dating, on the slim chance that she might track one down.

Of course I should add that Mrs. Speck might do other man-free things with the remainder of her days and find fulfillment that way. But truth was, women like Mrs. Speck weren't *accustomed* to finding fulfillment without a man. Mrs. Speck was unlike me but, I realized with a shock, I sympathized. If you are used to living a certain way, it can be near impossible to embrace a new way. Mrs. Speck might move into a cozy apartment, take up pottery, join the National Trust and an opera-based social club, but she'd be merely treading water through the days, grateful when it got to 10 P.M. and she could get into bed and lose consciousness *respectably,* passing time until, she hoped, she met the man who would make her normal again.

"Poor Mrs. Speck, stuck with a shit like that," I said and stamped out of Greg's office.

He looked startled and I was annoyed with myself. Job done, I cut clients' problems out of my mind like you slice off a piece of bruised apple. It was not my concern what Mrs. Speck decided to do with our findings and the rest of her life. Truth was, I was impatient to see Jason and it was making me ratty. For one thing, the hair on my tush was growing back. I didn't like to see all that pain and mortification go to waste.

He had sent me chocolates from Kenya every day. Or rather, he'd got his PA to send me chocolates from Thorntons every day. I'd told Gabrielle, expecting praise on Jason's behalf. Her response: "How horrid."

When he rang the following morning, my bad mood popped like a bubble.

"Jase!"

"Hello, Chocolate Girl!"

"What?" I said.

"Chocolate Girl. It's a song title. By Deacon Blue. And I've been sending—"

"Yeah, I get it." I paused. Tried to click in to my new personality. "Thank you," I added. "It was really nice of you. They were delicious. I may be heading for diabetes."

Silence.

"It would be lovely to see you, Jason," I said after a few moments. I had to be less brusque. More acquiescent. *Nicer.* Fewer orders, barked statements. More shy, eyelash-fluttering questions. Thing was, I needed Jason. In a world of people who didn't think much of me, he stood alone.

"Come round," I said. "I'll make you dinner."

"Pardon?"

"I'll make you dinner."

"Really?"

"Yes!"

"No!"

"Jason," I said. "I have been taking this seriously. This list of conditions."

"Ah, that. Ah, Hannah. You know, that list . . . it was a bit much. Especially the note from Jack, I mean, I felt bad when I saw it . . . I can't imagine it was easy to secure. It's just, I felt hurt by you, I felt angry. I just wanted to see if you would *try.*"

I squirmed in my seat. Despite my supposed new personality I was still unhappy with the concept of bleating out emotion as one experienced it. If someone tells you "I feel hurt . . . I feel angry," that is to me (and I'm quoting Jason here, don't think I thought of this myself) *codependent behavior.* Codependence, if I stayed awake long enough to compute, is when you act in a way so as to trick your stooge of a partner into a certain response. When Jason told me he felt hurt, he felt angry, he was forcing me to feel pity and guilt.

Isn't that the opposite of good manners, the aim of which are to make people feel comfortable?

Supposedly, it was the holy grail of therapy to access and express your emotions, the point at which you became *adult*. How, when sharing your hurt and anger is such an enormous bore and inconvenience to those around you?

I felt mean for having such thoughts. I said, "Come at nine. That would give me time to cook."

"Wow," said Jason. "Can't wait."

Then I looked in the mirror on my wall and realized I was the color of milk. I'd have to cancel. No way could I see Jason before I'd had a respray. I kid you not, at that precise moment, the phone rang. It was an underling calling on behalf of Gabrielle's beautician (now there's a made-up word, invented to give us faith in absolutely nothing), reminding me that I had a "St. Tropez" booked for 5:30 today. If that isn't fate, tell me what is.

The process of being St. Tropez'd is dull and humiliating, but after my Brazilian, it was a breeze. Then she said, "You're done!" I jumped up, triumphant, looked in the mirror, nearly fainted.

"B . . . b . . . but I . . . This isn't a tan! This isn't golden brown! It's dirty brown! I look all smeared and filthy! I look like a chimney sweep. I look like I've been rolling in mud. I look . . ." I finished miserably, "like a black-and-white minstrel. I'll be lynched on the tube."

The woman smiled like I was stupid. "It's only temporary. You shower tomorrow morning and your lovely golden tan will have developed underneath."

A likely tale!

"But until then," she continued breezily, "you can't get your hands wet. Or *any* part of you. And drink through a straw. Or else you'll get two white bits at the edges of your mouth."

"You mean"—I gulped—"you mean I look like *this* until tomorrow morning?"

"Didn't you read the information leaflet?"

Of course I didn't read the information leaflet! What did she think I was, a tourist?

"No," I said as haughtily as I could (in the circumstances).

She gave me a disdainful look. "If you shower tonight, it'll be forty-five pounds down the drain."

Forty-five pounds? All she'd done was paint me brown! She'd have a nerve charging a tenner!

I paid and slunk out. *Forty-five pounds.* I was one of the world's poor. Also, I'd left my car at the station to avoid rush-hour traffic. I couldn't afford a cab. I just couldn't. And don't tell me Londoners are standoffish. From Green Park station to Kentish Town tube, strangers all but collapsed laughing in each other's arms. At last I escaped into the polluted air, only to remember I had to go food shopping. Where people were equally insolent. Staring. Nudging. By the time the checkout man squawked, "Chim-chiminy cher*oo*!" I'd had enough.

I jumped into my car and dialed Jason to postpone. Then I cut off. He'd wanted to see me *tonight.* And I'd bought the meat loaf ingredients. Also, I wanted to see him. I didn't want to wait. I didn't want to give the impression that I was halfhearted about our new start. I'd just have to . . . dim the lights.

The doorbell rang dot on nine. I sighed. It would have to do. The flat was extraordinarily tidy. There were flowers on the table, an old lady bunch, all the supermarket had, but flowers all the same. I'd scoured the floor of the bathroom for pubic hairs and Dustbusted three wiry offenders. My bed linen had been washed at sixty degrees (the lowest temperature at which bacteria die, according to Jason) and tumble-dried, giving it a lovely burnt cottony smell. Meanwhile, I looked fairly frightening.

I'd got the edges of my mouth wet, even though I hadn't drunk, despite an uncharacteristic raging thirst. That beautician had made me paranoid; every second I'd felt drool leaking from my mouth. When I checked for white bits, I had a white outline around the *whole* of it, like a clown. Plainly, unlike most young ladies, I slavered like a dog. I'd covered it up by applying a generous amount of lipstick. Consequently, I now had a huge fake mouth. I'd applied mascara to my eyelashes, although my face looked so dirty I might as well have applied it to my alleged mustache. My hair looked great. The clothes Gabrielle had picked out for me weren't that bad. Beautiful red high-heeled shoes like a prostitute might wear. A white flared skirt with an uneven hem. A red halterneck top. The worst you could say was, there was whiff of the transvestite about me. That apart, I hoped Jason would be impressed.

"Hannah! Oh, is there a power cut?"

"Hi, Jase. No. It's atmospheric. For the dinner."

"But it's pitch black."

"You get used to it."

"Well, let's at least have a candle. Or the hall light on. There! Ahhh! Jesus! Hannah! What have you done? You're all . . . mucky. Is it, is it . . . er, fancy dress?"

I was about to be angry because I was embarrassed, but I looked at Jason's handsome, good-natured face, his smile caught somewhere between confusion and horror, and started to giggle.

"No," I said finally. "This is a *tan*. It was meant to impress you."

"But . . ."

"It's a Miw Hiw tan."

"A what?"

"Jason, it's a fake tan."

"Oh."

"Instead of getting skin cancer?"

"Oh! I see!"

(I knew he'd like that one.)

"But . . . so . . . why is it . . . so . . . *wrong?*"

I explained.

"But," I said, "if you could see past the brown vegetable dye, to the hair and the clothes and the shoes . . . ?" I did a quick twirl.

Jason beamed. "You look lovely," he said. And then he pulled me into his arms and kissed me. I wasn't expecting it, so my teeth hit his quite hard, but apart from that (and the tan stains on his yellow shirt and the red lipstick smears around his mouth) it was perfect. The evening had begun well.

"I like your clothes," Jason said. "I *really* like them. They're so . . . they are *girls'* clothes." He added, "I don't mean that to sound bad."

He looked around, wide-eyed. "And the place is spotless. And there are flowers!"

If Jason planned to give me a rundown of everything he saw, we were in for a long night. But then, Gab always complained that she could have a head transplant and Ollie wouldn't notice. I tried to be glad that Jase was a man who noticed change.

"And"—he sniffed—"whatever you're cooking smells great! And you've laid the table!"

"Would you like a drink?" I said, to stop the commentary.

Jason hesitated.

I waved a bottle of red at him. "Oh, be a devil!" I said in my mother's voice.

145

He grinned. "Why not! Go on then."

In the silent aftermath of this middle-aged exchange, my heart shot to my shoes. I suppose I'd expected Jason to *get* that young hipsters like us weren't expected to dawdle over the offer of one glass of red wine, as if it were a bowl of smack cut with talcum powder. I knew he saw it as serious consideration to be weighed against the demands of the office the following day, and it made me feel like I was en route to dying. To cheer myself up, I retrieved two brandy glasses and poured an inch of booze into his (the polite measure, apparently). I filled mine to the brim.

"Something's different," muttered Jason as I danced around the hob, squashing the lumps out of the mushroom gravy. I was getting quietly violent until I realized they were mushrooms. "Hannah! You turned off the TV!"

I blushed.

Jason shook his head. "Hannah. You are amazing. To be honest, I never thought you'd do it. But it seems that you have. I did think it was a risk, asking you to contact Jack, but I feel it's a risk that's paid off. You really have turned over a new leaf!"

One problem with Jason: his use of clichés. Ready-made language. For people too lazy to bother with original thought. Still, he took similar offense at my use of ready-made meals. Not tonight, though.

"This is superb!"

"It's meat loaf," I said.

Jason paused. "Is it meat?"

I paused. "It's *meat* loaf. There's your clue."

Jason coughed. "Right. Right. Only, I thought, what with"—he rolled his eyes—"my delicate stomach, I thought you might have substituted soya."

"Oh."

"It's not a problem. But, you know, the Chinese call soya 'meat without bones.' "

"What! Do they? Urgh! Why do they do that? How disgusting. Urgh, it makes you think of a body without a skeleton—"

I stopped.

"Because of the beans' high protein content."

"Ah." I smiled. "Mushroom gravy? Can I taunt you with some? I mean, can I tempt you with some?"

Jason held out his plate. I doused it in gravy and waited for praise. What I got was a gobbet of chewed meat loaf spat onto the middle of my white tablecloth (also a sheet) and an overturned chair as Jason sped to the bathroom retching. There he remained for twenty minutes, which gave me time to ascertain that the mushroom gravy was as dense in salt as the Dead Sea. Eyes bulging, I snatched up my mother's instructions. There it was. "*Tsp* equals tablespoon."

"Jason," I shouted. I could hear him sighing on the toilet. "Jason. In cooking, what does Tee-Ess-Pee stand for?"

"Teaspoon," he croaked.

All I could do was apologize. And hate Angela. She knew what a tsp was, it was her native tongue! I'd deal with her later.

I leaned against the bathroom door. "Jase," I said. "Are you okay?"

He groaned softly.

"Jase? There's something I have to tell you."

"What?"

"I . . . I'm so sorry about this mess, tonight. All I want is a new beginning. I feel I don't deserve you. You're so . . . so *good,* Jason."

"Don't say that. Ahh, could you, could you run to the end of the hall *now,* please, Hannah?"

I ran to the end of the hall, where the sound of Jason's diarrhea was still clearly audible. When it was over, I ran back.

"Jason. I forged the note from Jack."

There was a silence. Then Jason said, "You mean he didn't write it?"

"No."

"So you didn't sort out your emotional baggage? You lied to me?"

"No." I winced. "Yes."

"Oh my God!"

I stared at the bathroom door.

"Is it . . . over?" I whispered.

"I think there might be a bit more to come, you might have to run to the end of the hall ag—"

"Jase. I mean, is it over with *us*?"

My insides were mercury, hard, and heavy. But I'd had to tell. I refused to base our new future on lies. I wanted to be honorable, through and through.

"Hannah, no, not at all."

I allowed a smile.

He laughed. "Actually," he said, "it makes it *fair.*"

"What do you mean?"

"Because, oh God"—sqtsqtsqtsqt—"End of the hall!"

I ran on the spot. "Yes?" I said, trying to throw my voice.

"Because I slept with Lucy."

I sighed. "Jase. Of course you slept with Lucy. You were engaged to her. For a minute."

"No." The toilet flushed. "I mean, I slept with her every day the week before I went to Kenya. *And* yesterday."

20.

"*What!*" I said. "I thought you said irritable bowel affected your sex drive?"

Now I see that I was relieved. Having been the bad guy with Jack, it was a privilege to be in a position to forgive. Jason's infidelity took the pressure off. It freed me from the duty to be *good*. Then, I didn't see this as reflecting on the strength of my love for Jason. Or on my famed problem with intimacy, as Jase would have it. I thought I was pretty damn twenty-first century, actually. I suspect that Jase was more clued than I was as to what my reaction meant. Which is possibly why he went ballistic.

He burst through the bathroom door (having opened it). Do you even care about me, etc.

"Of course I care about you," I said.

"Then why pull me up on a technicality? Aren't you furious, Hannah? Aren't you jealous? Aren't you imagining me and Lucy and what we did together?"

I made a face. "No, actually, that would be rather yucky."

"*God!*" shouted Jason.

I scowled. "Do you think that people who choose not to expose their souls for public entertainment don't *have* feelings? Wouldn't that be like thinking that, say, New York exists only when *you* fly in to JFK?"

(This was a dig, as Jason had never been to New York. Personally, I don't think he was up to it.)

Jason's expression softened.

Encouraged, I added, "For all *you* know, I'm dying inside."

"Hannah," he said, "I'm so sorry. I didn't realize."

I'm no Miss Marple, but Jason would have made a bad detective. He heard only what he chose to hear and made assumptions. I had not said, "I am dying inside."

He squashed me in a long hug, which gave me time to consider how I *was* feeling.

There was shock. Jason had always regarded sex as naughty, and not in a good way. He was thorough in his duties—but he never seemed to lose himself. But to shag Lucy day in day out suggested *enthusiasm*.

I *was* hurt. Because I loved Jason? Because my ego was dented? Jason had the promise of me, why did he need her? Yet there was none of the bubbling red fury I'd experienced on seeing Jack *kiss* a girl. Lucy wasn't blond, maybe that was it. What is worse? If a man cheats on you with a plain woman or a very beautiful one?

I also disliked that Jason had kissed *her* yesterday and *me* today, for health reasons if nothing else. Get Martine on the subject of mouth bacteria, and you'd never kiss anyone again. ("Staphylococci cause gum boils and grow in clumps like a bunch of grapes.")

I concluded that it was hard to be jealous because Lucy was not an object of envy. After three weeks of slog, I was mistress of the flower arrangement (lift bunch out of paper, place directly in vase) and the homely home: Remove every item from every surface, thus defeating the point of surfaces, disguise all smells with bleach or scent. This was Lucy's world, and she was welcome to it.

I squeezed him hard around the waist. He gasped. "I *do* love you," I said. "I really do." Suddenly, I felt happier about saying it.

Jason blushed. "That's the first time in five years you've said that voluntarily," he said. "I love you too. And of course I forgive you." He took a huge breath. "God, Hannah. I feel so light and happy!"

I was about to make a toilet-related crack, but caught myself.

Jason sank to one knee. I knew what was coming.

"Hannah," he said, gripping my hands in his, "this time *please* say yes."

"Okay," I said, "but do we always have to do this near a toilet?"

Jason laughed and shuffled along the carpet on his knees. I pigeon-toed behind, feeling silly. I wished he'd stood up and walked; I don't like short men. (This is apparently instinct. Also, I got a bad reaction off a guy once after describing him, to his face, as "petite.") Happily, when Jason had shuffled a respectable distance from the bathroom, he rose to his feet, affording me the girly thrill of his full height, five foot eleven.

"Hannah, will you marry me?"

I rolled my eyes. "Go on then."

"Hooray!"

Jason picked me up and spun me around. I laughed, then my feet hit the hall table, cricking my back. I allowed him to carry me to the sofa. He plumped the cushions behind my head and said, "Look what I got you."

A diamond that would take your eye out.

"Wow."

It was big and sharp with dangerous glinting edges, perched on top of a gold band.

He slid it onto my finger. It felt heavy and strange. My hand dropped to my side, stretching my arm, I was sure, by about three inches. I heaved it back up to my eyeline. I tilted my hand left and right, like a lady, to see it glitter. "This," I said, "is quite a weapon."

"It is also," murmured Jason, his voice tickling, "a token of my esteem." He breathed into my ear, which could only mean one thing.

What with his stomach, my back, and the aftertaste of infidelity, it wasn't the greatest. But as I stroked his hair afterward, I felt tender toward him. (The way to my heart is most unladylike.)

There was a mischievous part of me that couldn't wait to tell my mother that Jason and I were *affianced*.

Why? Because I had a suspicion. Angela didn't think Jason was right for me!

He'd always adored her. Young men did. It was like gay blokes and Lisa Minelli. I'd had to struggle to keep them apart. Jason thought he could see *maternal potential* in Angela and was determined to unlock it. As if she were the perfect mother trapped in a tower, waiting for the right child to come along and free her. He'd watch, wide-eyed, as she pulled a burning tray of spitting-hot roast potatoes out of the oven with a worn tea towel. "Angela, use the oven gloves, you'll burn your hands!"

She'd give him a quick, tight smile and say, "Thank you, Jason. I'm fine." Whereas if, say, Gabrielle had intervened, my mother would have clutched her arm, smiled into her eyes, and said, "Oh, Gabrielle, you know what I'm like, I'm hopeless."

It was strange. Jason was the kind of man that mothers were supposed to love.

A wicked urge overtook me, and I said, "Hey, Jase. I can't wait to tell my mother that we're engaged." Jason smiled. "I think she disapproves of you." He stopped smiling.

"She *disapproves* of me?" Jason was aware he was the kind of man mothers were supposed to love. "Why? That's not true! It can't be." He looked upset. Then he said. "But . . . if it is true, why can't you wait to tell her we're engaged? Wouldn't you want to put it off?"

I wrinkled my nose. "I like to *tease* her."

"That's not teasing," said Jason. "It's taunting. Which is a form of expressing anger." He propped himself on one elbow. "And you know what else anger is?"

I tickled his foot with mine, but he wouldn't be put off.

"*Grief*," said Jason sternly. "Anger is grief. And I think your anger at your mother is a mask for your pain. It's so you don't have to feel the pain at her loss."

I shushed him. "Oh, Jase. You are funny! She isn't *lost*. She's right there. I don't care for her much, but she's right there."

Jason shook his head. "Hannah. From all you've told me, she is lost to *you*. You *do* care for her, but you've destroyed all your expectations of her. That way, it's impossible for her to disappoint you. You've dragged the level down, because it hurts to set it high."

I silenced him with a pinch on the cheek. "Jason," I said. "I am going to ring my parents and tell them the happy news."

I didn't lose my temper, because I thought I knew why he'd burst out with all this. He was angry at *his* mother for dying. He was obsessed with mothers. His whole bearing screamed "I am the ideal son." Like if he was good enough, his mother would come back from the dead.

If that sounds uncharacteristically astute, one therapy session had taught me this: Whatever you say you are, you're the opposite. I was happy to apply it to Jason, if not to myself. (Therapy wasn't for me. I'd sat down and nearly puked as the seat was *warm from a previous bottom*. I was offended at the concept of being a bean on a conveyor belt of damaged goods.)

Jason checked his watch. "I do realize that Daddy Dear expects a report of each event in your life as it occurs," he said. "But it's past midnight. You can't ring now!"

I ignored the jealousy-induced sarcasm and flopped back down on the bed. "You're right. I'll ring tomorrow."

It crept over me that I felt limp about sharing the news with Roger, even though it would be the fast track back into his affections. I couldn't decide if this was because I was less than thrilled about the news myself, or because I was less than thrilled with Roger. Both thoughts were sacrilege and I tried to dismiss them.

21.

I did ring home the next day, but no one answered, and my father was uncontactable at the office. His PA, Rita, was apologetic and indiscreet. A *Telegraph* hack had pressed the "track changes" button on a press release sent as a Word document. This spelled trouble.

As Roger had once explained it, "Every press release has to be approved by every prick in the company, and ends up being amended by three hundred and thirty-six different cunts."

If a journalist receives a short document that has a disproportionately large number of bytes and selects the "track changes" option on the toolbar of his Word program, he can see every sly change made to that document.

"Your father is *steaming*," whispered Rita. "He'll be tied up all day in damage limitation. But I'll tell him you called, dear. Nothing important, I hope?"

I popped the diamond ring in my pocket, as I didn't want Greg to see it. My father should be the first to know. But I should tell *someone,* get a test reaction. I decided to call Gabrielle.

"Gab? You okay?"

"Not really, oh, Jesus, *stop that! No!* Don't press that, Jude, stop it now, now—wait!—baby, come along, away from there, darling, you'll hurt—awwww, silly sausage, now what did I just say, aww, poor Jude, oh no, oh you poor boy, oh it's okay, hug from your mummy, hug from your mummy, ouch, don't bite Mummy—"

Rather like pulling someone from a taxi, I feel it's rude to force a person out of a bad mood. I'd save my news. I said, "Did he trip? Is he okay? Where's Nanny Amanda?"

Gabrielle sniffed. "On her way back to Melbourne."

"A holiday?" I asked without hope.

"For good."

"What! Why?"

Secretly, I couldn't imagine a decision more self-explanatory. Ten minutes with Jude and I was exhausted, ready for bed. Allegedly, most babies were similar. Jude would step on and off and on and off and on and off a doorstep for a good half hour, while you bore his entire substantial body weight, then freak out, suddenly, for no reason. Once Jason had come in wearing a hat and Jude had reacted like Freddie Krueger just stepped in the door. Gab had ripped it off Jason's head while screaming "Hats scare him!" Now, unless he'd been watching *Nightmare on Elm Street,* that was irrational. I had no idea how Nanny Amanda had managed him.

"Hated England."

"Ah."

This wasn't a surprise. Nanny Amanda and Gabrielle had enjoyed a fine working relationship, bar the fact that Nanny Amanda was bluntly underwhelmed by London, while Gabrielle remained its staunch defender. If ever I'd asked after the health of Nanny Amanda, Gabrielle would report today's slur on the United Kingdom.

Its great advantage was that it was "very near to a lot of other countries."

After standing in a queue in Sainsburys, "You know, in Australia, we have these things called express checkouts?"

If it weren't for the exchange rate, "there'd be half the number of Aussies and Kiwis here."

Subsequent to putting on half a stone, "Everyone comes here and gets fat. It's the weather. I never ate junk food in Australia."

Following an encounter with a bloke from Dalston, "The men here are such dags." (On requesting translation, Gabrielle discovered that a dag was "the clotted shit and wool stuck to a sheep's tail.")

Plainly, it was only a matter of time before Nanny Amanda fled our land of fat people, daggy men, long queues, and Australians.

"What will you do?" I said.

"No idea," said Gabrielle in a singsong voice.

"Can't you get another nanny?"

"I can get a *psycho* who doesn't like kids, no problem. I can get a sixteen-year-old with no qualifications. I can get a girl who speaks two words of English—the girls who speak three words are all snapped up. I can get a fifty-six-year-old who's waiting for a hip replacement operation. Darling, away from the video! Away! Good boy! No, don't press that! Hannah, it is near impossible to find a good nanny who wants to work part-time; it's going to take me bloody months, and what am I going to do until then, I've got work, I—"

"Can't your mother help?"

"Yes, but not day in, day out! She's in Puerto Banus right now, anyway. She has her own life. Sweetheart, no! Not the TV! Away! Thank you! No, don't press that! She adores him, she likes showing him off, but she doesn't like changing nappies. He comes home from her with the fattest nappy you ever—"

"What about Ollie?"

"Well, he's off on jobs most of the time. And when he's home . . . he's okay, but he's . . . distracted. He doesn't quite realize that you can't leave a baby to do its own thing. And he doesn't do things *right*. I'm always having to correct him."

And as we all know, there's nothing men love more than being corrected.

"Gab," I said. "What are you doing today?"

"Looking after my son."

"How about *I* look after him?"

"What?"

Quite. "Give you a break for the afternoon."

"But you're at *work, Hannah.*"

"It'll be fine. No one will mind." Lie, lie.

"Darling, it's very kind of you, but he takes some looking after. No! Jude! No, darling, we don't eat money, we spend it. You can't plop him in a corner with a good book. You have to entertain him. You have to watch him every *second.* I mean that. He's easily bored. And he needs a drink midafternoon. And it's important that you respond positively when he speaks to you—well, he doesn't exactly speak, it's mostly gabble, except for a few key words—"

"He sounds like every man I know, I'll be fine. So, er, what are the key words."

"Apple. Door. Daddy. Boob. All men are greeted as 'daddy,' all women are greeted as 'boob.' "

Good lord, what kind of a man was she raising here? Gabrielle must have sensed my disapproval, for she added, "It's normal, for breast-fed babies, okay? Look, maybe this is a bad idea. Like, have you ever even changed a nappy? No! Honey, no! Not Mummy's sunglasses. Give them to—oh, oh, okay, keep them."

"*I* haven't but . . . Greg, my boss, must have. He's got four boys. We'll manage."

"He needs to be taken out for a walk."

"Greg? Oh, Jude, yes, of course. No problem."

"Are you sure you're up for this? Aren't you terribly busy? You will keep him safe? You won't take him on any assignments? I

157

mean . . . it would help me out. I've got a client coming for her final fitting at three. But—oh, all right, I'll give him lunch, then drop him off."

"What's *that*?" said Greg, pointing at Jude.

"A puppy." (Well, if he didn't know.)

"What is it doing in my office?"

"I'm his aunt, it was an emerg—"

"*Hiiiiiiii!*"

I grinned, and so did Greg. Jude had greeted my boss with an exaggerated enthusiasm mainly found in those who work in television.

"Hello, son!"

"*Up!*"

Jude held out his arms. Nice work.

Greg knelt and lifted Jude out of the buggy. "*Ma!*" said Jude, pointing at me. His other hand was round Greg's neck. I could see Greg going all misty-eyed, then, as I relaxed, Jude stuck a finger up Greg's nose and scraped it down again.

"God!" gasped Greg. His eyes watered. "Cut your nails, son." He handed Jude back. I sagged under his weight.

"So, how are you planning to do your"—Greg paused. "I have *exactly* the job for you. This is *perfect*."

I didn't like the sound of this.

Five minutes later, I was watching Jude chewing my keys and wondering if I should call Gabrielle. I didn't want to bother her. Or worry her. She might not appreciate me using her child as cover. Here was the scenario. The Legal Aid Board, through their solicitors, had approached Greg on behalf of a client. He was divorced, paying child maintenance. But he suspected that his ex-wife had a live-in boyfriend. In which case, he was entitled to drag her back to court and appeal to pay less maintenance.

To prove cohabitation, he had to prove that the partner was staying in her house three consecutive nights, not including the weekend. Greg would be looking at late-night attendance, early mornings, some indication that the boyfriend was still at the house. All he'd need would be a couple of stills—*photographs*—enough to give the court reason to question that the woman was single. Greg would do the late-night work himself, or get someone like Ron to do it. What he wanted *me* to do was go to the child's school, with Jude in his pushchair, to see who picked up the child. No one looks twice at a woman pushing a baby in a buggy, but a man outside a school on his own is conspicuous.

We had a rucksack with a tiny camera in the strap. I could hold it at a good height. What Greg hoped for was that the mother and the new boyfriend would pick up the kid together and get into a car. We'd need the registration. Then, if it was the boyfriend's car, we'd follow them—or Ron would—to see if they went back to his or her house. Jude and I were to be "one team." Ron would be nearby in a car, ready to go. Greg had given me a photo of the mother, Lara. She was thin with long lank brown hair and dry skin, and her back teeth were missing. She didn't look like a woman who was rolling in cash.

"Aaaaaa!" said Jude, holding out the keys.

"Thank you very much," I said. "Very kind. Would you, er, care to play with my laptop?"

I hauled him onto my knees, and he grabbed at my keyboard, ripping off five keys, D, S, K, F, and U.

Now it was my turn to say, "Aaaaaaa!"

For some reason, this made Jude laugh. He was quite an accomplished laugher. He tipped his head back and laughed with his mouth open, showing all six teeth. It was just lovely, and I laughed too. We repeated the "Aaaaaa!"/laugh process fifty times.

Greg wandered by my office. "You should get going," he said. "If you're going to catch her."

"Right," I said. Jude groaned. I looked down and he was purple in the face. "Oh, Jesus," I shrieked, "he's having a fit, call an ambu—"

"That's an I'm Doing a Pooh face," said Greg. "All men make that face on the toilet."

I put my hand over my heart and sighed. Then I looked at Greg slyly. "I'd better rush, so would you mind . . . ?"

I pushed Jude slowly up the road toward the school. He cooed to himself and greeted a wino who staggered past us with a wave and a great big "Hiiiiiii!"

Lara, the subject, also had a boy. He was five. Charlie. I wondered how much the court would reduce his mother's maintenance payments if I proved that the boyfriend was live-in. Strange reasoning. In my experience, the average live-in boyfriend is a money pit. If anything, Lara needed her maintenance doubled. I thought about what she wouldn't be able to buy Charlie when I handed over my evidence. A tricycle? Ice cream? Shoes?

I swerved left and took Jude to the park instead.

We sat together on the roundabout, and I called Ron. "She's by herself," I said. "There's no one else. And"—as I twisted something I shouldn't—"the camera's jammed. I'll come back tomorrow, get some victor then."

"*Fuck*," he said. Like it mattered to him.

I sat Jude on the swing, swept him down the slide. Then I gave him his milk, as Gabrielle had commanded. He roared briefly when I placed him back in his buggy, then went quiet. I thought he was sulking, but when I looked he was asleep. His long dark lashes glistened with tears, and his rosebud lips were slightly apart. God, I thought, I am doing this *right*. And I felt a rush of love.

"Love," I said aloud. The word didn't make me shudder like it normally did.

I returned to the office, apologetic.

"I think they're wrong," I told Greg. "But I couldn't get any footage, the camera's busted. How about I try again tomorrow? Or I could sit on the address tonight, if you like."

"Funny," said Greg. "It seemed fine. But yeah. Tonight'd be good. Though Ron's keen. Cheaper for me if you do it, though."

"No problem." I wiped my supposed *mustache*. I was sweating. And not only because of the summer heat. It was scary, lying to Greg. He was trained to spot liars.

"By the way. The kid's mother called. I told her you were out on a job and the baby was fine. Oh, and your dad rang. He didn't sound too happy."

I stared after Greg as he marched back into his office. Did he *know* what he had done?

Gabrielle walked in with a face like granite. She saw Jude was asleep, gently shut the door, and dragged me into the corridor by my arm. Then she said in a very quiet voice, "I thought I could trust you, can I not trust you, what did I say, what did I specifically order you NOT to do, and you bloody go and do it, you just *had* to use him, a little baby, for your stupid job, you couldn't just enjoy his company, appreciate him for what he is, your nephew, you have no respect, no respect for anyone, you are a cold, cold, sad person, how dare you, how *dare* you endanger my child, and after all I've done for you and that idiot Jason, after all I *said* to you, you sicken me—"

"But I—I"—I tried to glance casually behind me, to see if Greg's office door was open. It was and he was looking straight at me. I turned back. "He was never in any danger, I swear to God. But I'm really sorry, Gab. I really am."

I tried to tell her with my eyes that I couldn't speak *now,* but she was too angry to take the hint.

"You know what, Hannah," she said. "I don't say sorry. Because I think it doesn't *mean* anything."

Then she pushed me out of the way, retrieved Jude in his pushchair, and wheeled him out, her jaw clenched. I lumbered back into my office, shut the door, and muttered into my hands. I'd try to explain later. But in the mood Gab was in, I knew I'd have a hard time persuading her to believe me.

Then I called my father. I hoped that my engagement to Jason would cheer him and endear me to him. At least he'd *called,* even if he had sounded stern. On our last encounter he'd decided that I was a cheat and turfed me out the house. He'd made contact and that had to be good.

It wasn't.

He'd called to tell me my grandmother had died.

22.

Most days, my conscience lies around eating crisps. It had roused itself in a half-arsed way about Grandma Nellie, though, which made me despise it. I hadn't agreed to go and see Grandma Nellie out of the goodness of my heart. I'd agreed to go and see her because I hadn't wanted her to die resenting me. In which case, she'd had the last laugh.

"But it was only a mild stroke," I'd said when Roger told me.

"Yes, well, the second one made up for *that,*" he replied.

It was a strange way to put it, but people say odd things when they're upset.

"Poor Mum. How is she?"

Normally we do not discuss my mother's emotions. The assumption is, whatever they are, they're her own fault.

"She's at the home, clearing Nellie's room."

"Oh."

He hadn't answered my question but I didn't press it. His tone suggested that I hadn't yet been forgiven.

"What was the name of that home again?" I said.

"Hannah, I haven't the faintest."

"Okay. Never mind."

I rang my mother on her mobile. I had the number somewhere.

"Hello?"

"Mum. It's Hannah. I'm so sorry about Grandma Nellie. How is she?" *Oh God.* "I mean, how are you? How are you?"

My mother was silent.

"Are you okay? I mean, I know you're not okay, but . . ."

Silence.

"Do you need me to do anything?"

"No," said my mother. "I can manage."

"Right," I said. "Right. What's happening with funeral arrangements? Or is Roger taking care of those? Do you need me to help you clear her room, perhaps?"

It was embarrassing, really. Being cold to her all this time and then, because something horrible had happened, warming a little. I believe this is what people call *not* having the courage of your convictions. But then, if on this occasion I *had* had the courage of my convictions, I'd be a monster. I think I'd rather be two-faced than be a monster. Although they sound like the same thing.

163

"Roger," said my mother, "is paying for everything. He's good at that."

"Oh, that's nice," I said—I was relieved. I didn't like to think that my father was unfeeling.

My mother didn't reply. She was vague at the best of times. I repeated the question. "So do you need me to help clear her room or anything?"

"No thank you, Hannah."

There was a pause.

"And"—I stumbled—"the funeral arrangements?"

"Ollie is organizing the cremation. Really, there's nothing for you to do."

I felt a batsqueak of annoyance. She'd rung *Ollie*. But it was gone in a blink. She was closer to Ollie because I'd encircled myself with an invisible steel barrier that my mother bounced off every time she came near. Of course she'd rung Ollie. All the same, if you extend the hand of peace, it's a shock to have it slapped away. Even if you have been holding it behind your back for twenty-five years.

There was something else I didn't want to say. "I'm sorry that I left it too late to visit Grandma Nellie."

"You can say your sorries at the cremation, Hannah," replied my mother. Grief must be making her rash because she was *never* this rude to me. I didn't mind. I liked to see some spark. "It's at Golders Green cemetery, next Monday, at eleven."

"Hey, isn't that where Keith Moon from The Who is buried?" Jesus, shut *up*.

"I don't know," said my mother in a flat, dull voice. "I'd better get on."

"Of course," I said. "Bye then."

I changed my mind. I didn't like to see some spark. Not when it was aimed at *me*. All those years I'd spent trying to provoke my mother and failing. And finally the death of Grandma Nellie brings success. It didn't feel the way I thought it would. It made me feel sick, to realize that I didn't want my mother to hate me. Really *sick*. I had nausea high in my throat.

Well. I'd make an effort for Grandma Nellie's funeral. Wear a skirt. Now that I owned one. I had a flash of Grandma Nellie, in earlier days. She wore old-womany clothes and the flashiest Nikes you ever saw. I was always waiting for her to break into a sprint. She had a plump abdomen and skinny legs. Like an insect.

I thought of my mother also. Months back, I was in my parents' garden, and I saw Angela sitting in her study. Her desk is by the window. She was staring out at nothing while taking small, fast bites of bitter chocolate. The only sort she'll eat. All I know is, a dog would reject that stuff. That image summed her up. It reeked of apathy and self-punishment. But (as people always say after a death because they can't bear the tedium of others being inconsolable) maybe some good will come out of this.

It would be good, I found myself thinking, if my mother recovered some of her spirit.

They kept saying the weather would break, but they were wrong. On Monday, at nine, I sat in the office, wiping the sweat off the back of my neck with my hand. Greg's fans just flapped the hot air round the room. They were no more use than someone blowing in your face. I'm the first to moan about English weather (dreary, dreary, dreary, pitch dark at noon from October to February), but I realized, after the first day of searing heat uncharacteristically occurred in April and continued—bar a drizzling few weeks—into July, that I loathe sunshine.

My weekend had been spent sweltering and alone. Jason was offended that I hadn't told anyone about the engagement.

"Jase," I'd said. "Please understand. My family are grieving. It's not the right time."

He didn't understand and had stomped off on a golfing weekend with his father. "It's like you don't *want* to tell anyone" was his parting shot.

I might have asked Martine to come out and play, but she was on a hen weekend in Blackpool. If there was time, she was stopping off at the Cadbury's factory in Birmingham.

Sun is all very well if you live in a hot country and are used to it, but it turns the British into idiots. On Saturday, I hadn't worn a hat. As with most of my fellow citizens, when sunshine occurs in the UK, I don't actually *believe* in it. (It's the meteorological equivalent of chips not being fattening if consumed standing up.) All that night it felt as if someone was trying to yank the hair off my scalp. After hours of severe pain, I found a piece of haddock in the freezer and pressed it to my aching head. When I rang Martine, expecting sympathy, she laughed. So. A bag of frozen peas is acceptable, but a haddock makes you a weirdo?

All in all, when Monday morning came, I was feeling low. I regretted my obstinacy with Grandma Nellie. Never mind that she was not a chocolate-box grandmother. I knew in my heart that I hadn't done the right thing and it made me dislike myself.

Also, my head was still sore, making me twitchy; I kept darting into the shadows like a vampire. I also had the distinct impression that no one liked me. Not even my family. *Especially* not my family. Even Martine, a woman who—should a man be fool enough to mate with her—planned to call her children Roquefort and Dolcelatte, had better things to do than spend time with me. And Jason was being such a *baby*.

I tried to console myself that I looked okay, even if no one cared. The irony was, Grandma Nellie would have approved. I had lipstick. I had a hair*style,* my nails were free of dirt, my legs were smooth, my eyebrows were arch, and I'd taken the incentive and snipped all the hairs out of my nostrils. I still hadn't got the hang of the coverup stick—all it did was highlight every spot, in a big beige circle, like the rings around Saturn. But altogether, I'd scrubbed up well.

"Ooh, baby," said Ron when I walked in that Monday morning, "lookin' *hot!*"

I approached him, smiling, and pressed my fingers hard into his neck until he choked. "It's the twenty-first *century,* Ron," I sighed, "it's the twenty-first *century.*"

"Just sue him," said Greg. Ron rubbed his neck and muttered. When he said anything he showed his lower teeth, like a bulldog. I resented that he was getting work because of my grandmother's funeral. At least Greg knew I was telling the truth—the death notice and funeral details had appeared in *The Times.*

At ten-thirty, I checked my appearance in the mirror. "Lookin' hot," I said. The powder had melted to a shine on my scarlet face, each bead of sweat was beige. I wished I didn't *sweat* so much. Show me the woman who glows because I'd like to shake her cool, dry hand. *I* sweat like a man. A horse, even.

At ten thirty-two, I left for the funeral, sweating, having done no work.

The crematorium was nice, as crematoriums went. Dark wood, but not too dark. Some of them are little more than cement garages in a carpark. I joined my mother, my father, Ollie, and Gabrielle in the front row. Jude was sleeping in his pushchair. The coffin was right there in front of us, next to a velvet curtain. I felt this was in bad taste. I'm not entirely comfortable with death. I have this medieval notion that it's catching.

I stared at my mother, but she wouldn't look up. Gabrielle

stood beside her like a bodyguard, gripping her hand. She wouldn't make eye contact either. My father gave me a brisk nod. So did Ollie. I presumed Gabrielle had told him how I'd placed his son and heir in the line of fire. I noted that they were prompt in thinking badly of me. Martine sidled in, breathing heavily, sweating like two horses. I was touched, although she probably saw it as a chance to wear a nice hat in front of Roger. (I was prompt in thinking badly of Martine.) Probably we both deserved it.

There were very few mourners, and I felt bad for my mother. I had this crazy thought that Jack might see the notice in *The Times* and turn up, but why should he? He liked my mother. That was all I could think of. It hadn't, I noted, occurred to Jason that it might be good manners for *him* to show. No doubt he'd written my mother a beautiful letter. The minister spoke in a loud, clear voice. He also got Grandma Nellie's name right, which I was grateful for. He must have ten of these burn-ups a day, I didn't take his accuracy for granted.

I didn't think Angela would speak, but I was still surprised when my father rose, shuffling papers. There was a pulpit, behind which he stood to address us. He was immaculate in a dark navy suit, with a pink tie and yellow shirt. He was always dashing, but that day he was stunning. The faint lemony scent of his aftershave lingered prettily in the air. It reminded me of Tinkerbell in *Peter Pan*. I glanced at my mother again; she looked dreadful. Her mascara was streaked right down her face, and she was wearing some sort of black sack.

My father spoke smilingly. He even cracked a joke about Grandma Nellie and her trainers. Martine laughed, then clapped her hand over her mouth. I "hm!" ed. Everyone else stared silently at the floor. He then read an excerpt from the Bible, about trusting in God. Even though I'd have thought this precisely a time you *wouldn't* trust in God. If he was in charge, there was a strong case for him being the one who'd struck down Grandma Nellie. After that, you'd be hard pushed trusting him with the school hamster.

I heard my father's voice but his words drifted through me. I felt like I was five years old, waiting for the headmaster to stop preaching. His voice rang out, confident—almost, I felt with a twinge of disloyalty, *too* confident. I'd hesitate to use the word "patronizing." Surely it would have been good manners to stumble a little, be overcome with emotion? But he was word-perfect, enunciating the tedious conversation between God and his disciple with great enthusiasm and *in different voices* as if he were reading from a play, say, *Separate Tables*.

I had to trust him that this was the right thing to do. I wasn't that great on social convention. I glanced at my mother again and saw a tear splash onto her prayer book. It struck me that I couldn't remember the last time I'd seen her cry. Suddenly she stood up.

"I'd like to say a few words now."

My father stared at her. He hadn't finished the excerpt. "But I—" He smiled. "Of course, dear." As he returned to the other side of the aisle, he muttered, "It's your funeral."

No one heard him except me, perched on the end of the row. And I didn't want to hear him. Those words were unwelcome. There was no way to interpret them that was good. The sweat trickled down my neck and I felt swollen with heat and misery. My father was strong, kind, capable, perfection. It was like watching *Spartacus* and seeing some Roman wearing a watch. You put a lot of stock in the people who rule your world knowing what they're doing; you don't want to witness their mistakes, you need to know that they don't make them.

As my mother took the podium, I felt rotten with the knowledge that my father wasn't perfect.

169

23.

Whatever my mother had wanted to say about her mother remained private. She smiled shakily, from the pulpit, and said, "I was never very close to my mother, but she was . . . she was . . . she. . . ." Then she shook her head, covered her face. Ollie escorted her back to her seat. My father got to finish his lecture.

Then everyone drove in a convoy to Gab and Ollie's house and ate salmon bagels. I wasn't hungry but tried to eat something. Grandma Nellie had hated to see food go to waste. My mother wore dark glasses indoors, which meant she had a migraine. She went to lie down in Gab and Ollie's spare room five minutes later. I took this to mean the party was over and left. As I shut the door, Martine was chatting to my father. I wondered what was left to tell.

I took a detour to Hampstead Heath and sat staring at the pond until the sky began to turn pink. Afterward, on the drive home, about fifty cars hooted me. Either I'd won the cup, or my attention wasn't on the road. Funerals are supposed to make you feel more alive. There's a mean reflex in human nature that, on an unconscious level (unless you're particularly unpleasant), makes us think, ha-ha, they're dead, I'm not—even if we loved that person. I felt dead.

"Grandma," I said, addressing the car roof. "I'm an idiot. I am sorry I never made it to see you. All those years. It seems so petty now. I always . . . meant to."

I *meant* to.

How pathetic. Just like I'd always meant to explain to Jack.

Jack.

170

I thought of what he'd said in the restaurant. "You betrayed me, Hannah, when I loved you more than any woman I will ever love. . . ." And I felt a great rush of contrition; it washed over me like a wave, and there was a need to see him that made me ache. He had to know that I was truly sorry. I couldn't stand for him to hate me; I had to tell him to his face that I had been stupid and scared of love but that I wasn't a cheat. I couldn't go another minute without him knowing this.

I stared at the imposing white exterior of Jack's building, then hurried up the stone path.

It was only when I'd rung the doorbell and heard footsteps that my legs went wibbly. I smacked my lips together—they felt oddly slippery, I so rarely wore lipstick—and planted my feet square on the hallway carpet. Jack hadn't *told* me where he lived but I'd found out, courtesy of a rather fabulous website we had illegal access to. It was used by the police to trace people. You tapped in a phone number, and the corresponding address popped onto the screen. Oh, naughty.

"It'sHannahI'msosorry," I said as fast as I could before he could shout at me. The words sounded pretty, running into each other like paint, so I repeated them, "Jack, I'm so so sorry about everything, the divorce, everything. Grandma Nellie died and I had to see you, I had to explain." I added, "Please don't be angry with me, I know you are but don't be, because I am very very sorry."

He stood there, tall, and it felt as if he were swooping down on me, like a vampire bat. Or maybe I was giddy. My hand flew to my mouth, "Oh, God," I said. "I forgot. Is your girlfriend there? The blond one?"

"How many girlfriends do you think I have?" said Jack. His

expression was inscrutable. I flinched as if he might hit me. Although he never had, he was expert at communicating physical menace. Other men didn't start fights with Jack.

I made an apologetic face.

"I ended it with the blond one. It wasn't working," he said. But he held open the door and made a grand curly gesture with his arm, inviting me in. As I passed him, he touched my back briefly. "I'm sorry about Grandma Nellie."

"Thank you," I said. His hallway was a lot different from mine. The white ceiling, for instance, was twice as high, and had decorative swirly bits of plaster in each corner. Corneting, I believe it's called. I looked up, turning as I did so, like Alice in Wonderland after taking the shrinking pill, and nearly lost my balance. Jack grabbed my arm and righted me.

"Oh, this is so pretty, Jack," I said, "It's all Chinese-y, this dark wood floor and dark wooden blinds and hardly any furniture, it's very plain and minimalist." I was gabbling. Jack had come a long way since the days when placing a big pot plant on the kitchen table alongside a large anglepoise lamp to highlight our chops was his idea of a romantic dinner.

Jack showed me to a squashy sofa—it didn't fit with the room, but you sank into it as into a warm bath.

"Thank you," I said. I cleared my throat. I knew what I wanted to say and tried to arrange the words in comprehensible order. "I had this falling-out with Grandma Nellie. Years ago. The way she was to my father . . . offended me. I stopped going to see her and, because she's of, she *was* of the generation that believed the younger people should make the effort, she never came to see me. And so out of stubbornness, we never made up and she died. And now it seems like a great waste."

I paused.

Jack nodded.

"The funeral was today and I had to see you. I . . . didn't want the same thing to happen with . . . us."

"I was hoping I had a few years left," said Jack, and I knew he was nervous. His jokes always took a dive then.

"The truth is, Jack," I said, "that I *did* understand how you felt betrayed by me, and I am more sorry about it than about anything in my life. I *was* then, too, but I couldn't express it. I don't know why. You assumed the worst and I froze, I felt sick with stupidity, I didn't have the words. To say that I would never have slept with Guy while I had you. It was terrifying, being with you, because you played indifferent. That one time I kissed Guy—bad, I know, but nothing more—it was to give myself distance from you, it felt *safer.* I loved you, but I didn't *get* how you felt about me till I saw your reaction."

Jack closed his eyes and opened them. "I should have listened to you," he said, "but I couldn't. I believed the worst. It was as if I was so down on myself that I *wanted to.* You think you have confidence, but the test is what it can stand up to. If you don't grow up with confidence, but acquire it, you can just as easily *un*acquire it. When you said you'd been with that bloke, mine blew away like a fucking dandelion."

He shook his head. Then he got up abruptly and walked out of the room. I wasn't sure what to do.

"Jack?" I called after him. "Jack? Are you okay? I wanted to tell you I'm sorry, I'm sorry for everything I did, you were everything to me, it was too much, I hate that I did that to . . . us."

There was no reply and I was shouting into white silence. I held my breath and crept down the corridor. At the end, a door was open to a bathroom, the sort of bathroom I'd only ever seen in magazines, and Jack was leaning over the cream-colored stone sink, one hand over his eyes, shaking. He was, I saw with a shock, *crying.*

"Oh, baby." My heart lurched and I blurted out the words before I could think. I wanted to back away, I was mortified for both of us, to have stumbled on him in this private moment. I also knew that I'd been kidding myself about Jason, that I had to end it, God help me, the next time I saw him.

"Look, I'm sorry, Jack," I said. "I'll leave now, I'll leave for *good,* I mean, I—"

Without looking up, he raised a hand and said, through gritted teeth, "Wait."

I nodded, hurried back into the cool, white front room. I was too agitated to sit, so I wandered over to a mirror propped against the wall and looked into it. It was slightly dusty and mottled. Jack didn't buy . . . *antiques,* did he? I felt sober, embarrassed, suddenly, as if he had become a discerning adult, and I was still a bug-eyed child—who preferred things cheap, mass-made, *new.* I emitted a small squeak and peered closer into the murk of the reflective glass.

A clown stared back.

I hadn't applied my red lipstick to my lips, more *around* them. Jesus, I looked ridiculous. I must have been in more of a state than I'd thought. I started smearing it off my face with the back of my hand. Why hadn't he said something?

I was reminded of attending a wedding with Jack, a few months after we married, and Martine. It was a fierce, hot day, and I was wearing a hideous menopausal peach silk "ensemble" (as described by the woman in the shop—Sammies of Highgate—recommended by Martine, a place that reeked of estrogen; you got the feeling if a man ever walked in, a trapdoor opened in the floor and whoop, down he went).

That was my problem, I so rarely dressed like a girl, I didn't know how to. Hence the purchase of an item that turned me into a mutant butterbean. Not only that, I was so damn *hot,* I felt sure I'd sweated right through that mean scratchy material and there was a huge dark blotch of wet down my peach back.

"Jack," I said. "Have I got a sweat stain on the back of my dress?"

He inspected it and said, "No, Special, you look beautiful."

But I noticed Martine's eyes flicker. We walked into the church and I found a cloakroom with a mirror. I turned my back and, good grief, there was a dark damp patch on my dress the size of Wales. I was just about to be furious with Jack when it struck me that his lie was an act of love. I arranged my matching peach shawl strategically and marched to my seat, head high. My heart felt newly molded into a soft shape.

I was wiping off the last of my clown's lipstick when I heard Jack. I stood up as he walked fast toward me; he said, "Let me help you with that." Either I offered him my hand or he pulled it to him, but I was right up against him in a hot, hard kiss, we were stumbling, frantic, grabbing each other, I was rattling his belt buckle like it was a lock, and I could feel his fingers tremble as he tore off my jacket and trailed his hands over my back, front, all of me. "Oh, God, Hannah," he whispered. "Oh, God." I shook my head, crushed myself against him, I felt like crying, laughing, I couldn't speak.

He carried me to his bedroom and lowered me onto the bed. *Our* bed.

"You kept it," I said. My eyes teared up. "I thought you'd sell it." He whispered, "I couldn't."

He kissed me again, hard, and it felt right, in a way it never had with anyone else. Sex had made me want to cry before but not, believe me, out of elation and joy. It never felt like a celebration, but with Jack it did. As if it was meant to be us all along. It was like we could communicate better in bed than we could out of it.

I remembered Jack saying, after one mindblowing session, "What the hell was *that*?" At the time, I felt embarrassed, like I'd exposed my soul to a nonbeliever. It hadn't occurred to me that there might be a happier interpretation. Now, with him again after ten years, I breathed in the scent and feel of him with a hunger I didn't know I possessed. I felt ravenous for him, as if I'd been starving myself for the last decade.

Afterward, he said, mouth to mouth, "How could you think I didn't love you?"

"I . . . I suppose I never knew a good definition," I said. My heart leapt about inside my chest like a small bunny rabbit.

It was immeasurably more wonderful with Jack than with Jason. I always found Jason too hot. (Not in the sexy sense, in the "you're unpleasantly warm, get away from me" sense.)

Jason. Jason! Oh God. I hadn't even told Jack the situation with Jason. He'd gone right out of my head.

"What?" said Jack. His left arm was flung over my chest. He had beautiful arms, beautifully defined muscles, and skin the color of a fading tan. Jack probably went on a lot of holidays. I touched his cheek, softly, apologetically, and shifted away a little.

"Nothing."

Now my heart was leaping in my chest like a small bunny rabbit trying to avoid being shot.

"I like your bedroom," I blurted. The truth, even if it was to distract his attention from my discomfort. Jack's bedroom was cool, plain, and masculine. Not like *some* men's bedrooms. You see it in Sunday supplements, with actors or footballers. They're wealthy, young, handsome, living alone, free to design the master bedroom of their shag pad as they wish—and they decorate it for their mother to sleep in. Apricot carpets. Silk curtains, with swagging. Floral duvet, with fancy valance. Oh, God. Poor Jason.

"Thanks," said Jack, his dark eyes meeting mine. "So. What's the situation with Jason?"

"Jack," I said. "You have got to believe me. Jason proposed last week, and I accepted, and then Grandma Nellie happened, and I realized I'd made this hideous mistake. He's angry with me because I haven't yet told my parents or anyone. I said it wasn't the right time, but now I see it was because I *knew* it was a mistake. Not consciously, even, but I knew. And I, I promise, I didn't expect . . . this . . . I knew it was over with Jase before I came here. I would have told you straight up, but there wasn't time, and I'm going to end it with Jason, say it was a terrible mistake, I'm going to end it *now*, tonight, I'm going to ring him, I—"

Jack touched my knee and I gazed at him in fear.

"Hey," he said. "You say you're going to end it tonight. You will. I believe you."

24.

I left with the promise of nothing, the possibility of everything.

"I'd better go," I'd said.

We'd kissed good-bye at the entrance, and when I turned as I reached the pavement, he'd gone inside.

I smiled. I was basking in the glow of his trust, and nothing could undo the wonder of what had just happened. I tried to cool it by telling myself that men are always up for a shag, but even I am not that shallow. Not *all* men are *always* up for a shag like they're *one* person. Not with the way computer games have developed. Jack had said . . . some lovely things.

Although great sex does make one prone to exaggeration.

I allowed myself to dream and then I called a halt. I was a realist. I didn't assume that one fuck a happy ending made. I was still unsure what a happy ending *was* for me. If you're scared of marriage, are you even *allowed* to be in a fairy tale? But if the next day Jack was awoken by a beautiful princess, at the least, he had woken *me* up to the fact that Jason and I were as unsuited as a kitten and a bulldog. (I was the bulldog.)

I glanced at my watch. It was 1 A.M. I hesitated, then dug out my mobile and rang Jason's number at home. I let it ring thirty times. Then I tried again. And again. Nothing. That was the thing about Jason, he slept like a dead man. He also wore earplugs. You had to persevere. Ah, sod it.

I winced at the violence of my irritation. Sex with Jack had acted like a foil to the inadequacies of my relationship with Jason, and a thousand cold truths now rained on me like hail.

A love life with Jason had been impossible because of his prissiness. Sex was performed under controlled conditions, a brisk, slightly shameful routine. I think that Jase would have preferred it if men and women were made like Ken and Barbie, nice to look at but no holes or dangly bits, smooth all the way round, no chance of any *funny business.*

If I tell you, the man hadn't eat a madras curry for fifteen years because, as he said, "While it tastes nice, when it comes out the other end, it burns your . . . bottom, and Hannah, I don't like to be aware of which meal I'm excreting."

The truth was that he *couldn't* eat madras curries because of his irritable bowel, but was too coy to admit it. Like I could forget. He kept an IBS diary on the floor by the bed. I flicked through it once. It listed his daily symptoms, including the number of times he went to the toilet, and the degree of his abdominal bloating. Every spasm of pain was marked out of ten. It was an interesting take on *Bridget Jones*. Oh, and he kept a homemade laxative in my fridge. Apple puree, mixed with prune juice and wheat bran. I drank it once, when there was nothing to eat. An unpleasant minute later, I was hungrier than ever.

I shook my head, breathed out in a tense puff. I was angry with myself for making a mess of things. I was unsettled by what had happened with Jack. I hadn't expected it. Now that I was coming down off a sensory high, the old fears were creeping up on me. Could I trust myself, could I trust him, would it be as good the next time?

It wasn't fair to take it out on Jason. I felt great, and I felt terrible. My life had all the order of a dropped trifle. It was going to be horrendous, telling Jason that I didn't want to marry him after all. And, gosh, poor *Lucy*. They were, from the sound of her, a great match. My shortsightedness, my childish desire for Jason just because he'd had the nerve to bounce back from my rejection with another woman, all this had serious consequences. I had to accept I'd ruined Lucy's life, possibly Jason's too, out of *brattishness*. Lucy, I suppose, already knew her life was ruined. Jason didn't.

I got home, tried his number again. No answer. My pulse was racing, and I fought the urge to go and bang on his front door. I needed him to know *this minute*. I'd promised Jack. I needed to be free of Jason and for it to be official.

I tried twice more, then gave up. I'd call him at seven the next morning, before he left for work. I set the alarm. A first. Then I went into the bathroom and stared at my face in the mirror. My lips were puffy from kissing, and my cheeks were pink. I decided I was too tired for a shower, I didn't want to wash away the memory of Jack just yet. I felt like a squirrel, storing nuts for winter. Sort of.

The alarm shrilled after what seemed like a minute, but I jumped awake and stared at the phone. This was going to be one of the worst conversations of my life. I could actually see how some women pulled on their wedding dress like a shroud and walked up the aisle to spend a lifetime with a man they didn't love, because it felt easier than breaking off the engagement. Breaking off an engagement angers a lot of people. A lot of women prefer to suffer than anger other people, particularly relatives.

Talking of which, I realized that I hadn't even considered what my father would say. Ah well.

I lunged for the receiver, and it rang, confusing me.

"Hello?" I said.

Roger's voice boomed into my ear: "Angela and I see that Jason is an amicable fellow, but the idea of him as your husband fills us with fear. We feel its icy clutch. What, Hannah? *Fear's* icy clutch. We feel the icy clutch of fear. Hannah, anything sounds strange if you're forced to say it ten times. And we remind you, Hannah, that three weeks after you chucked him, the man proposed to his neighbor. Would he have proposed to the postman, had *he* happened to knock? How do I know? About the postman? The engagement! I've just *read* it, madam! Announced in the *Daily Fucking Telegraph* no less! Social Whatsits! Tell me, how's Jack?"

"My head's exploding, Daddy, would you mind terribly if I called you back in five?" I said.

I put the phone down and screamed. Then I raced out into the communal hallway, ran to my neighbor's door and whipped her pristine copy of the *Daily Telegraph* from the mat. I snuck back into my lounge, I riffled through the paper, ripping pages, until I came to the Social Whatsits.

Then I screamed again.

Brian Brocklehurst, esq., of Highgate is delighted to announce the engagement of his younger son, Jason Arran, to Hannah Bluebell, daughter of Mr. and Mrs. Roger Lovekin of Hampstead Garden Suburb.

I scrumpled the page in a fury and clutched at my head. I felt shaky with rage toward Jason. How dare he? Not respect my wishes. Expressly disobey me. He would never have behaved like this a year ago! Used his initiative! Now he'd complicated matters. He'd turned our private mistake into a public fiasco. Mortifying and awful. And Jack. What if Jack read it? What would he think of me? I had to ring him. But no! He wouldn't read the *Telegraph,* he wasn't the type. Better to leave it rather than alert him to a false alarm. But I'd be ringing Jason. That little shit.

And my father! I'd promised to ring him back in five, *easily* six minutes ago. I grabbed the phone to call him, then put it down again. Now I actually thought about what he'd said, I was confused. For the last five years, my father had all but drummed his fingers for Jason to propose to me. Now he had and he wasn't *suitable*?

I wondered if Roger remained so revolted at me for allegedly cheating on my marriage that no heroics I might perform from here to eternity could ever please him. It was plausible. What was implausible was his sudden best-friend act with my mother. Unless Grandma Nellie's death had squeezed a little pity from him. Also, why was he asking after Jack?

None of this felt right.

Perhaps I should ask Angela.

Too underhanded. My father was the only person I trusted. If his behavior was inconsistent, he had his reasons. It was disloyal to even consider discussing him with my mother. Anyway, I'd prefer to confide my personal matters to a stranger on a train.

Jesus, let me call Jason quickly.

No answer. *Shit.* I didn't leave a message.

I called Roger and explained that the announcement was an error but, as Jason didn't yet know and was probably out now buying a wedding suit, to *please* keep this information to himself.

"Hannah," said my father—he sounded remarkably relaxed—"it will be a great bore telling all and sundry that yet *another* of your marriages is off, having joyously accepted their inevitable congratulations and mazel tovs. However, rest assured your secret is safe with me. And your mother."

Despite everything, his words made me smile. I decided there was no mystery. Daddy simply wanted what was best for me. And Jason wasn't the best—which we'd both realized at the same time, roughly *yesterday.*

I was relieved to have worked it out.

25.

Then it occurred to me that it was ten twenty-nine on a weekday and I was currently in possession of a job.

When I arrived at the office, Greg was waving his porridge spoon at the *Daily Telegraph.*

"I see congratulations are in order," he said. "So I'm obliged to forgive you for being late."

"Nah," I said. "They're not. You can dock my pay."

182

Then I shut myself in my office.

I'd called Jason's mobile ten times; it was turned off. Now I called Jason at work. His PA, Kathleen, answered.

"I see congratulations are in order," she said, like a newscaster announcing the apocalypse.

"Don't trouble yourself," I replied, "Just put me through."

"He's in Milton Keynes for a hearing."

"Where in Milton Keynes, have they got a phone?"

"You can't call him in court!" she said.

I didn't have the energy. "Really," I said. "Well, if he rings, tell him his *fiancée* would like a word. Got that?"

"You know," she hissed. "Lucy was *so* much nicer than you."

"Ah, don't, Catherine, you'll make me cry," I said, and put the phone down.

I put my head in my hands and groaned. I'd get so much further in life if I was a mute.

Then I saw my answer machine was flashing. I pressed *play,* with a sour face.

"Darling, it's me. Jason. I'm *dying* to talk to you, but this was my one chance, it's pretty intense here! How infuriating that I missed you. Anyhow, I hope you liked the surprise in the *Telegraph!* I have another, for this evening. We're going to see *Chitty Chitty Bang Bang!* I'll see you at seven-fifteen outside the theater. The Palladium! Love you."

I stared at the machine in disbelief. *Chitty Chitty Bang Bang!* How old were we? Four? Jason seemed to be finally revealing his core personality. (An addiction to silly announcements in newspapers and second-rate musicals—forgive me, *chit* lovers, but all musicals are second-rate to me.) He wouldn't have dared suggest such a torture—let alone book it—before we were engaged. Some men saw marriage as a dog license, entitling them to ownership. Jason, I realized, was one of them.

Oh dear, though. He sounded so excited. And genuinely in love. He'd been hurt that I had dawdled over telling my parents of our engagement, and I had to concede that his was a valid response. Going to the papers was a way of forcing my hand, so to speak— passive aggression, that was it!—but if I *had* been in love with him, it wouldn't have been a problem. That it was a problem was entirely my fault, and I would deal fairly with Jason.

Fine. I'd tell him after the show.

Well, gosh, I didn't want to spoil it for him.

The day passed with insufferable slowness. Martine had read the *Telegraph* (or someone had read it to her) and she insisted on meeting me for a quick lunch. She ate the same amount, twice as fast. There was collateral damage, mostly over her front, but I didn't care, it was preferable to the usual: my bottom fossilizing in my chair while I waited for Jason to finish eating. ("Chew slowly and pause between mouthfuls to give your food time to go down," his IBS group leader had advised—selfish man, whenever we dined out, restaurant staff worked late because of him.) When I told her my dilemma, her eyes widened, although she didn't put down her fork.

"Jason should never have come back to you," she said. "You do know why he did, though, don't you?"

"To punish me?"

"Yeah, well. I've met Lucy. I went round there to see Jason after you'd split."

"Oh yes. So?"

"She had chronic periodontitis."

"Pardon?"

Martine lowered her voice. "Her breath stank. She couldn't of been to a dentist for, like, years. I mean, it starts with chronic gingivitis, like, that's the earliest stage, that's just when your gums are inflamed. It's an infection, it's caused by accumulation of plaque at the gum margin. Every time she doesn't bother brushing her teeth or flossing—I can't tell you how important it is to floss, Hannah—food debris clings to the plaque, and bacteria feed and multiply on it."

"It sounds like something out of *Alien*."

"Yeah, and it can all happen in your *mouth*."

I shivered.

"She's let food debris accumulate in the gingival crevice."

"I may be sick."

"No, wait. That's the tiny space between the teeth and the gum. If your teeth"—*teef,* she said, which I liked—"are healthy, they're tight in there, like they're being hugged by the gum. But if you've got food debris and plaque, the gum gets irritated and swells up, enlarging the gingival crevice."

It's a rule that everything in dentistry sounds disgusting. That's because it is.

"And that forms a thing called a false pocket round the tooth. It doesn't hurt. But it's, like, stuffed with bacteria and pus. And that causes bad breath. I mean, she's so in trouble. If she leaves it much longer she'll get ulcers, bleeding, her alveolar bone will recede, I mean, I don't get why some people are so scared of dentists, it's like, they're only trying to help, I mean, Marvin, like, *loves* teeth, he *loves* them—"

"I know. But Marvin owns something called a 'Crocodile Matrix Clamp'."

Martine looked offended. "Well, anyway. Kissing Lucy would be like kissing a four-day-old corpse."

I assumed a snooty expression and sipped my white wine. "So. I'm marginally preferable to kiss than a four-day-old corpse." I sighed. "Ah, God. I hope he and Lucy *do* get back together after all this. I hope I haven't blown it for Jason."

"You probably have," said Martine. "Anyway. What about *you*? Who you going to pair up with?"

"I may," I said, "defy the world and live alone. Like you." But Martine had reminded me of something. "What were you talking to Roger about after the funeral yesterday?"

"Why?"

"Because when I told Daddy about Jason, it was obvious he couldn't care less. He seemed to be suddenly keen on Jack."

"What's that got to do with me?" Martine signaled to the waitress for more bread. The waitress gave her a look of death.

"I'm not bothered if it has something to do with you," I said. "It suits me fine. I wondered, that's all."

Martine twiddled an earring. She'd had her ears pierced when she was five months old. Twiddling an earring was her *tell*. So my question was pretty much answered. Big deal. I was too preoccupied with Jason and Jack to worry about Martine. I left it.

26.

"Any update on the single mother?" said Greg.

He hadn't mentioned the *Telegraph* announcement again. Intrigue was not a novelty to him.

"Charlie's mum?" I said.

"I suppose so," replied Greg.

I shuffled papers around my desk. "I've been frantic today, trying to get unengaged to people. I apologize, I haven't had a chance. I'll sit on the address tonight. And tomorrow morning. Get some victor."

Greg looked unmoved. "What's your cover story?"

"Um, I'm thinking of it now."

Mostly, I *do* actually set up a surveillance job with a brain in my head. I'll be on guard for "the third eye"—nosy neighbors, CCTV— and armed with a plausible excuse. You should go out there thinking you will be challenged. Greg's rule is "There's always another day." If you think you've been pinged, you walk away.

"Don't worry. I'll make it look good," I said.

I was queen of making a little look like a lot. I'd document the street name (times and dates were automatic to the footage), video the house (so the client knew I was there). I'd do everything to ensure that no one could suggest I hadn't done my job properly. If you give people enough detail—"the neighbors returned home at 11:37. At 12:03 the upstairs light came on"—they feel they're getting value for money. Which, on this occasion, they weren't. I felt quite bad enough about myself. If all the other kids wore Nike trainers, I couldn't be responsible for Charlie attending school in Mikes.

"I do worry," said Greg.

I hadn't seen him this unamused since the Hampstead Heath job (now legend). A woman had suspected her husband was having an affair. And he was, with a man. In fact, *any* man. Ron trailed him to Hampstead Heath. The guy parked his car, disappeared into the bushes, and reappeared a short while later with another man. Ron should have taken a still—it was too dark for video—but Ron was having a wee. The target approached him and said, "Do you need a hand with that?"

"No thanks," squeaked Ron. "I'm just having a slash." And he ran away! Greg was furious. Ron should have caught him in the act or called the police—if they'd arrested him for indecent behavior, Greg would have got his evidence that way. But because Ron was such a homophobic *baby,* he'd botched it. Greg didn't employ him for ages after that.

Thank God I was staff. (If you're of a certain character, a staff job is the ruin of you. And of the company you work for.)

"Greg, I'll sit there till 3 A.M., and I'll come back at 5. I'm really happy to do it. Consider it done."

Greg raised an eyebrow and left the room. I shrugged. I was telling the truth. A job would provide me with an excuse not to loiter, after breaking the news to Jason.

I'd decided that it would be the most natural thing to tell him over a posttheater coffee. See, whenever we ventured into *town* for the evening—woo-ee!—Jason would insist on finding "a place for coffee." He had an obsession with finding "a place for coffee" that was all about being out for the sake of being out, rather than being *in*. Plainly, one needs to go *out* to the theater, but I felt that Jason's need to go *out* for coffee reflected an insecurity with his life at home. Unless you're drinking coffee in front of the Taj Mahal (or you seize the opportunity to eat a massive cake), the only difference between drinking coffee *out* or *in* is other people's perception. As if your existence is without value unless viewed or approved by a third party. I imagined he always told colleagues the following day, "And then we went out for coffee. . . ."

Alas, that's not what he would be telling them *this* time.

I arrived at the London Palladium at 7:15 sharp. There was no need to upset Jason more than necessary.

"You look smart," he said as I squeezed through loud crowds of children in the foyer.

"Thank you."

Smart?! Has any woman ever been so humbled? Now that I was newly blessed with 20/20 vision, it amazed me that Jason couldn't see the gaping holes in our relationship. Still, I smiled and waved my jumbo pack of Maltesers at him. He smiled and waved his jumbo bottle of Evian at me. "I had to wait five months for these tickets," he said.

"You are *kidding* me."

"What?" said Jason. "You look upset."

I sighed. "You tell me something like that, and it makes me realize that I don't understand people. My job is about understanding people."

"You always said it was about facts."

"Yeah. Well. It is. But it's also about understanding people."

"You always said it wasn't!"

"Jason. That's probably why I'm not that good at it."

We found our seats, ten rows from the stage, and sat in them. Jason let me know that the tickets cost over a hundred pounds. I felt dreadful, so I bought him a program. I could refund him sixty quid later. (He'll spend over a hundred quid on tickets, yet won't pay a fiver for a program, preferring to spend the evening confused. As much as one can be confused by *Chitty Chitty Bang Bang*.)

Truth is, despite the fear of what was to come later, I quite enjoyed sitting there. I liked watching other people engage, booing and hissing the actor playing the Child Catcher. The problem I have with musicals is I can't get past people bursting into song as if it's natural. They get a funny look on their face moments before.

Jason had said the performance was sold out, yet three rows in front of us, there were two empty seats. That made me wonder. Is it like booking an exercise class for some people? Yes, I *will* go to the theater, it'll do me good, afterward I'll feel so pleased I've gone . . . and then they back out at the last minute. Jason "nipped" to the toilet and I considered whether the woman in front of me could possibly have a larger head. Not content with that, she'd blow-dried her hair into peaks. Perhaps after the interval she'd return wearing a top hat.

I jerked in my seat. I'd caught a familiar movement, looked up, and there was *Jack*. Fuck. I blushed and shrank in my seat. I was so quick to sense the possibility of his presence it was as if I was *looking* for it. I was embarrassed in front of myself.

He and some guy were picking their way into the empty seats. There was the usual arrogant aura, but Jack didn't look up. *Please don't see me with Jason, please don't. . . .* If I didn't have the worst luck.

The possibility of running into him hadn't occurred to me, although I knew from Jack that one of the main duties of being an actor's agent was to go to the theater. You went to the theater at least three times a week. It was about building relationships with people, as your standing in the industry was everything. There were so many actors. It wasn't difficult to sign clients. The trick was to sign good clients.

As your confidence grew, you took out casting directors, to see these clients of yours perform. You took them to press nights, first nights, aftershows (aftershow *parties,* darlings), and it was a great bore. You also supported your clients, whether they were playing Othello or Caractacus Potts. Often you snuck in at halftime, if you thought you could get away with it. I guessed this was what Jack was doing. But even so. Bloody *Chitty.* I was cursed, I knew it.

I wondered who his companion was. I saw his profile as he turned to speak to Jack, and my stomach clenched. Did I know him? You can see a person once and consciously forget what they look like instantly, be unable to describe them if asked. And yet your brain stores that information for you. You *will* recognize a person you've seen once for a second, even if you think you won't. Greg once attended a police lecture, where the audience was shown fifty faces in a flash of one second each. Then they were shown fifty more faces and asked to say if each face had featured in the first showing. "*Yeeesssss*" replied the audience as one. "*Noooooo. . . . Noooooo. . . . Yeeessss.*"

My brain said "*Yeeesssss,*" and yet I couldn't place him. Was he a casting director? A client? A friend? I tried to assess their relationship without staring. I failed. Jack turned round and looked right at me. Stupidly, instead of gazing through him, I ducked. Greg would have been ashamed. I wriggled upright again and forced a miserable smile as Jason plopped into his seat. "Okay, darling?"

"Fine," I said. Jack stared through me. If I'd had the option of covering Jason's head in a black bin liner I would have done. This couldn't get much worse.

Jack murmured in his friend's ear. The man started, or at least made a jerky movement, but didn't look round. I tensed. To my dismay, Jack was approaching our seats.

"Hannah," he said in an apparently normal voice. "Jason. Congratulations." He didn't meet my eye.

I laughed nervously. People reading was essential to my job. Greg was always preaching about the foolishness of going into an encounter with a preconceived notion of how it should turn out. "To get what you want," he said, "you must adjust yourself to the situation. Not the other way round." Much of people reading was, he insisted, about making elementary, commonsense observations and acting on them. I rarely did this. I was poor at making elementary, commonsense observations. But as we stood there, leaning on our worn red velvet seats, I knew that I had to get Jack away from Jason, fast. Jason was *not* going to hear the news of our canceled engagement from anyone but me.

"Jason," I said. "This is Jack Forrester. I—"

"Jack!" cried Jason. "I remember you from school. How are you? Thank you for, er, sorting things out with Hannah. I do believe it's best to start a marriage with an, er, clean slate—"

"Excuse me," I said. "I need to go to the . . . freshen up." (Jason hated the word "loo.") "You were on your way out for a cigarette, weren't you, Jack?" I mouthed "please," and he followed me from the auditorium. "I'll explain outside," I said.

He didn't reply, and I couldn't bear the silence, so I said, "Who's that man you're with?"

"Jonathan Coates. Our old drama teacher." Jack stared at me, expressionless.

"Nice of him to come over and say hi."

"Oh . . . well," said Jack.

I was being bullish to disguise my despair. Why hadn't he crushed me with a retort about *cheating*? He was rarely speechless, and I wondered, why now? He recovered fast once we were in the foyer, gripping my arm above the elbow, and saying, "So, Hannah. You've done it again. Except this time poor old *Jason's* playing the part of the gullible bastard."

I shook my head. Well, perhaps there *was* a similarity, but it was for entirely different reasons. With Jason, the betrayal was because I didn't love him. With Jack, it was because I'd loved him too much and, aged nineteen, I hadn't trusted the feeling he evoked in me. And hadn't I already explained this to Jack, after Grandma Nellie's funeral? He had a short memory. Standing here now, *I* could see that I'd changed. But I could also see that to Jack, I'd stayed the same.

"Look, Jason has be—"

"Jason is a lovely guy and an absolute fucking retard," said Jack into my face. "I can't believe you're going through with this."

I'm *not,* I wanted to say, but instead I murmured, "Ah, a closet *Telegraph* reader. Up the Revolution!"

His anger stunned me into irrelevancies. Like before. I couldn't defend myself. If he was always going to condemn me, whatever I said, what was the point?

Jack let go of my arm and screwed up his face. "Know what, I *can* believe it. Jason doesn't understand you. He has no idea what you're like as a person. What you want. What you fear. What in the world scares Hannah. I know. *Darling.*"

The way he said "darling" was worlds apart from how Jason said it. Jack said "darling" like it was a threat.

"That eejit out there is right in one thing. You fear intimacy, you fear it like other people fear violent death. What he doesn't get is that *that's* why you're marrying him, so you can keep him at arm's length till you both fucking kill yourself at the pointlessness of it all. What he also doesn't get is that your fucking problems didn't start with me, they started *waaay* back."

"What?"

"If you can't see it now, you never will, and that's because you're a coward, Hannah; you can't admit you're wrong, not even to yourself. You cannot take criticism of the one person who *should* be criticized, what he did was—and one day, when you're a sad old lady, you're going to look back on your life and regret you wasted it."

I made a small sound in my throat. "Thank you for that. For impact, it certainly beats a card. As ever, you assume the worst of me. You never give me a chance. For your information, Jason sprang that *Telegraph* thing on me, *and* I've not been able to reach him since I left you. I'm hoping to terminate our alliance after the *show*." I paused. "I am aware that every new minute that I don't tell Jason makes me a cheat. But I have his feelings to consider and I can't just blurt it out. Also, I don't think anyone in my life has ever been as hostile to me as you are."

Jack stared at me, disbelieving, then stood away, waved his hand as if to let me go. Then he grabbed my wrist, bent his head to my ear, and said, "I'd have looked after you forever if you'd let me."

I shook him off and ran. Jason frowned as I took my seat. "Are you okay? You took ages. Was there a queue? Or was it"—he lowered his voice—"tummy trouble?"

I nodded, stared ahead, grateful for the dimming lights. I opened my eyes as wide as they could go, blinking fast to keep them dry.

"Isn't the car spectacular?" whispered Jason.

I preferred the Vauxhall, I thought, but I didn't say it, just nodded. Whatever Jack said had a way of sticking. The words spun round my head, making me dizzy. All the time Jase had wittered on about intimacy, it had seemed like a joke in a foreign language. I thought it meant that he felt undermined by my confidence and strength. Fear of intimacy was a phrase used by people who felt threatened by independent women. That's all I was, independent. Because, ultimately, you can't depend on anyone. Not even your mother.

But when Jack made the accusation, it rang true and it meant something else. He didn't just say it and say it and say it like Jason did, until the words ran into each other like wet paint. He put it in context, so its consequences were lit in flames. I was scared of intimacy, and he was right; that was why, only last week, I'd agreed to bind myself to a man who didn't understand me, didn't know me, never would. I was backing out, and that gave me some cheer, because surely this meant progress? But the tears still queued to fall, and that was because Jack had shucked out the unwilling truth like an oyster from its shell.

Fear of intimacy meant fear of love, fear of giving it, fear of getting it, and that translated to a loveless life. That wasn't independence, that was insanity, I didn't want that. But my fear of intimacy was *there,* embedded in my heart, like a fear of the dark. I didn't know why, and I wasn't sure that I wanted to know. I collected other people's secrets and that knowing made me feel superior, it was a flimsy foil against my own weaknesses. I knew one thing, which terrified me. Jack was right. It didn't start with him. It had started *waay* before. Of course, it was linked to my mother; I should have paid more attention to how her behavior had made me act. No. *Feel*.

But there was more to it than that. We all need something to worship; it's about having faith in the ultimate goodness of life. No one wants their idol to fall. They *need* to believe, like they need to breathe. Which is why the papers don't print half the dirt they have on the celebrities we regard as national treasures. People take disillusionment badly. It can break them. If the great and the good are corrupt, then the whole world is corrupt and what is the point of existing? It was comforting to uncover the corruption of those who didn't matter to me. But if Jack was suggesting my father was in any way at fault, I didn't want to know.

27.

The show ended and I gave Jason a long hug to thank him. I think it was also an apology, for what I was about to do to him. He held on as if he couldn't believe it. (I was an ender of hugs, not an initiator.) I felt uncomfortable, and there was a fixed smile on my face, possibly a grimace, but I forced myself to stay put. Happily, the person sitting next to me—the fattest person in the theater, needless to say—said, "Sorry, can I get past?" so I had a legitimate excuse to pull away. Covertly, I glanced at where Jack had been sitting. He'd gone.

"That was *brilliant!*" said Jason. "Well, Truly Scrumptious! Shall we find a place for coffee?"

"Jason," I said. I couldn't wait for the coffee. I had to tell him now. I took his hand. "Look. I have something to tell you." I looked into his brown eyes and saw fear, and it shocked me. I added, quickly, "Greg insisted I work tonight. I am so sorry."

Jason laughed, I think with relief. "No worries. The caffeine would only have kept me awake."

I smiled, tight-lipped. Then sat, blank-faced and immobile in the cab home. I *was* a coward. But it was one thing resolving to tell him, quite another thing to face him and speak. The truth? I *couldn't* end it again, I realized. It would scar him, he was a delicate soul, twice would be too much. Jesus, what would I do?

I had a nasty half hour before an idea presented itself, ping! I nearly cracked a smile. *He* would have to end it. Jason Brocklehurst must regretfully break my heart.

Now I had to think of how to effect such an occurrence.

I sat in my car across the road from Charlie's house, a video camera on my lap, and thought about my job. I won't lie to you, I thought it was cool, it made me feel a bit of a hero. We at Hound Dog got results, with meager resources—we really did live off our wits—and that made me proud. When the police do a follow, they use a twenty-five-man team and eight vehicles. Each one will be behind the target for only forty to fifty seconds. The max *we'll* use is three agents, one car, and a motorbike. There's quite a stream of old coppers in this industry, and Greg is always saying how *shocked* they are at how we manage, the spoiled brats. It's not so easy when you can't flash a warrant card.

And yet, just then, I did not feel the tiniest bit a hero. I felt like a bad guy. I'd done the usual. Filmed the street name, filmed the house. Now I was watching it. An upstairs light went on, at 11:07, and off, at 11:24. In the window was an Action Man doll, suspended from a makeshift parachute. Genius that I was, I guessed this room was Charlie's. Maybe he couldn't sleep. Maybe his mother had brought him a glass of milk or Coke, or read him a story. Thanks to Gabrielle and Jude, I was newly attuned to the world of mothers and their children.

I found good mothers intriguing. Gabrielle, for instance, had once told me off for singing "Nik nak paddywack" to Jude. (For the uninitiated: "This old man, he played one, he played nik nak on my tum, with a nik nak paddywack give a dog a bone, this old man came rolling home.") As far as I could tell, this was amicable nonsense. To Gabrielle, I was singing to my year-old nephew about a pedophile.

"On my *tum*?" she kept saying. "What is an old man doing playing nik nak paddywack, whatever the hell that is, it sounds incredibly suspicious, on a child's *tum*?"

"Some people sing it 'on my *bum*,'" I replied, to reassure her that I was responsible enough to have chosen the clean version. My reassurance was poorly received. Likewise, she paid an extraordinary amount of attention to the tiny details of Jude's daily life that would simply not occur to normal people (Ollie, for instance).

She moved his high chair around the table so he didn't always have the same view. She dressed him in dungarees because she felt that trouser elastic would be tight on his fat little tummy. She reassembled his cardboard box house every night, so one morning he'd waddle into the lounge to a studio flat, the next, an open plan penthouse. Once, she saw a fox in the garden, and she yelled from her study, "A FOX! Everyone, a FOX!" Nanny Amanda was made to cease and desist from a nappy change, and Jude was held, naked, up to the window to see his first fox. "Woof!" he said, pleasing compensation for the Dobermanesque pooh he then did on the carpet.

I was in awe at the care that Gabrielle took with him. Apart from the fact that we'd all like our own personal butler, there was something redemptive about that kind of love. I felt that as long as there were mothers—and fathers, of course, and fathers—in the world who loved their babies with the inexpressible passion that Gabrielle loved her baby, there was hope for us all. Which brought me to the Hound Dog client who had cost Jason his post-*Chitty* coffee. The vile pig. On what worthy cause was he going to spend the money that he planned to withhold from his five-year-old son, Charlie? Beer? A new stereo system? Pec implants?

I watched a Ford Fiesta pull up and a young man jump out. He was holding a bedraggled bunch of flowers, but no overnight bag. He sprinted up the concrete path and—*knocked gently.* Oh, lord, he was a pro! The door was pulled open, and Charlie's mother flung her arms around him and they kissed. Then, as if he'd planned it to kill me softly, a small boy in pajamas elbowed his way past his mother and received a high five and a big hug for his trouble. I, the intruder, looked away. My video camera was aimed at the floor, where it had a fine view of the Coke cans, Ribena cartons, old printouts of maps, Snickers bar wrappers, crisp packets, and small change obscuring the dust mat. I lifted it, slowly, pointing the lens toward the almost identical house opposite. Night vision recordings were of terrible quality; no one would notice.

I sat around till 2:30, on the grounds that it had to look as if I'd waited in vain for the boyfriend to show. Then I drove home, let myself into the hallway of my apartment building, where the first thing I saw was a solid mouse-haired woman in black slacks, *pumps,* and a sleeveless beige V-neck, perched on the uncarpeted stairs reading a fat book with a gold embossed title. Her arms were pale, freckled and untoned, and there was something businesslike about her. She stared at me and got up. "Hannah Lovekin?" she barked. I assessed her potential as a threat.

"Who wants to know?" I replied, "at quarter to three in the morning."

"You *are!*" she shrieked, throwing down her book and running at me, "you little whore, I *hate* you, you stole my fiancé, it was sour grapes, *you* didn't even want him, *we* were in love, and then out of sheer sour grapes [*share sare grapes,* she pronounced it] you steal him back, and the first thing I know about it is when Mummy reads the bloody *Telegraph,* you little *whore!* I've been in Monte Carlo on a yacht for the last five days, I only flew in this morning, I didn't even know *my* engagement was off!"

I sidestepped the body slam, and said, "You don't want to go down for assault, dear."

She stopped, which gave me confidence. "And don't call me 'whore' again," I said. "If you're Lucy, you're a bit of a goer yourself, from what I've heard."

She grabbed the knot of her ponytail and smoothed it so her thick dull hair fell over one shoulder. "What? What have you heard? Jasie wouldn't"—her lip trembled—"he wouldn't tell you anything. He loves me. You've tricked him, I know you have, I *know* he loves me." She sniffed. "What have you done with him? He's not answering his mobile, he wasn't home all day, all evening—I banged on his door every half hour for three hours—and he's not answering now. I've been waiting here for three hours."

I could see that Lucy had a lot to learn about Jason. Jason *never* answered his mobile, the pay-as-you-go mobile I'd bought him, at great expense, for his last birthday. He was convinced that whenever he put it to his ear, it gave him an earache and left him slightly deaf. "It suggests the development of a tumor," he'd said. Consequently, he'd always forget it at home, and it was left to me to remind him to put it in his pocket, to switch it on, to power it up.

"Your necklace is twisted," added Lucy, wiggling her fingers in the direction of my neck. I stared at her as I straightened it. "If I see something like that, I always point it out to people."

"Right," I said.

Were we even the same species?

"Lucy," I said slowly. "Come inside. I'm glad you're here."

She flicked her hair, reminding me of an irritable horse, swishing away flies with its tail. I led her into my lounge, where she regarded the grubby pale pink walls with distaste. She turned to face me. "I'm confused," she said, "I cannot picture you with Jasie. He loathes . . . uncleanliness."

I was about to tell her that, for me, the place was pristine, but I was too busy breathing through my mouth. Speaking of uncleanliness, Martine was right. Her breath was *awful*. I didn't say anything. Instead, I asked her to sit down and brought her a glass of water. Then I sat on a chair out of breathing range.

"Lucy," I began. "I'll be honest. Jason *is* in love with you. Not me. You and he *are* still engaged. I've behaved terribly, you're right. I was jealous. We're not engaged—"

"Then what's that stonking great diamond on your ring finger?" she screeched.

"That," I said. I was so out of the marriage loop I'd forgotten the terminology. *Ring finger.* I ripped off the diamond and shoved it in a drawer. I also noticed for the first time that Lucy was sporting the dead grandmother's red and black wart.

"I'm so embarrassed!" I added. "I—well, you know he proposed to me once? He let me keep the ring." I smiled, nervously, in case Jason had told her the details, but there was no eruption, so I presumed he'd seen sense and kept his mouth shut. "I, I've been wearing it, fooling myself. *I* put the announcement in the *Telegraph*. He knew nothing about it. He was appalled."

I paused.

Lucy wiped away tears with hands that did dishes (and looked like it). "The poor baby. Shame on you. What's the time? I must ring him." She recovered a mobile phone the size of a brick from her large handbag in a smooth movement.

"Oh, no, don't!" I cried.

Lucy placed the phone in her lap. "Why ever not?"

"Because . . . I think he should call you. We had a long talk this morning. He made me understand that I had no hope for us, I had to stop fantasizing, move on. Also, I have this . . . problem. I'm scared of dentists. Haven't seen one in years and, well, Jason had difficulties with my . . . halitosis. He hates that in a woman."

Lucy placed a hand over her mouth. Damn right, after I'd humiliated myself like that.

I added, "Jason said that he was in love with you. What I did has embarrassed him. He probably thinks you're furious with him, so don't be surprised if he's distant, sheepish even. He might even seem to be avoiding you for a week or so. But only because he's desperate to explain and terrified you won't believe him."

"I see." Lucy looked me in the eye, squeezed her handbag to her. "I'm going to go now," she announced. "I don't expect to hear of you again."

I nodded meekly and showed her out.

Then I rang Jason. The phone rang forty times before Jason woke up and answered it.

"Jase," I said with a big theatrical sniff. "I, I have something I feel I need to tell you."

"Mm. What's the time?"

"Late. But it's urgent."

"Urggh." I could hear rustling as he sat up in bed. "What," he said, his voice less bleary.

"I felt that before we actually got married, you ought to know."

"What?"

"That I love you but that I am also 100 percent certain that I never want children."

"What! . . . You mean, you can't *have* children?"

"No. No. I mean, I don't *want* children. Ever."

"But why? Where did this come from? You're just tired! You love Jude! You adore him."

"Jason, I admire him for three minutes, then I hand him back to his rightful owners. I, I do not want a family, Jason. I felt, I felt that before you committed yourself to me . . . instead of Lucy, it was only fair to tell you this."

"But," spluttered Jason, "but, but it's already been *announced*! I love you, Hannah. But this, this is impossible! I can't imagine why you left it so late to tell me something so fundamental, so crucial."

"I'm so sorry," I said. "I was so scared you would . . . change your mind. But, but if you did, I would"—I wondered if I was pushing it—"find it in my heart to understand. I suppose I would eventually move on."

"Hannah, I—I'm speechless—how could you *do* this to me? This is crazy! Everyone has kids!"

"Not true."

"You never know. This might be a phase. You're run-down. You need a holiday. You might change your mind in a few months, years—"

"No. Never. I never would. In fact, I'm considering an operation."

"An operation!"

We were veering off track. It was time to steer him back. "Jason. I don't know if you've had a chance yet to break off your engagement to Lucy—"

"Yes, well! A fine mess this is! She's been away . . . I meant to ring her . . . yesterday . . . the day before . . . today, before she saw the *Telegraph,* but . . . well, it's not the easiest thing to do . . . and whenever I saw her we ended up . . . and today I've been out all day, and when I got home tonight *she* was out. And now it's just awful, just awful!"

I was a little shocked that Jason—a man so polite he couldn't put the phone down on an automated answering system—had convinced himself that there was *any* valid excuse for omitting to tell Lucy. Still, I couldn't complain; it was lucky for all of us.

"Jase," I said. "I am deeply hurt by the fact that you and Lucy can't keep your hands off each other. Particularly when our love life was . . . tame. But, perhaps that tells us something."

I paused so that my wisdom might sink in. Then I added, "For all she knows, *I* placed that announcement without your permission or knowledge. For all she knows, you and I were never engaged, it was a fantasy on my part. I mean, obviously, I am devastated, I would be devastated if you were to . . . but I felt I had to tell you the truth. I mean—*is* it over?"

I tried to keep my voice hope-free.

"Hannah," said Jason. "I am so sorry. But if you don't want children, I'm afraid it has to be."

28.

"Your dad will be pleased" was Martine's reaction when I told her. "Have you rung him?"

"Tell you what," I said. "Why don't *you* ring him?"

She was annoying me. It was a blessing that Roger would approve, but I'd decided to maintain a little distance. Jason was right, I *did* always ring him within five minutes of any significant event in my life, and maybe it was his turn to call me.

"I might," said Martine. "Chow!"

Martine is the only person I know who still says "*Ciao!*" five years after everyone else stopped saying it. (Excluding the Italians.)

I was not in the greatest of moods.

That might surprise those who haven't bailed out of an engagement. The relief of knowing I wasn't to endure a lifetime with a man who would bore and irritate me was wonderful but physically sapping, like swimming in the sea. I also felt stunned at the success of my plan. I *hadn't* just blurted out the mean old truth; I'd told a lie so pure it would bring a tear to your eye. I had achieved the impossible and made a silk purse out of a pig's ear. (Or however that saying goes.) Admittedly, I could have left Lucy and Jase alone to begin with but, remarkably, no harm done.

But I felt flat. I stood by what I said earlier. Despite Jason's faults, there was a part of me that was sad to let him go. I can only compare it to *Free Willy*. There are women out there who'd understand. Women who have devoted a chunk of their twenties, thirties, forties, to a man who is decent, amiable, handsome, *wrong*, who feel sorrow at releasing him into the wild but know it's for the best. Who regret that it's not socially acceptable to keep a nice man in a fish tank in the downstairs toilet.

And there were other factors. I'd had two hours rest before sleepdriving to Charlie's house for 6 A.M., to continue my impression of a stakeout for a few more hours. I was looking forward to billing Legal Aid to within an inch of their grant, so they'd have less cash to lavish on other wasters like Charlie's father. I'd got into work at 9:30 sharp and e-mailed Greg to tell him "no luck on the boyfriend," but that I'd try again tonight. I didn't want to lie to his face, that direct gaze melting my brain.

Greg hadn't replied for hours, then at 3 P.M. he e'd back. "You're having no luck with this. Perhaps I should assign Ron?"

While I liked the fact that I could hide behind the poker face of electronic communication, I found it tedious that Greg could hide behind it too. Was he being sarcastic? Or sympathetic? I'd written back, "I'll have another go tonight."

I'd also spoken to my mother. It had been a strange conversation. Full of holes, like Swiss cheese. I'd felt hungry after it, eaten half a pack of biscuits.

"How are you?"

"Fine, thank you. How are you?"

"Fine. My engagement to Jason is off, you'll be pleased to hear."

"Ah. Shame. Your father said it would be."

"Oh. Well, anyway, I'm presuming you know that meat loaf is unsuitable for someone with irritable bowel? Particularly if the mushroom gravy has five times the recommended salt content."

"Oh dear. Did I get the recipe wrong?"

"You know you did, Angela."

"I'm sorry. I must have been distracted by . . . other things."

"Oh. Oh. Right. Well. Are all Grandma's things sorted?"

My mother sighed. "I suppose so," she said, finally. "She left you a box."

"Oh! I wasn't expecting— What sort of box?"

"Cardboard."

Grandma and I hadn't exactly got on, but I was a little taken aback. "W-what do you think she was trying to say?"

"No, Hannah. There are things inside it. I don't know what, though. It's not heavy. It has your name written on it, and it's tightly sealed. I'll give it to you when you next come over."

"Fine. And what are you doing—I mean, rather, how . . . how are you ah feeling?"

I braced myself for another sigh, but it didn't come. "Bit better," she said, as if she almost meant it.

"Anything I can do?"

"Oh, no, no, thank you."

I was about to give up—it was like tweezing hairs from your armpit—when my mother said, "Hannah?"

"Yes?"

"Are you sad about Jason?"

I pondered this. "I'll live," I said.

"Yes," she replied, sounding unconvinced.

It struck me, as I tapped my nails listlessly on my keyboard, that the exchange with my mother had been near devoid of emotional content, and for once, that wasn't my fault. I'd tried to eke some feeling from her, but failed. Fair's fair. I supposed. After speaking to her, I'd yearned for a meaty conversation, where people said what they thought, and called Gabrielle. Either she wasn't in or she wasn't answering the phone. Most likely, she wasn't answering the phone to *me*. Call me contrary, I was peeved she hadn't called to congratulate me on my second engagement.

Or its demise.

I hoped her rage would have cooled, at least that she'd let me explain, but it hadn't or she'd have rung me. I wanted to talk to her about Angela. Check my mother was okay. I've never experienced grief, I don't know what it does to people. It had certainly changed *something* in my mother, which made me nervous. Since the funeral Angela had stopped trying with me, which was why we couldn't speak. You can't have *both* sides holding back. One person has to babble away happily to mask the other's reticence. My mother was no longer making the effort to do that with me. It meant our invalid relationship had slipped into a coma. I wasn't sure what I felt about this. But I was certain that Angela confided in Gabrielle.

I missed her. Everyone I spoke to lately was miserable. I needed a chat with my sister-in-law, who—despite her recent grumpiness—was a cheerful person at heart. I was kind of hoping she'd inject some cheer into *my* day. A good mood transfusion. Wouldn't it be great, I thought, as I drove home, if I pulled up in front of my flat and there was Gabrielle on the doorstep. I sometimes do this. "Wouldn't it be great if . . ." I think, slyly refusing to acknowledge that I *may* be asking some airborne entity to grant a wish.

In keeping with this unofficial pact, I kept my gaze averted from my apartment building until I'd parked the Vauxhall. Then I looked up. And started. There, sitting on my doorstep, was . . . *Ollie.* Yeah. Nice try, Tinkerbell. Back to fairy school you go.

"Ollie?" I shouted, as if it might not be him.

"Hey, Ner. How are you?"

"Single, how are you?"

"I thought you and Jase were abandoning the hurly-burly of the chaise longue."

"What?"

"Never mind. It's off?"

"Yes."

"You don't sound too upset."

"I never sound too anything, Ollie."

He smiled at last. "Quite right, Ner. You don't get your knickers in a twist like normal girls."

"I'll interpret that to mean I'm stable, rather than abnormal."

"And there's my point! Gab would accuse me of calling her mad."

"How is she?"

"Busy."

"Still annoyed with me?"

He shrugged.

"Funny thing is, Ollie, even though the job only entailed taking

Jude for a walk to a school to watch someone pick up a kid, I actually took him to the park."

"Gab made it sound like you'd taken him on a car chase. *I* can't see what harm it would have done. But you know Gab. She . . . feels things very strongly in her own head. She can be unreasonable."

I smiled stiffly. I disliked it when Ollie criticized Gabrielle in front of me; I liked to believe he couldn't see a flaw. "So," I said, "to what do I owe this pleasure?"

Ollie laughed and held up a plastic bag that clinked. "Don't get excited. It's mostly Coke. I'm driving. Anyway, what are you saying? I can't come and see my sister? I need a motive?"

I looked straight at him. Ollie and I were close in spirit. Jack would have said we were as close as two people who were itchy with intimacy could be. Because if *I* had problems doing a moonie of the soul, so did Ollie. His job as a freelance photographer took him all over the world. He did a lot of stuff for travel and wildlife magazines, adventures to strange, dangerous places. He rejected offers of blue chip advertising work that would have allowed him to be home by six. He spent a good five months of the year abroad. He'd missed Jude's first word, "Dada." (Jude had said it to a photo of Ollie on the wall.)

I didn't see Ollie much, and when I did, our conversations were as fanciful as butterflies dancing over a meadow. Our love was solid, but I often felt shy talking to him, certainly about *me* and *my* life. Now and then he or I would have the odd blast of frankness. We never discussed our parents, our feelings toward them, our relationships with them. Instead, we had intricate, detailed, pinhead conversations about characters on TV programs, which allowed us to open up about *other* people, make-believe ones at that. *CSI* was one of our favorites.

"Grissom is *so* cool," I remarked after my hero had said—with imperious disdain—of a killer, "Why do they think they can trick us?"

Ollie had replied, "Yes, but you do realize, he *is* a nerd."

The ensuing debate lasted the length of the program. When he'd gone, I realized that while I could have done a master's degree on Ollie's beliefs and analysis of Grissom's personality, I had no idea what jobs he had coming up, if he and Gabrielle had plans (more Judes? Italy excursions? loft extensions?), or what he thought of his son's latest development. He hadn't mentioned Jude, let alone Jude's latest development, and I wondered if he even knew. I hadn't bothered to ask if he was carrying any photos.

That said, Gabrielle didn't carry photos of Jude either. I asked her once why, and she replied, "If people genuinely care, rather than being merely curious or polite, they'll come round to see him."

That blew me away. Not only did she protect Jude from actual harm, she protected him from theoretical harm floating round in people's heads. *Her* emotional sensibilities were so overdeveloped, she had every possible nuance of human psychology covered; she balanced Ollie's weak emotional radar nicely. She was largely responsible for what they had today, a warm, welcoming home that made people want to linger. I thought of the stern formal aura of my childhood home and I was proud of Ollie for what he had created. Naturally, I never told him.

"No," I said. "You don't need a motive, Ollie. It's just that, in the nicest possible way, you always do."

Ollie squeezed his temples as if pain could be popped like a spot. His sideburns were flecked with gray hairs. "Gab's gone to visit her mother for the weekend. She's taken Jude."

"Glad to hear it. He's a bit young to housesit." I frowned. "For the *weekend*. But her mother only lives in Miw Hiw. That's about twenty minutes from you."

Ollie looked irritable. "It's nice for her to see her mother. They chat about, you know, girls' things."

"*Girls' things*, Ollie?" I said. "You mean . . . *periods*?" I waggled my fingers by the sides of my head in the approximation of a scary ghost.

"Don't say that word," said my brother, and cracked open a can.

It was four hours, three episodes of *The Shield,* and two madras curries later, as I set off to continue the charade of staking out Charlie's house, that my suspicions were confirmed.

"All right if I sleep on your sofa?" said Ollie.

"*No.* Why would you even want to when this is a poky one-bed flat and you own a palatial home of your own?"

I *hated* overnight guests. Talk about an imposition. They expected proper food (not pesto on toast), clean towels, hot water, phone privileges, they acted as if they were in a hotel, they wondered if you might have a hot water bottle, if they could borrow your hair dryer, had you serfing around after them like a Hampstead Garden Suburb Filipino maid. They snooped around your things, peered into cupboards, wandered into your bedroom when you were still in your Snoopy T-shirt, quaffing fresh coffee from your last coffee filter from your favorite mug and munching the stale Danish pastry you'd earmarked for your own breakfast.

Martine had slept over once and so enraged me I'd had to avoid her for three months.

Ollie stared at the writing on his Coke can. "Oh, you know," he muttered. "Change of scene."

"Ollie?" I said.

"Ah, Jesus," he said. "I've left Gabrielle."

210

29.

I screamed it. "What?"

Ollie sunk his head into his shoulders like a child about to be hit. "It just all got too much."

"What!" I screamed again. "*What* got too much? Having all your clothes cleaned and dried for you?"

Ollie lifted his head and said in a whisper, "Stop shouting."

He seemed to be thinking and moving in slow motion, so I snatched an empty glass and smashed it on the floor.

"Hannah!" He stared at me. "That was *your* glass. What's your problem?"

"What's my problem?" I screamed. "What do you think my problem is? My problem is you've left your wife and child for no reason, you fucking fuckwit."

"Hannah, Hannah, calm down. Jesus! Why are you reacting like this? You're *my* sister."

I felt like a bull that just walked into an abattoir. "That means NOTHING," I screeched. "Since when has family meant *close* to you? I'll tell you since when. Since you met Gabrielle Goldstein from Mill bloody Hill! Before then you were like a human desert! That girl has made you, Oliver! And she's *my* sister-in-law, and Jude is *my* nephew! They are your family, you are nothing without them, your life is pointless!"

"Hannah, shut up, I'm not hearing this!" Ollie banged a hand on the table.

I gave him my most evil look.

"Hannah, you don't understand. There's a lot going on. Work's bad."

"So?"

"It's been bad for a year. I'm lucky if I get one job a month. I haven't worked in six weeks. I go out . . . I wander round parks. The economic climate. And I'm disposable. Even if a story's cheap, magazines are all sending staffers or calling in agency shots."

"And what has this to do with Gabrielle?"

"She's such a nag, she was driving me nuts."

"Really?"

Ollie gargoyled his face ugly and assumed a whiny voice. "You should have taken that advertising job, you should put yourself out there more, you should be taking round your book to picture editors, you shouldn't have done so much work for *Wild Things,* you should have worked for a wider range of publications, yak yak yak."

"I see," I said. "And how do you deal with that?"

Ollie reverted to his own voice. "Sometimes I just waggle my fingers over her face, and say, '*Sleeeeep!*' "

"Uh-huh."

"Or I zone out. I let her talk, but all I hear is 'blah blah blah.' It makes it easier to deal with."

"Genius."

Ollie sighed. "You understand, right? You must deal with this sort of thing all the time. Husbands sick of their nagging wives. Not that I'd cheat on her, because apart from anything else, who's got the energy? But you get where I'm coming from?"

"Yes," I replied. "I think you've made it pretty clear where you're coming from. *Kindergarten.* You selfish, selfish pig!" My voice once again had risen to a scream. "She's not *nagging* you, Oliver, why is it 'nagging' if she voices her opinion? She's right! Why are you so picky? You're not Marion Testino—"

"Mario."

"I don't care. You're not a world-famous artiste, you don't have the luxury of rejecting work just because it's not Kate Moss in a bikini or an indigenous person wielding a blowpipe! So what if it's the in-house magazine for a firm that sells lawn mowers? You're a father who needs to help feed his family! It's not like all the pressure's on you. Gabrielle works too! As well as running the house and Jude and secretarying after you! She's right! Everything she says is right!"

"Look," said Ollie. "I've been a snapper for ten years—"

"Don't tell me. You feel, after your glorious decade in the business, that you've earned the right to stop trying. You're going to sulk now till all the lovely glamorous high-paying jobs come to you. My God. Gabrielle's grandfather worked for the same firm as a glazier for *fifty* years before they made him redundant, a year before he was due to retire. He didn't complain. He went freelance because he had no choice, within six months he was earning five times what the firm had paid him, because of his reputation. Every time a kid kicked a ball through a window, every time someone had a break-in, their neighbors recommended Mr. Gol—"

"And the point of this story, which I've heard before . . . ?"

"The work ethic, Oliver."

"That, coming from you."

I ignored this. "So," I said. "To sum up. You're having a few problems with laziness. Sorry, lack of work. Gabrielle is anxious about this. So I don't get it. Why have you left her?"

A little Coke had spilled on the table. My brother drew patterns in it with one finger, turning a Coke blob into a Coke octopus. "She's impossible," he said. "It's not just the work." He laughed. "Having a kid. It's changed everything. There is no spare time, no time for us. Don't get me wrong—I love Jude, he's the bollocks, that kid, when he smiles, I tell you—"

"And when he doesn't smile?"

Oliver looked to the sky and blew upward, so his fringe fluttered in the breeze. "A crying baby . . . when a baby cries and cries . . . you feel your head could crack like two halves of a walnut. It drives you insane—"

"I would have thought," I said, "that that's the point. An alarm bell that parents can't ignore."

"Well, Gab can't ignore it. She's basically trained him to cry."

"I'm sorry, Oliver. What am I missing here? Because I'm still not seeing why you've left your wife."

"She's so up and down, Hannah. She's irrational. She freaked out the other day because I threw Jude in the air and caught him. He was laughing his head off—he loved it."

"Yes, but what if you'd dropped him?"

"I wasn't going to drop him."

"Oliver. People make mistakes."

"Jesus. Look. I'll come into my own when he's a bit older, when he can talk. He's so . . . demanding of you, so intense. It's like, if he could, he'd suck out your soul through your eyes. It's exhausting, it's too much. He's so . . . powerful."

Ollie paused and shook his head. He was strange, my brother. He was literate, well read, intelligent. And yet he'd chosen to assume the guise of a Neanderthal.

"Right now, he's a mummy's boy. Yeah, he loves his dad, but she's what he really needs. She's better with him than I am. She's the one who gets him up, makes his breakfast—"

"What, she has to wake him up?"

"Are you joking? The kid's up at six. If a cat walks past the house, that kid is up. He's a bat. Gab goes in there."

"I see. And what does *Jude*"—I said it "Jooode"—"have for breakfast?"

"What? Toast and peanut butter. Bacon and eggs. I don't know."

"You don't know what Jude eats for breakfast?"

"Ner, get off my back. Look. Gabrielle works from home. She's got a nanny—"

"The woman quit, remember? Gab is doing everything there is to do, apart from wiping your bottom. Maybe you'd like her to do that too?"

"There's no need to be sarcastic. I do lots of stuff. Gabrielle doesn't see that. She's always so angry, so hostile, so—"

"Tired?"

"Yes, she's tired, but everyone's tired. I don't know. She keeps saying she thinks she's . . . *low*."

I squashed a flicker of guilt. "Right, and what do you say?"

"I tell her she just needs a good night's sleep and she'll feel better in the morning. But I'm sick of saying it, she doesn't listen and she always goes to bed at midnight. She won't listen to advice, she's taking everything out on me, and I can't stand it anymore. I need some space. She needs to get a grip. If I'm not there, maybe she will." Ollie sighed. "So what do you say, Ner? Can I stay the night? It'll only be for a week or so. I've left her a note to say where I am."

"You mean . . . she knows you're here?"

"Yes."

"No, you can*not* stay the night, just get out, get out, get the fuck out and go home, how dare you come to me, how *dare* you, and how dare you leave Gab a note, as if we were in this together, I am speechless at the sheer cheek of you, my God, it's fucking obvious, Gab needs you to be an equal partner, you should be helping her with the baby and the house, you've got to kindly encourage her to get more rest, instead of waving your hand over her face and going '*Sleeeeep*' you selfish, stupid patronizing prick!"

Then, to my surprise, I burst into tears.

Ollie jumped up like a man in a horror movie and started shuffling toward the door. "Er, Ner, look, it's okay, I'm leaving—"

"Get OUT of here," I shrieked. "How dare you, you have responsibilities, stop moaning, go home to your family, get out, get out, get OUT!"

After he'd gone I sat on the sofa shaking. I'd had no idea I was so upset.

I drove to Charlie's, but I couldn't even concentrate on *pretending* to do my job. The rage pulsed through me like a strobe light, and I kept bursting into short fits of tears. I called Ollie's mobile but it was turned off. Maybe men shouldn't be given mobiles until they've proven they can use them responsibly. Then my phone rang. I blushed in the darkness. Greg has a big sign pasted on the back of the main office door. PHONE ON DIVERT. It was the first time I'd forgotten to divert my calls on a job.

"Martine. I'm on a job."

"You're on the job! Bit rude to answer your phone, innit?"

"A job, *a* job, not *the* job, what are you, deaf?"

"Just because you don't have a sex life don't take it out on *me.*"

"Martine. What's wrong?"

"Just rang to see how it was going. How you were feeling, what with everything."

It had taken me a long time to realize that Martine kept nothing confidential. I suppose I always told her stuff because she never looked that eager to know. Jesus. She could have learned that from *me.* It's a rule, when you're trying to get information out of someone, don't push. You tell me something, I tell *you* something, or we're not equal and we're not friends. Greg's always said it helps in this business if you've been a waitress or a barman because you're used to chatting, making people feel good. You have to show interest without being aggressive. If someone starts to tell you something about himself and you push too hard, he clams up. People like to talk about themselves, but *you* have to give as well.

Martine, I realized, gave everything and nothing. She'd spill supposedly privileged personal details, and yet, if you thought about it, there was nothing of what *she* thought of the situation. She was like a news reporter based somewhere horrible. *CSI Miami,* perhaps. The last anecdote she'd thrown my way related to a sore bursting on one of her mother's varicose veins and blood spurting up the lounge walls. You could see why we were friends, but she was devious. I wasn't going to mention Oliver coming round or she'd extract the whole story like Marvin extracting a tooth.

"If *everything* refers to Jason, I am feeling fine, thanks. You?"

"Yeah, good, thanks. I called Roger, like you said, told him you'd done the deed. He's thrilled for you, mate, thrilled. He said he'd call you, soon as. He's been busy. What with your grandmother dying, and the play."

Despite myself—and despite the weirdness of Martine having an independent phone relationship with my father—I felt a flicker of joy.

"Well, then," I said. "You'd better get off the phone."

I waited for an hour, rubbing my eyes, no one rang. The reception came and went with this phone anyway. Maybe he was trying the flat. I decided to go home. The scenic route, via Belsize Park. I drove, slow, down Gab and Ollie's road, then back again, and again. A slow curl of anger uncoiled in my chest. Ollie's car (a metallic purple Mercedes hatchback) was absent. I knew he wouldn't go home. I just knew it. Everything I told him, it was as much use as talking to a cat. That was my family, we ran away from trouble.

30.

The next day I called in sick and went to see Gabrielle. She hadn't gone to visit her mother, Ollie had lied. Who else in my family had lied? It was so easy to lie; try it once, try it twice—it was a habit that slipped over you like a warm coat. Lies soothed people. I held this as private belief, was disappointed to find it was in the genes. Was I now obliged by honor to dig out the truth? I hoped not. I felt like a woman who'd been tricked into seeing the World's Longest Domino Line and accidentally knocked over the first domino.

"It's not a good time," said Gabrielle and shut the door. I wedged a foot in the gap, but I was wearing flip-flops and having a heavy door slammed repeatedly on my bare toes was too painful. I withdrew and rang the bell instead. I also shouted through the letter box.

"Gab! Please! Listen to me. I'm worried about you. I spoke to Ollie, he—"

The door was wrenched open. Gabrielle appeared, furious. The skin around her eyes was puffy under her "cover it" stick.

"Shut up," she hissed. "A new client just walked in, do you think I want her to hear this?"

"No, but I—"

"Hannah, just leave. What do you care anyway?"

"I'm not going away," I said. "There are things we need to discuss. *Hello!*" Seeing my chance, I waved at the plump dark-haired woman bobbing around in the hallway behind Gabrielle. "Sorry to interrupt, I'm Hannah, Gabrielle's sister-in-law. Can I say if you're after a beautiful wedding dress, you've come to the right person."

Gabrielle scowled. The woman beamed. "Oh! I'm sure I have. My cousin got her dress from Gabrielle, and she looked amazing." She paused. "Although she is thinner than me. Are you staying? You can come and watch, if you like. My friend Amy was meant to come, but her dog died." She dipped her head in apology for implied callousness toward the dog.

"I'd be honored," I trilled and stepped into the house. Gab raised a toned arm and barred my way.

"Jennifer, are you sure?" she said.

I smiled encouragingly at Jennifer, trying not to look like Red Riding Hood's wolf.

She nodded. "I never know how I look. It'll be nice to have an unbiased opinion."

"Well, how lovely," I said and gently barged past my sister-in-law. I knew Gab didn't think too highly of her brides being chaperoned by interested parties. She said that few people could look at a girl in a wedding dress objectively. Unmarried friends, for instance, would sit there and see how *they* looked. Mothers-in-law could not be trusted, even some mothers. Once Gab had told me how a beautiful bride invited her mother in to see the final dress rehearsal, for her to react in what Gab had described as "stony silence." The bride had said, "Don't you like it?" and her chin had wobbled. Gab reckoned either she'd got it wrong or the woman was jealous, and she thought she knew which. But the bride, said Gab, was "dissolved."

Gab, without looking at me, said to Jennifer, "You have to trust yourself. You will know when you find the right dress." She smiled. "When a bride gets into the right dress she starts to move in a different way. She starts to smile at herself. You'll know, Jennifer. You'll maybe try on umpteen other dresses and then come back to the right one. It will have that wow factor."

Jennifer blinked. She was wearing owlish spectacles and I could see the tears glinting behind the glass. Gab also looked a little soggy. Jennifer laughed, a nervous, high-pitched laugh, and said, "I suppose it's the same as meeting Mr. Right."

"Exactly!" cried Gab with impressive enthusiasm.

"How did you meet your fiancé?" I asked, thinking that this was a safe question. Gab glared at me.

"He was my parole officer," sighed Jennifer.

I said, "Aah, that's lovely."

Jennifer giggled. "Actually, that's not true. I just wanted to see what you'd say. We met at work. He was my PA. I fell in love with him on sight. He's dyslexic, which wasn't great with letters to clients. But I liked the way he chewed his pen. I watched him chew it for three-quarters of an hour once, until I realized the whole office was staring at us."

Gab had always said that designing wedding dresses was like being a hairdresser—people confided in you immediately. You talked about The Dress, but they were baring themselves to you, emotionally and physically, discussing their physicality in a way they wouldn't normally. Fair enough, but Jennifer hadn't yet taken off her jacket!

Gab, however, cried, "Oh, that's so beautiful. I *love* to hear stories like that. Very occasionally a client will say, 'I really love him . . . but how do you really know?' and it worries me. You *do* know. People fall into these safe, comfortable relationships, and nothing's terribly wrong so they go along with it, but what a way to live, when you compare that to the feeling of meeting someone who makes your heart fly!"

She and Jennifer cooed like a pair of wood pigeons, and I marveled at Gab's professionalism. No way could she still believe this— her husband had left her the previous night! But her words made me wriggly. "Nothing's Terribly Wrong" could have been the headline for Jason and my relationship, and I'd gone along with that for five years, nearly written myself into a marriage contract without bothering to read the small print. (I DON'T ACTUALLY LOVE YOU.)

The cooing reached its natural conclusion, and Gab ushered Jennifer into the lounge. I'm not sentimental, but it was like walking into the Snow Kingdom. White princessy dresses everywhere, their sequins and pearls kissing the afternoon sunshine and infusing the air with sparkle and glow. I sat on a taut sofa, and Jennifer ran straight to a dress and stroked it.

I sat there, smiling, not really seeing them, and time melted into itself. I was aware of a warm buzz of words, Gabrielle's voice murmuring against Jennifer's.

"Is it to be held in church? . . . How do you feel about lace? . . . Do you take a D-cup? . . . What's your shoe size? . . . So is it a big wedding? . . . Will you be wearing a tiara on the day? . . . crystals . . . beadwork . . . when you're dancing, we put a flat string under the hem . . . it's a very close shape . . . if you want more taken in, then we can do that . . . step forward a little bit . . . Millennium satin, more shimmery than duchesse satin . . . look at the heart shape of this one . . . two pieces do emphasize the hips . . . no one decides on the first visit, not even the second . . . I'll make a note of the ones you like . . . Hannah, what do you think? *Hannah!*"

"Yes?" I jumped, and tried to look attentive.

Jennifer was standing, arms stretched out like a scarecrow, in the sort of dreary dress that fashion calls sophisticated. The breed of dress that Gwyneth Paltrow might wear to the Oscars. It did nothing for her. Jennifer twisted and turned in front of Gabrielle's enormous wall mirror, as if she was missing something.

Now what? Did I insult the designer or the wearer? I said, "It's lovely, but . . . er . . . what do *you* think?"

Jennifer swished this way and that and said, "Hmm."

"You can stand there for ten minutes," said Gabrielle, "but 'hmm' is not going to get any better. Off with its head!"

The dress was removed with a rustle, and Jennifer's eyes lingered on its nemesis—a dress fit for a medieval princess. It had long drapy sleeves, a tight bodice, and flowing skirt. All that was missing was the cone-shaped hat. "I'm too short for a full dress," she said hopefully.

"Nonsense," said Gabrielle. "You have the fullness to suit you. I alter the pattern. If I move the hipline up a quarter of an inch it can make a massive difference in how it flatters you."

"Really?"

"Oh, yes. If you see a picture of a bride standing on her own without a tree or a car to gauge her height by, you shouldn't be able to guess how tall she is."

"Oh, that's good." Jennifer paused. "I *am* going to lose weight, though. Half a stone. But . . . will that mess up your measurements?"

Gabrielle whipped the dress off its hanger and said, "Darling, I don't care if you don't lose a pound. I'm going to make you look *fabulous*. But if you feel you want to be lighter for your wedding, fine. We'll set the toile date—I'll mock up the dress in calico and lining, then we can move the proportions around. I'll also give you a diet deadline. No crash diets a month before The Day."

Jennifer nodded, her huge smile punctuated by two fat dimples of happiness. The magic words *I'm going to make you look fabulous*. I smiled myself then. Gab had explained her work to me shortly after we met. She'd said, "My job is not important in the scheme of things . . . it's not like being a doctor. But it *is* important." She was right.

"What do you think?"

Jennifer did, not so much a twirl, it was too regal for that, more a slow sweep around. I smiled. She couldn't have looked more different from the woman I'd met in the hallway in dark, shapeless trousers. This dress dipped, cinched, and flounced in all the right places, its pale cream material, a teasing trail of small buttons down the back bodice, the front coyly demure, her dark hair shone against its paleness, and even the owly glasses took on a sexy glint, very *why, Miss Jones, but* . . .

"You're beautiful," I said.

"Oh!" She clutched her throat with one hand; the other she waved in front of her face. "Don't, you'll make me cry."

Gabrielle laughed. "That is what the right dress will do. It will make people cry."

Jennifer laughed and shook her head. "Oh my God," she said. "I feel . . . I feel so . . . it's amazing, oh, I never want to take it off . . . oh, I don't know, what do you think, are you sure I . . . ?"

I nodded, smiling. Jesus. An hour back I'd never met this woman, and now I was too choked to speak. It was strange. Gab had talked about women like Jennifer. All professionals, impressive careers, spending budgets, flying hither and thither, and yet, when it came to a personal decision they hadn't the first clue. They didn't have the time to be introspective. They avoided looking at themselves in great detail, and when Gabrielle Goldstein forced them to, they felt obliged to run themselves down.

Only now did this seem a little sad.

I sat there, gazing into the distance, as Jennifer changed back into her ordinary clothes and arranged another date with Gab. She left, moving as lightly as a dandelion on the breeze. Gab marched back into the lounge.

I said quickly, "That was lovely, it was a real privilege to witness. I was really . . . moved by that."

Immediately I flinched, it was so slimy on my tongue, so *touchy feely*, my worst thing. But the words didn't feel like self-disembowelment; it actually gave me relief to say them.

"Yeah, right," said Gab, huffing through her nose. "We all know *your* view on marriage."

"Well," I said. "Everyone thinks they do."

Gab sighed. "Yeah," she said as if she hadn't heard me. "Well, guess what, I'm beginning to agree with you." She paused. "You needn't have sent your brother home last night, I threw him straight out."

"Oh, no!" I said, "but this is terrible." I slumped in my chair; I had the posture of a banana.

Gabrielle kicked off her silver ballet pumps and placed her pedicured feet on the lounge table. "Why?" she said. "Marriages break up the whole time. I mean, look at *you*."

I stared at the floor. I did look at me. I saw a girl who'd got married when just about everyone said don't, and they'd had the last laugh and I'd had to stomach it. Age twenty, everything is quite intense, and when Jack left it hit me that I could have spent all my life with him, but now I'd be spending it by myself. Divorce was a dirty subject in my family, and I know my father felt that I'd brought dog shit into the house. All the same, he hired a lawyer for me, and all *she* wanted to know was "Where's any money you might have?" Like I had any, like I'd care if I did and Jack took all of it.

I blinked. Looked up again. Saw Gabrielle, who looked uncomfortable. It was plain she wasn't planning to forgive me about Jude, about being Oliver's sister, about anything. I decided to go. I took three steps.

Then I stopped. "No," I said. "I'm looking at you. And I see the woman who once told me that she *dreams* wedding dresses, whose dreams are filled with organza and lace, that she wakes in the morning having cut a pattern in her sleep. I see the woman who, when I told her I was divorcing Jack, went crazy. Who told me that people these days don't want to put up with that much, they don't want to put the work in. Who said she'd like people to be more patient with each other, that there's so much safety if you're with the right person. The woman who tells her brides that the dress symbolizes the importance of the day, that it's like saying, for this very special day, we are going to do this one-off, very special thing, so that what it means never fades in our memory. And yet this same woman also tells her brides, it's not about the frock, it's about you and him, and you will blink and your wedding day will be over, and the day will come when you hate him, but that will pass, to hang on in there, you may encounter financial problems, your children, your lack of children, will test your relationship, but that if you did have love for that person, not to make any rash decisions, because things will come round again."

Gab stared at me. "I don't want him to leave me," she said through clenched teeth. "I couldn't bear it."

"He won't, Gab," I said. "He loves you so much. But you need to talk to each other. Make plans to change what needs changing."

Gab looked up. "Could you get me a tissue?"

"Sure," I said and ran to the luxe toilet. I sat down and had a little cry myself. It was becoming a bad habit, like sugary snacks. But I realized, as I wiped my nose, the success of Gab and Ollie's marriage meant everything to me.

Then I drove home fast; I dragged a chair to my wardrobe and pulled down the black binbag containing my scrunched-up wedding dress. I threw the bag on the floor and spread out the dress on my bed. My heart thumped as I stroked the silken material—I remembered seeing it similarly discarded, on our wedding night. My eyes prickled—Jesus, I was like a hormonal teenager! I marveled as to how mere objects take on a status and meaning so far beyond their real worth, as to how they can almost feel like a part of someone. Especially if that someone is lost. I pored over the dress, trying to smooth out the creases. Then I saw that the back of the hem was grimy with dirt and a little bit ragged. I would take it to be dry-cleaned, first thing. Out of respect for . . . I wasn't quite sure, but I knew I'd feel better if it were steamed and pressed and hanging on a squashy silk hanger, almost as good as new.

31.

I returned to work Monday morning, and got the sack. Greg called it a "trial separation," but we all know what that means. That bastard, Ron. He'd tailed me. He had footage of Charlie's mother and her boyfriend, kissing, on the Thursday night. And footage of me not recording it.

It's hard to express quite how loathsome I find Ron. Dark curly hair, in greasy ringlets, close to his head. Scrofulous skin, like something out of the Middle Ages. Rounded shoulders. Hates women. I think he registered that I was one only after my St. Tropez transformation. I couldn't believe it. I always considered myself inoffensive to both men and women. I'm not beauteous enough to be a threat to either, but nor am I the level of ugly that gets you picked on. (Talking of which, there's my theory for why Ron hates women.)

Greg didn't say that much. He said more with his body language. Crossed arms, crossed legs: cross, basically.

"You didn't take that kid to the school; you took him to the park."

"What, did the great sleuth Ron tail me there too?"

"No. There was loads of grass caught in the wheels of the kid's pushchair. There's nothing green within five miles of that school."

"Well, Greg," I said, "if only my sister-in-law was as good a tec as you are. She's still convinced I took her baby on surveillance, and nothing I say will convince her otherwise."

Greg said, "You got emotionally involved, Hannah. I can't have that."

I didn't say anything. It wasn't fair. Because I was female, I was "emotionally" involved. Whereas if I were a man, I'd have made an "executive" decision. Greg had made enough of them. There was the time a client had him investigate the feasibility of blowing up his local tax office. Greg said it wasn't feasible and charged him a lot of money.

"So this is it, then," I said.

Greg rolled his eyes. "No, Hannah, this is not it. You're going to get lost for two weeks, during which time you are going to decide whether or not you actually want this job."

"Will I be paid for getting lost?"

"What do you think?"

I sighed.

"Hannah," said Greg. "You have it in you to be a good investigator. You're ambitious. Determined. Stubborn. Intelligent. When you first came here, you were also professional. And yet . . . right now. . . . You're not distinguishing between data, facts, as opposed to judgment, supposition. I know you've got stuff going on, but who hasn't? You know two things about Charlie's dad—he's divorced, he wants to pay less maintenance—and you're automatically believing a third—he's a bad guy. It's dangerous thinking. I can't have you going all moral on me. Understanding the psychology of the human condition was never your special subject, but at least you managed to fake an interest. Now you've gone to the other extreme and you're identifying with people. What's that all about?"

I made an I'm-an-idiot face and looked at my shoes. "So Ron gets my job, does he?"

"No," said Greg.

I allowed myself a tight smile. "Good," I said, "because he's a moron."

"Now, now," said Greg. But he didn't meet my eyes. Another time Ron had distinguished himself was when he broke a car's taillight in order to track it. Berk. Why break the law? You just buy a reflector strip from Halfords and stick it on the rear bumper. It's a little plastic strip, double-sided, you push it on and walk off, takes two seconds. Your headlights illuminate it, and because it's where the valance comes down at the bottom of the car, no one notices.

"Your position," said Greg, "will remain open for those two weeks. As I said, use that time to consider what this job entails, and whether you are prepared to give what it takes. I'm not saying you have to be bent. More . . . *flexible*. I pay you not to lie to me. I don't expect you to waste my time. If you have a problem with your commissions, say so."

"I don't have a problem with my commissions, I had a problem with *this* commission. Did you see Charlie's mother? Does she look like a woman rolling in wealth? Her ex is paying her nothing, I bet, and now he wants to pay her less than nothing. I just . . . what's that little boy going to miss out on because of us? You've always said, Greg, that we make a difference. But what if it's the *wrong* difference?"

"I like to think our intentions are good," said Greg. "I like to think that I am ruthlessly compassionate."

I wanted to say that he was compassionate, but I knew he wouldn't want to hear it. Greg was a man who spent his days solving other people's problems. One time, the grandparents of a toddler had applied for custody because her parents were "unsuitable." Greg had to deliver the first lot of papers, give the parents notification. Because there's always a second batch to deliver, you can't make enemies. Greg had picked his way up a "garden path" heaped with decaying rubbish and dog shit. He'd walked in the door, and inside was a three-year-old with maggots in her arm. She'd reached out to him, he'd said she had eyes like saucers. He couldn't touch her, he'd have ruined everything. He'd had to walk away. I was in the car, waiting. He'd called social services, told them to get there *now*. The jobsworth at the other end had tried to tell him she was going home. Greg had persuaded her otherwise; he was shaking. There was a happy ending. The grandparents got the kid. They were "rough as nuts," Greg said, but they loved her, would do their best. Even so, I knew he still had nightmares about that child. You could see it in him; he still tasted and smelled that job. I knew it meant something to him that he'd done his bit to get that kid out of there. I also knew that unshockable, unshakable Greg had been shocked, shaken, that this child lived in a terraced house in a big city, that neighbors must have seen the state of her, and yet not one person *acted*. We'd returned to work and Greg had shut himself in his office. But on no account should *I* get emotionally involved with a case.

I sighed and began to clear my desk.

"So were you listening? I want you to use this time to think. Think about what sort of person you are, Hannah. Not everyone is cut out for this. You were once, but people change. Then again, there are different sorts of approach to the job. Me, I find you almost can't help break the Data Protection Act in this business. But I know enough PIs who're as straight as they come. And maybe you're one of those, Hannah. But maybe you're not a PI at all.

Maybe you're happy to take what you see at face value. Maybe the truth is something you can take or leave. Maybe, Hannah, your true calling is as a *lawyer.*"

There was no need to insult me.

I picked my mobile off my desk and tried not to feel like a loser. It didn't even help that my mobile was silver and the size of a matchbox. (I'd upgraded after seeing Jack's.) I was a girl with the best gadgets, the smallest phone, the biggest TV. And yet I felt like the girl with the biggest phone, the smallest TV. I felt as if I was walking around and everyone was *assuming* I owned a big fat mobile phone. Gabrielle had something similar. Everyone, for years and years, thought she was vegetarian. As a voracious meat eater (she used the Atkins Diet like a bus, on, off, on, off), she found this offensive. You can tell a lot about yourself from what people assume about you, which is why I never ask. Jason, when we first met, offered the assumption that I was a girl who never filled her car with petrol, who ignored the red light until the vehicle conked out in the street. I saw where he was coming from, but actually I am *obsessive* about maintaining a full tank. It's part of the job, being a bit of a Girl Scout, prepared for any eventuality. Cash, credit cards, full tank, bag with a change of jacket. You never know what the subject is going to do. I was grateful, then, for my job, that it made me mysterious, unpredictable.

I walked out of Hound Dog, whistling. Greg was not going to see me cry like a girl. But I clenched my teeth so hard, I was surprised they didn't shatter in my mouth. My job was my *identity.* I was big phone, small telly girl without it. I felt exposed, naked, like one of those furless cats. It was horrible.

I got home and slammed the door. I didn't want to see anyone. I thought of calling Jack, but I couldn't. I didn't feel like an attractive proposition. Even if you're selling a can of beans, presentation is all. I sat on my sofa, didn't switch on the TV, just stared at its silent gray face.

What would I do for two weeks? An enforced break on no pay doesn't put you in the holiday mood, even if you are free to watch films in the afternoon.

I rang my father.

"Sugar pumpkin! How *are* you?"

"I've been better, Roger."

I paused. Here was I, disengaged from Jason, a family pariah (I suspected that if I didn't force myself upon Gabrielle, my mother, or my father, there was a good chance I'd never hear from any of them again), dismissed from my job, sodden with regret about not seeing my grandma before she died, appalled about Ollie leaving Gabrielle—and my father hadn't called. He wasn't like some men. He was perfectly able to pick up the phone in a social situation and *chat*.

"Darling, I am so sorry I haven't been in touch, I've not had a minute to call my own—I've been in the office sorting out dramas, all the while organizing a *real* drama—Inimitable Theatre's production of *Separate Tables* opens on Wednesday night! But I've been with you in spirit. Martine has assigned herself our personal go-between, and hoorah for giving Jason the heave-ho, he would have made you miserable. That fellow was too . . . *inconsiderate*."

"I didn't realize the play was still going ahead," I said. "What with Grandma dying, me out of a job—yes, I was told today—Ollie leaving Gabrielle—you knew?—my engagement being announced in the press and called off the same day, making me the talk of the Suburb—everyone in the family seems to be cracking up, I'm surprised there's time for the play."

My heart battered my chest. I had never spoken to my father like this; it bordered on rude and was unprecedented. I tensed to be shouted at.

"Oh, Hannah," said my father instead. "Oh, Hannah," in a deep, warm voice. "You poor love. Now let me say this, *no* one in the Suburb is laughing at you. Everyone was greatly saddened to hear the marriage was off."

Forgive my cynicism, I curled my lip. There's a red minibus that speeds round the tree-lined roads of the Suburb delivering Filipino maids hither and thither, and when the woman next door had a heart attack and her son called the ambulance, the minibus *hooted* the ambulance for blocking the road. This, after the driver and his passengers had watched the ambulance men transporting the woman's prone body on a stretcher from the house, like a pack of Romans watching a lion eat a Christian.

I doubted that the Suburb was saddened to hear my marriage was off. I said so.

"Oh, Hannah," said Roger for the third time. "I know what you need. You need a *treat!*"

My ears pricked up. Even though I'm not five.

"What you need, my darling, is to eat a fancy meal, in a fancy restaurant, wearing fancy clothes! I'll have to leave dress rehearsal promptly, but sod all that! My daughter comes first! I have the perfect place, Michelin starred, I shall call up using my deepest voice and the name Rockerfeller, and let's see if they dare refuse me a table! I'll pick you up at eight-thirty. Now chin up, and best frock! Ta-ta!"

Some people sneer at grand gestures. I don't. I find the "grand" bit overrides the "gesture." Anyway, I had a tricky question to ask my father, and—short of asking it in the middle of a nick surrounded by coppers—a fancy restaurant, where no one could raise their voice or hand, was the perfect venue.

32.

I won't deny I myself am annoying, but other people are more annoying. Even people I like. I think highly of Gabrielle, yet even she has habits that make my stomach clench. For instance, her endless comments on everyone else's diets. She once watched me devour a heap of pasta with cheese sauce and said, "You eat a lot of white food." I think she'd have preferred me to step into the street and spear an antelope.

Jason annoyed me in a million ways, one of them by not picking up his feet when he walked, another by replying "Sterling" when the bank teller asked how he wanted his cash. Ollie by visiting my flat and leaving a souvenir jammed in the toilet, which Jason then presumed was mine and freaked out about ("I'm not getting rid of it, we'll have to call a plumber," etc.). Martine by loudly snorting air up her nose to clear it and thinking this socially acceptable. Greg, his public use of toothpicks (would he *floss* in a restaurant?). My mother . . . you know about. But my father was faultless.

Until now. He stood a little wonky on his pedestal, wobbled occasionally. He'd righted himself each time, but it had shaken my confidence. I was supersensitive to his every word, alert to any possible slip of judgment. So far, this evening I hadn't caught him out. He pulled up on time in his black Volvo C70 ("one of the world's safest convertibles"), held open every door, remarked favorably on my hairstyle. And the restaurant, when we reached it, was very special. It wasn't a place I'd go to eat if I was hungry, but it was a lovely experience.

We were greeted by a swarm of besuited men and women who smiled unceasingly and competed to offer us drink, seats, wine lists, menus, canapes, a cocktail glass of pale froth "compliments of the chef." I worried he'd spat in it, but Roger told me it was *espumantay duh Pimms*—don't quote me on the spelling—and drained his through a straw.

The room was white, with floor-to-ceiling windows like a greenhouse. We overlooked what appeared to be a pond, but up close, it was the depth of a puddle. There were flame lights across it. "A fire and water mow-teef," Jack would have said, in a northern accent, mocking. Nice or tacky, depending. England always struggled in the heat, and I liked that this place was smoothly Mediterranean, as if born to it.

The food was presented like art. It was delicious but sparse, and I had to pad out each course with bread. My father sighed and leaned back in his daddy bear armchair. *I* was seated on a wall sofa, and my feet didn't reach the ground. I swung them, like a little girl, and swizzled the straw in my chocolate milkshake. I was psyching myself up to speak and reckoned the best way was to cram as much sugar into my system as I could.

(Another of Gabrielle's comments: "You're *addicted* to sugar!" Said while ticking off on each finger what I'd eaten that day: "Ricicles! White bread and honey and peanut butter! Baked potato! Coke! Honey-roasted peanuts! Baked beans! Dates! Apple juice! Lion bar! Pasta! Mascarpone sauce! Coffee with full cream milk and two sugars! Coke! Apple pie! Raw cookie dough ice cream!" *I'd* been pleasantly surprised at my balanced diet.)

My father refused to be alarmed that Ollie had left Gabrielle. "A storm in a teacup," he said twice. "They'll make it up. Best not interfere in other people's marriages."

Then he'd wiped his mouth with his napkin, to show that no more was to be said on the matter. I was desperate to say, "Yes, but we don't even know where Ollie *is,* aren't you worried?" but I refrained. If he didn't wish to discuss it, fine. I'd sacrifice this concern for another, more pressing. I was braced for the shake and the crème brûlée to turn my veins sticky with glucose when Roger pre-empted me.

"So," he said. "Now that Jason's out of the picture, I suppose you'll want to bring Jack to the play!"

I swallowed. I wasn't imagining this. I glanced at my father over the table. It was a mark of this restaurant's quality that there was no candle placed smack in its middle like a flashlight shone in your eye.

"Why are you so pro-Jack?"

The question shot out baldly. I'd meant to soften it with a "tell me" or a "can I ask," but it never worked that way with me.

If this were a film and my father the villain, the camera would have zoomed to his face, where a muscle would tense in his cheek, betraying his anger and discomfort. I've always thought that a cheap trick—I mean, what ham-faced actor can't clench their jaw? They're all masters of it at Inimitable Theatre. For the record, my father's jaw remained unclenched.

He said, "I think he would be good for you, Hannah. That's all. I want to see you with the right person."

It frustrated me that he wanted to see me with *any* person. I disliked the universal habit—common to any old busybody with a vague blood tie—of meddling with their younger relatives' love lives. I couldn't get away from the thought that they were making plans for my vagina, hunting down suitable penises for it. Surely this was a private, personal endeavor, no one else's business? It was the reason I failed English A Level; I found Jane Austen virtually pornographic.

And yet vaginas weren't my present concern.

"Right," I said. "You're very keen that he comes to see the play."

"Absolutely!" said my father, smiling broadly. "I thought it would be nice for you to bring someone, and Jack knows all the family. It would be very relaxed, very chilled."

I wished he wouldn't use words like "chilled." *I* was too old to use words like "chilled."

And then in for the kill. "Daddy. Did you know that Jack is an actors' agent? A very successful actors' agent?"

I gripped my seat as if it were perched on a cliff edge. The way my heart beat, it might have been.

"*Noooooooo!*" said my father. And then, in a tone of hurt and shock, "Han-nah! You didn't think I . . . ?" And then chiding but affectionate, "Now, how long have you known me?" And then stern but understanding, "You've gone through a rough patch, been betrayed by a lot of people, Jason, your boss, your mother—"

"Well, to be honest, Mum's been fine, actually, I think the salt in the meat loaf was—"

"*Wwwwh*atever. All I'm saying is, your trust in people close to you has understandably been compromised, but I have to say, I am *quite* taken aback at your extremely offensive intimation that I could ever, would ever, stoop so low as to use my own daughter to promote my silly little acting career—it's not even a career, it's a hobby, a self-indulgence, an escape—if I even *dreamed* for one picosecond that your imagination had taken off on such a warped, vicious route, I would never, never have suggested it. In fact, I insist, *don't* bring Jack to the play, I couldn't bear it if you were to harbor even the twinkle of a suspicion that I had tricked you into bringing him to satisfy my own selfish ends. Now, Hannah sweetness, do you *swear* to me that you will on no account bring Jack Forrester to see your old dad make a fool of himself onstage this Wednesday night at seven in the Old School Hall?"

I was almost snapped in two with guilt.

"Daddy," I said, "I'm bringing Jack to the damn play, end of story, accept my most servile apologies, and let's forget this conversation; let's scrape it from our minds like, ah, mud off our boots. Pardon, do I want coffee? Roger, are you having? Decaffeinated, please, only if it's decaffeinated."

The trouble with me, I realized the second the words left my mouth, was that I'd do anything to please my father. It was pathological, although the sugar rush hadn't helped. Even if I *thought* I was annoyed with Roger, that deeper need overrode my annoyance. I felt sick with myself, like a reformed alcoholic sneaking a slug of whiskey. I might as well have promised my father entitlement to the throne.

But . . . I wanted to speak to Jack. His last words to me at the theater rolled around my head like marbles. *I would have looked after you forever if you'd let me.*

I was beginning to see that Jack was so protective of his feelings, almost every emotion was hidden behind a shield of possibilities. You could never be certain of what he meant unless *you* took a risk.

The next morning, I thought about it and thought about it and rushed to the toilet retching, and then I called Jack at his office. I was thinking that if he said, "How are you?" perhaps I could reply, "Single."

How to put a man off you forever.

His assistant answered, with the air of a doorman. "Jack Forrester's office. Can I help you?"

"Yes, please. It's Hannah Lovekin. I'd like to speak to him. Is he, is he there?"

"May I ask what it's concerning?"

"I'm his ex-wife."

"Oh! Sorry. I thought you were an actor wanting representation! One second, I'll put you through."

After a long pause, Jack came on the line. "We really shouldn't be speaking."

I pressed my lips together to stop a gasp of relief escaping. "Jack," I said. I loved the sound of his name in my mouth. "I wanted you to know that I ended my engagement to Jason." I paused. Waited. Silence.

I closed my eyes briefly and added, "And I do think that a lot of what you said at the theater, about me being . . . jumpy around intimacy . . . that's probably correct. So, er, well noticed."

I stopped. Nothing.

"Look, I wondered if I could come and see you. Anywhere you like. Any time. I'm not working right now. Later today, I thought?"

"Hannah. I don't know."

"Please."

"I've got a lot of work on."

"Well, maybe I could meet you at your office, after work."

"What, come to my office?"

"Yes."

"You'll have to wait around."

"Fine."

"Hannah, I think you have this idea that some men just spring back into shape, that they're immune to pain."

"Oh! I don't think I think that! I hope I don't think that, I'm not sure I've ever thought about it."

"You should."

"Jack!"

"Yes?"

"I'll come to your office, then, tonight at, say, seven."

"What?"

"Please."

"Christ, okay."

I wiped off my lipstick immediately after, feeling flat. It had cost me a lot to ring him, and he knew that. Yet he hadn't given me *a thing*. Still, I suppose you can't expect every encounter to be smoldering.

Exactly eight hours later, I sat in the corner of Jack's office on a small hard chair, watching him work. There was a massive oak desk between us. He had said one word to me ("Hello") between a series of endless and indecipherable phone conversations.

"Well, if I *did* take you on, I'd get you out of the soap as soon as possible. And no press or publicity. No more being papped in short skirts outside Click at 3 A.M. A third series? Turn it down. You can't be frightened of turning things down. People who come out of soaps are very hard to get jobs for. Snobbery, darling. Your choice. It's going to be hard to get you seen for, say, a Shakespeare film, but that's the aim. The Donmar with a good director. Anything with Sam Mendes. A combination of film and good theater. One-off TV if it's good. Ideally, a dour maid in *Pride and Prejudice,* whatever. Something brilliant at the National. We've got to keep the balance, keep the door open. Have a think, we'll talk, mm-hmm. Bye.

"Venetia? That breakdown's come through. Tomorrow at ten suit you? We'll discuss which parts we're going to suggest on. Yeah, two main parts, not cast. I think they're looking for genuine Irish clients for this. Tilly's reading the script tonight. Where are you? Unlucky. He was probably looking through the curtain to see where you were. See you then, bye.

"What? I know. We got the tip-off. *News of the World.* They've got the quote. All it needs is corroboration. *I* don't, I never say a word. Pact with the devil. All I can say is, it's not major. Okay.

"Lucien? Typical. Hasn't worked for months, then he gets two things that conflict. I spoke to *Vanity Fair.* No. Got to be Gloucester on Thursday, it's the only day they've got the windmill. Terence. He's playing opposite him. Thursday in Prague, *has* to be, Terence can't do any other day. Alternative windmills? I'll get Tilly on to it. Good, bye.

"Clara, sweetheart? Jack. You sitting down? The deal is done. Yes! I know! Legally contracted! Drinks somewhere starry, it's a *date.* Not at all, well done *you.* If you've got talent, things turn around. I've passed on your details to the production office. Costume will call you tomorrow. The production assistant already called the office, wanting to know where to send the latest draft. It's being biked to your flat first thing. I know, very exciting! Sleep tight, darling, big kiss."

After this particular call, I huffed loudly through my nose and looked sour. Jack checked his watch. "Darling," he said. "Don't you pull a strop with me. I'm not about to drop my life because your Thought for Today involves *me.* You'll probably be back with Jason tomorrow."

I was indignant. "No I won't!"

Jack stood up. "No, you won't. That was unfair. Sorry."

"Huh," I said.

"Ah, Hannah," he said, grabbing his coat. "I *am* sorry. I'm also . . . jumpy. To have any sort of meaningful relationship with a person, you've got to trust."

Good grief, I thought, here it comes at last, as long awaited as a royal baby! The admission of fallibility. It finally dawns on Jack that while others may be at fault, *Jack* doesn't trust, and thus Jack is not perfect!

"You don't trust me, you don't trust yourself, you don't trust anyone. Not much has changed in ten years. And now that's out the way and we understand each other, would you care to go out to eat?"

240

33.

I couldn't say "*What?*" without sounding petty. We were going out to eat, which was pretty damn civilized considering our last encounter. I had to be content with that. I also knew where we should go to eat. Fred's Books. Fred's Books was, surprise, a bookshop owned by a man called Fred. It had a café, boasting sausage and mash, fish pie, and bread and butter pudding. There were also purple squashy sofas on which you could snuggle up with your purchases and a mug of hot chocolate.

When we'd first met, Jack and I had gone there quite a bit. It had a happy aura. Fred was fat, camp, and loved books. He said that a lot of booksellers might as well sell sprouts for all the interest they took in what they did. Fred treated his bookshop like an extension of his home. He loved to discuss books with anyone. He hosted book readings. He liked what he liked, he wasn't a snob. He didn't snort when I said I liked ghost stories. When one author suggested that there ought to be a separate bestsellers' list for children's books, as J. K. Rowling was hogging the chart, Fred said, "How about a separate chart for John Grisham? *He* takes up more than his share."

It was like hanging out at your bossy uncle's house. I hadn't been there for a while. I hoped it would imbue Jack with a rosy glow of nostalgia.

I don't know. I think I just wanted him to like me.

"I know," I said. "Let's go to Fred's."

I expected Jack to say, "*Fred's!*" but he said, "Who?"

"Fred's Books," I said. "You remember. Near Golders Green."

If Jack did remember, he wasn't saying. "That's a bit far out, isn't it? Will it be open?"

"It's open till eleven every night," I replied, trying to sound unbothered.

Jack shrugged. "Fred's then."

I stifled a sigh and watched him drive. He was a good driver. His car was a bit of a calling card. A red Audi with lavish curves. I felt that my Vauxhall, a dignified gray old lady, would think it vulgar. He hadn't commented on my appearance, which was, frankly, brilliant. (In comparison to what it usually was.) The St. Tropez had encouraged me to brave real sunlight, and I had a bit of a *tint*. My hair was glossy, like a horse, I was wearing black wedge shoes with ribbons that did up round my ankles, and my fingernails were neither ragged nor black with filth. Maybe Jack would have noticed if I'd turned up with my head cut off.

I wanted him to admire me.

No. More than that, I thought with a blush. I wanted him to *want* me.

I'd have to make the effort to be alluring.

I wasn't quite sure how or where to begin. I tried to think of Sophia Loren, how she acted in her films, but couldn't remember any. The only thing I could think of, an indictment of us all, was to *say nothing*. I arranged my legs together, rather than let them hang open like a brickie's, and gazed coolly out of the window. Then I became aware of movement on my shoulder. I looked down and screamed.

"Fuck!" shouted Jack, "What is it!"

"Argh, argh, oh God, it was a fly! On my shoulder!"

"A *fly*?"

"Urgh," I said, and shuddered. A horrible lazy fat fruit fly sat on my shoulder like a parrot. Now, thanks to my ninja brushing and stamping technique, it lay squashed and dead on the Audi floor mat. Jack sniggered. I shot him a look.

"I'm not scared of flies," I said.

"Of course not."

"It was the shock. It was just *sitting* there, like in a horror film," I said. "It's disturbing, a fly on your shoulder."

I shuddered again. I hate flies. I hate the way they get in your house and crawl over food, when they've crawled over dog shit. I also knew that screaming because there was a fly on your shoulder was not alluring. No one did this to attract a man. I'd tried to align myself with Sophia Loren. I'd managed dog shit.

Jack giggled.

I glared at him. "It was in *your* car," I said.

We stepped inside Fred's, and I cheered up, glancing at Jack sideways on, to see if it jolted him. He smiled at me, like you might smile at anyone you didn't hate.

I marched to a corner table, the corner table we always sat at. Jack pulled away a chair for me and sat down himself. I wondered if a phone book had landed on his head recently, perhaps he had amnesia. Then he picked up the menu, peered over it, and said, "Hot chocolate with extra chocolate, a freshly squeezed orange juice, and buttered raisin toast with jam for Ratfink?"

My heart went *boof* in my chest like a boxing glove.

I tweaked the menu from his grasp, gave it a cursory glance, and said, "Two soft-boiled eggs with, mm, soldiers of toast for Muttley?"

Jack started laughing, and so did I. "Don't say that," he said, "like it was a special request made by me because I'm five. That's what it says on the menu. 'Soldiers of toast'!"

"Yes, but you could have said 'Do you mind if I cut up my *own* toast, I am old enough now.' "

Jack pouted. "It's nice to have your toast cut up for you. People come here for the childhood they never had. You know, food like Mother never used to make."

I smiled. This was more like it. Teasing, chatting, proper conversation, now we were getting—

"Hannah? Hannah Lovekin?"

I looked up, ready to be tough, and saw a powdery-faced old lady smiling down at me.

"Er, yes."

"I *knew* it was you!" cried the old lady. "I'm Millie Blask, your old Brown Owl!"

I tried to shuffle my shocked features into an expression of joy and stood up. "Brown Owl!" I said. "How are you?"

Guilt was already turning my face pink, I could feel it. When I was a Brownie, at the end of each session, we stood in a circle holding hands behind our backs, and Brown Owl would squeeze the hand of one of the girls next to her. "The Squeeze" was thus passed from hand to hand until Brown Owl said "Stop!" Then, whoever had the Squeeze would have to take it home and feed it on good deeds, or it would "shrivel up and die." Once or twice, a Brownie forgot she'd had the Squeeze. "Er . . . I hung up my coat," she'd stammer the following week. "I . . . er . . . took my plate to the sink." "Well!" Brown Owl would say tartly. "The Squeeze has been fed on bread and water!" Little did she know, the Squeeze had shriveled up and died years before, when I'd schlepped it home and done nothing that wasn't 100 percent selfish for seven days. The Brownies had been trying to revive a corpse.

"I'm very well, thank you," said Brown Owl. "My son is a member of the Inimitable Theatre Company, so I hear bits and bobs about you now and then."

"Oh, from my father."

"From your mother, in fact."

"Oh! Right, right."

"Well, nice to see you again, dear. You were a good Brownie. I'll let you get back to your young man." She smiled at Jack. Jack smiled at her.

"Nice to see you too, Brown Owl," I said and sat down. My face was beet, I knew it. I'm not saying Brown Owl was a fly on my shoulder, but nor was she Sophia Loren.

Jack grinned at me, sucked in his cheeks, and ordered our food. I gave up on trying to be alluring.

"Your dad's still doing Am Dram, is he?"

"Mm," I said. "He is. They've got some good people. Funny enough, they've got an opening night tomorrow. Terence Rattigan's *Separate Tables*." I paused. "I'm going. You could come with if you like."

"Whew," said Jack. "And there's an offer I can refuse."

"There's no need to be snitty. You were always going on about discovering people at theater schools and youth theater and Am Dram."

"Yeah. More theater schools and youth theater than Am Dram, though, darling."

"Oh, don't darling *me,* Jack. I'm not one of your actresses!"

"Darling," said Jack, lowering his lids in an approximation of sleazy, "they call themselves 'actors' these days, even, especially, the women. And I've only slept with an actress once. After we split."

"Oh?" I said.

He grinned. "Yes. Midscrew, I noticed she had her head slightly to one side, and I realized that a script was open on the table and she was reading it over my shoulder."

"Oh!" I paused. "So . . . *do* you sleep with a lot of actresses?"

"No!" cried Jack. "What did I just say? God, I mean, you *could.* My boss says there's not an actress you—or rather he, he's a lot more powerful than me—couldn't go to bed with. But, bloody hell, it would be awful. They'd just talk about themselves 24/7, 'Do you think I should do *this*? Or *this*?' The neurosis level is incredibly high. I made the mistake once. After the divorce was a bad time. Now I pretend my clients don't have sex lives. It would be like imagining your parents doing it."

"Oh, okay." I stopped short of adding, "good."

Jack pressed his fork into the paper napkin, making steel teeth marks. "I don't mean to be snide about your dad's Am Dram. It's just . . . I go to so much theater, all the time. To talent spot, to see clients perform. The other week, I got in real trouble." He giggled to himself. I smiled, remembering this habit. He looked at me from under his eyelashes. In the nicest possible way, receiving his old mischievous look felt like a stab to the chest. "You just sneak into the theater for the second half, if you can get away with it. Anyway, this guy was Duncan in *Macbeth*. I thought, I'll get there after the interval. It was out in Stratford, such a long drive. Anyway, I get there. And I realize that Duncan gets killed before the interval. Normally you can bluff, but this client is quite . . . luvvy. So there's me going 'Marvelous direction!' and he's saying, 'Yes, but do you think I really got it? What about the castle scene?' 'Oh! I thought all the castle scenes were great!' "

I laughed, shook my head. "It sounds a nightmare."

Jack shook his head too. "You're selling people who dress up for a living. It *is* ridiculous. But it's fun. I like all of my clients."

"Do you have anyone famous?"

Jack wrinkled his nose. "Not really. No 'institutions.' I avoid *celeb*-y clients. You end up discussing what they're going to wear on *Good Morning*. It would drive me mad. 'Yeth, but Jaack, do you think I should have my hair *up*! Or *down*?!' And then, nothing's ever good enough. 'Ja-ack, the towels in my hotel room are too rough!' I can't stand all that. You're a counselor and a shrink and a business adviser anyway, but the celeb-y ones treat you like a servant too. I mean, *everyone's* paranoid. They'll be doing panto in Exmouth, and they'll ring up and say, 'I've just got my ruler out, and so-and-so's billing is *twelve* percent bigger than mine.' "

"What," I said. "They measure the typeface! How do you deal with them?" I suspected myself of asking bogus questions purely for the pleasure of watching his mouth move.

"I don't, anymore. There was one fat old grandam of soap wanted me to get her on some closed list for a premiere, and I couldn't. She shouted, 'Oh, you're bloody useless!' I said, 'Well, *you* carry more weight than I do, *you* call them,' and put the phone down."

I raised an eyebrow. "You told a fat woman that she 'carried more weight' than you?"

"I know. Right after, I realized what it sounded like. She never spoke to me like that again. But you have to be direct. One ex-client was complaining about not getting a meeting—an audition—for a part he could have played in his sleep, and I said, 'To be honest, they think you're an absolute arsehole.' You can't get to the point where you're frightened of your client, because then you end up giving them bad advice. You need"—he grinned—"strong moral fiber. Some agents get too clingy with their clients. You've got to be supportive in the bad times, honest in the good times. It's the good times that people tend to go off the rails."

He paused. "It sounds like I'm moaning, but I love it. What about you? Are you still loving being a PI?"

"I'm not sure," I said. "In fact, Hound Dog and I have parted ways. Maybe for good."

"Why?"

"Ah, I wasn't doing my job properly. It was fair enough. I've been told to have a think about whether I'm committed."

"I'm surprised. I'd have thought it was the perfect job for you."

"Why?"

"Well . . . you're *observing*, aren't you? You're not involved. There's no risk of getting hurt, there's nothing emotional about your job, it's all about fact, isn't it?"

"Actually, that's why my job's on the line. Apparently, I got too emotionally involved with a case."

"Did you?"

"I think people overuse the word 'emotional' where women are concerned."

Jack grinned. "Are you speaking from experience or in general?"

"In general."

"Yeah. Thought so."

"What do you mean?"

"Work it out, Sherlock!"

He winked at me, which in Jack terms was like a big fat kiss, and I smiled. He was fond of me, and really, that was a good start, a good basis for . . . something. And thank the Lord for Fred's Books, it was a gift to conversation. I think it was because you were warm, fed well, comfortable—babied, frankly—it made you feel there was nothing to worry about, it relaxed your brain. This was not always a good thing. It meant that I blurted out whatever was in my head. Do chickens have personalities? (Jack had never known a chicken well enough to say.) Why is the biggest chocolate in the box always disgusting? (Some sort of greed check.) I'd really like to go back in time with, say, a flashlight, and show off to medieval people. (A *flashlight*? They're going to kill you as a witch—take a machine gun and an armored car.)

"Well, maybe, Jack," I said, picking a raisin out of my raisin bread, "I *did* get a little emotional in this one instance. Maybe this is the new me, and you're wrong, I *have* changed."

Jack tilted his head to one side, pretended to consider. "Well, maybe, Hannah, you've changed a small bit. You definitely seem less . . . *uptight.*"

I gasped and threw my napkin at him.

He laughed. "So where's this thing tomorrow night? I'm coming, aren't I?"

I beamed. "Great! I'm so pleased. It's at the Old School Hall, Barley Lane. Everyone will be getting there for six forty-five. And don't you dare turn up after the interval!"

"Six forty-five it is." Jack got a thoughtful look on his face. "Is, er, all your family going to be there?"

I nodded. "Well. Angela is."

"How is Angela?"

I sighed. "Not great. She and Dad are still together. More . . . *spatially* than emotionally."

"Right. Right. Okay. Is it all right if I bring someone?"

A dry scratchy ball of chewed-up raisin toast sat in my mouth and made it hard for me to speak. I gulped it down, like a boa swallowing a rat. *Bring* someone? Like who? Some *girl?*

All the hope rushed out of me like a ghost. He was still seeing other women! And . . . I'd thought we were connecting. The man had said *how could you think I didn't love you?* What was I supposed to think. Although, legally speaking it wasn't the same as *I love you.* Jack was like fucking Shakespeare, everything he said had a million possible meanings. I had to face it. I wanted to get back with him. And there was little chance of that. I'd misread every signal. I had as much social nous as a dysfunctional serial killer, one of the fancy American types.

"Bring anyone you like." I smiled. I wanted to cry suddenly, in that way where you gasp for breath, that dry hacking sort of sob, where all the tears are locked inside you, where all the world's suffering constricts your chest and the pain is so terrible it physically crushes you, and you welcome it because you need to die.

I settled instead for clearing my throat.

34.

The saving grace of being angry with someone is, you can always take it out on someone else. (Which is why my one experience of therapy did not impress. I realized that, were therapy ever to be successful, one's anger would become nontransferable, like a check. It could be cashed only by the person to whom it was owed. How extraordinarily life-sapping.) After saying a curt good night to Jack, I tried Ollie's mobile for the tenth time. He hadn't been answering, but now he did, and I screamed at him.

"Where the hell are you, and why the fuck aren't you back with your family?"

Ollie cut me off.

I held my breath for a bit, then rang again.

Ollie answered sounding hurt. "You've got no right speaking to me like that, Ner. You have no idea what it's been like. I like how you blame me 100 percent, you don't even consider that Gab might have been a right cow."

I tutted. "Oliver. I don't think you should be calling your wife 'a right cow.' I don't even know what that *means*."

"I think you know what 'a right cow' is, Ner."

"Okay, I admit, I do. It's a nasty, sexist term that a man applies to a woman when she dares to behave in a way that isn't to his liking."

Ollie sighed down the phone. "Ner," he said, "I am not a difficult bloke. But her temper and her moods have worn me right down. She's irrational!"

"I'll be the judge of that," I said. "Like how?"

"Okay. How about, Jude's still on the tit."

"I beg your pardon?"

"Gab is still breast-feeding Jude. And Jude will only drink from her left breast. So, anyway—I don't know how much you know about all this."

"I know nothing."

"Fine. So the left boob is full of milk, and the other's empty. Because if he won't drink from it, it stops making milk, because there's no demand for it."

"Gotcha."

"The other night I come home and she's flopped on the bed, topless, sobbing, so distraught she can't speak. I thought she'd been attacked. I finally get out of her what's wrong: 'I've got one massive boob and one tiny one!' "

I tried not to laugh. "Oliver, Gabrielle's appearance is very important to her. And you. And when you've had a baby, I suppose your image takes a knock. I think she looks great, but maybe I didn't look that hard. You've got to be more patient, Ol. You've got your work problems making you short-tempered too."

"You talk like *she* had the baby."

"Oh, a thousand apologies, were *you* the one who gave birth?"

"She gave birth, *we* had the baby. She went through a lot, physically, and I'm in awe of her for that. I know it takes time to recover, and I tried to support her. But you talk like she's a single parent and I'm just some tosser hanging round the house. *I've* gone through all the baby dramas with her, the joy, the fear, the panic, the lack of sleep, mainly the panic and the lack of sleep. Gab talks out her feelings. Just because I don't, doesn't mean I don't have them. I *do* want to tell her things. Tell her that I appreciate all she does, that I understand it's hard. But then she snaps at me and I say the opposite of what I meant to say."

"Ol," I said. "I'm sorry if I spoke out of turn. I think you were right. A few days apart seems to have been good for you. The important thing is, you and Gab both want to make things better. It's about agreeing how."

"How do you know Gab wants to make things better?"

"I talked to her. You should try it. She loves you very much. She said."

Silence.

"Ol," I said. "Where are you, by the way?"

"At Mum and Dad's."

"What!"

"Yeah." Ollie sounded embarrassed. "Roger said I could stay. Mum was *not* pleased."

"He said you could stay? But I . . . we went out last night, he never said!"

"Maybe he knew you wouldn't approve. Mum didn't."

"How could you tell?"

Ollie made a noise that was not quite a laugh. "She was quite vocal about it. For Mum. She wanted to know what she'd say if Gab rang."

"Well, absolutely. It would seem like she was taking sides. That was my exact same problem. What did you say?"

"Roger shushed her. I felt bad about it, but I did need a place to stay."

"Yes," I said. "Okay. Well, what are you going to do now?"

"Maybe go home, see my child and wife."

"Can I suggest something?"

"Go on."

"Take a fat bouquet and a pushalong toy, preferably one that makes loud noises."

"Gotcha," said Ollie.

The next day, bright and early, I rang Roger.

"Hellooo!" he said. "All set for tonight?"

"I'm coming," I said. And then, as a test, "Jack isn't."

"God!" he shouted. "Why are you such an *idiot*?"

The dial tone purred in my ear, and I found myself shaking. I didn't know what to think. How could I be thirty-one and so *clueless*? Right now, not one area of my life got a tick. I'd always thought, "at least I'm not her," of my neighbor, the one with the Siamese cat. She was middle-aged, smelt faintly of boiled fish, and had once revealed that she thought of herself as her cat's "special mummy." She wasn't, she explained, the cat's *real* mummy, she was his special mummy. Uh. Huh. May I go now?

The Cat's Special Mummy was a major success story compared with me.

I'd never been renowned for being a people person (though secretly I believe that no one is a people person, it's just that some people are better than others at disguising their condescension). So it wasn't a big wow that I'd made enemies of my entire address book. The one thing I *was* supposed to be good at, however, was my job. As Jack said, there was nothing emotional about my job; it was all about fact.

Emotions were trying to grip jelly, emotions were writing an essay on what Shakespeare meant. Well, according to what's been said, the man meant ten hundred thousand contradictory things per page. But facts. Facts were *lovely*. Two plus two equals four. (Although Jack tried to argue with me on this once.) Mr. Smith tells Mrs. Smith he's stuck in traffic in Edgware, and yet the tracker we put on his car says he's doing ninety down the M11. Fact. Facts were my friends. I did not have a problem with facts. And yet it seemed that somehow, suddenly, I did.

I supposed, if I called myself a detective, I'd have to check out this curious anomaly.

I got to the Old School Hall early, around six-thirty. I could have arrived earlier and helped backstage, but I hadn't. Not that it wasn't fun. Everyone was so excited, so energetic, so enthusiastic. It embarrassed me, actually. I kept thinking, you're all doing this voluntarily in your *spare time*. I'm mean with my time. Don't ask me why, it's not like I do anything with it. The Am Dram lot showed me up. They didn't work for a charity. But it was humbling to see people giving of themselves so happily.

I'd also dug out Mum's mobile number, intending to ring her, but I hadn't done that either. I had this sickish feeling of having misjudged her. Perhaps because she had finally stopped trying to please me. When a person tries to please you, it puts them under suspicion. Now she was daring to demonstrate—to me, and others—that she thought she deserved better treatment, she thought she deserved to have a voice. It made me wonder. It was unheard of (excuse pun), Angela speaking up against my father.

I wanted to tell her that it was okay to be selfish (something I'd never had the guts to tell Brown Owl). I was beginning to see that Roger could be a little overbearing. He could shout you down, without saying a word. While I knew my mother would never allow her grief to show, no more than she'd allow her knickers to show, I felt sure that this soft breeze of rebellion had been caused by my grandmother's death. I didn't know what a bereaved person required to feel less wretched, but I suspected that being forced to appear onstage alongside your husband in his ego orgy was not it.

But there she was, carrying plates of what looked like steak and gravy, on a tray, to backstage. It was bound to be something foul—moldy bread and stale scotch eggs, covered in tinned onion soup. Here was a mystery. When food was required onstage, it was always *other* food masquerading as the *supposed* food. ("Before this, I was with the RSC, the Scottish Play, I was the leg of pork at the feast.") Why? Fact was, whatever stinky bacteria-fest they were served, the actors always ate, rather than pretended to eat. Either they were shockingly hungry, or they were act-*ors*.

I nodded at Angela, and she nodded back, white and tense. The fact that she was acting in this play and that her mother had just died had not exempted her from the gruntwork. Still, I supposed that hauling trays of food about was in character—Angela was playing Miss Cooper, the manageress of the seaside hotel in which the play was set. She was in costume: longish skirt, dull heavy blouse, firmly set hair. It was one hell of a frumpy part. I wasn't sure if my father had put her forward for it. She'd never acted before.

My father, in addition to having directed the thing, was playing John Malcolm, a character who—after many chats with Daddy about his interpretation, his choices—I felt I knew better than myself.

At the risk of killing the suspense, John, a former politician, is having a middle-of-the-road relationship with Miss Cooper. Then his young, glamorous ex-wife shows up at the hotel as a guest, having tracked him down. They'd divorced years before—she was "frigid," he was violent (all in the name of frustrated passion, though, and he *was* a northerner). He'd gone to prison for it, changed his name, and reinvented himself as a journalist. Anyway, after much ranting and declamation, John ditches Miss Cooper and gets back together with the love of his life (the one he kept hitting).

I was glad not to see Roger. He'd be in the dressing room, applying *his* makeup. I sat down in the front row, not wanting to. The hall was drafty and smelled of damp sawdust.

"Hi," said Gabrielle, slipping into the seat beside me.

"Hello!" I checked for signs of distress.

"All right, Ner," said Ollie, plonking down next to her.

"Nice to see you both," I said. They seemed a little stiff with each other, nothing worse. Gabrielle picked at his collar, which I took as a good sign. Sort of like a dog weeing on a garden post. I know that doesn't sound great.

"Where's Squeaker?" I said.

They smiled, as I knew they would. Squeaker was one of Jude's many aliases. (He was like the Red Baron, that one.) If I mentioned Jude, in Jude's absence, Gab and Ol just melted. That said, if the genuine article had been present, biting people's fingers to the bone or banging his own head on the concrete floor (as was this month's vogue), their smiles would have been no less brilliant. I liked that I could unify them this way, the platonic vision of their firstborn, in all his soft chubby glory, turned them *purry* toward each other. You could interpret their coy glances: we make a good baby.

"My mum's monstersitting," said Gab.

I smiled also. I didn't want them to see how pleased I was that they were here together. It was a start.

I looked around. Just in case. He probably wouldn't bother turning up. Oh, but there were compensations. I could see Martine, at the kiosk, arguing with the ticket guy—he was rearing back like a cat from a snake. I sighed. Settled back down beside Gab.

She glanced at me. "Are you all right, dahl?"

"Oh . . . you know."

"Please don't tell me you're missing Jason."

"*Goodness,* no!"

Gab squeezed my hand. "There's something I should have said a while back. But I didn't. I've been too wrapped up in my own stuff. I wanted to tell you, though. I knew you took Squeaker to the park. Not immediately. After you came round. It struck me that . . . you're quite . . . contrary. I was way too harsh. I apologize." She leaned close. Her hair held the scent of meadows and flowers and sunshine. "You've made some good decisions, Hannah. You have. And that means things will get better for you. Oh, look, darling, they already have."

I followed her smirk. And there stood Jack.

35.

I scanned his vicinity for willowy blondes. However, the mystery "someone" appeared to be . . . Mr. Coates, my old drama teacher. I felt confused, and embarrassed at my schoolgirl assumptions. Although I do maintain that asking if you can bring "someone" is like asking a date in for "coffee." These words have double lives. They are like unexploded bombs; you have to handle them with care, you can't chuck them about like beach balls.

So why was he here? This had to be good. Wonderful, even. My pulse was doing double time. Maybe Gab was right. Things would get better. I thought of what she'd said at the wedding dress fitting. About a man who has the power to make your heart fly.

Jack had the power to make my heart fly. He also had the power to shoot it out of the sky. Because, let's not forget, love isn't just about the flying. I knew that, more than most. And so I was not a person who was forgiving of love, but right then, I felt I could learn to be. Jack was my man and it wasn't something rational.

He stood in the aisle, tall and imperious, surveying the hall for a place to sit. Or was he looking for a person? *Me.* Mr. Coates was standing next to him, jerking his head this way and that. He looked uncomfortable. Possibly it worked both ways and clients were just as repulsed by the idea of their agents having love lives. Jack hadn't seen me yet. I darted my head this way and that, trying to catch his eye. Then, not wishing to remind him of a pelican, I stopped. But I couldn't stop smiling. Although I still couldn't understand why Jack had asked if he might bring "someone," if the someone was merely a client. No offense to Mr. Coates, but the term, "someone" implied a person of *note.*

Perhaps he was important in the business sense. Jack had said he had a lucrative career doing voice-overs. He was also, Jack had said, a fine character actor. (Which I'd presumed was showbiz shorthand for "ugly.")

Mr. Coates wasn't ugly. He was a good height, nearly as tall as Jack; he had sandy gray hair and blue eyes. He was clean shaven but a little scruffy. Even though he no longer worked in schools, he was wearing what I thought of as teacher's clothes. Khaki green cords, faded at the knees, brown suede shoes, a brown cable-knit jumper, the wool starting to unravel at the wrists. I had a flash of memory, of him not quite meeting my eyes. I must have been all of five years old.

That was quite common, wasn't it, actors being shy? Wanting to escape from their tortured selves. Only being able to do so through the medium of showing off.

"Jack Forrester," called Gabrielle, making me start. "Come and sit with us!"

Jack turned around and smiled. It was the most unrelaxing smile I'd ever seen. This made me anxious, but I attempted one of my own. Even though I had an urge to kick Gabrielle in the shin, I was pleased she'd asked him. He took a step toward us—Mr. Coates behind him, still twisting his neck about like a periscope—then stopped.

I followed his gaze to the stage, not understanding. Unless he was surprised at how Angela had aged. I wanted to tell him that the costume did her no justice. She trod down the steps at the side of the stage, closed the front doors, hurried backstage again. Martine, trundling up the aisle behind them, talking on her *mobe,* trod on Mr. Coates's heel.

"Oh," she said to Jack, ignoring Mr. Coates, who was bright red with pain. "Fort you said you weren't coming."

Jack gave her a mean look, but said nothing. Instead, he murmured in the ear of Mr. Coates, who nodded. Martine stared as they brushed past her and sat next to us. Jack stepped aside for Mr. Coates, so he sat beside Ollie. Jack seemed to be shadowing him like a minder. Plainly, you were expected to work hard for your 10 percent. It wasn't all premieres, bon mots at the *aftershow,* and lapping champagne out of women's navels (or men's).

I tried to smile at Jack and glare at Martine—what did she mean, Jack had said he wasn't coming? When, why had *she* even talked to him? Martine sat down with a thump behind us, with a cold "All right" at me. I turned my back.

Gabrielle leaned forward and smacked Jack on the hand, in a friendly way. "*Look* at you!" she cried. "What a nice surprise! Finally!"

Jack got up to kiss her. "Don't speak too soon," he said.

"No," said Ollie. "Don't."

Gab and I stared at him. What were they talking about? Ollie raised an eyebrow at Mr. Coates. Mr. Coates looked at his suede shoes. He was twiddling the loose thread at his wrist, twisting it very fast, between finger and thumb.

"Took you long enough," added Ollie after a pause.

Jack said, "Gabrielle. This is a client of mine, the actor, Jonathan Coates; Jonathan, this is the lovely Gabrielle Goldstein. She is married to . . . you remember Ollie, and his sister, Hannah Lovekin."

I was thinking, well, how come *I* don't get a "lovely" in front of my name, but it was obvious. I was also *rabid* to know why Ollie was behaving so strangely. He seemed to be torn between being rude or obsequious.

"Has Angela seen this yet?" said Ollie. I wasn't sure if the question was directed at Jack or Mr. Coates. Was he referring to the play? She was *in* the play! "It was a shame," he continued as Gab and I sat there, still and meek as sugar mice. "You wasted years of everyone's lives. Anyway." He stood up. "I can't sit around to watch this. Gab, babe, I'm sorry. It's too much. You'll see. I'm going home. I'll see you later. Good *luck*." He touched his wife tenderly, just above her jawline, and hurried from the hall.

"Wait!" I said, but Ollie was gone. "Can someone tell me what's going on?" I directed the question at Jack. Mr. Coates was hunched in a miserable mound of loose-knit brown jumper, and seemingly mute, goodness knows how he made a living. Jack sprang from his chair and crouched at my feet. "Hannah, I—look, Jonathan was desperate to—and, I, I think that—it might be none of my business, but, but if I, if we, then it *is* my business, and—you were never going to see otherwise—"

"Oh God, oh God," wailed Gab suddenly. I made an "eek" face. If Ollie had gone mad, this was proof insanity was catching, like measles. One, two, three, they all had it, I was the only one not crazy. "Oh, God"—Gabrielle covered her face with both hands—"I know what this is!"

"*What*?" I hissed.

"Hannah," said Jack, his expression serious. "Don't you remember Jonathan?"

He nudged Mr. Coates, who smiled at me. "Ah, Hannah," he said and leaned over Gabrielle to touch my hand. As he did, his voice rippled through me like deep thunder, I got a whiff of his aftershave, and it felt like a coiled spring released, snap, in my brain. I snatched back my hand, gasping, trembling. Good grief, what *was* this? This man was unlocking some feeling inside me, a bad, bad feeling.

I clutched my hair. "Someone tell me *now* what this is about or I am going to lose it."

Gabrielle, Jack, and Mr. Coates turned toward me, a frieze of regret. Jack opened his mouth to speak—and the lights dimmed.

"I—" he said.

"*Sssssssssshhhhhhhhh!*" boomed Martine. He winced apologetically at me as the curtain rose.

The play began, and while I made a point of looking in the right direction, I neither heard nor saw the action of the first scene. My heart seemed to twitch and fidget and I kept stealing sideways glances at Mr. Coates. His presence meant something awful, terror weighed in my stomach like the first day at school. My mind groped for answers that lay just out of reach. It knew what it was searching for; I hadn't a clue. And part of me wanted it to stay that way. I blocked this unauthorized search by forcing my attention back to the stage.

I could sense Gabrielle and Jack, bolt upright in their chairs beside me, as nervous as I was. Now and then I sensed their fearful gaze, and I felt like the ghost of a woman rising from the wreck of a fatal accident. Mr. Coates never looked at me once. He stared straight ahead as if hypnotized, his whole body still. He didn't laugh at the jokes, though, and he didn't stop twisting the loose threads of his jumper sleeve.

I tried to follow the story. I breathed evenly and managed to form the thought that Roger was a good actor. John Malcolm was a part that suited him. He'd described the part to me as "Heath-cliffeish" (a description meant to enlighten me). Unfortunately, it had made me think of Cliff Richard. The character my father was por-traying came across a lot less polished and polite than Cliff Richard.

I looked behind me and saw Martine mouthing his lines as he said them. Her crush on my father was out of control. I could see that Roger was handsome, with a certain charm. I could also see that the character of John Malcolm was—to an unworldly woman who didn't get that being knocked about is not romantic—dreamy in that he purported to love his ex-punching bag, sorry, wife, *"too much."* In Martine's fiction, I imagined that the hero ain't the hero unless he's giving the heroine a good old belt. That's how she knows he isn't *indifferent.*

I've always thought that love isn't a straight choice between being ignored or being pulped. (Historically, I've chosen to be ignored, but I believe that some women favor the middle ground of kindness, nurturing, and support.) Martine, however, was an old-fashioned girl. For this reason, despite her feelings for my father, she'd always remained respectful to Angela. I think she approved of my mother's subservience—as if she was excused from the sin of being my father's wife because she knew her place. (Also, I suppose, Martine saw that they were over the honeymoon period.)

I was also able to register that Angela wasn't a bad actor. Her character was supposed to have a "quiet manner" and fuss around my father—both of which came naturally—but Angela also con-veyed a managerial efficiency. I could tell she was a little scared of the audience though—she never looked our way once, whereas some of the other actors did. I could tell my father was aching to, but was restraining himself. No doubt he didn't wish to be distracted from his own genius.

However, after the scene where he and the woman playing his ex-wife fought out their differences (Martine had nothing to worry about, Geraldine Robbins could cinch in her waist all she liked, her whiny, prima-donnaish personality was anathema to my father, he didn't like women who made him compete for attention), Roger could no longer resist. Geraldine Robbins exited; my mother, as Miss Cooper, entered. It was the point where the manageress realizes that this glamorous guest of hers is her lover's ex-wife, that he's still in love with her.

"*That's her, isn't it?*" said Angela. The bitterness in her voice chilled you.

My father as John Malcolm was supposed to reply "*What?*"

"*What?*" said my father, but as he said it, I squirmed. He wasn't directing the question at Miss Cooper, but was staring straight at Jack, as if he couldn't look away. "*What?*" he said again, turning his head with effort back to Miss Cooper.

My mother was disconcerted. She gabbled her next line, asking him if this was indeed, his former wife, at ninety miles an hour.

"*Yes,*" managed my father. All credit to him he'd caught the question. His gaze darted back to the front row. I writhed in my chair, willing him to snap back into character. It was horribly obvious, more obvious than he thought, that he was distracted.

"*What's going to happen now, John?*" said my mother. There was a hint of panic in her voice, and I didn't believe she was that much of a natural. My father's head had turned a fraction away from her, toward Jack, no, he was looking at Mr. Coates, and the expression on his face was of horrified disbelief. I frowned, not understanding, tried to see what he had seen in Mr. Coates. Mr. Coates had stopped fiddling with his jumper. He was staring back at my father, a cold, fierce intensity on his face. I felt as if my insides had curdled. I held my breath involuntarily. There was supposed to be a pause, I knew, as John looks at Miss Cooper without response. But the pause wasn't supposed to be *this* long.

Then I realized that it was my mother who was supposed to speak. John doesn't reply, Miss Cooper draws the inevitable conclusion. My father's eyes were now fixed on her, shock on his face, and she looked like a nervous spaniel. She darted a glance to the front row, to see what had so disconcerted my father, and visibly staggered backward. Her mouth opened but no sound came out.

The prompt murmured, "*I see. Well, I always knew you were still in love with her . . .*"

The entire audience cringed as one, it was like a wave of denial. Which goes to show what a curious nation we are. Kids start school unable to recognize a fork, men bite the heads off kittens at barbecues, but the population is universally aghast to see anyone make a berk of themselves onstage.

"*I see,*" said Angela. "*Well, I always knew I was still . . . you were still in love with her. . . .*"

She faltered, blushing through her heavy makeup, and her ghastly expression as she faced my father—not John Malcolm, there was no more pretense here—sent a jolt of recognition thundering through me. She'd looked at me like that once, a long time ago. Fractured memories sped backward in time, jumping together, like footage of a smashed mirror rewound. I remembered something Ollie had said to Jude not that long ago, it had made my skin crawl and I hadn't known why.

"Go and see what your mother is doing."

My father had said it first, twenty-five years ago.

36.

I remembered. The bits that mattered, anyway. The rest I could piece together. I watched myself step over the doorframe. I was wearing dark green shoes with buckles and white ankle socks, probably a gray school skirt. I *felt* five years old, but maybe I was six. My father was behind me, resting his hand on my shoulder, I could feel its warm pressure.

"Go and see what your mother is doing," he whispered, pointing toward the stairs.

His voice wasn't angry, it was calm and controlled. And yet it meant you did as you were told immediately. I must have pushed open the frosted glass doors, scampered across the dogtooth oak floor of the hallway. Our stairs had orange carpet. Daddy smiled at me then, I'm sure, nodded me onward as I peered down at him over the banisters.

The midafternoon sun shone through the stained-glass windows at the back of the house, tinting patches of my skin red. It always did. Daddy placed a finger over his mouth, and I clapped a hand over mine, to muffle my giggles. Then I skipped toward my parents' bedroom. I could hear my mother, but my smile faltered, she sounded as if she were in pain. I pushed open the door and screamed.

"Mummy!"

She screamed, too, and pushed Mr. Coates off her. She grabbed at the sheets and Mr. Coates fled hunched into the bathroom, his arms crossed over his chest, his hands covering his willy. He was hairy, and I felt a *whoof* of air as he swept past. There was a damp, musky smell, like something beginning to rot, mingled with a sickly sweet perfume—different from the light, flowery stuff my father slapped on his face after shaving; it made my throat feel raw.

"Baby!" said Angela, and stumbled toward me, dragging the sheet with her. She tripped over it and sprawled on the floor, pink and naked.

"Daddy said you'd be in here," I blurted, and turned and ran.

I've probably imagined details here and there, joined the dots. I don't flatter myself that this memory lay perfectly formed in a no-go area of my mind, like a phoenix in the ashes, waiting to be reborn. But the *sense* of it was unquestionable. The emotions it dredged up that now dragged me through the experience as though it had just occurred a second time were supernatural in their force; I felt like an ant being sucked down a drain.

My head ached fit to crack.

Gabrielle grabbed at my arm as I rushed past her, past Jack, past Mr. Coates and his throat-rasping aftershave. As I ran out of the Old School Hall, I could feel Angela and Roger watching me from the stage. I blundered outside and was sick into a bush. I didn't have a tissue, so I spat—"pah! pah! pah!"—to get rid of the drool. Reluctantly, I wiped my mouth on my sleeve, resenting the fact that I'd now have to wash my jumper. It isn't true that if you have a big blow to contend with, the little things cease to matter. If anything, they matter more.

Then, moaning aloud like a dying person, I staggered to my car. I flopped over the wheel, resting my head on my forearms, gasping, "Oh, how could he, how could he do it to *both of us*?"

He might as well have shot us, but plainly he'd wanted us to suffer.

I'd blanked it out, I must have blanked it. Age five, your mind is mostly on *play*, not *record*. That's why—and I owe this knowledge, of

266

course, to Jason—if shit happens before then, it's harder to undo later, because you don't quite know what the shit *was*. Now I stopped moaning. I just rested my forehead on my hands, opening and shutting my mouth silently. I couldn't stop shaking my head. It was as if the repetitive swaying movement kept it from bursting open.

How could he be so . . . cold? How could he do that to me, how could he make a rational decision to *damage* us, me, her, his own family? Thanks to him, I'd had two and a half decades to stew over the fact that my harlot of a mother had been unfaithful, wrecked the family, deceived us all. And, also thanks to him, I trusted no one. If I even suspected I might get too close to anyone, I destroyed the relationship as a chick in the nest. It was safer to strike first.

I had adored my mother. Thanks to Roger, I'd been made to feel that my own mother had betrayed me, the most unnatural betrayal there is—I'd been made to feel that she didn't love me back. When I burst in on her and Mr. Coates that day, I was implicated in their crime. It marked the beginning of my preference for isolation.

That Angela had been unfaithful had been enough to condemn her. I had never thought to inquire back further as to *why* she had been unfaithful, something that was so very unlike her. Our condemnation was as absolute as if she'd committed a murder.

Now I couldn't see why I hadn't wondered about her reasons. I knew from my work at Hound Dog that an affair was often the end of a painful journey. I mean, I ignored it, but I knew. Greg and I were like—if I may be so bold—crime scene investigators. We uncovered the truth. We didn't prevent the evil from taking place. We arrived *too late*. Our job was simply to witness the end.

And now, it hit me, that wasn't enough. At least not when the story had taken place at the heart of my own family, when a grasp of what had occurred *before* the affair might impact on . . . everything.

How could he? How could he do it to me, his little girl?

And my mother! I had barely been civil to her for most of my life. She had suffered disproportionately for her mistake. Her decision. I wouldn't say an affair is a *mistake*. Swigging from a carton of milk five days past its sell-by date is a mistake.

How easily and glibly I had judged my mother for cheating, when probably her only wrong decision was to do the "right" thing, by staying with Roger and damaging so many people, including herself. I hadn't felt a good person for sleeping with Jack while I was technically engaged to Jason, but if Angela's experience had taught me anything, it was that if Jack was the right man for me, sex with him was *not* bad or wrong—the only wrong thing would have been to go through with marrying Jason.

Poor Angela. I could feel her infidelity shrinking in significance in my head; it was fizzing to nothing like an aspirin in water. What crowded out the image of me, witnessing the offense, was the realization that my father had planned that I should witness it. That atrocity far outweighed the atrocity of seeing my mother grappling with my school drama teacher. I'd not understood what I'd witnessed, but its brutality had terrified me. Their reactions had terrified me even more.

I couldn't believe that my father would be so callous. If this was how he punished his wife, I was lucky he hadn't gassed me in the Volvo. That would really have served her right. I'm not easily taught, but I'd got the gist of being a good parent off Gabrielle. You protected your kids, for as long as the world let you. To a reasonable extent, you put their needs before yours. You didn't traumatize them to the toes of their white ankle socks in order to inflict massive pain on your spouse. (That last was a basic.)

I was hurt.

All right, I was *fucking* hurt.

I was so incredibly hurt it took my breath away.

If you love someone, you do not purposely inflict pain on them. I could conclude only that my father didn't love me. Not in any sense that matched my definition of love (and my requirements weren't excessive). However, from the nature of his crime, I didn't have to work for Hound Dog to conclude that my mother did love me. His MO proved the opposite of what he had intended.

37.

I jumped as someone rapped on the window and opened the passenger door.

"God!" I shouted. "Don't do that!" as Jack sat down beside me.

"Special," he said, rubbing my back. "You okay?" He looked concerned. As well he might.

I turned to face him. "Well," I said. "I invite you to see my parents in a play, and you bring along *him* and upset everybody."

Jack shook his head. "Hannah, Jonathan loves your mother. And she is so unhappy with your father. When you and I were together, I thought Angela was one of the saddest people I'd ever met. I just didn't know why. She's *still* sad. And the coldness between the two of you, it's such a waste. As for Roger. He should be afuckingshamed of himself. I thought, here are two unhappy people who could be happy together and—"

"Don't patronize me."

"All right. It's hard to explain. Jonathan didn't approach me to be his agent just because he knew me. He knew I'd married *you*. Eleven years ago, he'd seen Roger's announcement in the *Ham & High*. He'd always wondered about Angela, but as he never heard from her again, he presumed she and Roger had patched things up.

For a while, he was married himself. He divorced four years ago. When he called me, looking for an agent, he'd recognized my name; he was hoping I might know something about Angela. He just couldn't forget her. I didn't know anything about anything, of course. Until . . . now. This wasn't a spontaneous decision to interfere. It was about five, six months ago that Jonathan told me what happened, the truth of the affair. Which explains a lot. About you. I thought you deserved to know the whole story, from someone who wasn't Roger. But I didn't think that Roger would react that like when he saw Jonathan. I didn't think Angela would react like that when she saw Jonathan. I didn't know she was going to be onstage. You never said. I thought I'd bring him. He could see her. See if the spark was still there, or if he'd just created a whole new woman in his head. It's easier to have a love affair with an idea of a person than the actual person. The idea of a person doesn't give you any grief. So I thought, this man is desperate. At least let him see her. But that wasn't why I brought him along. I wanted him to speak to *you*. Tell you what happened. It was a wicked thing to do to a kid, and I feel that if only you remembered what had happened, you'd understand . . . your own mind. And then, I thought, it would take away some of this fear—"

I clapped my hands in front of his face. "God bless you, Jack, are you ever going to stop talking? Because, guess what, I did remember. *Everything.* That aftershave Mr. Coates wears, it brought it all back. Roger telling me to go and see what my mother was doing, me seeing what she was doing. So thanks for your concern, but Mr. Coates won't have to explain the facts of my life, because I know them. I know that I've been taking out my bitterness on the wrong person. Of course, knowing *this* makes it all okay. The truth! The truth! The fucking truth! I know the truth! Everything will be *wonderful* now! I was happy with the way things were—"

"You were not happy, Ratfink." Jack took my hand as he said this. "You've lived your life since the age of five in the emotional equivalent of solitary confinement."

"Jack," I said, looking at my hand in his. "To hear you talk you'd think that there was only one of us in this car that was screwed up. You're no gift to intimacy yourself. I'm not saying it's *only* your fault, what with parents who care marginally more about you than about the butcher down the road—"

"That phrase is gonna stick."

"Sorry."

"No, you're right. But I like to think I've progressed. I accept that they're never going to treat me how I'd have liked. I tell myself it's not personal. And when I think of a 'parent' I think of . . . other people's parents."

"But you admit that how they were affected you."

Jack nodded. "How could it not? I am . . . cautious. You were my one gamble. . . . That set me back. Maybe the effect you had on me, the way I reacted, maybe there was more to it than . . . you. But. You can take a lot that's useful from bad parents. It gives you an edge. You don't expect the world to come to you. I'm cynical, but that's an advantage."

"Well, no," I said. I was surprised to hear myself say it. "It isn't. Not always."

I removed my hand. "Where's Mr. Coates, anyway?"

Jack rubbed his eyes. "He was still sitting there staring at Angela when I came out. I suppose I should go and find him, break up any fistfights." He paused. "So . . . will you be okay?"

When people ask this question, usually with one foot out the door, they require only one answer.

"I'll be fine."

Jack hesitated as he got out of the car. "So . . ." he said. "I'm

271

sorry if I've . . . kickstarted something. I didn't mean it to . . . explode like this. I didn't think it through. I swear I had . . . the best intentions."

The second he was gone, I clunked my head down hard on the steering wheel. I was sick of my parents, I was sick of Jack's parents, and I was sick of Mr. Coates. His name annoyed me. If the only reason Jack had showed was to play Cupid to a fully grown adult male who should be able to organize his own love life—

The passenger door opened and I jumped.

"Fuck Coates," said Jack. "Fuck 'em all."

He plonked down beside me and grinned, and I started laughing.

"*Hi,*" I said, tilting my head to one side.

"Hi."

"I've missed you."

"I've missed you too, Special." He stopped. Studied my face. "It's not the same without you."

I reached over the gearshift and kissed him. "I am," I whispered, "just so happy . . . that you're here."

"I love you," he said. "I fucking love you, Hannah."

"I love you, Jack. It's always been you. Although your language has not improved." I felt sick with joy.

Jack loved me. And even if my relationship with my father, the man I'd seen as a god, had just crumbled to ash, even though it felt that I could never ever get over the rage and disgust and grief, even though I had to face that I had wasted over twenty-five years rejecting the woman who had once provided the most loving, giving, rewarding bond of my life—this meant that there was some kind of hope.

"I haven't felt this happy for ten years," said Jack. "You don't realize. You're so powerful. The smallest thing you do, it has the biggest effect on me. That's why I . . . lose it sometimes."

"But do you see that I've changed? That I'm not like I was at age twenty? I know it was wrong of me to be going on *dates* with another man when I was seeing you, but our relationship was so *vague* at the beginning, and I felt so much for you, it scared the life out of me; Guy was a defense, I swear it. I need you to know, Jack, that I never slept with him while I was with you, I need you to believe it, and to get over what *could* have happened, to forgive me, to accept that while I was stupid, all those years ago, I wasn't *bad*."

"Hannah," said Jack, "I was the stupid one. I was stubborn. I punished myself as much as you. It was all or nothing with me, and while that's fine as a principle, it doesn't work for real life. I forgave you a long time ago. If I'm still angry at anyone, it's *me*."

"And you're sure about that?"

"I'm sure."

He frowned. I gazed at him and stroked his hair, and he stopped frowning.

"Jack," I said, "I know it's difficult in a car, but kiss me again."

"Quickly," he said. "But then I'm going."

"Oh!" I tried to keep the shock from my voice. "Where?"

"Back to my car. I'm going to follow you home and then we are going to make love all night long. Well. Once at least, and not rush it."

In normal circumstances I might have giggled. But now I felt delirious with desire and disbelief.

We ran into my flat and he pulled me to him in a kiss in one fluid move. I felt myself lose control. My happy/sad ratio, usually reined in tight, exploded in a hail of stars; passion and joy seemed to whirl within me, spin me clean off the ground, but maybe that was Jack, scooping me into bed, and my emotions roared and soared and dipped in crazy swoops, until I gasped for air, could no longer see straight, it scared me, was like being conscious during your descent into madness.

But I stayed with it, this time I didn't fight it, I felt every single flutter of my own heart, every fairy fingertip sensation, I let it flow, I allowed it to engulf me, there was no shutdown, no cutoff, no running away to find space, to get some *distance;* here was Jack and everywhere I wanted to be. I understood the meaning of surrender, I gave myself to him like I never had before, and I felt him do the same for me. I had never liked, never *uttered,* I had loathed and detested the phrase "make love"—it was repulsive and creepy, it made me shudder—but now I cried because I understood it; it had me in its grasp. It was worth the risk, worth the terror, because even my fear felt like heaven.

Afterward, Jack rolled over so his face was above mine. He kissed my neck, his lips touching the skin where the carotid artery pulsed below, and he said, "It's so good to have you back, Hannah."

I smiled. "I can't believe I let you get away. You're so precious to me."

He stroked my hair. "I think when we first met we were too similar. You look around you and you sense what you've lost. You lost your mother. And so you cut yourself off from the grief and it feels better, *bearable.* That becomes what you can manage, you can't tolerate any emotion warmer than cool, because real passionate love, gentle and fierce and nurturing, is too painful a reminder of what you lost. It feels easier and safer to banish it, to choose a life hidden in shadow."

I held him to me.

38.

I was awoken the next morning at an ungodly hour, good heaven, it must have been ten o'clock. Jack was gone. Some sadist had their finger jammed on the buzzer. If it was the postman, I was going to report him.

Actually, I wasn't. I'd reported the postman before, on suspicion of sadism. Every time he posted mail through my letter box—usually at dawn, especially on Saturdays—he purposely rattled the flap in an ear-splitting cacophony that lasted ten minutes. One morning Gab had brought Jude over, and he'd fallen asleep. Alas, that same morning, I had post (addressed *Dear Pizza Lover*). The racket awoke Jude, who was inconsolable. I ripped open my door, shouted at the culprit's back, "Excuse me!" He'd ignored me. Furious, I rang the post office. To my utter surprise, they took the complaint seriously (not a factor I'd taken into consideration, as I'd only wanted to hear the sound of my own whiny voice and have the satisfaction of someone *else* hearing it). A bureaucrat spoke to the postman and rang me back. The postman hadn't heard me shouting. He also hadn't meant to rattle the postbox. Maybe it needed oiling? Oh, really. Plainly, we were dealing with a master criminal! The following morning, I lay in wait for the postman. And I noticed . . . he was wearing headphones.

I stumbled thick-headed out of bed, mumbling "All right, I can hear you!" staggered about searching for a dressing gown, in vain as I didn't own one, tripped to the door in boxer shorts and my Snoopy T-shirt.

"Sugar pumpkin! I was *so* worried!" cried Roger.

I stared at him. Who *was* he, really?

"Were you?" I said.

He stepped in and flung his arms around me.

"Pumpsky! Relax! That was like an embrace with a large frozen fish finger!" He let go, felt my forehead. I twisted away. "Excuse me while I get dressed," I said. I thought if I took long enough, he might get the message and leave. But when I emerged from my bedroom forty-five minutes later, head to foot in black, he was sprawled on my sofa, *asleep.*

"Er, hell-*o*," I said.

He opened his eyes, smiled. The smile became a frown, and he leapt up. "Sweetheart, how *are* you? It must have been such a ghastly, ghastly shock."

"Yes," I replied. "It was."

"When you fled the hall, I was desperate to follow, but alas, the show must go on!"

"Yes," I said. "Apparently it must."

When was he going to stop acting concerned and apologize? Not that a "sorry" would cover it. Nothing would cover it short of cutting out his own innards with a knife.

"That bastard certainly had a fuck of a nerve turning up like that—shocked the hell out of me. And your mother. He broke up my family once, I'm surprised he dared show his ugly face. Thank the lord our professionalism took over and we managed to get ourselves back on track. The audience didn't have a clue what was going on. But they were most forgiving. I'm not saying it wasn't humiliating—the bastard had vanished by the end of the show, or I'd have kicked his head in. What *I* want to know is what the hell he was doing all cozied up to *your* ex-husband? What's Forrester got to do with any of this? There's no way *now* that I could—"

I realized with a start that Roger didn't know I *knew.* He thought

I'd run out because, after a disappearing act that lasted twenty-six years, Angela's lover had forced his insolent presence upon us.

My whole body trembled.

Roger stopped in the middle of his sentence. "Are you okay?"

"Why shouldn't I be?" I said, testing him.

"That git turning up like that must have brought it all back for you."

"Yes," I said. "It did. It brought it *all* back."

Roger shook his head, sympathetic. "Your mother was in a dreadful state. Guilt, I expect."

"I suppose you have to have a conscience, to feel guilt."

"Mm. So tell me. What's your fellow's involvement in all this? They're not *friends,* are they? I call that suspect, teachers being *friends* with pupils."

"Mr. Coates is a client of Jack's."

I watched my father's face closely. He nodded, a short sharp jab of the chin. "Oh yes. How can he be a *client?*"

"He's a very successful voice-over artist. And character actor."

"Ugly, you mean. Voice-over artist! He was a second-rate drama teacher!" Roger paused. "I do hope Jack—well, he bloody obviously doesn't—I was going to say, doesn't he realize the *sensitivity* of all this? No, I'll bet that piece of scum never told him what he got up to before he was a *voice-over artist.* But, Hannah, I mean, *you* don't want to come face-to-face with this fellow."

"Don't you remember, Roger?" I said. "I already have."

My father didn't shift position on the sofa. "What do you mean?"

I sat on a tall, straight-backed chair, so I looked down on him. "I mean," I said, " *'Go and see what your mother is doing'?*"

"What!" Roger laughed. "What the fuck does that mean?"

I jumped out of the chair and screamed so loud my voice cracked. "Oh come off it, you know what the fuck that means, it means you don't give a shit about her *or* me, me, me, your own daughter, it's disgusting, disgusting, no, not her silly affair, I don't give a damn about that, it's disgusting, it's warped, to purposely send your own five-year-old daughter to see her mother fucking another man, Jesus Christ, no wonder I don't trust people, I've probably got Past Traumatic Stress Sign. Syndrome, I mean, what do you think that kind of sight would do to a five-year-old? Oh, don't answer that, I think you know exactly. Jesus, *I* think the worst of everyone, and yet I still can't believe that anyone would be so sick; you've got to be one sick fuck to pull a stunt like that, knowingly wreck the relationship between your own daughter and her mother, just because your ego's been knocked. And all this time, all my life, for as long as I can remember, I've trusted you, *you* have been the only person that I've trusted and respected, the only person I actually dared"—I couldn't say the word "love," I just couldn't say it—"*like,* the one person who I thought was safe, I mean, the numbers of people, the postman, who've suffered because . . . the poor postman! Fuck, I don't know, if you've been conned into believing the worst of your own mother, who *aren't* you going to think the worst of?"

Roger stood up and hit me round the face. I gasped and shoved him. He fell backward and cracked his head hard on my lounge table. "*Shit!*" he shouted. "Ow! Ow! Ow! Shiiiiiiiiiiiiiiiiiiiiiiit! That bloody hurt! What the fuck did you do that for? Hannah, you were hysterical, I don't know what the hell you were talking about; it's as if you're delirious, could it be something you've eaten? Undercooked chicken? I mean, really, it's nonsense, all this, someone has been lying to you—"

"Yes!" I screamed. "YOU!"

"HANNAH!" shouted Roger, equally loud. "I don't know where you've got this from! It's nonsense! Nonsense! You have no *evidence*! You know this, you're a detective! All you're basing this revolting accusation on is some false memory syndrome, and all that's shit, the Royal Psychiatrists' Society banned all that years ago, it was in the *Daily Mail;* my God, I have never been so insulted in all my life. Christ, my head's killing me, you could have given me brain damage! And I've got to do a show tonight. But I'll overlook it because you, young lady, are hysterical and overtired. You are still suffering from the shock of that wanker turning up at the premiere of my show, the spiteful bastard; he knew if she saw him it'd put her off her stroke. I hadn't a hope of holding it together; she just lost it, it was a nightmare, and I'm afraid you were upset by being confronted, without warning, with the embodiment of your mother's sordid past and, I'm sad to say, you took it out on me. Now I suggest you get some sleep, think things through, and maybe"—he marched to the front door and clicked open the latch—"tomorrow morning, after you've got some rest, I trust you'll see fit to apologize. Good day!"

The door slammed behind him and I stared after it. *Good day?!*

It wasn't natural, and if something isn't natural, it's fake.

Thank you, Roger. I *would* think things through. He was right. I was a detective with no evidence. But that was going to change.

I picked up the phone and rang my mother.

39.

I was scared. I won't say, "not much scares me," because a lot scares me. Spontaneously combusting, one. (Although Jack did say that you have to be fat and old for it to happen, so I have a while yet.)

Jumping out of bed in the morning, unaware I'm going to die horribly that day, two. But people are what really scare me. The power that other people have to ruin your life. It's not true that they can do this only if you let them.

That I also had this power had not occurred to me. Now I felt like a mugger forced to face his victim as part of his community service. If my mother hated me, she had good reason. I had treated her shockingly, and by doing so, crushed all my hopes of her. I had a suspicion, gleaned either from Jason or the Discovery Channel, that what you consciously do is the opposite of what you unconsciously want. For the first time in a long while, this psychological get-out clause, which neatly ensured even the most idiot therapist of having the last word, presented itself as a possibility.

When I'd last seen Jude he'd mastered the word "mummy." This was a new achievement, a progression from the earlier, inferior pronouncement "Ma-ma"—a vague, generic term that could refer to anything from Gabrielle to Marmite. "*Mummy*" was a direct and specific request, enunciated with all the precision of a Royal, spoken with triumphant knowledge of the glorious reward it would bring. He said it constantly, "Mummy! Mummy! Mummy! Mummy!" And every time he said it, Gabrielle would reply, in a voice like honey, "Yes, my darling?" and sweep him into her arms.

I saw them together and the thought leapt in to my head like a stranger stealing your taxi, *I want that.*

This phone call would tell me if I could have it.

"Hello?"

My mother sounded sad and dull. I wasn't sure what I had expected. Some dumb part of me had presumed that she'd be elated. However, I wasn't good with how women's minds worked. There was the time, just after Jude was born, that I bought Gabrielle a size 18 jumper, as she was going on and on and on about all her clothes being too small. *There's no way* this *will be too small!* I'd thought smugly.

"Mum. It's me."

"Oh, hello."

It was hardly "*Yes, my darling?*"

"I'm sorry about running out on your performance. I didn't . . . feel well. I heard that the rest of it went okay."

As usual, I was talking about something entirely irrelevant.

"Well," Angela replied. "As your father says, 'Once the spell has been broken' . . ."

Was she being sarcastic? We could go on forever like this, wasting time till it ran out.

"Are you by yourself?" I said.

"Yes."

"I'll see you in twenty minutes."

I did not want to face my mother. So I knew it was the right thing to do. I stopped on the way, bought her two bars of her dark bitter extra-nasty chocolate. I wasn't sure which it was she ate, 70 percent cocoa or 85 percent. I figured she could take one bite of the 85 percent—like chewing dust—then a hunk of the 70 percent stuff. In comparison it would taste gorgeous.

She opened the door. There were double bags underneath her eyes, she looked as mournful as a bloodhound. I handed her the chocolate. She looked surprised. "What's this for?"

Until recently my self-righteousness had been armor-plated. Now she made me feel guilty, without trying. I remembered all the times I'd come over to be fed (Roger played the bountiful host, Angela cooked). I'd watch other guests hand over their flowers and chocolates with a superior eye, *I'm family,* exempt from gift tax. I felt entitled to take, take, take, with no show of gratitude, because we both knew that she remained in debt from twenty-five years ago, that however many free dinners I ate at her house, she could never give me back what she had taken.

I thought of joking about the chocolate, of saying "I thought you might need it," buying into that self-deprecating *in-joke* that all women are forced to be a part of, chocolate, how we're slaves to it, the great cure-all, oh, ho ho ho we're pathetic. Lover left you? Home repossessed? Got breast cancer? Have a slab of Dairy Milk! That'll put you right!

I said, "I didn't want to come round empty-handed."

There was a peek of a smile. "Thank you," she said and took both bars. I followed her to the kitchen. She never sat in the lounge. "I'm so dreadfully embarrassed," she said over her shoulder. Then she turned around and we were uncomfortably close.

"Embarrassed!" I said. "Why?"

She looked at me, I could see the green flecks in her hazel eyes, there was a slight lifting of one eyebrow. "Last night," she said, a lilt in her tone as if I was being disingenuous. "I hadn't seen him since . . . *since*. I never knew if you . . . remembered who it was. I saw that, last night, when *we* saw who it was . . . you saw too. I saw you run away from me." She paused. "I've never *stopped* seeing you run away from me."

I felt as if I was turning to stone, being here, seeing, hearing this. It was good, though. It meant that this time my legs wouldn't let me run.

"I will always be ashamed," she said.

"Please don't be," I said.

She blinked. "Would you like a drink?"

I shook my head. "Roger is the one who should be ashamed." *And me.*

"What! What's brought this on? You get on so well with your father."

She sounded as if she were pleading.

"Please! I know what he did."

"Did Jonathan tell you?" Her voice was fierce.

"No. It . . . came back to me."

She shook her head.

I did my best to explain. "It was like trying to get a dream to reveal itself. It's there in your head, but it's eluding you. Then you surrender, and it lays itself at your feet."

"Oh, God," she whispered.

"I feel . . . I wished you would have told me."

"What," she said. "And have you hate *both* your parents?"

A scratch of guilt, and it was like striking oil. The shame welled up, I felt as if I might drown. Here she was, my Platonic mother, ready to sacrifice herself for the sake of her child. This was what I had been seeking for all of my life, this is what I had wanted of her, this is what my behavior had implied, my endless resentment, my deepest disgust that once, when I was little, she had put her own adult needs before *mine*. She had learned her lesson right then; ever since, she had thought only of me. I realized this now. I also realized how wrong it was.

"I don't think I hated you," I said. "Not really."

She didn't reply.

"I think," I said, "that sometimes you convince yourself you feel the opposite of what you secretly feel."

Still, nothing.

"Jason told me that."

"Good old Jason," said my mother, and we both laughed. Then we stood there awkwardly, smiling.

"Why don't you sit," I said. "I'll make us a drink."

She sat.

"I'd be so sad for you. If you decided to hate Roger."

I whirled round. "I wouldn't say it's a *decision*. Isn't that the entire point of an emotion? It's in charge of you, not you in charge of it?"

Angela shook her head. "Not necessarily. As Ollie always said, 'I'm the boss of me, not you.' "

I made her a coffee in the percolator and poured it into a china cup, put it on a saucer. Left to herself, she would have chucked a teaspoon of instant into a mug. I'm not Gabrielle. ("*God.* In Tuscany, I caught Ollie drinking *Nescafé. In Italy!* Like spitting at the pope!") But now, it gave me satisfaction to see my mother drinking real coffee that I had made for her.

I said, "I will have to see how I feel about Roger."

My mother dipped her head.

A thunderbolt. "He, er, *is* my father, I suppose?"

"Gosh, yes, Hannah! Oh, you poor thing! When you . . . that time . . . it was the only time we . . . not that it matters."

My heart thumped. "I think you should leave Roger."

"Hannah!"

"Well, why not? He's awful."

"Hannah. A week ago, you wouldn't have a word said against him."

"I didn't know the real him a week ago."

"I think," said my mother, "that sometimes you have to look beyond the person."

I made an effort to comprehend. "What. Like in *Manhunter*? 'I weep for the child. But the adult is a sick fuck, etc.?' "

My mother sipped from the china cup. "I'm not sure I've seen that one," she said. "But I do know that Daddy's upbringing was cold and stern, that he was a sad, lonely little boy. It has always been important to him that *his* family held fast as a nice, jolly unit, that everything was perfect, and everyone happy, no matter what. And I'm afraid I spoilt that for him. I had too many . . . unchartered . . . moods. It was hard for him to accept."

I nodded, swallowed. "Why . . . why did you . . . spoil it?"

My mother sighed and shook her head. "Ah well," she said. "Ah, well."

I waited.

"It's over with," she said when she saw I was still waiting. "All in the past. It's done with now."

I sighed. "But it *isn't*. Look at the effects of the past. Look at me and Oliver. We're emotional retards!"

"Oh!" said my mother. "That's not a very nice thing to say. Don't say that!"

"But we are," I said. "Isn't that true? That we're the sum of our past."

"Actually, darling"—it was a long time since she'd dared to call me darling, she was aware, by the twitchy way she said it—"actually, I think the phrase might be along the lines of someone being 'more than the sum of their parts,' which implies something altogether different."

"What?"

"Well. Unlike *your* interpretation, I think it suggests that one's destiny is not fixed."

"Right," I said. "Right." I stared at her. She sipped her coffee self-consciously, smoothed her hand along the (immaculate) kitchen surface, some sort of black polished stone. They'd had an architect and an interior designer do the whole house. I'd assumed this was because that's what you did in the Suburb, any attempt at DIY, an undercover trip to Homebase, the Trust would be informed and your membership revoked. Now I wondered if the architect and the interior designer had been employed because my mother couldn't have cared less about the house.

I saw the pale puffiness around her eyes and her strawlike hair, the dark blue sweatsuit. This was not an Angela that had ever appeared in public. I felt like I was staring at a drawing in a puzzle book. *"Can you see what's wrong with this picture?"* I tried to apply myself. Disregard what I knew, consider the feelings behind what she said.

"Choice," I said, "is very important for you."

My mother cleared her throat, put her coffee cup down. "Choice," she said, "is very important for *everyone*."

I thought of the many people who might drive past my parents' house, with its imperialist white pillars and its stone lions and its neatly clipped rosebushes and its gleaming windows, two smart cars in the drive, and I knew that these people would wonder about the inhabitants of such a palace, would assume the ease and opulence of their lives, would never guess that poverty and sadness might lie beyond the elegant red front door. It's a given that you can be skint and miserable, but people *will* insist on equating money with happiness; they never learn.

"You say choice is important," I said. "And yet . . . ?"

My mother, ignoring her Bosch dishwasher, went to the stainless steel sink and washed her cup and saucer by hand. She didn't bother with the yellow rubber gloves. "There's another phrase," she said. "I've always thought it silly and untrue. 'It's never too late.' Well, no, actually, sometimes it *is* too late." She turned to face me. "Come on," she said. "I want to give you the box Grandma Nellie left for you. She's probably frowning down, wondering why I've been so hopeless and inefficient."

*   *   *

286

I placed the tatty old cardboard box in the backseat of the Vauxhall and shut the door. My mother watched from the pavement. I darted forward and mimed a peck in the vicinity of her ear. Then I jangled my car keys, but she touched my arm to say *stop*.

"When you were little," she said slowly, "you had a low tolerance for being kissed. You'd struggle to be put down. But sometimes, at bedtime, I'd stroke your hair and you'd fall asleep on me. And *then* I could steal a kiss."

I smiled, one of those tight-lipped affairs. "Right."

"Ah," she said, and a smile crept on to her face. I realized she was speaking almost to herself, "The baby had the softest cheeks."

"*The* baby?" I said sternly. I looked around me, the street was deserted.

"You," she replied.

"Why didn't you say 'my baby' then? I'm *your* baby, not *the* baby."

"Of course you're *my* baby," said my mother. "And that makes you *The Baby,* not in the general sense of a baby, but *The Baby,* as in, The Only Baby in the World because there *is* no other baby but you."

We were speaking in the present tense. It was strange, I didn't care. I wanted to hug her, but I didn't know how to make the transition.

She laughed. "All mothers speak nonsense to their babies. You don't recognize yourself. You just go mad with love."

I couldn't just fall on her like a werewolf, so I said clunkingly, "So . . . what now?"

She looked confused.

"You know, like, *hug-wise.*"

I tried not to squirm. *Hug.* A word of small pink novelty books, the sort given as stocking fillers, that clutter up your shelf, make you feel terrible for the tree.

She screwed up her tired face, and then I had my chin on her shoulder and *my* face screwed up. Her arms pressed on my shoulder blades, and she very gently stroked my hair, rocking me softly the most gentle movement, back and forth, back and forth.

"Relax," she murmured. "Relax."

I stiffened. "Mum?"

"Yes, my darling?"

"Relax . . . ?"

"You always fought sleep. There was a short episode where I could say 'relax' over and over, and you would drift off. Then one day you realized what I was doing, and the word 'relax,' well, I might as well have shouted '*attention!*' But I still liked to say it."

My sigh was like the breath wheezing out of an old dog lying beside a fire. My mother turned her head quickly and kissed my cheek luxuriously, a real smacker.

"Ah," she whispered, "the baby has the softest cheeks."

I closed my eyes, relaxed. Mummy, Mummy, Mummy, Mummy.

40.

For the rest of the day, my sense of balance came and went, like when I had an inner ear infection. I lay on my sofa under a quilt despite the hot weather. I felt exhausted, but I couldn't sleep. When things were bad, I was good at not thinking about them, but when things were good, there was comfort in knowing that I didn't *have* to think about them. So why couldn't I stop thinking about my mother?

Things were good with her now, right?

In theory. But I felt like a person who was out at the shops when a meteor crashed into their house. After the initial euphoria of cheating death—"oh, it's only a house, all that matters is that I and my family are safe, this makes me appreciate how lucky I am!"—I'd start to feel annoyed and unlucky that a meteor had crashed into my house.

I was dizzy with joy to have reclaimed my mother. But the joy was muted by regret. By realizing the value of what I'd gained, I saw the enormity of what I had lost. I'd always felt withering pity for people adopted as babies who traced their birth mothers when adult. They were always quoted in the papers, saying brightly, "We're making up for lost time!"

Well, *no,* actually, that's impossible. You can never make up for the loss of her missing your first swimming race, the day you learned to ride a bike, all the days you didn't learn to ride a bike. You *can't* make up for lost time. That's the whole damn point of it.

My mother had been present, in person, in spirit, and yet I had managed to banish her warmth and love, I was a girl suffering from hypothermia, refusing to stand by the fire. If I looked back, I could never say, "I regret nothing." That's bullshit, anyway. Everyone regrets something. Anyone who claims different is arrogant, stupid, or a liar. In fact, all sorts of workaday "wisdoms" popped into my head, to taunt me. "Least said, soonest mended" was one.

Don't think I wasn't aware of being the living embodiment of that phrase, until, hm, this morning. (Don't discuss your marriage problems: they'll quickly go away by themselves!) My mother was right, to urge me not to dwell on the past. She could see I would happily allow it to swallow me whole. She wanted me to do the tiresome thing. To be *strong.*

Society is very keen on other people being strong. If you get cancer, even if you have a sedentary job, everyone else expects you to fight it like you're in the special forces. I've always felt this was unfair pressure on people who frankly have more than enough to deal with. They have a potentially fatal illness, so we urge them to fight it with yoga? I'd argue that pursuing a lounge lizard lifestyle with lashings of saturated fat would be equally brave in the circumstances. Nor would I condemn smoking to cope with the stress.

I resented Angela's expectation of strength. I wanted to hide indoors, face no one. I needed to mope around the house, feel sorry for myself. My mother wanted me to bear no grudges. And there was another mystery. People who don't bear grudges. Of course I wouldn't bear a grudge against Roger—from the exact moment I got even with the fucker. How was it strong not to bear a grudge? You might claim dignity, nobility, class, a bunch of impressive excuses for your reluctance to hit back.

People would nod admiringly, but secretly they'd think, yeah, you just didn't dare.

I didn't want Roger to think that he could ruin a sizable chunk of my life, Angela's life, and get away with it because we were cowards. People who didn't fight back could claim the moral victory, but that is, literally, nothing. You don't hear of people accepting moral compensation. I'm sure that the term "moral victory" only came about so that people with self-esteem so low that they didn't consider themselves worth defending could claim they'd won *something* off their enemies.

I wanted my enemy to rue the day he'd crossed me. I wanted him to die, sobbing, "I'm so, so sorry, Hannah, please forgive me," as I turned my back and waved him on his way to hell.

I was still pretty upset with my father.

I might have simmered till dawn, but the phone rang.

"Hannah, is that you?"

"Jason!"

The second I heard his voice, I thought, "He'll never get his mother back," and the anger shifted to make a little more room in my heart for my good fortune.

"Hello! I'm so sorry I haven't been in touch, how have you been?" Jason sounded serious and concerned, he spoke like one might if nervous of upsetting a person known to be mentally ill. I remembered that he was under the impression that *he* had left *me*.

For the sake of his ego, I tried to sound reasonably heartbroken. "I've been better, but I'll live."

Jason sighed deeply. "Hannah. I am so very sorry, but you do accept that I couldn't marry a woman who didn't want children. It wouldn't have been fair to either one of us. To be honest, I thought you'd get back with Jack, once I was out of the picture."

I was touched he gave me credit for waiting until he was out of the picture. "Oh, well," I said, joking. "My second choice, of course!"

"He's a sweet guy," insisted Jason, who plainly didn't know Jack at all.

"Anyway," I said, uncomfortable. "How have you been?"

"*Really* well! In fact, I called to give you some good news. Good and bad. Good for me, bad for you. Lucy and I are engaged. Again."

"That's *wonderful*!" I cried. "Congratulations!"

"You think?" said Jason. "Really? You're not devastated?"

"Jason, I am delighted for you both, really delighted."

"Thank you!" He sounded pleased. "Between you and me, Lucy didn't want me to call. She thinks"—he lowered his voice—"that you're a little obsessed with me."

How to claw back a scrap of dignity yet avoid giving offense?

"Jason, I do assure you that I'm not a danger to either you or your fiancée. I will always feel very fond of you. But I promise you that doesn't mean I'll be boiling your children's pets. I wish you both nothing but the best, the greatest happiness together—"

"Even though you hate marriage?"

"What! Who said I hate marriage?"

"You."

"I hated *my* marriage. Because it didn't work. Because of *me*. I wasn't right for that marriage. Just like a car wouldn't go if you put orange juice in the tank. Do you see, Jase? I'm not against *all* marriage, just like I'm not against all, er, orange juice"—this was getting complicated. "I mean, cars. Cars are great if, ah, there's petrol in their tanks."

"I think I see what you mean."

"What I mean, Jason, is that I'm not such an idiot that I write off all marriage as bad. And I have no doubt that you and Lucy are such a great match that yours will be highly successful."

"Thank you, Hannah. That's . . . very gracious of you. In that case, may I take the opportunity to invite you to our wedding?"

"How lovely!"

"I'm afraid . . . numbers are tight . . . it won't be a *plus one*."

"That's fine, Jason."

"And, ah, it won't be to the ceremony."

"I understand."

"Or the, ah, dinner. You'll be one of the, ah, *after*-dinner guests. There will be sandwiches, though, and cake."

Little did he know how uninsulted I was. A wedding can eat up a day of your weekend—nay, the weekend itself! Happy the guest who is not invited to the ceremony *or* the dinner, for she can spend the entire morning and afternoon eating biscuits in front of cable.

"Jason," I said, "I am truly honored to be part of your special day, even if it is the smallest, measliest, dog-endiest part of it."

"Hannah, arrgh, the thing is, Lucy's family, it's bloody massive, I—"

292

"I'm teasing you, Jase. Really, I swear, after dinner suits me *great.*"

"Yeah," he said, and I could hear the smile in his voice. "I thought it might."

He was just about to put down the phone when I said, "Jason."

"Yes?"

Now I'd started, I didn't know how to say it.

"Well," I said. "I'm sure you know this, but as someone who has seen you . . . quite frequently in the last five years, I wanted to say, just in case no one else did, that"—shit, how do people do this?—"even though your mother is dead"—great, Hannah, could you be a little more blunt?—"I'm sure she will be looking down on you"—Angela believed *her* mother was looking down on her, disapproving, but looking down all the same, so looking down had to be a good thing—"and just fucking bursting with pride at how well her boy turned out, she must have done a bloody great job in the time she had. Okay? That's it. Just so you're aware."

There was silence on the end of the line. Then Jason said, "Thanks."

I was embarrassed. All I knew was, I had my mother back. I wanted everyone to feel a bit of what I felt. I hoped I wasn't turning sentimental in my old age. Next thing I'd be signing "*Hannah Lovekin*" with a little heart over the "i."

I hadn't changed my name when I married Jack, more out of laziness than principle. Even though I preferred the name Hannah Forrester. "Hannah Forrester" carried more weight than wimpy old "Hannah Lovekin." My mother's maiden name was Black. I thought that was rather cool, "Angela Black," the gold of Angela contrasting nicely with the darkness of Black. "Lovekin" was for *sissies.* I suspect my mother didn't like it either but had no choice.

If Gabrielle was right, and all mothers want for their children what they never had themselves, then what Angela felt *she* lacked was choice. She was desperate for me to make the right choices. Practically jumping up and down about it. She hadn't thought Jason was right for me, and so when she heard about our Second Try, in her own, Women's Institute way, she'd tried sabotage. Plainly, Roger had not been right for her. Still wasn't. And yet, she thought she had no choice but to stay with him.

I hadn't even asked her if *she* loved Jonathan.

Even if she didn't, this wasn't an issue of manhopping. It was about deciding what *she* wanted, regardless of what everyone else thought. I guessed she thought it "too late" because she'd been married to Roger for forty years, and if she left, he'd make it nasty. But also perhaps she'd lived so long with a man who refused to let her be *her* that her real personality, opinions, desires had been suffocated by his, and when she looked at her tired, aging face in the mirror, even she no longer knew her real self.

My mother had energy and fire for me, but none for herself. And I wondered where this apathy came from. She was not indolent, and yet she'd sat back and let her husband rob her of her daughter. Why, when there had once been something of the Gabrielle in her, an appreciation of the little things that make life fun? For goodness' sake, at the age of two, I was drinking freshly squeezed orange juice for breakfast—the orange squeezed before my eyes—because my mother wanted me to, *one,* see that orange juice came from oranges, not cartons, and *two,* have that luxury hotel feeling every day. (I say again, I was two.)

It didn't make sense. Angela wanted to spare me the details of and the reasons behind their marriage's deterioration to avoid causing me further anguish—I no longer doubted the purity of her motives—but I needed to know *everything.* For so long I had been precious about facts, sneering of emotions. How could I not have realized: the facts of all our lives are *borne* of emotions.

My mother claimed you could make a decision to set yourself free of your past, and yet she was pinned to the ground by hers. Today had the potential to be the start of something amazing. Or, not. If I accepted her capsule explanation (he wanted "happy," she had "uncharted moods," whatever that meant), we would never move beyond a surface understanding. And suddenly that wasn't enough.

I owned a silver £250 Panasonic microwave, and the only setting I ever employed on this fine machine was HEAT. This miracle of technology could grill, defrost, bake, and no doubt iron, but I was too idle to go to the trouble of investigating the full majesty of its brilliance. I made do with a hundredth of its capacity, all the while feeling guilty and wasteful and not very bright. Same with my flash harry laptop. I refused to let the same thing happen with my newly acquired top-of-the-range mother.

I was going to have to play detective.

41.

I didn't know where to begin. The cardboard box, my legacy from Grandma, I'd dropped in the hallway, and there it had stayed. It was the obvious place to start, but I felt a bit *The Mummy Returns* about it. Grandma Nellie and I hadn't been on good terms when she died, and I feared that if I opened it, hoards of black beetles would scuttle out and devour me. I exaggerate (about the beetles). But I *was* afraid. Most families look bad close up, which is possibly why I preferred to keep mine at a distance. I'd had enough unwelcome surprises. I didn't want to open the box and find a skull and a lilac-scented note:

Hannah,

I am at long last dead, and the time to reveal the wretched truth is woefully upon us. You were once possessed of an infant brother. When you were three, you put him in the washing machine (mixed fabrics, 60 degrees), where he met an excruciating end. Your parents did not wish you to grow up tainted with the name "MURDERER," so reference to the incident was banished from speech. Oliver had hypnosis, to drive all thoughts of the tragedy from his mind. Although the hypnotist was hard of hearing, and we fear he only caught, "drive all thoughts . . . from his mind." Alas, grief and rage sent your mother mad. The woman you believe to be your mother is, in fact, her twin sister. Your true mother rants in an asylum, under lock and key. Your father could only escape his deep despair by throwing himself into panto. I know you would wish to discover the horrid truth in order to make your peace with God, and I enclose this skull, etc. etc.

I stamped into the hall, kicked the box back into the lounge, and ripped it open. I'm not ashamed to say that if there's a scary scene in a film I watch it with eyes half shut *and* from behind splayed fingers. I employed that same heroic technique here. Naturally, I could see nothing, so I removed my hand from my face and peered into the box, heart thumping. And saw . . . a mess of old photographs. Not so much as a jawbone. No bugs, not even a lady-bird. No envelopes, lilac or otherwise. I sighed and picked out a photo. It wasn't even black and white.

A group of alarmingly seventies-looking people stood in a stiff row, in the thick of which was a big fat plain baby boy. The baby was sat in the lap of a small woman. Hey, it was Angela. She didn't look robust. Her smile was wan. Presumably, that buck-toothed toddler leaning his pumpkin head on her arm was Ollie. The baby boy must belong to a cousin. It was ugly enough. So where was I? Not yet born? Ollie was two years older than me. I was nowhere! And my mother did not look pregnant. This was the secret! I was adopted! But . . . I *looked* so like my mother. I stared suspiciously and unwillingly at the nonbonny baby. Oh yeah. He was me.

Grandma and Grandpa stood stiff and formal either side of my mother, staring into the camera lens like it was a gun barrel. It struck me again how good-looking my father was. Skinny, collar-length hair. Bit of the mod about him. His square chin jutted, and one large hand rested on my mother's shoulder. She all but sagged under it. His expression said, *All this is mine.* He even looked proud of his Halloween offspring. The camera lies plenty, but my mother wasn't a beauty. As with many people, she'd improved with age.

So.

What did this picture tell me? I felt a professional recoil at making assumptions. I already knew that my father required all of us to be happy, even when we weren't. I suppose that figured here. He was a lot about show, was Roger. He cared too much for what other people thought of him, of his achievements. His expression challenged you to pick fault with his masculinity. Although, as a trophy family, we weren't great. My mother looked half-dead and we children were, at least aesthetically, monsters.

I'd just had this—not uplifting—thought when the phone rang.

My heart thumped. Jack was in L.A. for five days. All I'd said was "Don't get your head turned," but I was hoping he'd call. He hadn't yet.

"Hello?"

"Smee."

My heart seemed to swell like a blood blister.

"Yes," I said.

"Me, Martine!"

"Yes, I know."

"I'm calling to see how things are, what with all the to-do at Roger's show, oh my god, like, *what* did Jack think he was doing, bringing that man along—"

"You must think I'm stupid."

"What?"

"You make out you're my friend, when all you are is a grass for Roger, because you fancy him, it's perverted. I tell you *anything,* it goes straight to him. You have no loyalty, no dignity, *no* knowledge of who you're dealing with, or the circumstances that you're messing in. Roger got you to beg Jack to come to the play, because he had this moronic idea that Jack would snap him up, next stop Hollywood, because his vanity makes him deranged and a liar! He's using you, dear. He's not your friend, what did you think you'd get out of it? A sympathy sh—?"

I was ready for shock, tears, or the dial tone. I did not expect Martine to reply in a calm, soft voice, "No, Hannah. You think *I'm* stupid."

I was silent.

"When," she continued, "have you ever treated me with respect? I know what you think of me. Fat Martine, works for a dentist, reads trash. Well, love, least I *read. You* watch telly. You have affairs with characters off crime dramas, insteada real life. I tried to be your friend, but what was the point? You never would treat me as equal. You're patronizing, rude, only ever turn to me to unload

298

whatever crap's in your head, you don't care what *I* have to say, you patronize me, you think I don't have feelings, don't talk to me about not being a friend, you treat me like I'm rubbish. Roger pays me attention, treats me like a valid person in my own right, and I'm pleased to do things for him, it goes both ways, we have brilliant discussions about teeth, and fame, he's not sure if he should get his capped or whitened and he respects my opinions and expertise, which is more than I can say for you, you're a lot of fun to be with if you put your mind to it and I would of *loved* to of been your friend but then I got sick of my efforts being thrown back in my face."

When she cut off, my first thought was that Martine was surprisingly eloquent. My second was that she was surprisingly *right*.

A devout believer in revenge, if I were to uphold my religious principles I would be forced to sanction Martine's behavior. However, my piety did not extend to ringing her back and apologizing. I needed a distraction from my conscience, so I rang Gabrielle, who ordered me round.

"I would have rung," she said, throwing open the door as I thundered up the path, "but Jude's not well. Ollie called me home just after you left the play."

"What's wrong?"

"Gastro flu. We were in casualty all yesterday afternoon; he kept vomiting, then went all listless and lethargic. I thought it was meningitis. He's fine, though. He's sleeping. He vomited up spag bol over my Diane von Furstenberg wrap dress."

"*Rap* dress? What's a rap dress?"

"A wrap dress. It wraps around you."

Raps around you? I would never understand fashion. "Poor Jude. So is it all good with Ollie now?"

Gabrielle laughed. "Oh, you," she said. "No wonder it all went pear-shaped with Jack. You don't *get* relationships."

I laughed myself, out of hurt. That's an extreme accusation to make of someone, particularly to their face. Anyway, little did *she* know.

"Who does?" I said coldly.

"Ollie and I," said Gabrielle, "are . . . up and down. Ollie doesn't like there to be problems. He is trying to be nice and I am trying to be . . . *up,* and maybe it will be okay. Anyway, bore, bore, bore. God. *Wednesday night!* Poor, poor Angela. I've left messages on her mobile, I haven't wanted to ring the house. I don't suppose you'll know if she's okay? I was hoping to go round there and check when Ollie got back from his shoot."

"He's at a shoot?"

Gabrielle allowed herself a brief smile. "Photographs of nails and screws for the dummy issue of a DIY magazine."

Neither of us said the obvious: that this was work he'd have spat at a month ago.

Good news, but I had that same feeling that I got every time I talked to Gabrielle, that I was missing something. *Not* a life-size china leopard guarding her fireplace, but something just as obvious.

Gabrielle had once said that after Jude was born she was sure her memory developed little black holes. It was pure luck as to whether or not information rolled down a little black hole to be lost forever. I didn't have the baby excuse, but my mind was not dissimilar. I likened it to an Advent calendar. All the information was there, except it was in compartments, behind lots of little doors, and if you didn't chance to open the correct door, the information would stay hidden. If I was lucky, one of the little doors would swing open at the appropriate moment and the information would reveal itself:

You came into the kitchen to find your checkbook.

One of the main reasons you drove to the supermarket was to buy kitchen roll.

You wanted to see Gabrielle to discuss the pathology of your parents' marriage.

If I was unlucky, however, the little door would swing open only when it was too late—when I was halfway to the bank or at the front of the checkout queue . . . But, as my sister-in-law and I stood in her hallway, the little door opened on cue. The cue was "He didn't want to see there was a problem. He wanted me to be fine."

I don't know about all that stuff—wanting to be like your parents, wanting to rebel against your parents, being like your parents whether you want to be or not. It made me uncomfortable, so I mostly avoided thinking about it. Although now I *did* think about it, it seemed you couldn't win. If you're unlike your parents, people can say "you're rebelling"; if you're like them, people can say "aha, copycat." Or whatever the clinical term is. Either way, you can't escape their clutch.

All those years ago, I accepted I was a cheat, like my mother, and emergency-braked there. Now, I heard my brother's wife speak—"Ollie doesn't like there to be problems . . . I am trying to be *up*"—and her words echoed Angela's. "It has always been important to Roger that . . . we were happy, even if we weren't."

I had an expert witness standing in front of me.

"Gab," I said. "Do you think that Ollie is like Roger in wanting his wife to be fine . . . no matter what?"

She stared. "Well, Hannah. They're two different people."

I nodded humbly.

"Ollie is not spiteful like his father," she added. "Sorry. I know

301

you think the world of that man. But, I mean, if *your* mother even hints at having any emotion that isn't positive, Roger blanks her. He can't cope with any of you expressing misery. He seems to think it reflects badly on *him*. Ollie said he was so cruel to her after her affair. And probably before it, too. Why else would she have it? Ollie isn't cruel. Ollie's very different from his father. As a child Ollie was scared of Roger. There's no way Ollie would ever be like him. Ollie just . . . finds it hard to see me upset."

"Ah!" I said. "Right."

But to be honest, I was having a little trouble seeing the distinction.

42.

The Woman in White is not a ghost story, but at first you think it might be. By the time you discover it isn't, you're hooked. You read it, eyes a-boggle, gasping "agh! agh!" and "Oh my God!" Wilkie Collins wrote it in the nineteenth century, and it was serialized in a magazine. All of England was hooked, the prime-minister-to-be canceled a theater visit to read the next installment, and you could buy *Woman in White* capes and *Woman in White* perfume. I thought that was the coolest thing. Walt Disney stole brand merchandising from the Victorians.

Fred had recommended it, and I'd hesitated because it was a classic. "I don't usually read books like this," I said. "I'm not sure I'll understand the language."

"Darling, if you don't like it," he said. "I'll give you your money back, *and* a free copy of *Bravo Two Zero*."

"And if I do like it?"

"Say marvelous things about me and the store!"

After I'd finished it, I recommended it to friends. Greg. Gabrielle. My father. (They were all interested anyway in why I was using words like "malevolent.") *I* think that recommending a book has a dual purpose. It's about power. (Allow me to pass on my superior experience . . .) But it's equally about seeking approval (I have something here that will please you).

It was gratifying when Gabrielle announced, "Wilkie Collins has given me hours of pleasure! More than I could say of any man in a long time!"

And when Ron had knocked on Greg's door and he'd barked, "Not now! I'm busy on a case! . . . Walter Hartright's!" I was as proud as if I'd written the book myself.

My father, the last time we'd spoken, had still been "meaning to get round to it."

I hadn't bothered to recommend *The Woman in White* to Martine. And right now that seemed like an indictment. I didn't care about her approval, her enjoyment. I felt so greatly superior toward her, I didn't even bother with power play.

I left Gabrielle in Belsize Park and bought a copy of the novel from the nearest bookshop. Then I drove to the office of Marvin Van De Vetering (DENTIST, SPECIALIZING IN CHILDREN), rang the bell, and was buzzed in.

Martine did not look pleased to see me. "Do you have an appointment?" she said.

"Martine. You were right. I'm sorry about how I've been. I value your friendship." I stopped. I remembered what Martine had said to me when I'd told her that Jack and I were divorcing. *Before* she'd suggested a divorce party. She'd said, "That's the worst thing I've ever heard," and her eyes were round and watery. "Like, you and Jack . . . you're like, this golden couple. I look at you two and I think it was meant to be. If *you* can't make it, what hope is there for the rest of us?" She'd wiped her nose and added, "It makes me feel very insecure."

It was one of the most honest responses I'd got, and for some perverse reason, it had cheered me up.

"Look," I said. "I bought you a book. It's brilliant. I thought you might like it."

She held out a hand. I gave her the bag, and she took out *The Woman in White.* "I've read it," she said and handed it back.

"What!" I said. "You've read *The Woman in White* and you didn't bother recommending it to me?"

Martine tried not to grin and failed. "I was in a mood with you."

"Yes," I said. "I think I finally realized that." I paused. "Look. I don't think you're stupid."

"Not anymore, you mean."

I suppose it was best to be straight. "Not anymore."

At last she smiled. "Marvin's waiting. But come round later? About eight?"

"Great," I said and turned to go.

"Oi." I turned back. "Give us the book, then."

"But you've read it."

"I'm not turning down the only freebie I've ever got off you."

I thought that was terrible, so I turned up with flowers. Not my style.

"Not your style," said Martine, opening the door.

I'm sorry to say that I hadn't been to her flat since she'd bought it. It was in a rough area, and teeny-tiny. I went round soon after she moved in, a year ago, and it was disgusting. The bathroom was minuscule and reeked of backed-up drains. She'd forgotten to shut the door when she'd left for work and it had stunk out the entire flat. The whole place, including the lounge, was floored in terra-cotta tiles.

Now it was unrecognizable. The walls were soft shades of lilac and yellow and pink, all lit with upside-down lighting. There was that straw matting stuff that's so fashionable. All the windows had wooden blinds. The bathroom was glossy and white, with stone tiles. The bath itself was a clawfoot. Not *my* ideal, but pretty damn respectable. The kitchen was chrome and showroom standard. Martine caught me staring.

"Ikea," she said.

I hate Ikea, having never forgiven them for a wood veneer flat-pack filing cabinet that cost three hundred quid and wouldn't shut properly. But other people used Ikea to work miracles.

"This is fantastic," I said. "It's beautiful. You've made it so beautiful."

"My brothers helped," she said. "But I designed where stuff was to go."

We sat in the lounge, on firm, angular cream sofas, surrounded by crammed bookshelves. Martine pressed *play* on her stereo. "You had a classical CD already in there!" I said, impressed. "You walk the talk!"

We ate a salad Martine had prepared, as she was on a diet. Ten minutes later, she was on the phone to Pizza Hut. I was interrogating her about her new bathroom when she suddenly said, "This is awkward."

"Yeah," I said, taking a bite and pulling the pizza slice away from my face, creating a string of cheese as long as the Golden Gate Bridge. "Lucky we're not being filmed."

"I didn't mean that," said Martine. She heaved herself up and thundered into the kitchen. A drawer was pulled open and I heard sounds of rummaging. Then she returned with a newspaper cutting. She wafted it in front of me but wouldn't let me hold it. "It's from *The Ham & High*."

"What?" I said, squinting. " 'FETID MEAT AT WEDDING HORROR.' "

"No! Next to that one. It's an article about Jack. Well. Not Jack, one of his clients, an actress. She's local, and Jack got her her big break. In a Hollywood movie. She played Sharon Stone's granddaughter . . . oh, the point is, I saw it, six months ago, and I recognized Jack's name. Your dad was always going on about being famous—"

"Not to me, he wasn't!"

"No. I don't think he told many people."

I looked down at the rest of my pizza and scowled.

Martine paused respectfully, then said, "So I said to him that maybe *Jack* would take him on, and he said hardly, seeing as he's divorced from Hannah and they've not been in contact since, and then, all that bother happened with Jason, and when Jason was nagging you to make your peace with Jack, it was perfect timing for your dad. I did feel bad about him pretending it was because he thought Jack was better for you than Jason, but I was so angry with you for—"

I held up a hand. "Oh, Martine. It doesn't matter."

"You don't hate me?"

"I think you're a bit of a mean cow—"

She grinned.

"And I'll never cross you again—"

She nodded happily.

"But I don't blame you, I blame *him*. Roger."

"Yeah?"

"He . . . charms people. He gets them to do things for him when they don't want to and makes them think it was their idea."

Martine nodded slowly.

I said in a rush, "*That* scheme is nothing compared to all the other stuff."

Martine said, "What stuff?"—and with that, I was there till 4 A.M.

At approximately three thirty-five, Martine had sat up, demolished a Picnic bar in two bites, and called me a "thickie."

"You know," she said. "You tell me all this about Angela. How, when you were little, she swings from being hyper, making you continental breakfasts and all that, to not being able to get out of bed."

"Yes," I said.

"And, like, how she says now that she had uncharted moods and Roger couldn't take it."

"Yes," I'd said.

"Well!" Martine had shouted. "*Hell-o!* She's had postnatal depression. Your dad's just ignored it, hoped it would go away. He's punished her for being miserable, like it's been her fault! No wonder she's gone and had the affair! Poor love!"

"Postnatal depression," I'd said. "But . . . how can that be right? Angela loved us. It got a bit much for her sometimes, but she would never have hurt us."

"Berk," Martine had said. "Having PND doesn't mean you hurt or hate your baby. It can do. I'm not claiming all women love their babies, I'm not claiming that. I mean, some women don't bond with their babies instantly. It's not like they're irresistible cute, like a, a, a *puppy*. Sometimes it takes a while."

"Right."

Martine had paused. "Ask me how I know this."

"Sorry! How?"

"Mum had it."

"Get *off*!"

"True."

"I knew you looked after all your brothers, I thought your family were just sexist. I'm sorry."

Martine had smiled. "I'm sorry for you too."

"Oh! Me. Yes." I still hadn't quite connected myself with the problem. "So . . . what happened with *your* mum?"

"She had it proper. Illuminations, wanting to kill herself."

"Illuminations? Aren't they . . . lights?"

"No, love. They're when you see things that aren't there," replied Martine kindly.

"That's terrible. I don't think Angela was like that."

"There are degrees. But Mum. Oh, my God. Everything was . . . left. Like, she'd make as if she was going to scrub the oven, but then she'd stand there, flapping her hands, was that a good idea, if she was going to cook our tea on it? And you knew, in the end she weren't going to do neither. Dad was good. He cooked, cleaned, got her to the doctor. She wouldn't go. Years, she said there was nothing wrong with her, she was just weary. She was afraid of mental illness. Her gran's brother hung himself. Also, in those days, there was the stigma."

"Still is."

"Yeah. True. But Dad didn't give a toss what anyone else thought."

"Roger is *obsessed* with what everyone else thinks."

"Yeah. Roger's typical of his generation. All anyone wanted then was a perfect happy family. A career was just . . . a *job* back then. The social apsiration—"

"Aspiration."

"The social apsiration was to work in an office nine till five year after year and come home every day to the little woman, who would have dinner on the table, and there'd be four rosy-cheeked kids beaming at you. Roger wanted that. He expected it, like every other bloke of his age. I mean, Angela falling apart must have shocked the life out of him. To Roger, it's not the plan, it reflects badly on him. He's scared of being seen as a failure. Neighbors talking, gossip. Him, feeling like his family's abnormal. *He* thinks it means he's failed as a husband and a father, I mean, it's the ultimate shame, the most important thing for Roger would be that no one gets to know about it. He likes to be included, Roger, likes the right sort of attention. And, you know what people are like. They think you're not normal, they get the idea it's catching. They start crossing the street. That, Hannah, has got to be your dad's worst nightmare. So, like, he treats Angela as if she hasn't got it."

Martine scraped some olive off her teeth.

"What . . ." I'd whispered. "And what would *that* mean?"

"Well, girl. *Look* at what it's meant! That poor, poor woman, look at what she's been through. If I'd known any of this, I'd of spit on him, I tell you. He's blamed her for something she can't help. I mean, like, did he allow her to get treatment? Doesn't sound like it. And then, when she's so desperate for a bit of kindness, and she goes with that drama bloke, he punishes her even more. And because her mind is faulty, she lets him. Believes she's as bad as he says she is. What a prick. I mean, that's evil."

"This is . . . terrible. I feel . . . responsible."

"Hannah. You were a child. How were you to know what was going on? He played you like he played her."

"Poor, poor Angela. I just . . . what, how did she manage to . . . live?"

"Everyone's different. Mum, she was always bursting into tears. Banged her head on the wall, made us all scream to see her. Slept all afternoon, up at dawn, to, like, *stare*. Now, I don't sleep much. I think, I'll sleep when I'm dead. She just seemed to *hate* herself. Dad would tell her she was pretty, and she'd burst into tears. If she cut an apple and it was bruised, it would make her hate herself."

"And . . . did she get better?"

"The pills . . . took away the extremeness. Made her . . . okay. Not sad. Not happy. Just okay."

"She's *still* on pills?"

"Isn't everyone?"

"But . . . postnatal . . . doesn't postnatal depression go away when your kids grow up a bit?"

"Yeah, but with her, she was prone to depression, and this brought it on, and then it was there for good. But she can function now." Martine had paused. "I don't know how Angela is now, but you should talk to her."

"Yes," I'd said. "I will."

But first I was going to talk to my brother.

43.

Gabrielle allowed me to babysit with Oliver the following evening, while she went out with a friend "for sushi." We waved her off. I've had sushi a few times, and it's fine, except I always come home after it and eat a large bowl of hot food.

"That'll cheer her up," said Oliver as he slammed shut the door. (Precisely two seconds earlier, his wife had asked him to shut it quietly, so as not to wake Jude. Maybe I was a vampire and Gab spoke at the frequency of a bat, because he didn't slam it maliciously, it was just as if he couldn't hear her.) He shrugged. "I bought her the flowers, and she was nice to me for five minutes."

Oliver, I realized, was like a baby in that, though his behavior was not ideal, he did not benefit from being shouted at. I decided to go slow, not blunder in like normal. I said, "Have you spoken to Mum?"

Oliver rubbed the back of his neck. "Thought I'd give her a bit of space."

I studied his face. He is *scared*, I thought.

The Cat's Special Mummy had once told me that her ex-boyfriend's smoking had given Chairman Miaow asthma. She always knew when he'd had a wheezing fit because he'd hide under the coffee table. (Chairman Miaow, not the boyfriend.) Right now, I suspected that Oliver's understanding of what he was scared of was on a par with Chairman Miaow's.

I didn't know how to begin. Maybe I should treat it like I would any investigation—find the subject's weakest point. Hmm. I looked at Ollie again. He had frozen where he stood, an expression on his face of sheer terror.

"What is it?" I said.

"*Shhh!*"

I was about to retrieve my metal nail file from my bag when I heard it.

"A-a-a-ah."

The sound of a woken baby.

Now Ollie paled and clutched my arm. "*Quiet. He might go back to sleep,*" he mouthed.

"A-a-AH-AAAAAAAAAAAAAAAAH. AAAAAAAAAAAAAAAAAH-AAAAAAAH."

"You reckon?" I said.

I smiled sweetly as my brother bounded up the stairs. His weakest point had made itself known.

"Bugger," said Ollie, appearing at the lounge door fifteen minutes later, with a grinning Jude. "He won't go back to sleep. Every time I lie him flat he gets up and bangs his head on the bars of his cot on *purpose*."

"The gentleman wants to play," I said. "Isn't there an A-4 sized note on your fridge saying OLLIE NO SWEARING?"

Ollie deposited Jude on the carpet, where he did a little dance of triumph.

"Hello, Supercute," I said. "May I have a kiss?"

Jude stamped over with an exaggerated swagger and smacked his lips on my cheek.

"Oh, my!" I touched where he'd kissed. I felt all bashful, like a southern belle. "Well, thank you, Jude. What a great kiss."

Jude, still walking like a penguin, went over to his toys, pulled out a tennis ball, and gave it to me. "Shall we play?" I said. "OK. I'll throw it and you catch it. Ball to Jude. There!"

Jude picked up the ball and threw it back. He had a nice overarm; the ball hit my foot. "Oh!" I cried. "Good shot, sir! Good shot!"

Jude (rather like Chairman Miaow) had a certain bearing that I felt required the address of *Sir*.

Jude clapped his hands, and said, "Baw."

"*Baaaaaaalllllll!*" I crowed. "Yes! Baaaaaawwwllll! Ollie!" I glanced at my brother. I glanced again. "Oliver!" He was tapping at his laptop. "*Oliver!*"

"Yes?" he said, not looking up.

"Jude wants to throw you the ball."

"Mm?"

Ollie looked up, glazed. Jude stood still, holding the ball, an uncertain smile on his face. It fucking broke my heart to see it.

"Your son wants to throw you the ball," I said.

"Aaah," said Oliver finally. "Throw the ball."

Jude did a wiggle and threw the ball. It landed smack on the keyboard. *"No,"* said Oliver. "Naughty! Bad!"

"Jesus, Oliver. He didn't do it on purpose," I said. "Anyway, it was your fault. You should have put down the laptop." It was too late. The corners of Jude's mouth twitched down in, at the risk of sounding mean, a highly comic fashion. This happened several times, then he started howling.

I glared at my brother.

"Awwww," said Ollie, scooping him up. "I'm sorry. Silly Daddy. Come on now. You're really tired. Bedtime. Say night-night to Auntie Hannah."

"Night-night, Beautiful," I said, and kissed his fat cheek.

Oliver was back tapping on his laptop in under two minutes. There was silence from upstairs.

I sat for a while, watching him. God, I thought, you might as well be in China. My heart pounded. Please, Jason, tell me I was never like *this*. A squirmy feeling in my gut gave me the answer.

I knew his weak point, yet I still didn't know where to begin. I would just say *something* and go from there. "Does being a dad make you sympathize with Roger?"

"What do you mean?" said Ollie. He looked up.

I smiled. "Oh, nothing. Just that when I see you with Jude, it reminds me of Roger with you."

This was a lie, as I didn't *remember* Roger with Oliver at this age for the very good reason that I hadn't yet been born. However, I had it on reliable authority that Roger was useless with babies—from

Roger himself. ("Babies! Pointless creatures! Utterly boring until they're four! Much prefer dogs, etc., etc.")

Ollie shut his laptop. "I am not like Roger," he said.

"No, it's just when I see you play with your little boy from behind a shield, I think, yes, it must be hard for Ollie to put down that barrier, let that love hit him like a speeding train."

"What?"

I paused. "Jude loves, depends on you. That's a big scary responsibility. You might not be up to it. You have a shield up the whole time he's in the room, so he can't get to you."

"What?"

"Seeing you afraid of Jude—"

"I'm not afraid of Jude!"

"Well you plainly *are* because you don't dare face him. You're distant, you're half there."

"Is my laptop a shield?" said Ollie. I didn't think he was asking *me.*

"Roger was so scared that he *might* be seen as a failure that he *was* a failure. He couldn't connect with Angela or you. He failed all of us. I only just realized it, that he failed *me* and Angela. I know he failed you too, because I see how you are with him, but I don't know for sure because no one ever talks. I see you distancing yourself from Jude. I see you backing away from Gab, because she has had"—and here I introduced my great idea—"*postnatal depression,* like Mum, I see that you're paralyzed with fear in case it all falls apart."

Ollie shook his head. "I'm not like Roger," he croaked. "And Gab is not like Mum was. No matter how nuts Gab's been, she's always there for Jude, big smile on her face. After you were born, Mum, she was . . . weird. Grandma Nellie said, when you learned to smile, you'd smile at her and sometimes she was so *in herself,* she wouldn't smile back. She'd just . . . *stare* at you with this little frown. And Grandma Nellie says one time she was there, you got this puzzled look and stopped smiling, she said it made her want to weep. Gab is not like Mum. Gab just needs chivvying along a bit—"

"*Chivvying along.* Who always said *that?*"

Ollie rubbed his eyes roughly with the heel of his hands, as if he wanted to blind himself. "Roger always said it," he whispered. "Roger always said it about Mum." He shuddered.

A funny thing happens at Hound Dog Investigations, starting in November. People stop ringing us about their cheating husbands, cheating wives. Our matrimonial work tails off to nearly nothing. As Greg explained, "People don't want to rock the boat before Christmas. They don't want to ruin a family Christmas."

That had to be the most pathetic thing I ever heard. That people *thought* like this. Not just one misguided idiot. *Lots* of them! I imagined these fools, waking up on opposing edges of the bed, exchanging spiteful gifts, miserably chewing sprouts, while the tree lights twinkled and the kids tried not to care that Mummy and Daddy didn't talk. I couldn't believe that the ritual of greed and the positive PR were so important to them that instead of doing themselves justice—banishing the traitor to a Traveller's Inn to eat a festive dinner of turkey sandwich purloined from an Esso station—they preferred to suffer a lie, a wretched day of extravagant untruth, pretending to celebrate love and togetherness with a person they hated, cracking their face with a smile, all the while howling inside.

Now I had a less fascist perspective. I saw that people found it easier to bear their own unhappiness than to inflict it on their families. No one wants to rock the boat. Not at Christmas, not ever.

I'd rocked Oliver's for him.

I was silent.

315

It wasn't as if *I* ever saw more than what was in front of my face. Usually I didn't even see that. It seemed as if most people didn't. But I thought of Jude, and I didn't want him to grow up like his father: with a miserable mother, feeling like his father didn't care about him.

"You must think I'm completely useless," said Oliver, finally raising his head.

"You're a bit annoying," I said. "I wouldn't say you were useless."

He laughed. "Thanks. You cow." He wiped his nose on his hand. "I knew things weren't right with Gab. I feel like it's my fault."

"Well, darling, it's not your fault about the depression—okay, okay—*whatever* it is, but I think it starts to be when you know there's something wrong but pretend to her and everyone that there isn't."

Oliver raised his eyebrows. "Listen, gobshite, you don't know the . . . *fear.*"

"Fear?" I squeaked. "I know fear! Don't tell me I don't know fear! I—"

"Fine. What are *you* afraid of?"

"Well . . . I can't sleep when the wardrobe doors are open."

"Thought so. Nothing. You couldn't give me a serious answer. I'll tell you what *I'm* afraid of." He shook his head, all speech seemed to stick in his throat.

"That house," he said finally. "If I ever thought that *I* would make my family feel how I felt in that house . . . It's like you can't escape it. There was once, she didn't feel well—"

"Who? Gab?"

"Mum. I was on the landing. I heard her in their bedroom, she was crying, going, 'Oh God, Roger, help me, I feel so ill.' I think I was about six. I was so scared. She *never* said things like that. She never complained. And he goes, 'No, you don't.' And she stopped crying. I heard him coming out of the bedroom and I ran to my room and hid in the cupboard."

"Did he scare you that much?"

"*Yes.*"

"He never . . . hit her . . . or you, did he?"

"No. But you know his temper. He was such an angry man, it was a constant, it was underlying but barely contained, you could sense him bristling with it, you always felt like if you said the wrong thing he might hit you. The fear of . . . expecting to be hit was worse than being hit. His rage was all with her. She had this little china collection and he stamped into the room and swept it off the shelf—I can't remember what she'd done—and I yelled at him, 'Stop being mean to Mummy,' and he was shocked. He thought a child couldn't see it. And then it felt like it spilled over to me. Especially after the affair. I liked Mr. Coates. I was good at drama. I was the reason he met Mum in the first place. I didn't really understand what was going on, but I sensed enough never to mention his name to Roger. If ever we had *fun* in that family it was because we *had* to. Grandma Nellie couldn't stand him; *she* knew what he was like to her daughter, never malicious so that other people could see, but *always* malicious. But she was an old woman, she couldn't do anything."

"If he was so horrible the whole time, then—"

"He *wasn't* horrible the whole time, that was the thing. We could go out for the day to, say, the zoo, and he'd be in a marvelous mood, and so would *we* all be, but mostly it would be relief. We'd *seem* relaxed, but it was an act. You could never relax with him around. I spent the whole of my childhood tense. I don't know if he realized his whole family were shit scared of him. He didn't act like it, but he must have known. And he was different with you. You were his mate."

"Oh, great. I was the partner in crime."

"*You* didn't know. He had a different relationship with you, I think he genuinely adored you. Whereas I was competition in a way. But he still used you against her."

"I know." I paused. "But they must have been happy once."

Oliver laughed, a sad laugh. "Yes, but it must have been before we came along."

"Poor you, Oliver. You must have felt helpless."

"I don't know. I was nice to Mum when I could be. I spent a lot of the time out of the house. But . . . yeah. You do feel helpless."

"Still?"

He said it so quietly. "Yes."

"But Ollie, it's different now. Gab isn't Mum. You grew up in his house, but you're not him. You're not that helpless kid anymore. You're big and strong and you have the power to help Gab. You have it in you, Ol, to be a great husband and a really good dad. Just stop running away. There's nothing to be afraid of."

44.

I went home and Jack had called, saying he'd be back tomorrow, but to ring anyway. *Yes!* I thought, what about *me?* Even Superman needed Lois Lane to cuddle up to. I rang him at his hotel, but he was out. I left a message. "Hello, Jack," I said to the machine. "I'm so glad you're in LA. Because right now, I'm working full-time on my peculiar family and frankly there aren't enough hours in the day. Hope you're okay, though. Probably repulsed by all those thin, tanned huge-boobed women. See you when you're back. If I have time."

I put down the phone and winced. I wasn't great at electronic flirting. I always sounded serious, even if I was joking. Still. I shrugged, fell into bed, and slept fitfully; I was all talked out from being with Oliver. There are some people, touchy-feely conversations are their lifeblood. You see them nodding earnestly, frowning in sorrow, big hug at the ready, as they feast of the tales of anguish sucked out of unwitting acquaintances. I've never been like that, even at work. I feel ashamed and nosy and vampirical, because I can't help suspect that the listener experiences a little pleasure, along with all the horror and compassion. Perhaps it also depends on the teller.

Ollie had not enjoyed his trip down memory lane. He looked shaken after it. If Ollie had been a person who loved to talk about himself it would have been different. But every word was squeezed out like water from a twisted flannel. He hadn't cried, thank God. He'd glazed over, not looked at me more than twice. It was painful to watch, painful to hear. He hadn't wanted to tell me any of it. I'd made him dredge up a history, a version of himself that he had buried and tried to forget. I felt indecent witnessing his intense shame; it was like going to see a public hanging.

But he *was* more aware now of why he'd been behaving like he had, and maybe that would prompt him to change. Although, in my experience, people can be Ten Years' Therapy Self-Aware and still behave like arseholes. Time would tell—which, of course, is absolutely no help to anyone.

Still, the information was stacking up. I had more understanding of my immediate family than ever before. I wasn't yet convinced this was a good thing. I spent the morning cleaning the flat. It was exercise and it was boring, which freed my mind to think. I hadn't heard from Roger. One would assume because he was too ashamed to call, but knowing him as I felt, alas, I did now, he was waiting for *me* to apologize. My poor mother, still living in that house with him.

319

I threw down the duster and called her mobile. What Ollie had said about her being "weird" after I was born had sunk in, and it bothered me. Only when she answered did I realize I knew the number by heart.

"Are you okay?"

"I'm very well, thank you, Hannah, how are you?"

There was actually life in her voice.

"Fine. I—*is he there*—because if he is being unpleasant in any way at all, I—"

"Hannah. Don't worry about me. I know how to deal with your father. He's spent very little time in the house since Wednesday."

"Oh. Where's he been?"

"At the office, I should imagine. I doubt he has anywhere else to go."

She wasn't normally so breezy, so self-assured. A thought occurred. "Tell me, what . . . er, what ever happened with the play?"

"The play!" Angela sounded amused. "Rosalind Emerson took my part. Jumped at it. She's been dying to play opposite your father for years, but she's taller than he is and the opportunity never seemed to arise."

"Did you mind?"

"Oh, no! I asked *her*. It turned out quite well for Inimitable Theatre, thank goodness. Roger forgot to advertise that I was no longer playing Miss Cooper, and all the tickets sold out. Which is, as you know, unheard of."

"What! Why?"

"Hannah. You are sweet. You have this job, you like everyone to think that you're this . . . cynical creature . . . and yet. The tickets sold out because everyone had heard about Jonathan turning up after all this time, and how Roger and I reacted, and, well, it makes for additional drama; real-life drama is always more exciting than staged."

I was shocked. "*Everyone?* People knew about your affair? How?"

"I don't know. That was what Roger was most concerned about. That people would find out. I said how could they. I didn't think Jonathan would tell anyone. But . . . of course . . . now I think of it, Roger had involved *you,* and Ollie, poor little boy, was seven, and he knew something was up. So . . . other children tell their parents, and parents tell their friends . . . I suppose that's what comes of living in a village. People are very vigilant of other people's business. It was mortifying to realize that my . . . love affair was practically folklore. Although I almost felt sorry for Roger. He thought the secret had been kept. You know he didn't play the last night?"

"No!"

For Roger to forgo the bacchanalian excesses of the *aftershow,* he would have to be clinically certified brain dead, at least with embarrassment. The aftershow was where all sexual frustration, all the pent-up energy of being onstage could at last break loose; this was an orgy of adulation and self-congratulation, and as a man whose primal need was that other people thought well of him and told him so in public, Roger *lived* for the aftershow.

My mother giggled. Like hearing the pope giggle. She said, "It's a lot to take in."

"Yes," I said. "And how does it feel to be such an object of notoriety?"

"The scarlet woman, you mean? I thought it would bother me, but it doesn't. They don't know one scrap about me, they only think they know. Half of them are cheating or being cheated on and they're all agog because they know that it could have been them on that stage."

"They're savages!"

"Oh, no, Hannah! Don't think that. People are scared. They look at their own lives. They think of their husbands, they think, is she after *him*?"

"That's ironic, seeing as half of them couldn't care whether their husbands lived or died so long as the life insurance was in place."

"Hannah! You . . . you would be happier if you learned to let go, rather than hang on tight to every little hurt. Imagine each hurt as a twig—you're dragging round a forest! And let me say that one or two of the younger ladies I know have been sweet."

I was tempted to say "that many?" but didn't. She sounded happier. If this poor, thin life was contentment, why should I pick holes in it?

I said good-bye, knowing that I hadn't asked her about her depression, about her frowning at me when I was a baby. It was too much. I'd already bored my way into Oliver's soul; it would have felt too impudent to intrude on my mother's. What did I think I could do, fix it for her just by saying "I know"? There are some things in life you can't fix. And yet. Sometimes an "I know" can be deeply comforting. I suppose I wanted to undo twenty-five years of ill treatment in a few days.

It was no excuse. I waited in all evening and then tried Jack at home.

"Hey, thanks for ringing me," I said.

"I've just got in from the airport! Also, that message. I thought I'd leave you be. How is everything?"

"That's what I'm ringing about."

There was a pause. Then he said, "Do you want to go for lunch tomorrow?"

"Yes," I said. "Okay. But *not* that celebrity place I met you the other time."

"Quite. Where then?"

I know *nowhere* to eat. Fred's Books, but that's it, and strictly speaking that's only half a place to eat. Beyond Fred's—despite having lived in one of the world's greatest cities for thirty odd years—I haven't a clue where is good. Once I resorted to *Time Out* and ended up eating tacos on a main road.

"The café in Regent's Park?"

"Isn't there more than one?"

"You know. That one near the fountain. And the ducks."

"That narrows it down."

"There's an international business school near the entrance."

"You're a pain in the ass, Special. I'll take a cab. See you at the café at one. Take your mobile in case—"

"Jack. Locating people is my *job*."

"Hah!" said Jack and put the phone down.

The next day, against the odds, we found each other.

I bought cheese sandwiches for us both, and we walked to the fountain and sat on a lichen-covered bench. I launched into tales of my family. What I'd discovered.

"I need you to give me Jonathan's number," I said. "I have to speak to him. Find out about Angela's state of mind when the affair started, what she told him about Roger. She must have confided in him. I should find out what he knows. And find out whether he's planning to see her again. It was so selfish and blundering, what he did—"

"Wait. Stop."

I stopped. Stared at him. Sitting on that bench, he made it look smaller than it was.

"What?"

"Ratfink. Don't you think you've discovered enough?"

"How do you mean?"

"Well . . . you wanted to find out the truth about Roger and Angela, and you and Oliver. And you have."

"Yes. And no. There's still a lot I don't know. Angela wouldn't tell me *that* much, and Oliver, he only talked a little about what it was like. Martine was helpful; she helped piece a lot together."

"But why do you need to know every forensic detail? You've found what you need to know. Why Angela *might* have had the affair."

"Yes. Because she'd been depressed for so long and Roger was so cruel to her in that casual, dismissive way of his."

"I'm sure that was a big part of it. And now you see that she had, in a way, justification for doing what she did. I know that's important to you. No one wants to hate their mother. But here's a thing."

"What?"

Jack took my hand. "You'll never know, Special, because you're not Angela, and she isn't going to tell you. And I'm not giving you Jonathan's number—"

I snatched my hand away. "Jack. I can *get* Jonathan's number. I thought I'd ask you as a courtesy."

"Is this why you wanted to see me?"

"Well, yes. I need to speak to Jonathan and—"

"And *I* am saying that you are *not* going speak to Jonathan."

"Why? You were all for it the other day."

"At that point I didn't realize you knew the truth about your dad. But you do, and so now, to ask Jonathan anything more about their affair would be rude and pointless."

I threw a fat wood pigeon crumbs from my sandwich. Jack was annoying me.

"Look," I said. "I am very angry with Jonathan. What right did he have to come back like that, like a ghost? He *thought* he still loved her is bullshit."

"Hannah. You don't have to take care of *all* business. Just trust people to . . . look after themselves. Why can't we talk about *us*? All their stuff is getting in the way."

I ignored this last comment and said, "I don't know why I should trust people to look after themselves. They never have before. And my mother's stuff *is* my stuff." I glared at him. He didn't seem to understand that I couldn't be fine until *she* was fine. "Angela called me 'sweet,' " I added. "I don't know how she could. I feel mean. Mean as a snake."

Jack shook his head. "You were little and you wanted to please your dad. You're the only one who thinks you're unusually mean. You're normal mean. You're not special mean."

"Yeah?" I scowled at the ground. "I'm glad Roger's suffering now. Ha ha *har.*"

Jack looked surprised. "Why, when did you last speak to Angela?"

"Just before you arrived. She said *everyone* in the Suburb knows the happy family was a charade, and always did know. I think, thanks to me and Ollie blabbing our mouths off at school. So Roger thinks he's a laughingstock, not respected at all. He's almost too embarrassed to be seen—he's hiding at the office. Bet they're surprised to see him; he's about as regular as a blue moon at that firm."

Jack shrugged.

I glared at the ground. I felt irritable, because this meeting was not turning out like I'd hoped. Be fair, I reasoned to myself, it was in essence a business meeting. It was civilized. Friendly. But we weren't even holding hands. I could sense his distance.

"I feel," I said, "like I've unearthed a lot of sadness."

"You knew you were never going to uncover anything . . . *lovely.*"

"Huh."

"Hannah. Look at what you did. You thought you might have got it wrong, so you went in search of the truth. And you succeeded. And look what it's got you. The chance to maybe make things better with Angela, begin on a new level. Even Ollie."

"Oh," I said. "Ollie will go back to his silent old self. It will be like this never happened. It was a fluke he told me anything at all. With Ollie, it's like *Back to the Future,* where he's got to be in the car as the lightning strikes the clock tower—you've got a split second—all the stars are in alignment and for some reason, Ollie opens up, shares his feelings, and then *bam!* it's over, and if you missed your chance, that's it, never again."

"Maybe. But that split second could be enough to make all the difference. Maybe he'll be a little different to his son and wife. He'd never consciously want to be like Roger. You did *something.* You uncovered the main facts, and you used them for the good of *now. Now* has been rerouted. And so the future is altered for the best. Angela is right, in a way. The tiny details of the past no longer matter."

The heat had gone out of the summer, which made you forget it had ever happened. One chill day was all it took.

Driving home, I thought about retrieving my earmuffs from the back of the wardrobe and wondered if Jack was right. I might have ignored him and hunted down Jonathan anyway, but I didn't have the heart for the chase. My heart was otherwise engaged.

A week before, Jack had said he loved me. Now I wondered, did that statement carry a lifetime guarantee? Or was it like a £5 voucher for my local Indian takeaway, which ran out after six days? Jack had to be aware that *my* feelings toward him hadn't changed, and yet he showed no inclination to make a further move. I suppose that meant that, despite what he said, he didn't trust me. Or that I'd done something wrong, revealing my immaturity. Too bad. *I* wasn't going to call him again, it was his turn.

I speculated on what might occur if I resolved *never* to call. Would he never call either? It fascinated me, the possibilities, or lack of them, that you could create for yourself if you were stubborn enough. You could fold in on yourself, smaller, smaller, tighter, tighter, an origami person, until you shut out every chance of giving joy, of getting it. You could miss so much. You would feel safe but sad, in your empty high-walled castle of a life. I didn't want to be like that, not anymore. It was secure, but no fun. There were no surprises, every adrenaline hit was courtesy of the *office*.

But then what could I do with a man who refused to believe in me?

The phone rang as I walked in, and I leapt on it.

"Hell-*ow*?" I said, in what I hoped was a friendly voice.

"Hannah!"

"Yes," I said, the warmth drained away; I switched from summer to winter like the weather itself.

"I'm on my way to yours, I'll be there in a sec, get your coat, and I'll pick you up."

"I don't *think* so. Perhaps I could refer you to our last conversation. I believe it ended with you slapping me round the face."

Roger plainly believed in that great untruth, that time heals all wounds. No it doesn't. What about the ones that go septic? Get gangrene? Then a leg has to be lopped off. *My* wound was green and stinking and oozing pus. Time wasn't improving it; a wound isn't like a fine wine.

"Well, *you* hurt me too, I still have the green bruise—oh, but this isn't important right now, I can't—"

It had taken me a while to realize that Roger was so self-obsessed it practically qualified as a disorder. Narcissism! There you go. They classify everything. Maybe I hadn't wanted to believe. It is easier to block unpleasantness than to deal with it. Although I had a nasty feeling that all the unpleasantness in my personal life that I'd succeeded in blocking had managed to squish through around the edges, tarnishing my view of the world, influencing my every thought, opinion, action, reaction. Put it this way: I was the only girl I knew who slept with a machete *in the bed with her.* (Sheathed, but nonetheless.)

It was like a punch to the stomach, to see my father as he was. None of us are perfect, but at the other extreme, no one wants to discover that their hero is nothing but a composite of flaws. He was actually incapable of feeling what I felt at his betrayal, even of imagining what it might be like. There was *no* identification. I might have been a different species.

And no excuse, even if I were. I'd never say that the Siamese next door and I were friends, but she *always* gets a rip of burger, chicken nugget, or kebab if I come home late after a job. She shows her appreciation with a purr and a silky slither around my ankles. It's a nice moment—human, cat, sharing a common pleasure, a love of good food. But what gets me is her courtesy. She's friendly, she knows I'll be friendly in return. Chairman Miaow is more emotionally astute than Roger Lovekin!

It was a bit much—I had more of a synthesis with a feline than with my own father, and I'm not even a cat person!

So was it worth trying to punish him if he really *was* incapable of understanding what he'd done to me? There's no point in eliciting a "sorry" from someone who doesn't mean it, and I suspected that my father never would. He didn't comprehend other people's pain, only his own.

And how very convenient that would be! Like pleading insanity after you've bludgeoned someone to death. If he didn't comprehend *my* pain, I would quit trying to make him understand it, but that didn't mean he was free to go. No. If *his* pain was all he understood, then I would have to concentrate on poking and prodding *that*.

"Roger," I interrupted. "I'm surprised you dare show your face around here, what with all your so-called friends in the Suburb gossiping about Angela's affair. Everyone completely understands why she did it. Your behavior toward her was vile. Which is why everyone you know must be asking each other why she confined herself to a mere affair, why not leave him, oh, the kids of course, but now the kids are grown, why stay? I'm sure they're all thinking that—"

"You *knew*!"

"What do you mean, I knew? Of course I knew! You never bloody let us forget, did—"

"Not the affair. You knew she was planning this?"

I hesitated. I didn't want to ask "planning what?" because I wouldn't want him to think he had *anything* on me, any knowledge that I didn't have, anything he might be able to blackmail me with. He was the slimiest of toads, I had given him so much, so many years of my life had been devoted to him, I was not going to give him one more minute. Think, Hannah. Be logical. I cleared my throat and took a chance. I said, "Are you suggesting I knew that Angela was planning to leave you?"

My father's voice rose to a shriek. "I *knew* it!" he yelled. And my heart gave an almighty thump. She'd done it! She'd actually done it!

A niggle of memory bothered at my brain like a tadpole at a piece of meat. *Yes.* Jack. Talking to Jack. He'd asked if I'd spoken to Angela this morning. Because of something I said. Oh, think, dense girl!

"I can't believe she's done this to me and you didn't tell me, I can't fucking belieeeeeeeeeeeeeve it!"

I held the phone away from my ear and looked at it with distaste. *Ha ha har. I'm glad Roger's suffering now.*

That was it! That was what I'd said to Jack. That was when he'd asked if I'd spoken to Angela. Which meant . . . dur, you're so thick . . . which meant that he knew she was planning to leave him. Because Jonathan had told him! Aha! Ar har! A-sodding-ha!

Oh. But Jack hadn't told me. He'd just refused to give me Jonathan's number. So. I was right. He didn't trust me. He didn't trust me not to tell my father! Despite all that I knew. Thanks for that show of faith, Jack.

Out of interest, I put the receiver back to my ear.

"—with him, isn't she? All her stuff gone, the dirty dishes on the side, and not even a note! Now I'm warning you, you tell me where they—"

"Ah, Roger. Go to hell and scare the devil," I said and put the phone down.

46.

The next morning my mother rang, sounding coy.

"Well," she said. "I did it. I left your father." She paused. "I hope you don't mind."

My reflex response—"Of course not!"—was on my lips. I held on, gave it some thought. It was a strange thing to say, not exactly a real question and possibly a dig. I decided to ignore it and said instead, "Thank God you did—it will allay some of my guilt."

I wasn't trying to manipulate any particular response, but she said smartly, "Don't *say* that. You mustn't have any, I won't have it. I take full responsibility for everything."

This flustered me. "You do?" I said. "For . . . being weird after I was born?"

My mother sighed down the phone. "Hannah."

I waited.

"Hannah," she said again, with a little gasp, as if a cork had been unpopped. "It's true, I . . . I didn't know then. Babies are egocentric. So when a baby's miserable mother doesn't smile back at her, the baby thinks, it's *my* fault, it feels guilt. *The little baby!* The next day, Mummy feels better, manages a smile. It's confusing for the baby. The . . . *my* inconsistency was damaging. I can't tell you how I feel about that. When you were four, five, I had everything more . . . under control, and we were great friends."

"Oh, I know," I said. "I'm not asking you to feel guilty for anything that . . . happened later. That was all *his* fault. Blame him."

"Well. Hannah. I improved, but the distance between us was already there, and that was thanks to *me,* and while your father was wrong to use that . . . weakness against us both, it would be unfair to blame him wholly. You, however, should not feel guilt. Please."

I was silent.

Then I said, "I'll do my best."

"I'm so glad," she replied. And then, "Would you . . . do you think you might like to come round and see us?"

Jonathan lived on the sixth floor of a mansion block in a smart area of London; it was three stops to Bond Street, I checked on the tube map. Voice-over work must pay well, because teaching certainly didn't. My mother opened the door. If I'd had the breath, I'd have asked why they couldn't invest in a lift. Instead I grinned at her inanely. "God," I wheezed. "You don't look like you."

Her eyes were wide, her lashes curly, and her lips pink. Oho. The stealth application that Gab had been talking about. She looked kittenish in a white jumper and a longish suede skirt, with leather boots that disappeared under it. The boots and skirt were a light brown. Beige? Fawn? Taupe. Toupee? (My knowledge of shades still lagged.) There was a touch of the Lady Penelope about this getup, I was impressed. I always saw her dressed for duty. This was for pleasure. I blushed.

She leaned in for a chaste kiss. It would be a while before we were throwing ourselves at each other.

"Come in. Jonathan's making coffee."

I snorted.

She glanced at me, nervous, and I clapped a hand over my mouth. "Sorry. It's just that, well, catch *Roger* making coffee."

My mother smiled thinly.

I covered by babbling, "Oh, this is nice, isn't this nice, how nice this is."

Actually, it was not at all my taste. For a start, the man had a real live *vine* growing in his kitchen. I suppose the skylight made this possible, but I kept glancing at the leaves, hoping they were plastic. There were pots and pans dangling from, as far as I could tell, the ceiling, I presume so that Mr. Coates (I couldn't call an old teacher by his first name; I was too puritan) could whip up a three-course meal without having to haul utensils out of cupboards. I didn't like it. It felt cluttered, lazy, utilitarian. Put that scrap metal away! There was no unity, no style, no *vision* to Mr. Coates's home; it seemed to be composed of a load of random stuff, every unrelated item bought and found a corner, for no finer reason than because he liked it.

Mr. Coates's first words to me were "I have to confess to being a little scared to meet you."

I stood a few feet away from him so that he couldn't make a sudden lunge and kiss me. I knew what these arty people were like. "We've met about a thousand times," I said. "Mostly when I was four, but even so!"

Mr. Coates gestured toward a wooden chair that looked as if it had escaped from the Three Bears' cottage. "Yes, but we've not met in *these* circumstances." He glanced toward my mother.

I was about to blurt, "Oh, yes we have, when I burst in on you and Angela naked." This would have been a faux pas, and thankfully I realized it before the words emerged. I cleared my throat and all but bowed as I said, "If you make my mother happy, then you don't have to be scared of me."

Mr. Coates coughed and said, "Good, great."

I beamed at my mother, who laughed, although it sounded as if she was being strangled.

I took the mug of coffee that Mr. Coates had set down on the farmhousey pine table before backing away. He was acting like I might throw it at him. Meanwhile, Angela looked as if she was tied to a totem pole.

I worked back through what I'd said and realized I might have come across as threatening. I was about to clarify, then thought better of it. If he was all he said he was, like I said, he had no reason to be scared of me. If he wasn't . . . then he should consider himself warned—there *would* be payback.

I sipped my coffee, and I saw him wink at Angela and stroke her arm. He didn't even mouth, "You okay?" but she nodded and smiled. He placed a mug in front of her and pulled out one of his tatty old woman chairs for her. I watched Angela smooth her suede skirt and sit in it. I was perched on an identical seat, and I have to say, it was the hardest piece of wood I'd ever sat on. I'd just formed this thought when Mr. Coates cried, "Bollocks, the cushions!"

My mother and I stared as he dived toward a green-stained pine cupboard door and heaved it open. Behind it sat a prehistoric washing machine. The thing was *crammed* with cushions.

"I wanted to wash them before you arrived," he said, dragging a sodden one out.

My mother gasped. "Jonathan . . . Maybe it might have been better to take the cushion covers *off* the cushions to wash them . . . perhaps?"

She sucked in her lips, and her shoulders started to shake. Mr. Coates frowned at her and then a smile crept across his face. The two of them burst out laughing. My mother was bent over in mirth, and Mr. Coates was wheezing, clutching his knees, and they were gazing right at each other. It was lovely to see. She didn't look like the person who, as I remembered, had once said "excuse me" after every hiccup for twenty minutes.

"I'm sorry," said Mr. Coates, regaining composure, darting a mischievous glance at my mother.

"Don't be," I said. And I smiled. A real, genuine warm smile. I saw that the vine, the pine, the rabble of tin, it didn't matter. I saw, yet again, that it wasn't things that made a home, it was the people in it.

It was a strange thing to see my mother like this. As if she were a teenager again. She patted her hair, giggled, and hung on his every word. I thought he was a genuine person—despite the actorly diction—but she seemed to think he was some kind of god. When he pottered off to the toilet, she gazed after him as if he were Hercules having said ta-ta before embarking on his seven labors. She turned back to me with effort.

"How is Jack these days?" she said.

As I hadn't mentioned anything, I presumed she'd heard some gossip from Mr. Coates. This didn't delight me.

I replied, "We see each other now and then."

I thought this was a fair answer. Jack hadn't called since our meeting in the park. Nor had he said, "See you later." His exact words, as he'd hailed a taxi: "Now you look after yourself, Ex-Wife."

I was not a woman who had the time or intellect to drive herself crazy analyzing male linguistics. But even at a glance I could tell that this fond farewell was a few levels cooler than burning love. In fact, it was the Jack I had always imagined him to be. A person to whom a lover like me was inconsequential fun, a mere pastime, a party favor. All right, I was being overdramatic. I knew I meant something to him. But did I mean *everything* to him? Or was I more on the level of an onion bhaji?

Once, the uncertainty wouldn't have bothered me, but now it did. Which I didn't like. I felt ruffled. I consoled myself that I wasn't an expert in this, and the most likely explanation was that a normal person's intimacy level naturally waxed and waned like the moon. It wasn't possible or sane to be all snuggly-woo with other humans twenty-four hours a day. You'd be mentally drained. Empty inside. To keep a sense of who you were, you had to back off, to gather your wits. I was sure even Jason's shrink would agree that to be an emotional Open Sesame! day in, day out, was a little warped.

My mother said, "Oh, that's nice," in a voice that was unconvinced. She took a dainty sip of coffee. "And how are his parents?"

"I don't know," I said, suddenly embarrassed that I didn't.

"Does he talk about them?" said Angela.

I became aware that she was ever so gently making a point,

although what it was I had no idea. As we were rebuilding our relationship I didn't say what I wanted to say, which was, "I haven't seen him for bloody days, so shut up about him, all right?"

"No," I said instead. "Not much."

She was silent.

I added, "They're strange people, but I think he's resigned to how they are."

Mr. Coates wandered back into the kitchen. He'd been ages. *Must have been a pooh.* I shook off the thought, thinking why am I so *disturbed,* no wonder Jack needs to keep his distance. It's struck me more than once what a holiday it would be to exchange minds for a fortnight with, say, Julie Andrews.

"Jack's parents?" said Mr. Coates. He had to be at least fifty. His hearing was good for an old person.

"Yes, that's right," said my mother, welcoming him into the conversation as if three wasn't a crowd.

"His mother recently remarried," said Mr. Coates casually, as if people remarried every day. Which I suppose they did. "Three boys. In their twenties. He said she doesn't stop talking about them."

Immediately I heard this, I tried to justify all aspects of it. Why Jack hadn't told *me.* What it meant. The queasy sensation in my stomach told me that something wasn't as it should be. Jack was superb at philosophizing about my life. He could be wise, fatalistic, understanding, all in the same breath. But when it came to *his* problems, he was as stuck as a fly trapped in golden syrup.

And he didn't feel able to confide in me.

Normally, I do not sympathize with women who complain that they can't get their men to talk. My private belief is, are you *crazy?* What caliber of chat do you think you're missing out on?

But now I urgently wanted him to tell all. Partly because if it related to him, I wanted to know. But also because his silence didn't bode well.

"Right," I said, standing up. "It was great to see you. Both. Together. Well. I'll let you get on."

I hoped she wasn't aware that just about everyone who says, "Well. I'll let you get on," is actually saying, "I really want to go now, please may I?"

On my way to the car, I awarded my visit five out of ten. I'm a stern marker, because it *had* been a success. I hadn't offended any-one. Mr. Coates hadn't offended me. (And goodness, the potential was there. On seeing him again, I'd felt a little bristly, on my mother's behalf, as if our roles were reversed. This was cheeky, as I'm sure he could never have hurt her as much as I had.)

No. My mother had merely unsettled me a little. All for the best, I'm sure, but right then, I didn't want to *have* doubts about Jack. The time I spent with him, I wanted to be caught up in the moment, not second-guessing it. And hark at her! Her way of deal-ing with her past was to brush it aside, claim it was old news. Maybe she felt entitled to preach because earlier that morning she had alluded to her depression and its effect on me, but the mention had not been overt. She had *never* referred to it openly.

That was fine by me. I knew enough. What riled me was that *she* kept stuff back from me, why did she care that Jack did?

When he called that night—I calculated that we hadn't spoken for three days—I was reserved.

"You're in a mood," he said. "What's wrong?"

I huffed, and then I told him. Well, some. I *didn't* say that I was worried that we'd lost pace, that he'd buggered off to LA and returned altogether cooler, and that I felt much as I did eleven

337

years ago. Out of my depth. I just told him about what Jonathan had said.

"Jonathan!" said Jack. "He's such a queen! I was going to tell you. It's his fault. All the dust he's kicked up in your family—we've been caught up, talking about *that*. And it's your fault. When I'm with you my mind is on other things . . . filth, mainly."

I grinned, curled myself around the phone. God, look at me. I had the man, I felt the urge to get me a *Cosmo* subscription and a large pink bow, I was turning into such a *girl*. Worrying about nothing.

47.

Unemployment is wasted on some people. They do nothing with it. Rather like lottery winners bleating, "It won't change me," as if that's a good thing, their biggest extravagance buying new seat covers for their Ford Cavalier, hiring a four-berth caravan this year, insulting the rest of us who really *know* how to burn cash. They quit their job as a dustman or dinner lady, and all the time they once spent clearing rubbish or ladling out rubbish, they now spend watching rubbish and eating rubbish. They might as well be on the dole!

I was different from lottery winners, and doleys. For a start, I had less money. But I had been so damn creative with my time, God, I impressed myself. I had achieved a lot. The people stuff, you know about. I'm talking about other things. Details that I'd never have noticed before because I was moving too fast. These last two weeks, I'd spent quite a few hours sitting at my glass dining table—no wooden desk was ever big enough for all my shit—by the study window, just *thinking*. I'd never been too keen on thinking. There's a point after which thinking only makes people miserable.

But I'd had some good thoughts. I'd sit there, gaze at Grandma Nellie's photographs, and a plane would fly across my table. Well, it flew across the sky, but I liked to see its reflection cross my glass table—I was amused by the idea of a plane flying through my study. At least daily, a great fat honey bee would bonk its head on the window, *clonk*. And once a fluffy dandelion spore wafted in and bounced across the images of my mother as a young woman. These tiny nothings, they made me smile inwardly. I'd sit there, survey my tiny slice of the world, feel a wriggle that wasn't too far removed from contentment. It was good to know that small things could make an impact on my mood. We can't all winter in the Caribbean.

I'd missed a couple of episodes of *CSI*. And I hadn't cared too much. I was trying to cool the heat of my passion for a bunch of made-up characters portrayed by actors.

I could go back to Greg—my *own dear* Grissom—and tell him that I had used my unpaid leave wisely. Perhaps I would never have the instinct of Gil ("something isn't right here"), but I had finally seen what was plonk in front of me. Jack, Martine, Grandma Nellie, the fact that they'd all but forced my face into the plate of details, didn't take away from my pride. When people said, "And what do *you* do?" I'd always replied, "I'm a detective," thinking that they didn't need to know the whole of it ("but not a very good one"). Now I knew I could be a—if not brilliant—fine bread-and-butter sleuth, because I had revised my approach. I understood about people's need for an emotional life, and how it drove them, whether they knew it or not.

Monday morning, I got in at nine, and heaved all Ron's files out of my office and into the corridor. The room smelled bad, of grease and cheap food. I opened the window, aired the place. There was a glossy pamphlet on *my* desk for, I kid you not, a submergeable bike.

I swept it into the bin. Ron was a sucker for all that James-Bond-type rubbish. No real detective uses equipment like that. Cubby Broccoli has a lot to answer for. You wouldn't believe how many women watch James Bond films, then ring us up and ask if we can "put a bug" on their husband. It's just not practical to bug someone on the move. It would be like trying to tune into a pirate radio station in bad weather.

Greg is a bit of a purist (his tools are "the phone and my brilliant personality") and the most fancy device I ever used was a hidden camera inside a teddy bear. This kid was going to stay with her dad on the weekends, and the mother believed the new girlfriend was being nasty to the child. She wasn't. That was a while back. Those bears are pretty much for sale in Mothercare now.

Greg came in as I was spraying my chair with Dettox. He nodded. "Probably wise."

I turned around so he could get a view of my face, which is, I hope, less offensive than my butt. "I'm back," I said. "Hello!"

He grinned. "Drop by when the decontamination process is complete."

An hour later, I made it to Greg's office.

He looked up. "You look different. How are you?"

"Very good. I enjoyed my forced nonlabor."

"Yeah? Any conclusions?"

"Well. Yes, actually."

"Good, because when we had our chat, two weeks ago, you looked at me like I was a talking donkey. I wanted you to use this time wisely. I didn't want you to piss it up the wall."

"Women can't do that, Greg."

"Women can do whatever they want."

Greg nodded for me to sit.

I sat. "I'm committed to the job. I am. I know that now. I did some . . . unofficial fieldwork on my break. Unpaid. For *me*. Learned a lot. Discovered a lot."

"So you're not leaving me to do decoy work *just* yet."

"Well. I certainly hope not."

Greg and I are pretty sniffy about companies who do decoy work. We reckon that decoys are for stalkers and obsessives. The stuff they find out, it isn't anything you can use in court. There's nothing worse than the judge saying, "And how did you get this information?" It can be classed as entrapment. Not only that, they're so *vulnerable*. Women who do decoy work put themselves at such risk. Flirt, flirt, flirt, then back off at the last moment. It pisses men off, and not all men are decent blokes. So I jolly well hoped Greg was teasing. *He* knew I'd rather work in a supermarket.

"So tell me what you learned."

I told him. About digging up all the family skeletons till there was a great pile of white bones on my living room floor.

"I feel that I am," I concluded, "a little more aware of . . . the *human condition*."

Greg smiled. "That's no small claim."

I coughed. "Although. I have to tell you."

Greg leaned forward. "Oh yes?"

"I want to do this job. But. There are certain things I won't do. I couldn't grass up Charlie's mother to her ex-husband for having a new boyfriend, that woman had *nothing*. I do have to live with myself. And I don't want ever to think that I'm responsible for a little kid missing out. So I stand by what I did. Although I see I was wrong to waste your time and money. Although, Greg, Hound Dog does get paid exactly the same, regardless of what we report, so it wouldn't have made any difference to you financially. In the future, though, if I may, I won't take on the jobs I don't feel morally comfortable doing."

I winced. I'd used the M-word. I braced myself to be slung out on my ear. I met Greg's eyes and I wasn't surprised to see he looked furious.

"You little shit!" he said. "How *dare* you?"

"What?" I gasped.

"I'm not some fucking *ogre*. I'm not some dark creature with two heads. I'm not . . . *Ron*. I'll tell you what happened with that particular case, missy. Hound Dog submitted *your* footage, not his, with our report. No new boyfriend, here's our proof. I've got *four* boys, okay, four! I'm not going to deprive some little fella of any-thing—for a start, my wife would kill me."

I allowed the corners of my mouth to tweak upward. I'd met Greg's wife. She was Scottish, dark long curly hair, luscious curves, bright, funny, and never stopped talking, but you could tell she was carved out of flint. A disk had crumbled in her spine and she was in constant excruciating pain. Christ, if it were me, the whining would never cease. With her, och, said Greg, she just drank a little more at parties.

I beamed. "I have to live with myself. And *you* have to live with her. But I would never suggest that your wife keeps you in check."

"No," agreed Greg. "You wouldn't."

"What did Ron think of your decision?"

"He wasn't thrilled."

"Shame."

"But I made it up to him."

"Yeah?"

"Yeah. Right now, he's spending two days in a field. Watching an industrial site. Keeping an eye on some gypsies."

"Oh," I said. "How lovely!"

Greg and I smiled, our hearts warmed by the thought of Ron, digging a scrape in the cold ground, covering it, and himself, in the undergrowth of the area, peeing in a bottle, taking a dump in cling-film, drinking Nescafé in a can (push the button and it heats up, ah, *luxury*), stuffing Pro-plus to keep himself awake, and eating army rations, mm, delicious!

Greg winked at me. "Good to have you back, girl. Now sidle out to your car and follow someone!"

48.

People are funny about weddings. I don't mean funny ha-ha. As someone who has been a bride, I feel qualified to speak about this.

Jack and I didn't want kids at our big day, so we didn't invite anyone under sixteen. This made every guest with kids hate us. Fair enough. But, get this, it was *our* wedding, *our* decision. Any other day of our lives, if we saw them, we'd expect to see their kids too, but just this once, we hoped they might indulge our wishes without complaint, because they were, after all, here for *us,* in *our* honor, it was actually *our wedding,* it was our brief prerogative to be selfish, think only of ourselves.

Jack's favorite uncle and aunt turned down the invitation in a sulk. Hurt, he invited their brood (who loathed every minute), but his affection for them cooled for good. Another guest ignored our request and brought her baby, who screamed as we said our vows. The attitude problems didn't end there. Even Martine said, "Do you mind if I'm *not* a bridesmaid if I don't like the dress?" My father's cousin bitched about the food. Anyone would have thought it was *their* big day.

"Ratfink," Jack had said. "Next time I do this I'm going to elope."

For all the above reasons, I was determined not to voice, even *think,* a single negative thing about Jason and Lucy's wedding (or, at least, the willy end bit that I was attending). I resolved to separate my dislike for weddings as an entity that sucked up your weekend from this particular occasion, the much-longed-for union of a great favorite to, hm, a good old girl. To demonstrate my goodwill, I'd donated two Versace cups and saucers off the wedding list (information, phone numbers, enclosed with the invite; they weren't taking any chances). Set me back nearly four hundred quid, but you can't buy *one* cup and saucer for people who are marrying, and after what I'd put Jason through, I sensed that poverty was the price of a clean-ish conscience.

I was greatly touched to discover that Jason had invited Jack (also, to the willy end bit).

I was driving round the roundabout at the end of the Rotherhithe Tunnel for the third time, trying to guess which turning to take, when I realized that a voluptuous red Audi was doing the same. I looked closer, and yes, there was Jack, cursing at the wheel. Why? Because the wedding was taking place at the London Hilton Docklands, in glorious Rotherhithe. That was sarcastic, the place is a dump. It's also, for North Londoners, impossible to find. (I'll remind you that mostly, detectives *follow* people . . .) I could imagine that the London Hilton Docklands was not Lucy's ideal venue, but the only one in Britain you could secure at short notice.

I hooted Jack, who glared into his rearview mirror, saw it was me, chose an exit, and pulled over. I did the same and hopped out of my car.

"Why didn't you say Jase had invited you?"

Jack grinned. "He wanted it to be a surprise. For some reason, he thinks he's matchmaking. He's so bloody *decent,* it's almost more than I can stand."

I smiled. "He's such a romantic, he doesn't think that we could have saved on petrol."

I was joking, because privately I reckoned that Jason had done us both a favor. If we'd shared a car, the driver would have probably murdered the navigator by now. As it was, it took us another half hour to chance upon the hotel. Just modern enough to be depressing, the place screamed "conference center," but alas, not loud enough to help us locate it.

We poked our heads round the door of what appeared to be a large assembly hall. It was stuffed with smart people, and there were a lot of feathery hats on chairs. A band was playing "I Wanna Know What Love Is" loud and fast. Most of the guests looked happily drunk, even the ten-year-olds. I scanned the room for food and the groom. Aw, there he was in the far corner chatting away to some granny, and didn't he look sweet. God bless him, he'd gone all out for tradition. Gray top hat and tails, with a great gold tie and golden waistcoat. He had a white rose as a buttonhole, and his nose looked red and sniffly.

"Oh, hello."

Ah, crap, I can never help but smile when I see a bride, such is the power of conditioning. Lucy had chosen a strapless corset dress with a massive skirt, it seemed to have been inspired by the costume of a seventeenth-century infanta and was wide enough to have doubled as a road sweep. I felt that Gabrielle would have steered her toward a wiser choice; the woman had shoulders like a carthorse.

And yet the glow, the bridal glow . . .

"*Lucy!*" I cried. "Oh! How are you? You look really nice. Tired, though. You look a bit tired. I suppose it's a really long day. Have you enjoyed it?"

She smiled stiffly. "Yes, thank you."

I felt the hot breeze of her breath on my face and, oh my sainted aunt! It was as fresh and lovely as a snowdrop in spring! The groom didn't *know* how much he owed me.

Jack leaned in and kissed her hand, the creep. "Lucy, I'm Jack, Hannah's friend. You look gorgeous, absolutely beautiful. Radiant in fact. Jason's very lucky."

Lucy beamed, tilted her head, "Oh, thank you, Jack!"

I realized I should have been a little more effusive in my compliments. I forget, women don't like understated when it comes to praise. I cleared my throat. "And Jason looks fantastic," I said. "Very handsome, obviously he *is* handsome, but today he looks stunning, he could be a model. Congratulations on nabbing him, you must be delighted!"

To my surprise and disappointment, she shot me a furious look. "My husband and I are very happy. *Very* happy. Oh, and thanks for the cups. You shouldn't have. Help yourself to sandwiches."

She swish-swashed away, the skirt knocking down chairs and tables (I exaggerate but furniture definitely teetered).

I widened my eyes at Jack. What was *her* problem?

Jack widened his eyes at me. "You moron," he said. "You date the guy for five years, you tell the bride she looks okay—"

" 'Nice,' I said, 'really nice,' is what I said!"

"That's the same as 'okay'; it's shit. And why on earth would you tell her she looks tired? You don't want to look tired on your wedding day!"

"But she does look tired."

"Firemen have cut people out of cars who look better than that, but you don't *tell her to her face. Then* you go overboard on how awesomely fabulous Jason looks, making it sound as if you still fancy him—"

"Oh *no.* Lucy already thinks I'm obsessed with him."

"Really. Why?"

"Ah, no reason, I don't know. She's paranoid."

"And you tell her she's lucky to have nabbed him, like she's a jewel thief!"

I bit my lip. "Should I go and speak to her?"

"Don't you go near her, you've done enough. *I'll* speak to her."

"What will you say?"

"That you're an idiot, need new glasses, that sort of thing."

"Right," I said glumly.

Jack whipped my glasses from my face and polished the lenses on his shirt. "How can you *see*," he said. "It's like cleaning a hubcap." Then he pushed the hair from my eyes and kissed me.

The band announced they were taking a break, that in the meantime they would leave us in the capable hands of "Don't You Forget About Me." My heart thumped, one of my favorite songs. Out in the charts around the time that Jack and I first got together. It said everything. "I won't harm you, or touch your defenses, vanities, insecurities. . . ." I couldn't think of any more perfect description of the contract implied by a first kiss, and then, over time if intimacy progressed, torn in two.

"Dance with me to this," I said. "Then speak to Lucy."

Jack led me to the dance floor and, goobers that we were, we jumped around shouting the words in each other's faces. It didn't matter, though. Everyone else under forty was doing the same. As the song ended, Jason caught my eye and waved.

"You go and make my apologies to the bride," I said. "I want to say hello to her husband."

"Sure," said Jack. His lips brushed against mine, and he walked off.

"Look at you!" I roared at Jason. "Don't you look the part! How do you feel?"

I did not expect him to sweep me into his arms, but he did. He hit me with a great big smacker of a kiss, and said, "You know, Hannah. I waited for five years for you to ask me that question, and I don't think you ever did. But now you do! Four hours after I get married to someone else!"

This floored me and I couldn't think of anything to say. So I said, "Hell of a wedding cake."

Jason grimaced. "Lucy's mother chose it. It's Victorian."

"Bit stale then," I said.

We gravely regarded the cake, a three-tiered affair, each tier lifted high by three golden pillars and encrusted with frills and drapes of white icing and a ton of pink sugar roses. It stood on a gold stand.

Jason whispered, "It cost three hundred and twenty-five *pounds!*"

We giggled together. Then I remembered *my* wedding vow and said, "I'm sure it tastes delicious."

"Hey," said Jason, looking over my shoulder. "What did you think of me inviting Jack?"

"Very thoughtful."

He nudged me. "So! So! What do you think? Do you think you and Jack will end up doing this"—he gestured around the room, then blushed—"er, again?"

I looked at my feet. "Jason! The questions you ask!"

"Hm," said Jason, in the manner of a tease. "I think I'll have to have a word with Jack."

I clutched his arm. "No. God. Jason. Don't you *dare*."

"Jaaaaaaayyyyyyson, come and daaaaaaaaaaaance with meeeeeeee!" said a small girl, tugging at his coattails.

Jason grinned at me. "Duty calls," he said and took her hand.

The crowd parted for Jason, cheers, slaps on the back, shouts of "aaarrrr!" because he was dancing with a kid.

I stared after him, smiling. Then I turned to see if I could spot Jack. At first I couldn't. Then I saw him, he was huddled at a table with Lucy, their two chairs facing, her great skirt billowing up around her like a cloud; from where I was standing it seemed to engulf Jack's lower half. She was talking to him, her gestures fast and excitable, her head wobbling on her neck. She was drunk and probably boring him. I wondered if I should mount a rescue operation. I decided to wander past, make eye contact with Jack. I grabbed a glass of champagne and walked casually by, staring right at him. I was sure he saw me, but he didn't look at me, just focused on Lucy's yapping mouth.

One must indulge the bride on her special day, I decided, and went to watch the dancing. Jack would find me when Lucy had finished talking at him. Ten minutes later, I glanced over, and they were *still* at it. Not only that, Jason had joined them. What the hell did those three have to talk about? Not married life, I'll bet. I didn't like it. I felt cross and left out. I checked my watch. Ten to midnight. Hang on, they should be wrapping up this thing in a few minutes. I sighed, tapped my toes, saw, with relief, Lucy's mother bend and murmur in her ear. Lucy heaved herself off the chair, kissed Jack on the cheek, and rustled off to say au revoir to some old biddy. Jason and Jack shook hands, then Jason scurried off in his wife's wake.

At *last*. I wondered if we could sneak off without saying goodbye. After all, Jack had been chatting to the hosts for a good half hour, it would be silly to chase after them just to inform them that we were leaving; they were about to scuttle off to their honeymoon suite, what did they care? I was hoping that tonight would be *our* night too. I was trying not to fret, but I felt that Jack and I urgently needed to touch base (in the romantic sense.) We hadn't had sex since *before* LA. Before it! I wasn't quite sure why—it could have been work, but I'd never believed in "the work" excuse. Jack's attitude was what worried me. Or was it *my* attitude?

I stood up with a smile as Jack approached, but he swept past without looking at me.

"Jack?" I said.

"Fuck off."

I was stunned. "*What?*"

He was walking so fast I had to jog to keep up with him. "Jack! What is it? What's wrong?"

He stopped, and his expression was so ferocious, I reared back. "Leave me alone, you *bitch*."

I felt vaguely hysterical. What had I done? I was clean, wasn't I? Jesus. Jason or Lucy must have said something, but what?

I followed him all the way to his red Audi, a sob in my throat.

"Fuck off fuck off fuck off don't speak to me," he spat and there were tears in his eyes.

"Jack," I said, and there were tears in my eyes too. "I don't understand. Please. Tell me what it is I'm supposed to have done."

Jack slammed shut the door and buzzed down the window. "As ever," he said, "I find out the truth about you from your *friends*. Lucy tells me that you were, still are, obsessed with Jason, to the point that you pretended to be engaged when you weren't, that *you* put that engagement announcement in the *Telegraph* without asking him in the hope of forcing him to propose—which works out the day before you shagged *me*—she didn't want him to invite you but he felt obliged, and you go and spend a ridiculous sum on their wedding gift, more than her *parents* spent, which is fucking weird. And I tell her, as politely as you *can* tell a bride, I don't think so, I think you've got it wrong, I'm sure that Hannah did not want to marry Jason. So she calls over Jasie, who confirms that *he* split with *you,* and you were devastated, heartbroken, but really, Jack, we think you'd be good for her, you've both grown up a lot. So you tell me a pack of lies, and far from being the love of your life, I find out I'm, quote Brocklehurst, your second choice."

He revved the engine. "I won't be your second choice again," he said and screeched off.

49.

I bawled for a while, then quit. This man was about as volatile as a Mexican firework, and I couldn't handle it any longer. When I looked at Jack, he saw me ten years ago. Whatever he said, he was still screwed up about what I'd done to him aged twenty, and if you ask me, it was all mixed up in what his parents *hadn't* done for him, way back. It had to be, or why would he react with such venom? Why was he so ready to believe the worst of me? I reckoned if he wanted to be with me, he'd have asked for *my* version of events before legging it. He didn't, which meant that Lucy and Jason's ramblings were a convenient *out.*

I knew this because I wrote the rules. I was the one who backed away when Jack tried to love me a decade before. I'd made sure that my behavior saw him off. Now, at last, I was ready to trust him, ready *for* him, finally fit for a real relationship, despite the uninsurable risk of committing, putting my mental welfare in the shaky hands of an emotional anarchist. And he wasn't. I'd scared him, scarred him. Maybe there was a wide-eyed idealist somewhere inside him that wanted to believe it would work, but it wasn't enough. It couldn't fight that powerful cynic, a person who was nothing to do with me, who was created long before I came on the scene.

I hadn't helped. He'd taken a chance, and I'd proved to him it was the wrong move. But Jason was right. I *had* grown since then. I was under the distinct impression that I *had* made my peace with Jack. He was a bit of a terrorist in that sense. "Yeah, yeah, I agree to this, but I don't really, one tiny bomb doesn't count." I felt I'd served my time, but it seemed that Jack felt that I deserved a life sentence. In which case I was regretfully going to have to leave him to it, or he'd destroy me. I had no problem feeling bad for my own sins, but there was no way I was going to feel bad for someone else's.

I've seen it happen. Women date men, men date women the insides of whose heads are knotted up tight as a golf ball. They meet some sweet, unsuspecting character, who makes the mistake of sympathizing, tugs at a stray thread, and this great festering wad of string starts to unravel. They end up taking the rap for a million prior transgressions committed by other people at other times. It was like Jason's shrink getting him to act out his anger on a chair. You can't punish the bastard responsible because he isn't here. But this poor little chair's right in front of you! I wasn't about to be sat on.

I drove home and was wiping off my makeup with a big fat cotton ball in front of the mirror—when I thought "No."

No, actually.

I threw the gray cotton ball in the bin, drove to Jack's flat, pressed my finger to the buzzer, and kept it there.

When he finally wrenched open the door, I didn't give him the chance to speak. He opened his mouth, and I said, "No. You are not going to talk this time. You are going to listen to *me*. There is a bit of a pattern going on here. *You* get the wrong end of the stick, you think I'm guilty, you dump me. Last time that happened, I was too young, too naive, too confused to put you straight. You believed I was cheating and I was so frozen by my family history, I let our marriage go without a fight. I didn't fight to make you understand, I didn't fight to tell you that you were wrong. I just accepted it. But I've already explained this to you. Which means, either you're deaf or you're not listening. If you thought about it rationally, you'd know that there is no *way* I was or am obsessed with Jason. I told you before the wedding that I had to think of a clever way to break off with him without hurting his feelings, and that is exactly what I did. I made *him* think he ended it by saying I never wanted children. I lied to Lucy about the *Telegraph* to get Jason off the hook with *her*. So the upshot of all this, Jack, is that you have been a complete fool. I'm here for you because I *have* changed. It's *you* who's still the same. I don't want to let you go again, I would marry you again in a second, but there's two things preventing that. *You* and your godawful attitude. Truth is, you can't believe that I've really changed. And how can I commit to a man who at heart thinks I'm a liar? Here's my suggestion. When *you've* changed, get in touch. There won't be anyone else."

I left him standing openmouthed on the doorstep.

50.

There's nothing worse than two lonely people hanging out together. Still, I had nothing else to do, so I went to my father's house in the Suburb. He opened the door. He looked immaculate as ever, but there was a certain wildness around the eyes. As Jason would have said (although I felt that Jason had said enough), Roger didn't look *centered*. He had an air of being lost. I thought he might turn me away, but he grabbed me.

"Hannah, Hannah, I'm so glad you're here, come in, come in, so good to see you, can I get you something? anything?"

I glanced up to see if he was being sarcastic, but I don't think he was, there was no superior lift of the nostril. He didn't normally sound so artless. There'd always been a certain amount of flower to his speech. It was as if he no longer had the energy.

He flung a listless hand out to usher me in. The house was spotless. Which meant the cleaner was still being paid. Probably by direct debit.

"How's your mother? Have you spoken to her?" His eyes searched mine.

I sighed. "She's fine. I saw her. With Jonathan. She seemed . . . happy." I couldn't resist this one dig.

My father nodded. And then, with supreme effort, he mouthed the word "good."

He cleared his throat. "And you, Hannah. How are you?"

"Pretty good. Job's fine. Car's going okay."

In addition to doing my job and driving my car, I was spending an unhealthy amount of time staring at my now pristine wedding dress, which I'd hung on my bedroom wall. My father didn't need to know this.

"Good." He raked a hand through his hair, then rubbed his finger and thumb together as if to dispel the grease, a nervous habit rarely displayed. "Do you . . . do you think she'll divorce me?"

I blinked. "She didn't mention anything to me. But." I paused. "She's not a big talker."

Roger, you *fool*, I was saying inside. Look at you. A popped balloon. He wasn't, though, I realized, *contrite*. He merely felt sorry for himself. Splashing around in his bad luck. My guess was he was telling himself that he didn't understand why all this had happened. He probably believed we'd overreacted (women! huh!). He'd moved away from anger on to sorrow. Missing my mother. It was funny. Give people a while, they'd feel nostalgic for the most miserable of situations. In the nicest possible way, Roger was like the serial killer in *Manhunter*. Murdering entire families, sticking broken bits of mirror in their dead eyes, so they could look back at him. Ya know, it ain't quite the same as having real live opinionated people to contend with.

"Can I offer you anything?" he was still saying.

I was about to refuse. Then I thought, actually, you owe me. "There is something," I said.

"Yes?" Roger's eyes lit with hope.

"A bath. I'd like a bath."

"Be my *guest*," he cried. "There's plenty of hot water. You know where the towels are. I think . . . your mother left some bubble bath."

I reclined for an age in the hot water, resting my head on smooth enamel. The bathroom wasn't my thing—gray tiles—but it was restful to be here. I hoped they wouldn't sell the house. That might sound strange, because I wasn't fond of it. It was just that, with parents, I think that something is better than nothing. As a child, you'll take whatever you can get, however shoddy. For as long as I sat in my parents' bath, I could kid myself I was a little girl under the protection of a competent higher power (*Daddy*), and that was a cute fantasy to indulge for twenty minutes, because the second I walked out of his front door I knew I'd revert to being a fully grown adult, on my own, me looking out for *me*. Jack knew the terms. He might call. Or he might not. And I was fine with that. Really.

Seeing my father left me a little deflated. I suppose I'll sound weak and crazy if I say that I was glad to have him back. He had shrunk, in spirit and in person. No more than he deserved, I'm sure. I had no plans to see him more than on occasion. But I preferred to know that he was around, if I felt like a hit. He would occupy a very different, much reduced space in my life than he had before; our relationship had been ripped out at its roots. Whatever had survived would regenerate in a more measured, modest form. There would always be distance between us, call it a safety barrier. But I couldn't let him go altogether. You can hate a person with your whole body, but love is a stubborn thing, it clings on in your heart.

Seeing him made me want to connect with Angela. But I was pretty busy at work. So I didn't call her until the following week. Actually, that's inaccurate. I'd called her once on her mobile—I didn't feel comfortable calling Jonathan's flat—on my way into the office. She'd answered sounding sleepy. "Oh hello. We've just woken up."

Shut up shut up shut up, don't tell me that stuff.

I'd said, "Okay, look, well, I'll speak to you later in the day."

I hadn't said *which* day.

When I got around to ringing, a week later, her tone was very different.

"You all right?" I said. "You sound funny."

"Oh dear," she replied. "Is it that obvious? I must be losing my touch."

If this was a joke, it was ruined by her poor delivery. "Is *what* obvious?" I said.

"Jonathan and I are separating."

Instantly I wished I'd been less curt last time we'd spoken. Now, if I was to offer any more than a restrained amount of sympathy, I'd come across like a hypocrite.

"What!" I said. "Why?"

My mother sighed. "It's too . . . strange. Too odd. I feel over-whelmed by it all. I need to be by myself. At least for a while. Then we'll see."

"Well," I said. "That's sensible." I paused. "I'm sorry." I was sorry. She deserved to be happy. "Do you feel . . . you must feel . . . sad?"

She burst out laughing, then halfway through, the laugh turned to sobs. I tutted, winced, sighed, and muttered, "Poor you."

Shock upon shock! Except for at Grandma Nellie's funeral, I couldn't recall the last time I'd seen or heard my mother cry.

"Sorry," she sniffed after a while. "Right. Right. That's it. No more. All done. I'll be fine now."

I gathered that she was referring to the crying fit.

"How's Jonathan."

"He's upset. But he understands. He's very patient. He doesn't want to rush me. He's so *kind*. But after all this time. I'm not accustomed to it. It's like chocolate cheesecake."

"Is it?" I said.

"Wonderful, but too much, too rich, leaves you feeling sick and bloated and not a very *worthy* sort of person."

My God. Some women's relationship with food was as complex as their relationship with men. I remembered watching Gabrielle one Friday night, painstakingly peeling off each layer of my mother's lasagna, eating only the vegetables in between.

"You're right. You need decompressing. Where will you live?" I said.

I prayed she wasn't going back to my father. It was one thing to prefer him alive to dead. But even I wasn't fool enough to prefer him with, rather than without, my mother. A week of those two under the same roof and he'd spring back to tyranny in no time. If

357

she didn't know, I certainly wasn't about to tell her that Roger was pining. As I saw it, he'd pine for a while longer, then he'd get bored and stop.

"Gabrielle has very kindly said I could stay with her and Ollie for a while. It won't be for long. Just until I find a little place of my own. I'd like to get back into accounting, actually. Even if it means starting from scratch." She added, "I couldn't bear to be a pain but Gabrielle said it suited her. She's looking for a new part-time nanny. So while I'm around, I can help out with Jude until she finds one. She's with, I think, fifteen agencies. There has to be *someone*."

"That's a good idea," I said. "And the flat's small, but you could always stay with me if you need a change."

"That's very sweet," said my mother. "But won't I get in the way of you and . . ."

"Nah."

"Oh *no,* why on earth not, for goodness' sake!"

I felt quite cross. "As you yourself know, love stories don't always end the way one would wish," I said. "People are too spoilt. What with the cinema."

"Well, that's just too bad," said my mother, huffing in my ear.

I changed the subject; she could have ruined everything. I'd carefully lost myself in work, planning my ideal bathroom and watching a string of backed-up episodes of *Seinfeld,* recorded for the time that I needed to wallow in someone *else's* misery. If I zeroed Jack, I'd get by. So I'd erased him, pretended the last few months had never happened. I was like some tribe I'd read about, happy in their straw huts until they were introduced to television. A few weeks of lifestyle ads later, they saw what they were "missing" and got depressed. I was taking it a step further. Wiping that lifestyle ad named Jack Forrester from my mind. I was doing okay.

51.

Saturday night and I was eating a chicken dinner at Gab and Ollie's house. My mother sat opposite, fiddling with the stem of her wineglass. We made a good show of it, but while our hosts disputed how much longer the rice had to cook, we allowed our social expressions time off. At my advanced age, I suppose I felt I should be up to something more thrilling and I guess my mother felt the same. Then I felt bad about feeling bad; these were people I adored, what better way to spend my time?

By the time the rice was done, my social expression was back on duty.

And *they* were happy. I'd gone out with Ollie that afternoon. We'd taken Jude to the playground while Gab did the food shopping. Ollie seemed more confident with his son, more focused. I also noticed that Gab hadn't given my brother a million orders. She'd said, "Maybe scrambled egg for Squeal's dinner?" then let us get on with it.

"Da-*dee*!" said Jude. "Da-*dee*!"

"Joo-*ood*!" replied Ollie. "Joo-*ood*!" This cracked Jude up. That kid had a weird sense of humor.

"You look more relaxed," I said.

Ollie nodded. He said. "Things are going better."

We left it at that.

Later, though, when Ollie and Angela were giving Jude his bath, Gab said a few words as she chopped vegetables. I felt outrageous, sitting there, stuffing my face with cashews, watching her sweat, so I said—a token gesture if there ever was—"You have so much to do, Gab, I should be cooking for you."

And she was off like Chairman Miaow after a rat. "Are you joking, Hannah, you're a dreadful cook. I like cooking. It's relaxing.
And I don't feel so *fraught*, thank *God*. Ollie's . . . in a good place
right now, which makes a huge difference. He's not so . . . separate.
Maybe it has to do with Jude being a little older. We're getting on,
like, *so* great, we're talking more, and sleeping more, and my work
is going well, and his is improving, and Dr. Patel said I, well, he said
it sounded as if I'd had a depressive episode. He said it was a bio-
logical disturbance that had more or less run its course, and add
that to the adjustments you have to make when raising a baby, how
tiring and challenging it is, and how you feel cut off from the world,
he said I was suffering from wear and tear. Dr. Patel said I should
stop trying to be so perfect. Basic management advice, really. He's
such a good doctor, I sent him a thank-you card. So I'm trying to
calm down, not give myself a hard time. Ollie is being supportive,
so of course, I'm about a *ton* nicer to him. It's the opposite of a
vicious circle!

"Oh, and I've got a couple of lovely friends from postnatal
group with babies the same age as Jude, I'm making the effort to see
them more often, they're kind of a litmus test as to what's normal.
Clare is worse than me; she thinks every nonspecific virus Sebastian
has is cancer. I only think it's meningitis. And Polly is brilliantly laid
back; her little girl, Octavia, is addicted to *Teletubbies,* and yet she's
such a bright little thing, it's not done her any harm, and Polly kind
of shows me that if I don't happen to take Jude to the zoo or a farm
or the opera every day, he isn't going to suffer; if we go to the shops
or just hang out at home, that's *fine*. Also I interviewed a lovely
nanny yesterday, and she's fine with the hours I want. I just have to
check her references, but the last reference said she bought building
blocks for the little girl, and books. *Out of her own money.* You don't
know how rare that is, she sounds like the pink diamond of nan-

nies. And Ollie and I went out for dinner the other night, to the most gorgeous Italian restaurant, Lolalilalilablabla, it's got a Michelin star, have you heard of it? Angela babysat. It made a change to us going out in shifts. It was quite an occasion, sitting opposite him at a table with a lily on it, talking like adults. And this glamorous woman admired my Chloé dress. And I've joined a new gym with a babysitter, so I'm having some time for myself. And I've made a half-day appointment with Michel—I'm going to have a beauty blitz. And I have a new cleaner, one who doesn't empty my tampons from the pack and arrange them in glorious display in the marble bowl I bought for my cottonwool balls, or neatly fold all my dirty clothes and put them back in my wardrobe, and . . ."

The hell she'd had a depressive episode! There was nothing wrong with her, bar she was a total neurotic! *I* pull my dirty clothes out of the linen basket and stick them straight on again! She should be so lucky to have them folded neatly and put back in her wardrobe!

"Gab," I said when she finally stopped melting my ear. "You cheer me *right* up."

I hoped that she would keep talking for the rest of the night so that no one could ask me about Jack.

"So," said Gabrielle, just as I was about to attack the chocolate cheesecake. "What's going on with you and Jack?"

"Nothing," I replied. "Who is this 'Jack' you speak of?"

Everyone looked disbelieving and disapproving, so I added, "He's embroiled in his own ancient misery, and I refuse to be part of it."

No one's expression changed. I was forced to recount the sorry tale of the willy end of Jason's wedding.

"Jason's an idiot!" shouted Gab, who was drinking the red wine like a dog laps water. "And Jack's just scared. It's only because he loves you too much!"

Ah, yes. The "I love you so much I can't stand to be with you" phenomenon.

Even Ollie said, "Why don't you call him?"

My mother added, "Why don't you write to him?"

"Why don't *you*?" I said rudely. "I've made enough approaches, he knows the score. I will not demean myself further. Now can I please eat my cheesecake?"

If there was one place I thought I'd get a bit of rest, it was the office. But no.

I was at the door the following evening when Greg motioned me toward him with his porridge spoon. As I reluctantly neared the flying-oat weapon, he said, "You back with Jack yet?"

"Nope," I said. "See you tomorrow!"

"Half-wit," he called after me.

Was he referring to me or Jack?

I didn't go straight to my car. I went and bought a coffee. There's something special about drinking a coffee from a Styrofoam cup with a lid on it. The handing over of £1.75 and receiving the gift of caffeine, it feels like a little occasion. It confers status. I see people walking along carrying their bought coffees and I think, ooh, lucky you, you must be so important! Christ, listen to me. I needed a hobby.

I sat in my car and started to drink the coffee, staring ahead. Four sips and my hands were shaking. The last thing I needed was a coffee; the pleasure was all in the transaction. I sighed, got out the car, chucked the coffee in the nearest bin. Every time I do something like this I envisage a landfill of all my crimes. Plastic bottles. Cardboard boxes. Those squeaky polystyrene chips that pad out cardboard boxes. Tubs of hair mousse, cans of antistretch spray, the obligatory expenses incurred when you get a haircut, buy shoes, and don't feel brave enough to say no. If I really couldn't be bothered, I wouldn't recycle my wine bottles. I was a disgrace to the race.

I noticed there was an envelope tucked under my windscreen wiper. I was pretty slow that day. I'd only been staring through it for twenty minutes. Was it blackmail? I tore it open with mild interest (curious to see what terrible thing someone thought they had on me that everyone else didn't know about), and a small scrap of paper fell out, a photograph, ripped from a glossy magazine. Wait a minute, that was my BATH. Well. It wasn't *my* bath; it was a photograph of the sleek white £700 bath I lusted after every time I sat in my horrid green flaky one.

Jack had scrawled below it, "God, I'm a wanker, can I buy your forgiveness?"

I pulled out my mobile and rang him.

"Hello?"

"*Shit!*" I turned around, Jack was standing right behind me.

"I've been standing here watching you for the last half hour. What did you say you did for a living?"

I snapped shut my phone. "Fuck off fuck off fuck off."

Jack took a step back. "Oh," he said, "I, er—"

"I'm merely quoting the last words you said to me, after the wedding."

"Look, I—"

"And no, you can't buy my forgiveness. A large bribe does not *compensate* for what you think of me. *You* have to do the compensating. A bribe is an instead-of."

"No it's not! I rang your mother to see what you most wanted in the world, and you make that into a negative. Don't you see, Hannah, the bath is an *extra,* to show you that—"

"You mean, my mother rang *you.*"

363

"No. I rang her."

"Oh! Have you ordered the bath?" (Immediately I hated myself, but there you go.)

"Er, yes. Philippe Starck."

"You mean, Phil Stark, from the Starfish Bathrooms chain." (Why was I even having this conversation, I was so *corruptible*.)

"The Starfish Bathrooms chain! I don't think so, love! Your taste in baths isn't exactly highstreet knockoff!"

"You mean . . ." He'd only gone and bought the real designer seven-thousand-quid bath. The berk! I smiled weakly. "My mother told you this was the bath I wanted."

"Yes," said Jack. "She was most exact. Spelled out his name for me. And the price."

That woman was becoming more outrageous daily.

And I was becoming cheaper. I fought my conscience. Assumed an intractable expression.

"Here's the thing, Jack," I said. "Your instinct is, you can't trust me, and it all burst out at the wedding when you were provoked. This here now is lovely, but it's *planned*. Say we get together again. It'll be great until the minute I do something that you think is suspect, and it's going to happen because you think I *am* suspect. You can't help it. You just do. I'm fighting for us, Jack. But *you* have to fight for us, too. And that takes more than cracking a few jokes and throwing cash about. My relationships are pretty straight these days. I can't be bought. And I don't think you see that yet."

He stood there openmouthed. I half wished he'd say something, but I knew he wouldn't. He *couldn't*. He couldn't deny the truth.

I put the photo of the bath back in its envelope, handed it to him.

"Thanks, though," I said. "It was a nice thought."

52.

When Jack and I divorced, he was coldly fair about everything. I developed murderous feelings toward his solicitor, whose every communication was hoity-toity for "fuck you." I remember Martine suggesting that I throw a divorce party. "Like a hen night," she'd said. "Except inverted."

"Nice idea," I'd replied. "How about we also run three times anticlockwise round a church at midnight reciting black masses."

She didn't mention the divorce party again. Considering I'd entered into the marriage with all the gravitas of a teenager entering a pub, I was surprised I felt so lousy about its demise. The colossal bore of becoming officially *single* again, the paperwork, the endless trips to the post office, the sympathy that seeped from people, the fascinated disdain, as if I had syphilis (I suppose divorce *is* a sexually transmitted disease)—it was nothing compared to the hollow feeling of seeing myself referred to in print as "the respondent." This was all I was to Jack now, and his disgust could not be any clearer had he spat in my face.

Eventually, though, I'd coped by blocking myself off. It was a fabulous ploy that worked admirably. I didn't cry, ever; I repressed every ugly sensation, sweeping it down deeper, away from the surface, until it disappeared. It wasn't difficult. In fact, it was involuntary. After a while I didn't feel *able* to cry, even if, intellectually, I understood it to be appropriate to the situation. It was as if I was an alien, who did not experience sadness like a human being. "Boo-hoo-hoo waaaaah!" I'd try inside. Nope. Nothing. Eyes as dry as chalk. I ought to react to this, I'd think, but I couldn't. I felt like a hovering ghost, watching every shot fail to pierce my bulletproof skin.

It was a shock to realize, after Jack approached me with his bath offer, that this long-taken-for-granted talent of mine had slipped away. Like Aretha Franklin waking one morning and not knowing how to sing. Habit is different from routine. Routine is for neurotics. It gives you the illusion of control. I'm not that bothered by routine. The ceiling is just as likely to fall on your head if you drink your morning coffee at 8:15 precisely, as if you play fast and loose with fate and drink it whenever the hell you like. Whereas routine is something you impose, a habit grows on *you*. Habit is born of sloth—not having to trouble your mind for the tiniest thought because at last it's instinct. It is about carving the easiest, most uncluttered path through life.

When I tried to zero Jack and it didn't work, I was *incredulous.* This was what I did, this was my area of expertise! I thought of *Bewitched,* a program I dimly recalled from childhood. What was it the girl's mother did to work magic—blinked? Twitched? Wrinkled her nose? I was like the actress off-set, blinking, twitching: *nada.*

Every minute of every day pointed to what I was missing. I had the honeymoon postcard from Lucy. (She'd written it, Jason had signed it, his barely decipherable name squeezed in a tiny corner, dwarfed by Lucy's unfettered scrawl; from the size of each word she'd been taught English by a Great Dane.) The holiday so far sounded like a forced march, no cultural stone left unturned. I liked it, that my hell could be someone else's heaven, waste not want not. But it made me pale that *my* heaven was out there loose, when doubtless he was many other people's heaven too.

I saw Angela obsessed with her mobile, not *entirely* hearing what people said to her. She put off calling estate agents. Every second sentence began, "A friend of mine—" I didn't think it would be too long before my mother overcame her fear of being consumed by another man. I felt I might hold my breath until she and Jonathan got back together, maybe in a new, bigger flat, so that Angela could have a room, a space that was only hers. I felt that my mother was boldly acting out all the impulses that I kept a grip on. I refused to mouth the luscious words, "A friend of mine," because every time *she* said it, I thought "JONATHAN!!!" I couldn't bear a newsflash above everyone's head reading "JACK!!!"

And I saw Ollie, with Gab. I saw their ways with each other soften. And I thought, people *do* change a little sometimes, if they see that it's worth it, if they want something, someone, badly enough.

Maybe Gab sensed my despair, because one day she said, "I want to tell you something. Before I had Jude, there were two miscarriages. And when we conceived the second and third time, people encouraged me to . . . think of the fetus as 'just a few cells,' because it was too painful to commit to something that, as the doctors put it, might not be 'viable.' But I couldn't. I thought of it as 'Baby.' Even though when I miscarried the second time, the feeling of loss was excruciating; it would have been worse to think that I hadn't given it encouragement by loving it. At some point, Hannah, you have to have faith."

I wiped my eyes and considered the best approach.

Would I turn up at his house and say, "Jack, I love you, but before I put this emotion into practice, I must insist: you really mustn't take your rage at your parents out on me"?

Or would I write and say, "Jack, I adore you, but before I commit, I need to know that you've worked through all your *issues*"?

No.

I would ring him at home and say, "I love you." It was that simple.

But before I got the chance, a note was delivered to my office.

Hannah,
 Hello.
 I think of you often.
 Would you like to meet for dinner?
 It might be nice.
 Love,
 Jack
 ps. bath in storage

I danced around my office for a bit, then I posted my reply.

 I might. When? Where?
 oh.
 baggage in storage also

Jack posted me the details. It was a new place. In west London, inconvenient for both of us. But I felt he'd made a good choice. I didn't want Jack or me to roll off the sofa and slouch down the road to the nearest chippy, and I guess neither did he. It was important, that night, to travel. The food might be terrible, for all he knew, but he was right to take the chance.

 I kept his first note in my pocket; I touched it until the paper went soft. It was quaint and not a little thrilling, this old-fashioned way of communicating. Like negotiating with a kidnapper. I didn't want to blow this gossamer bond by foghorning down his ear on my mobile. For the first time in my life, I realized that waiting wasn't all bad.

I soon changed my mind.

 I checked my watch again. He'd booked the table for eight. And here I was. *Early.* I'd arrived at ten to. I could have sat in the car, but

I wanted to play it straight. Also, I'd wanted to check out the place. So. I walked in. Not bad. A big square white room, dark wood chairs and tables, a crowd that gave the impression of being gorgeous. A waitress led me right to the back wall, and I wasn't sure whether to be pleased or furious. For me, I looked good. I *felt* good, which is half the battle.

I ordered a vodka. Sat there. Watched people. Read the menu.

I put my mobile on vibrate, placed it on the bench next to me.

At five past eight, I told myself that Jack only seemed to be late because I'd arrived ten minutes early.

At quarter past eight, I decided that fifteen minutes late was normal and acceptable.

At half past eight, I presumed he'd been caught up at work. However, a phone call would have been nice.

At a quarter to nine, I scurried into the street and rang his mobile. "Jack," I said. "I'm at the restaurant, waiting. I'm sure you're on your way. I'll wait till nine. Then I'm gone."

I wasn't going anywhere. I'd wait all evening till they started stacking chairs on tables. He *had* to turn up. I couldn't quite believe he wasn't coming. I felt sick and shaken. Was it a trick? To punish me for forcing him to confront his shortcomings? For setting down a few relationship rules? I couldn't care less about sitting in a restaurant alone; I'd done it for work a thousand times. So what if people looked? All I cared about was Jack. So was this it?

I crumpled my napkin, fiddled with my phone, tried not to notice the couple on the next table, who were slowly twining from the feet and hands. She had streaked blond hair and looked effortlessly fabulous. He had an intense tan and black hair, possibly dyed. All around me, people were together, and here was I alone. Do people even *get* stood up at my age? Isn't that something that ends when you hit twenty?

I refused to believe it.

Jack had asked to meet me. That meant he was ready. I was no longer bothered if he had emotional baggage yet to be laundered, pressed, folded, and forgotten. As if *I* wasn't a work in progress. If he got out of line, I'd tell him so. I know he'd tell *me* so. But I had a feeling that supersonic fallouts would be rare. I had a sense that after all these years, after all the confusion, the passion and the rage, we finally understood each other, accepted each other. I wanted him as he was; we'd fight our way together.

Unless he wasn't coming. But I *knew* he was. I trusted him. He'd written "*bath in storage.*"

There had to be a reason for his no-show. Perhaps I should start calling hospitals. I accepted the waiter's offer of another vodka, I fixed my gaze on the door of the restaurant. It was five to nine. I drummed my fingers. Checked my reflection in the knife. Ate some bread. Wished for salt and butter, instead of squashed virgin olive oil. I was certain that at any moment, Jack would rush into the room.

As I stared at the door, a tall man rose from a table nearby and strode toward it, mobile clenched in fist.

Jack.

What!

They'd seated us at separate tables.

I leaped up, dodging waiters, stumbling over chairs.

"Jack!" I called. "Jack! Jack!"

He stopped. Turned. He saw me, broke into a smile.

I couldn't get the words out fast enough, "I've been waiting for you over there since forever!" I said.

"I've been waiting for you for longer than that! *I* got here at quarter to forever."

"I called you!"

"And I called you."

"Either our phones are inferior, or the reception in here is nil."

"Doesn't matter. I was going to wait."

"Me too. You did book the table in *your* name, didn't you?"

"I remembered it specially."

"Well then!"

"Their error then. Not ours. Although"—he grinned at me—"*one* of us is a detective."

"Excuse me," said a man in a black jacket who was gripping a clipboard. "Could I ask you to move, please? You're blocking the door."

"Excuse *me*," said Jack. "Could I ask *you* why my friend and I were shown to separate tables, where we've sat waiting for the last hour and a half?"

The man seemed to wilt inside his black jacket. "Oh no!" he cried. "You waited that long!" He riffled pointlessly through his notes. "I presume you didn't book under two names?" he added hopefully.

I could see Jack fighting the tide of sarcasm. "Just one," he replied.

"My apologies, a drink, the meal on the house, I—"

I shook my head. "Don't worry. It's fine. Isn't it, Jack?"

He looked at me. "Yes," he said. "We've found each other. We don't need anything . . . more."

I smiled at my shoes. I saw Jack follow my gaze. I was wearing my black shoes with the ribbons that crisscrossed, beautiful shoes for a beautiful moment. I felt a wave of bliss wash over me. For once, my life was movie perfect; people might look at me and think, *Wow, she's as polished as a conker!* Jack bent suddenly, grabbed at the hem of my black flared trousers. My smile faltered as he opened his hand, flashed me a glimpse of a small ball of pink material.

Yesterday's knickers.

Jack grinned and stuffed them in his jacket pocket. I turned a pants shade of pink.

"Hannah," he said. "I know you've changed. But . . . never change."

I lifted my gaze and smiled at Jack, smiled at the world. My life would never be movie perfect, and it didn't matter. It was good enough the way it was. I made a mental note to throw out the fifty-quid-a-pot moisturizer Gab had forced on me. It was starting to smell like mildew. And it was about time I donated Jason's baby doll nightdress to Oxfam. They could do with a laugh.

"I won't change if you won't," I said.

The headwaiter was still standing there, carefully oblivious, and I peered beyond him, gave Jack's table the once-over.

"Mine's nicer," I said and led him to it.